EXTRACURRICULAR

BOOK 2 OF 3 EPISODIC NOVELS

JOSIE BROWN

A BOOK BY

SIGNAL PRESS

ONE OF MANY GREAT SIGNAL PRESS BOOKS

San Francisco, CA

This is a work of fiction. All incidents and dialogue, and all characters with the exception of some well-known historical and public figures, are products of the author's imagination and are not to be construed as real.

Library of Congress Cataloging-in-Publication Data is available upon request.

Cover Design by Andrew Brown, ClickTwiceDesign.com

Trade Paperback ISBN: 978-1-970093-04-9

V100119

to-die-for plot, and a ripped-from-the-headlines premise. I absolutely loved it and must read the entire series!"

—Samantha M. Bailey, author, *Woman on the Edge*

"Sharp, smart, and sexy, Brown's timely new series about the cut-throat world of college admissions is a must-read. As always, Brown's cast of characters is a delicious mix of sweethearts, scoundrels and the just plain morally corrupt. Never predictable, *Extracurricular* is immensely enjoyable."

—Meredith Schorr, author of *The Boyfriend Swap* and the *Blogger Girl* series

"Dirty little secrets have a way of catching up with us. *Housewife Assassin* and *Totlandia* fans rejoice! Josie Brown has a new trail of secrets, lies, and parents behaving badly—and you're gonna love it. Ripped from the headlines, *Extracurricular* delivers the perfect summer read on just how far some people will go, no matter the cost, to get exactly what they want."

—Jen Tucker, author, *The Day I Wore My Panties Inside Out*, and Chick Lit Central columnist

"Josie Brown has hit it out of the ballpark with this timely tale of family, friends, love and the morally corrupt. As always, Ms. Brown's writing is sharp, smart, and oh-so witty. She'll have you laughing out loud one minute and cringing the next at her characters' antics and comments. Filled with twist and turns and complicated emotions that lead to decisions that play pivotal moments in the characters lives, this story will reach out and grab your attention from page one and not let go until the end. I now sit on tenterhooks awaiting the next release to find out who will be going down and who will be saved."

—Gail Chianese, author, *Love Runs Deep*

FALL SEMESTER

CHAPTER 1

My mother is dying.

The thought that one day, very soon, Lavinia Thorpe would no longer exist beyond her family's cherished memories or in a few fading photos of the many that lined Ashford Academy's halls numbed Audrey so thoroughly that she stopped cold in the middle of the private high school's entry rotunda.

Students streamed around her, oblivious to her grief. Although Audrey felt them breeze past her and saw their lips moving in earnest discussion or whispered gossip or gushing flirtations, her brain blocked out all sound except that of her pounding heart.

So that her sadness wouldn't blind her to the here and now, she forced herself to focus on something—anything. That was when she noticed a slim ray of sunshine had somehow found its way beyond the umbrella of leaves shielding the rotunda's tall windows.

The bright beam intersected Audrey's wrist, creating the illusion that her hand had been severed.

The symbolism was not lost on her. When Lavinia died, a part of her would be lost forever.

To escape this unbearable thought, Audrey shifted her gaze to the window instead. Through it, San Francisco's celebrated Haight Street was partially obscured by the early morning dew, which still glistened on the ancient panes of glass.

During the month prior to the school's founding—Audrey's

freshman year, some twenty-five years ago—she'd helped her mother, the school's founder and headmistress, scrub every pane to a sparkling brilliance. It was one of many tasks mother and daughter performed side by side to ready the careworn Victorian mansion for the thirty-six teenagers who would find themselves amongst its first four graduating classes.

Only six seniors had graduated that first year, three of whom were from impoverished families. All had received multiple offers from Ivy League universities.

As the school's reputation for hands-on learning, exemplary test scores, and high acceptance rates into the country's top-ranked universities grew, so did its student body and academic staff.

Today, four hundred students were enrolled. Still, its mandate was unchanged:

Students seeking intellectual engagement and the pure pursuit of knowledge will be welcomed with open arms, despite any social or economic barriers they must overcome.

For now, anyway.

Ashbury Academy is Lavinia's legacy, Audrey thought. For that reason alone, the values that led to its creation need to survive beyond her.

Despite what some of the school's newer trustee board members might attempt to do to decimate those founding principles.

I swore to Lavinia I'd keep her illness a secret. I must hold to that.

Audrey had made her mother another promise: to allow her husband, Daniel McKittridge, to take a seat on Ashbury Academy's trustee board.

But because Daniel was an attorney, she couldn't divulge Lavinia's secret to him. Otherwise, it would be his fiduciary duty to alert the other board members of her failing health.

She wished Daniel was there to hold her. Instead she made up her mind to call him.

Before doing so, she walked outside.

Under the tree, out of reach from the morning sun, those few moments of reflection faded to a mere glimmer.

Everything in life is fleeting.

"You've been crying." After eighteen years of marriage, Daniel knew Audrey well enough to pick up on the gruff catch that only affected her voice when she was upset.

"You're right. The kids found my first-day-of-school sentimentality something to scoff at." She attempted a chuckle, but it too got stuck in her throat.

"I'm sorry about that, babe."

Hearing his concern, Audrey winced. She'd always hated lying to Daniel.

Then again, she'd never been able to top the first one, almost nineteen years ago.

It was a doozy.

Well, at least this one is in Lavinia's honor.

"Aren't you in the middle of your PTA meeting?" Daniel asked warily.

"I've got a few minutes." Another small lie. In fact, she was already late. On the agenda: introduce her dear friends, Bliss Thackeray Belluci and Tallulah Wishart, who had jointly agreed to replace her as Ashbury Academy's Parent-Teacher Association chair.

As such, they'd also take her place on the trustee board.

"Listen, Daniel, I've been thinking. You were right. If you're keen on taking Lavinia up on her offer to join the board, you should do it. I've had all the fun these years. Now it's your turn."

"I think that's great!" Daniel laughed. "And after duly warning me this morning of all the reasons I shouldn't want to be on the board, I promise I won't complain, no matter how contentious I find it. I also promise it'll be a one-year stint, tops."

"I'll hold you to it." Yet another lie. She prayed that, like her, Daniel would want to stay on the board until the perfect replacement could be found for Lavinia: one who would stand up to the board's ever-increasing demands.

She knew she could count on Daniel. He too revered Lavinia and would do what he could to protect her legacy.

"My mother will appreciate it greatly, Daniel. Thank you, and… I love you." She hung up before he could respond to her fervent whisper.

Whoever said that each subsequent fib got easier was dead wrong.

Or was lying.

MIRANDA D'ARCY, ASHBURY ACADEMY'S NEWLY HIRED COLLEGE admissions consultant, always kept a to-do list on her cell phone. Continuously updated, its line items—taking calls with parents who were current clients, returning calls to parents who wanted to beg her to work on behalf of their children, and making calls to her network of contacts at various Ivy League schools—were ranked in an order of importance that rose and fell like the frenzied trading of stocks.

Even on this very first day of school at Ashbury Academy—her sole in-house consulting retainer—Miranda's most pressing task wasn't rubbing shoulders with AA's parents at the PTA's Back to School parent kaffeeklatsch that was already going on. Nor was it wooing new private clients with deep pockets and under-achieving children to her private college admissions concierge program.

Instead, it was reminding her somewhat forgetful and usually belligerent freelance test proctor, Winslow Jennings, that two students had appointments with him on this coming Saturday, and another two on Sunday.

She let his private phone ring until it rolled to voice mail. After hanging up, she did the same thing again.

And again.

Finally, he picked up. "What is it, Miranda?"

"That's a fine howdy-do for your boss," she growled.

He sighed. "I view our relationship more like a partnership. I mean, I am the Director of Testing at University Prep & Test."

The testing facility—a subsidiary of a shell company owned by her—was a necessary evil that allowed her to make good on her promise to her clients: that, under her tutelage, none of their children would score below 1400 on their SAT tests—a grade that put them in the running for their first-choice universities.

To keep that assurance, she desperately needed Winslow.

So she bit her tongue at Winslow's impertinence, declaring instead, "Speaking of which, check your online calendar. You'll note that you have clients coming in this weekend—four of them, two each day."

"Not too early, I hope," he whined.

"Yes, early," she warned him. "The first test appointments are nine o'clock, sharp! The second appointments are scheduled for two o'clock."

"Why do they have to show up at all?" Winslow countered.

"Because the students have to take the test!" she shouted.

Winslow snickered. "Not really. I take it for them."

"But they don't know that. They think they've earned their scores fair and square." She added with a snarl: "And that's just the way their parents want it."

Usually, SAT tests were taken at the students' schools, and the tests were timed. However, with their school's permission, students with learning disabilities were allowed to take untimed ACT and SAT tests, and they could do so at an accredited location, like UP&T.

As it happened, most—make that *all*—of the students in Miranda's program were given a disability waiver by a Special Education consultant: in this case, Winslow.

After these students took their exams at UP&T, the final test papers sent to the national testing companies weren't the students' versions, but ones filled out by Winslow, who also acted as the tests' administrating proctor.

It was the only way Miranda could hold to her assurance: that the students would score that magic number of 1400 or above.

Miranda's guarantee came at a very steep price. But, for parents who were desperate to see their children enrolled in a top-tier university—and were willing to do so by any means possible—no price was out of bounds—

An obsession that was making Miranda very wealthy.

"You scheduled them over both days?" Winslow fumed. "No, Miranda! Sorry, but I'm not going to let you kill my whole weekend!"

"*Pshaw!* It works for my clients, and that's all that matters. You're being paid handsomely for your time, Winslow. Not to mention that you have the rest of the week to surf, or play video games, or any of the other ridiculous folderol."

"'Folderol'?" Winslow snorted. "You don't even know the proper usage of the word! Otherwise, you'd have sung some witty ditty."

When Miranda had first considered hiring Winslow, she'd been warned against it by the referring source: a professor who'd mentored him during his Ph.D. program in Mathematics. "Winslow is that most exotic flower in the wild, overgrown garden of academia: a delicate genius," the professor had told her. "But, sadly, he is also a savant, and all that implies."

"Meaning what, exactly?" Miranda had asked.

"You know—on the spectrum, as it were. Obsessed with arcane trivia. Parses every word. But of course, he would. He memorized the Merriam-Webster dictionary before the age of three. Book smart, but not street smart. I guess that's why he's such a great test taker."

That's all Miranda needed to hear. She shrugged off the professor's warning. "I'm not asking him to cover me in a knife fight. So, where will I find this savant?"

The man chuckled. "He could be in any casino between here and Las Vegas. He makes his living as a professional gambler. He's one of the best card-counters in the world."

Now, having worked with Winslow for two years, Miranda realized it was the professor's delicate way of warning her that Winslow was an idiot savant.

No. Just a damn idiot.

But because he delivered the requisite scores, Miranda put up with his periodic tantrums.

Like this one.

She took a deep breath. When she exhaled, she muttered, "You want a 'witty ditty?' Okay, how's this?"

Then, in a mezzo-soprano voice to the tune of *Mary Had a Little Lamb*, she crooned:

"If you want to be an ass,
You will soon be out of cash.
I will cut you off LIKE THAT.
Cross me, and you'll FEEL MY WRATH.
I won't take your ands or buts
Rather, I'll chop off your nuts!"

"Not bad for off the cuff," Winslow admitted grudgingly. "Although, I'm sure you'll agree with me that the first two are slant rhymes, and therefore somewhat of a cheat —"

"You're testing my patience, Winslow!"

"And you are testing mine," he answered calmly.

Miranda realized it was time to cut to the chase. "Let me guess: there's some big gambling shindig you want to make this weekend."

"Yep. And I'll be honest with you, for what you're paying me, I don't see why I shouldn't take the whole weekend off."

"You're scoffing at five thousand dollars per test?"

"Yes. Admit it, Miranda: your clients pay you at least ten times that."

"You're dreaming if you truly think that," she lied.

Silence.

Winslow made a handsome living by bluffing. Suddenly, she wondered if he could smell fear, even through the phone.

"How much?" she muttered. It was a big gamble. Then again, she wrote a lot of fat into her clients' fees, just in case little emergencies arose.

His pouting was a perfect example.

"Fifty thousand each."

"*WHAT?*" Miranda sputtered. "NO... *NO!* Forget it! I'll find someone else."

"Not in time for Saturday."

"I'll reschedule their tests until I do." Miranda was bluffing now. Hopefully, she was just as good at it as him, although his Vegas outings had undoubtedly given him plenty of chances to hone his chops.

"Forty, then."

"Ten thou each."

Silence.

"Forty K, Winslow! Unlike Vegas, UP&T is a sure bet. Take it or leave it."

More silence.

She wondered if he'd hung up. And if not, she agonized if she should do so first, as proof that she meant business.

"Okay," Winslow muttered, finally.

"Thank you." The tremble in Miranda's voice was real.

She wanted him to hear it, to think he'd bested her.

In truth, he hadn't.

Miranda's concierge fees ran six figures. Sometimes as high as seven, if the parents were bound and determined to shove their child, even kicking and screaming, through the heavy oak doors of a prestigious university.

And Miranda was right there beside them to give their little darlings that final shove.

CHAPTER 2

"So, Boss, you agree with us, right? That we should at least meet with this woman, who knows about this counselor and these parents who are bribing college administrators to accept their kids into their schools?"

FBI Special Agent SallyAnne Jagger may have broached her comment as a question, but in truth, it was a declaration.

She was daring him to tell her she was wrong.

FBI Division Director Vance Melamed acceded with a nod and a sigh.

SallyAnne and her investigative partner, Lionel Porter Polk VII, considered themselves lucky to have snagged Melamed's very first appointment of the day. After placing the follow-up report of the anonymous source on his desk, SallyAnne had been pacing his office for the past half hour, railing on about the injustice of this potential crime.

How such incidents usually went under the radar because the perpetrators were invariably privileged;

How these crimes were wrongly labeled victimless when in fact the victims were those who had played fair in a supposedly chaste admissions system but then got sidestepped in favor of the cheaters' children;

Moreover, how the perpetrators were wealthy enough to play by their own rules.

"Not this time," SallyAnne vowed.

As she continued to make her case, Lionel sat silently, but his eyes followed the petite brunette's every step, and not just because her legs looked so great in that new skirt. (At least, that's what he told himself.)

Whenever SallyAnne went to the mat for a cause that she believed in, she was an indelible force of nature that always left him in awe. Lionel loved the way her dark eyes smoldered with resolve. When she paused after making a crucial point, her dimples deepened beside her pursed lips.

She's smart. She's fearless. She's adorable—

"Do you agree, Special Agent Polk?" Director Melamed barked.

"Do I…" Because Lionel always sat ramrod straight, there was no telltale clue in his posture that he'd been fantasizing.

He prayed that he hadn't torpedoed SallyAnne's argument for taking on the case. His declaration followed an attempt to clear his throat: "Agree? Emphatically? Oh, yes, sir!"

His cough caused a ghost of a smile to alight on SallyAnne's lips. She knew he'd been daydreaming. After three years as partners in San Francisco's white collar crime division, she knew all of his quirks and tells, just like he knew hers.

If not, he hoped he'd have many more years to discover them.

"What Special Agent Polk means to say, Sir, is that, as a Harvard man, he too is offended by the audacity of this illegal enterprise and hopes you'll agree with us that we should pull out all the stops to shut down the scheme before it defrauds more deserving students out of their fair chance to enter the school of their choice."

Lionel nodded vigorously.

Like him, SallyAnne had been intrigued when Lionel played back the recording of the anonymous source claiming proof that some college counselor was offering to help parents of graduating high school seniors attain admission to certain upper echelon universities through some fraudulent "side door."

Lionel did not doubt that even mediocre students were given a leg up if they were children of alumnae. The same reality could well apply to major donors, regardless of their previous affiliations with the university, if even any at all. However, in this case, where money changed hands for a guaranteed admission? Well, that certainly merited a detailed investigation.

"Special Agent Jagger, you're coming in loud and clear," Director Melamed conceded. "But the anonymous call came from Los Angeles. If what the tipster says is true, a lot of the case will be made down there. Why not just hand it off to that office?"

"Because the purported suspect has relocated here, Sir," Lionel explained. "And, unlike the Boston bureau's case, this time we can catch the purported suspect in action."

"And, just like the Boston case, if we flip the suspect into a cooperating witness, we can indict her clients and her network of on-campus co-conspirators," SallyAnne added.

Melamed stood up. "Okay, you two, then you better get on it. If we're lucky, it'll be as big as Boston's case. Just make sure the evidence is as tight as a gnat's ass." Nodding to SallyAnne, he added, "Excuse my French."

SallyAnne's grin was proof she was not bothered in the least.

When the agents got back to their cubicles, Lionel took on the first task: calling the anonymous informant to set up a meeting with her as soon as possible—that afternoon, in fact. There were flights to LAX almost hourly. The call had been traced to a home in LA's Bel-Air neighborhood. It belonged to a couple named Robert and Helene Edelson.

Lionel and SallyAnne had a lot to do between now and their departure.

It was a shame that the hour-long flight between San Francisco and Los Angeles didn't merit an overnight. Lionel always looked forward to an excuse to spend a few more hours with SallyAnne. His partner's ball-busting demeanor softened after a meal and a glass of wine. She cracked a few jokes and even laughed at his feeble attempts at humor.

He had good reason to trust her with his heart.

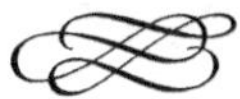

CHAPTER 3

"Testing—one, two, three! Testing, one, two, *THREE!*" Bliss Thackeray Belluci tapped the microphone in her hand. "Can you hear me from the back of the auditorium?"

Tallulah Wishart, perfectly positioned in the back, nodded enthusiastically, as did some of the parents who had already taken their seats, now that the first hour of class was in session.

A few seconds later, Tallulah was on the stage with Bliss.

Whereas Lavinia would be giving her opening day address to the students in the larger of AA's two auditoriums, the students' parents were welcomed into the smaller auditorium—really, the mansion's old ballroom—to attend the school year's first PTA meeting. There, they could enjoy coffee, tea, and juice, along with fresh-cut fruit and pastries (including gluten-free, dairy-free, sugar-free, and high fructose corn syrup-free options).

The first item on the agenda was for Audrey to pass the gavel to Bliss and Tallulah, the incoming PTA chairpersons.

"I'm sorry that I'm so late!" Audrey ran up the steps to the stage, all the while unbuttoning her coat—

Until she realized it couldn't come off unless she dropped her satchel first.

Instead, she flung it at the closest table—

Only to watch it skid off the other side and onto the floor.

As it landed with a plop, the latch gave way, and everything fell out. The pages from Audrey's welcome speech slid into the notes for a speech she'd written for her boss, Congressman Harris Blanchard, and a white paper she was due to review with him later that afternoon.

"Damn! Damn!" Audrey mumbled as she bent down to pick up the fallen sheets.

Immediately, Bliss and Tallulah scrambled to help—

Only to bump heads.

The parents in the almost-full auditorium chuckled at their antics.

Like Audrey, they kept their heads bent and grabbed for everything.

"Oh…Thanks!" Audrey, flustered, added, "Just stuff everything else back in here." She opened the satchel wide.

"We're not making such a great impression, are we?" Bliss muttered.

"They're almost all Virgins. Trust me, because they're so anxious to fit in, they'll kowtow to our every beck and call," Tallulah predicted.

She has a point, Audrey thought.

"Virgin" was the nickname Tallulah and other parents who were former alumni had given the new parents at the school.

"There are plenty of Titans out there too," Bliss warned her.

This was the name alumni gave those who felt that their wealth and additional school donations should provide them and their children special privileges.

"In fact, Gretchen McCoppin has already asked me what Tallulah and I are doing up here," Bliss continued.

Tallulah guffawed. "What did you tell her?"

"All I said was that Audrey was detained and asked us to test the microphone before the meeting. Little did I know I'd be telling the truth!" Bliss chuckled, then turned to Audrey. "Got a late start, eh?"

"Yes, something like that." Audrey winced. "Ha! And I thought handing over the reins to the school's auction would keep her too busy to stick her nose in PTA business too. Boy, was I dreaming!"

"That's okay," Bliss countered. "According to PTA bylaws, if you resign because of a personal emergency, you have the right to appoint interim successors. And since there has to be a semester moratorium before another election, Tallulah and I will have plenty of time to prove we're worthy of the position."

Audrey laughed, "I'm impressed at how well you know the bylaws!"

"Modeling is a lot like the Girl Scouts. It teaches you to always be prepared," Bliss replied primly. "At least, now I'll get to leave my bear spray at home."

"What did you need *that* for?" Audrey asked.

"Oversexed photographers and billionaire man whores." Bliss shook her head at the thought. "Tell you what, Tallulah: what say we split up our new PTA duties? The way I see it, I'll be the brains, and you can be the muscle."

Tallulah murmured, "I never thought I'd agree to that. But in this case, it makes sense. Heck, twisting the arms of parents to help out with the teacher appreciation days—not to mention AA's twenty-fifth-anniversary gala, will be a cakewalk compared to keeping music executives and concert promoters in line."

Tallulah managed two world-famous bands: Her mother, Maggie, was the lead singer for Chameleon, one of the Summer of Love's legendary rock bands. She also managed Jammerhead whose namesake and lead singer was her significant other.

"Don't be so cocky," Audrey warned her. "Last year, two moms almost came to blows when their daughters showed up in the same prom gown. Each thought they'd purchased a designer original. Guess who had to step in and pull them apart?" Audrey pointed at herself. Frowning, she added, "Maybe Bliss should lend you her bear spray. It may come in handy."

That sobered up her friends.

Audrey looked at her watch. "We'd better get this show on the road."

"Oh, listen," Bliss exclaimed. "Before you head to the podium, Clare mentioned that Lavinia wanted you to add one other item to the agenda: an introduction to AA's new college admissions consultant. Her name is…" She frowned, distressed at her own forgetfulness.

"Miranda D'Arcy," Audrey replied. "Yes, I've just met her. She's an alumna."

Tallulah shrugged. "Never heard of her."

"I hadn't either…" Audrey looked out into the audience. "She just walked in—the blonde in the suit and Louboutins."

Bliss and Tallulah followed her nod.

"Well, what do you know?" Bliss exclaimed. "Her suit is from our Spring collection." Her husband, Raffaele Belluci, was an internationally renowned couturier.

"Then I guess she has your seal of approval," Audrey replied.

Bliss shook her head. "You can't sway me with a pretty face. Actions speak louder than words." She hugged her friend. "If you're going to sell us to this anxious mob, you'd better put on a smile."

Easier said than done, Audrey thought.

***

Despite having to wing her opening remarks, Audrey stayed on point.

First, she welcomed the parents. Then she recognized the hard work of those who had been active the year before—specifically pointing out Gretchen McCoppin, who had broken all previous auction fundraising records.

Gretchen preened grandly.

Finally, Audrey broke the news that some unexpected personal and professional commitments would keep her from completing her third consecutive term as PTA president.

As expected, the crowd moaned its regrets.

Also, as expected, Gretchen McCoppin wasted no time in asking, "Audrey, will we be voting immediately on your replacement?"

"Per AA's PTA bylaws, the vote will take place next semester after candidates have declared themselves and have had time to campaign for the position. In the interim, I've appointed Bliss Thackeray Belluci and Tallulah Wishart as co-presidents."

"I object!" Gretchen huffed.

"That may be the case, but this isn't a court of law," Audrey replied. "Frankly, Gretchen, if you'd attended any of the PTA steering board meetings, you'd have known that I'm only following the bylaws."

"It's a blessing she doesn't. Otherwise, I'd have jumped off the steering committee," Tallulah muttered just loud enough for Audrey and Bliss to hear her.

Audrey stifled the urge to laugh. When she knew she could talk again without giggling, she added, "Now, for the final issue on today's agenda, I'd like to introduce Ashbury Academy's new college admissions consultant who also happens to be an alumna—Miranda D'Arcy."

She beckoned Miranda to the stage.

Miranda seemed to glide down the auditorium's center aisle before floating up the stage steps like a queen at her coronation. When she reached Audrey, she took both her hands and then kissed her.

Audrey was so stunned at the gesture that she froze.

Had Bliss and Tallulah been on the other side of the stage, they'd have been able to warn Audrey of the blood red lipstick mark that now branded her left cheek.

"It excites me beyond words to once again be a part of the Ashbury Academy family." Miranda made eye contact with at least five parents before opening her arms wide to the rest of the room. "As our school's college admissions counselor, first and foremost, my mission is to make your children happy with their choice for the next part of their life's journey. I'll do this by making sure that their time here at Ashbury Academy has paid off—*by acceptance to a college worthy of all of their hard work.*"

Parents nodded happily, obviously pleased with her determination.

"My second mission is just as important." She paused and leaned in as if she were about to divulge a vital secret. "To make you ecstatic—wait, dare I say *delirious?*—that you chose AA as your children's school."

Everyone chuckled.

"But we're all quite aware that in this day and age, even students with exceptional grades and excellent skills that are showcased by the right extracurricular activities can still miss the target by *that* much." Miranda held up a hand, its thumb and index finger a mere inch apart. "Last year, Georgetown, UCLA, and USC only accepted between fifteen and seventeen percent of the students who applied." Miranda frowned. "As for Stanford, Harvard, and Yale, it was between four and seven percent. With those kinds of acceptance rates, what else can a parent do to catapult their student into these elite schools?"

Miranda's smile faded along with her sigh. "We used to believe it takes a village. In fact, it takes cunning, guile, and the guts to do anything and everything needed to reach that lofty goal."

She paused to let that sink in. "Case in point: I'm sure you've heard that odious urban legend whispered by parents on San Francisco's playgrounds over the past couple of years. You know, the one about the mother who jumped off the Golden Gate Bridge when her son was passed over for admission by all the Ivys?"

The parents sat up ramrod straight, like marionettes whose strings have been pulled by their puppet masters. Some nodded, albeit hesitantly, as if thinking, I'm sure I've heard it…Wait…have I?

Setting the stage for her tale, Miranda leaned into the microphone conspiratorially. "Her son was a star athlete all throughout high school—it was public—having lettered in basketball, baseball, and lacrosse. He'd also been tutored six days a week, sometimes in shifts. But the results were worth the sacrifice! He aced all of his classes, and he placed in AP Math, Science, and English courses."

An awed murmur rose through the audience.

"To top it off, not only had the young man mastered the cello and the tuba—he was a dance-battle winning krumper, too!" Here, Miranda's voice rose to a crescendo.

"But…why?" The question, exclaimed in a strangled panic, was proffered by one nervous father, one of the Virgins.

Miranda's glare relayed her annoyance for his having interrupted her riff. "This last skill had been honed at the suggestion of one of the city's most expensive educational consultants," she explained.

Duly chastised, he hung his head.

"All this, and what was supposed to have made him a shoo-in was his volunteerism: he'd spent not one, but *two* summer vacations, doling out condoms to disease-ridden natives in some third world country…" Miranda thought for a moment. "Or perhaps it was Lodi, California. Sorry, but some of the details are hazy." she shrugged. "In any event, acceptance letters arrived—for all of his classmates. But his never did." She shook her head. "Not one."

The parents' alarmed murmurs were a wall of sound that would rival any on a Phil Spector album.

Miranda waited for silence again before delivering the *coup de grace*: "Ironically, this young man's acceptance letters—*all six of them* —arrived the day after his mother jumped. Apparently, the mailman had delivered them to the *wrong address*. Go figure."

Dead silence.

"The upshot of this rumor," Miranda continued, "is that each subsequent year, the number of applications to San Francisco's private high schools have risen twenty-three percent." Once again, she held out her hands to her audience, as if embracing them. "Welcome to a very elite club! As in all of life, you get what you pay for. Ashbury Academy is a proven commodity—and so am I. It's why Lavinia wants me here for you and our precious students. My promise to you: that I'll encourage your children to aim high. I will inspire them to be their personal best. Most importantly, I'll assess them as if I were the admissions director of their first-pick school. To do so, I'll first have to discover their strengths, which I'll place front and center in their applications. As for any weaknesses..." Here, Miranda paused just a nanosecond. "Well, if I discover any, it'll just be our little secret, okay?"

The parents laughed as if she were wise to them.

Hell yeah, she was. She knew that the last thing they'd want is for any of their children's character blemishes to be exposed.

It was a promise she'd make—for the right price.

They'd find that out soon enough.

The rest of the audience soon joined the first few parents who stood up and clapped.

As if touched by this show of respect, Miranda placed both hands over her heart with index fingers and thumbs touching, to mimic sending her love back to them.

She made a specific point to hold the gaze of that Gretchen person who was so obviously a thorn in Audrey's side.

If her pockets are deep and she's got a kid who's as dense as her, she may be a perfect candidate for my concierge program, Miranda reasoned. At the very least, if there's bad blood between her and Audrey, I can make that work to my favor.

"Look at that line to shake Miranda's hand and grab a business card!" Tallulah exclaimed. "You'd think she was running for president!"

"I'm just glad Raffaele isn't here. Between her suit and the speech she just gave, he'd have hired her on the spot and thrown in a new wardrobe to boot, just to get her to sit on Sienna twenty-four-seven. He's determined that she get a business degree from Harvard, Yale, Columbia, or Wharton. He feels it's the best way to position her to our stockholders as his successor."

"Granted, she is a junior. And if she's interested in college, yes, she should be touring schools this year," Audrey conceded. "But Sienna never struck me as the biz school type."

Bliss rolled her eyes. "My point exactly! Sienna is fine just being herself: a teenage girl who loves fashion, great causes, and cute boys. If that means passing on the best business college—or any college at all—I'm fine with that. Neither Raffaele nor I have college degrees. But he'll blow a gasket if she fights him on it."

Tallulah laughed. "Too bad, because her online presence is certainly paying off. Her Instagram and Snapchat followers are through the roof! Let me tell you, Jammerhead is jealous of her."

At that moment, Audrey turned her head, revealing Miranda's lipstick mark on her cheek. "Talk about being catty!" She took a tissue from her purse. "Keep still. It looks as if your new friend branded you!" Frowning, she turned to stare at Miranda. "What year did you say she graduated?"

"I didn't. Lavinia never said," Audrey rummaged for the hand mirror in her satchel. "But she can't be that much younger than us."

"You're right," Bliss chimed in. "She's had some work done on her face, and God knows where else."

Tallulah smirked. "I'm willing to guess: say, those perky tits, that perky ass, and that flat as a pancake gut, for starters."

Audrey shook her head, dismayed. "Now, now, ladies, no need to be catty."

"Spoilsport," Tallulah groused.

"I'll have to ask Lavinia," Audrey admitted. "In fact, since you're seeing her at the board meeting tomorrow afternoon, feel free to ask her then."

"We will. Trust me," Tallulah muttered. "By the way, who is the teacher trustee this year?"

"Last year it was Berney. But he just retired." Audrey shook her head sadly. "I have no idea who'll be his replacement. I guess the staff will have to vote on it."

She already missed the school's geography teacher and his sweet wife, Jean, but she knew they were happy to be traveling the country in their Silver Airstream trailer to his favorite archeological digs throughout the Mountain West.

Audrey shrugged. "Tallulah, Bliss—I can never thank you enough for taking me up on my offer to co-chair the PTA. You have full-time jobs and lots of employees who depend on you, not to mention that you must travel all over the world..." Audrey allowed her voice to fade rather than to choke up with gratitude. "I guess what I'm trying to say is thank you for having Lavinia's back."

"Of course we'd say yes!" Bliss exclaimed. "We love this school! It was our home, our sanctuary."

"We became the people we are because of AA," Tallulah added. "And besides, you and Lavinia are our family."

Bliss and Tallulah leaned into Audrey for a hug. "Always and forever," they promised in unison.

Audrey left before they could see the tears glistening in her eyes.

THE REST OF AUDREY'S DAY WAS SPENT FIELDING CONFERENCE CALLS with Harris and various members of his staff: fine-tuning a speech to the state's teachers' union, discussing a position paper on California's homelessness, and tweaking talking points for an upcoming town hall debate. All of this Audrey welcomed, as it kept her from fretting over Lavinia's failing health.

She tried to make it back to the school before Lavinia left for her benefactor's meeting, but missed seeing her mother anyway.

Maybe it was for the best. Her eyes were still red from crying.

She put on her sunglasses before the twins bounded into the car.

On the way home, Charly drove while Audrey asked about their day.

To her first question—if they shared any classes—Chuck declared, "Unfortunately, yes. Math and Lit."

"You jest now, but you'll miss having your sister at your side if you go off to different colleges," Audrey warned him.

"Heck no, Ma! I'm sticking to her like glue—but only because I know if I beg, she'll help me with my homework."

Charly snickered. "As if you could get into Berkeley with your grades!"

"You just wait," Chuck retorted. "We're both legacies, not just you. Remember?"

"That doesn't necessarily make you a shoo-in," Audrey warned him.

"I was joking." But Chuck's disappointed tone proved otherwise. He rallied by exclaiming, "I can't wait to prove you wrong, Charlene Lavinia Thorpe McKittridge."

"Now, that's my boy. A positive attitude!" Audrey turned around to grasp his hand and shake it. "Do you like all your teachers?"

"So far, so good," Charly replied. "Although we haven't yet met our Lit teacher. We'll have a substitute until Mercy comes back from maternity leave."

"Lit is which period?" Audrey asked.

"Seventh." The twins said in unison.

Tomorrow evening was AA's parent-teacher open house. That meant Comp Lit's session would be the last one of the night.

Hopefully, Audrey asked, "Does that mean Dad and I can skip your Lit class at the parent and teacher open house tomorrow evening?"

"Nope. Lavinia told us that the sub will be there. Since Mercy's sabbatical might run through both semesters, she expects the parents to be there," Charly assured her.

"I had Mercy for tenth-grade English," Chuck retorted. "This new teacher means I can start with a clean slate."

Audrey tried hard not to wince. Chuck was right. When it came to grades, his sophomore year had not been a stellar one.

Still, to show her support, she replied, "Agreed. And this year, do yourself a favor. Stay on top of all your assignments and ask questions if you're stumped. It's okay to be teacher's pet."

"Don't have such high hopes for him. Fawn is also in our class," Charly warned her. "It should be interesting to see if hearing you talk in iambic pentameter is going to make you any sexier to her." She stuck her tongue out at Chuck through the rearview mirror.

Intrigued, Chuck's brows went up. "Whatever that is, it sounds dirty. I look forward to proving you wrong."

Audrey laughed at that.

Charly too was giggling so hard that she almost ran a red light.

This is going to be one heck of a year, Audrey thought.

Suddenly, she realized that Lavinia might not live to see the twins graduate.

She forced herself to forget that sad possibility as they picked up Noah from private all-boy Town School.

To her relief, she was able to hold back her tears until she could cry in the privacy of her shower.

By the time Daniel got home, her composure was stable enough that she could smile while asking about his day, fill him in on the children's antics, and answer his questions about the other board members.

Later that night, while wrapped in her sleeping husband's arms, she grieved silently.

CHAPTER 4

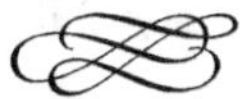

"*M*rs. Edelson—*Helene*. May I call you that? Thank you for taking the time to meet with us," Lionel began. "I'm Special Agent Lionel Polk, and this is my partner, Special Agent SallyAnne Jagger."

They held out their badges for her inspection.

Having been Helene's initial contact (and the more diplomatic of the team at that), it was a given that Lionel would start the interrogation.

SallyAnne didn't mind this at all. As the saying went, you catch more flies with honey than vinegar. Since her approach was more like a flyswatter—make that a sledgehammer—it was best to leave it as a last resort.

Helene hesitated a long minute before stepping aside and waving them into her home: a stucco-and-glass post-modern behemoth at the end of a narrow lane that zigged and zagged its way up a pinnacle hill in Los Angeles' Bel-Air neighborhood. Lionel and SallyAnne hadn't had time for lunch before the flight. In hindsight, it was a good thing. To keep from spewing the coffee she'd drunk on the plane, SallyAnne had stared at the horizon as Lionel willed the rental car up the windy road.

The reward for making the climb was the spectacular view from the two-story floor-to-ceiling wrap-around windows in the Edelsons' living room. It extended from Los Angeles' downtown cityscape in the southeast to the Pacific Ocean to the west, with Beverly Hills in between.

"Mesmerizing, isn't it?" Helene murmured.

SallyAnne nodded.

What Helene didn't know was that SallyAnne's eyes hadn't lingered long on what was outside the Edelson's living room. Instead, they lighted on the personal items interspersed between the white modular furnishings.

Books filled suspended shelves (mostly classic novels and histories). There were numerous family pictures as well. Formal portraits were interspersed among candid photos of Helene, her husband Robert, and their two children.

In many of the photos, the children wore sports jerseys. Soccer seemed to be the sport of choice for both. The trophies were displayed in a glass case on one of the higher shelves.

SallyAnne pointed to one photo: a boy, kneeling near a goal post, a soccer ball in hand. "Is this your son?" she asked.

Helene nodded. "Yes. Rob Junior—Robbie—is now a freshman at USC."

Lionel pointed to another photo: a teen girl, in a period costume, onstage. "And this is your daughter?"

"Yes. She's a junior this year at Bobbitt-Hennings Prep School."

Lionel nodded. "Is that the school where the incident happened?"

Helene frowned. "Yes. Robbie graduated from there last year. It's just down the hill and a few miles from here. Across the 405, in Brentwood."

Lionel and SallyAnne already knew this. After tracing Helene's phone call to the bureau, they'd pulled up what they could about her and Robert, including all social media postings and online photos. A picture from the school's latest fundraiser had popped up.

"Helene, Special Agent Jagger has read the transcript of our call," Lionel explained. "But, for the record, I'd like you to reiterate the key points—also recorded, for our records."

The woman's lower lip quivered at the thought. Still, she motioned for them to have a seat on the sofa, taking its twin across from them.

SallyAnne pulled out her phone, hit a recording app, and then noted the date, time, and that the interview being recorded was with Helene Edelson.

"Okay, well, as I mentioned, one of the members of the trustee board divulged his knowledge of Ms. D'Arcy's activities with another school parent."

"You mean, she had approached the parent about some contacts she had at a university, and that she could facilitate students' admissions?" SallyAnne asked.

"Frankly, it was blunter than that. She boasted that she's built a network of contacts with several universities: five or six elite choices on both coasts."

"The trustee who brought it to the board's attention—who was he, or she?" Lionel asked.

"I was curious, but Rob wouldn't tell me. He felt he'd already said too much. Everything the board discusses must stay confidential, for obvious reasons." Helene shrugged. "He just said many of the trustees were stunned. Others just rolled their eyes. They'd heard the same scuttlebutt." She paused. "Then one trustee admitted he too had been approached by Miranda. He had seriously considered her offer after another parent boasted she'd done the same for him the year before. It was at a pool party. The man was tipsy. For that reason, at first, the trustee didn't believe him." Helene shook her head in disbelief. "But then he asked one of his children. The boy was a friend of the student involved. His kid laughed. He thought it was funny that the boy got in as a crew coxswain! Our school doesn't even have a crew team!"

"Did the trustee in question approach Ms. D'Arcy after learning this?"

"Yes. He admitted doing so." By Helene's tremor, it was apparent she sympathized with him. "But apparently, he found the fee for her services outrageous."

"What was it?" SallyAnne asked.

"He was quoted one hundred thousand."

Lionel's eyes grew large. "That's more than the first year of tuition at many universities."

Helene nodded. "I'm sure that's why he passed on the offer."

"He'd have done it if it were cheaper?" SallyAnne asked.

"Probably. Private schools attract a lot of parents with more money than brains. To them, finding a side door into the college of their choice may not seem like a crime. Wealthier parents will offer to pay for a building, so why not?"

SallyAnne's eyes narrowed with disgust.

Lionel's cough warned her: *Behave.*

"The bigger crime is that a proper education is so expensive in the first place." Helene looked around the room. "It may not be a stretch for some of us, but many parents with kids at our school are barely scraping by. They make the sacrifice because they hope their children can get into a top flight college. And think of those children coming out of public schools! Talk about having the deck stacked against you!" Frustrated, Helene shook her head.

"We can understand your anger, Helene," Lionel murmured. "I mean, you work very hard to get your son into USC. Then, to hear some of the other parents would gladly pay for the privilege of having their children gain acceptance under fraudulent circumstances? That's got to hurt!"

"It hurts all right," Helene retorted. She scrutinized SallyAnne, then Lionel. "Are you married?"

Lionel's eyes widened. "You mean, to each other?"

SallyAnne blushed a deep red.

Helene smirked. "Sorry! I didn't mean to hit a nerve."

Lionel's face suddenly felt flush too.

"My question was meant in a general sense. Are either of you married? Do you have children?"

"No." They answered in unison, and as if there were shame in it.

"We're quite aware that college tuition has skyrocketed," Sally-Anne countered.

Helene guffawed. "Who said anything about college? Let's start with the fact that private preschool tuition now rivals what your parents shelled out for your senior year in college. Now, couple that with the reality that applications to your preferred preschools—and do note the use of the plural pronoun here: as in, have at least *five* safety schools!—should take place sometime during your second prenatal trimester—and you've got some idea of what you're facing, both financially and competitively—"

She paused here, for emphasis: *"For the next twenty-two years of your life."*

Lionel and SallyAnne flinched in unison.

"Metaphorically speaking, whatever belt-tightening was necessary for private kindergarten is merely pinching an inch compared to how you'll suck it in for private elementary school. You can double that figure for a well-regarded prep school," Helene added.

"Around ten thousand dollars? Maybe closer to twenty?" Sally-Anne asked.

Helene arched a brow. "You're joking, right?... No? Well then, I'm glad you're sitting down." She leaned in. "We're talking thirty or forty thou."

SallyAnne's eyes grew wide.

"Don't worry. You'll find the money somewhere. Go ahead, take out a second mortgage on your house, or sell a few bonds, or break into that 401(k) you were hoping would get you through your golden years." Helene smirked. "Better yet, beg your spouse's parents for it! A recent survey shows that one very successful ploy is to convince them that retiring to Florida is *so* last generation. Instead, convince them that extended family living is back in fashion and that you've already started converting your basement into an in-law suite so that they can move in the day you've shipped your child off to his Ivy of choice. To seal the deal, invite them to choose their own wallpaper. It's the least you can do, now that you know that the kid's tuition has sucked the yolk out of their nest egg."

SallyAnne blanched. She remembered her parents insisting that they pay for her college tuition. Knowing it would come out of their retirement savings, she opted to work and go to night school instead. They never said it, but she knew they were relieved that she never took them up on the offer.

"And you wonder why parents will lie, steal, cheat, and beg, to get their kids into college? Now you know." Helene shrugged. "Sorry I got so carried away. It comes from growing up with two public school teachers as parents."

It took a while before Lionel could find his composure. Softly, he asked, "Previously, you stated that the board fired Ms. D'Arcy."

"Yes, at Rob's recommendation. He was quite disconcerted about the matter."

"You also mentioned the board paid her a severance," SallyAnne pointed out.

"Yes. Six hundred thousand dollars." Helene grimaced. "And to add insult to injury, the board also gave her a letter of recommendation!"

"What a disgrace!" SallyAnne's voice rose in frustration. "But no one thought to inform local law enforcement?"

"There was only hearsay. There was no proof to back it up. If the rumors were wrong, she could have sued the school and taken it under! Either way, our school's reputation would have been ruined. The bitch knew that. Better to just let her go on her merry way." Helene shuddered at the thought.

"Thanks again for your help, Helene," Lionel said.

"Any time...I guess." She stood up. "By the way, did you find her at that San Francisco school—you know, Ashbury Academy?"

"We're not allowed to discuss an ongoing investigation," Lionel replied.

Helene's face went slack. "By that, I take it you're at least investigating her. Good. Miranda is ruining lives. She shouldn't be able to get away with it." She looked Lionel in the eye. "Listen, if Rob knew *I* was the one who turned you on to Miranda's scheme—"

"We'd never reveal an anonymous source," Lionel insisted.

Helene's lip quivered.

"I'm sure there are many other parents just as disgruntled with the turn of events," Lionel pointed out. "The last person he'd suspect is you."

Her silence spoke volumes: she didn't believe him.

"Odds are we won't have to interview him," Lionel assured her.

Finally, Helene nodded.

Lionel caught SallyAnne's smirk at this outright lie. Rob Edelson sat on B-H Prep's trustee board. He was an attorney. Of course they'd follow up with him.

And as an officer of the court, he'd answer their questions truthfully.

Thankfully, Helene missed SallyAnne's tell because she was wiping away a tear.

"DO YOU WANT TO HAVE KIDS?" LIONEL'S QUESTION CAME WHEN THEY were halfway down the hill.

It was all SallyAnne could do not to turn and stare at him, and not just because she might throw up, what with the way he was hurtling down the hill. "I... I guess I would. With the right person."

"Even after what she said about that whole school situation?"

"It's not the kids that have made education a mess. It's the parents! They do too much to shelter their children from reality. They don't allow them to grow and discover and make decisions on their own." SallyAnne shrugged. "They don't do enough to support their public schools."

"Not all parents," Lionel countered.

"But enough of them," she argued. "Enough to make this kind of behavior—this disregard for fairness—a thing." She gave him a sidelong glance. "How about you? Do you want children?"

"With the right woman, yes."

I'm the right woman.

Someday, she hoped to prove this to him.

And face the consequences.

She winced at the thought that he might say, *Sorry, SallyAnne, but you've got it wrong. We're great partners, and we should leave it at that...*

No, better to keep things just as they were. Right now, they were together eight, sometimes ten hours a day. If she were lucky, there would be an out of town trip that allowed them to stay in each other's company into the long hours of the evening.

Putting a case together was hard work. However, it was also an adrenaline high. Especially when the last thing you wanted to do was sleep.

When all you could think of was being with him.

It was always harder when the investigation meant an overnight stay. It was all she could do to keep from banging on his door and hoping he'd open it naked. At which point, she'd—

"Interviewing Rob Edelson is a must," Lionel was saying. "But I don't think we should tackle it today. We'll walk in unannounced to Edelson's law office first thing in the morning. I'll call Melamed and get it cleared with him."

"Okay," SallyAnne murmured. *YES! YES!*

"When Rob comes clean with the trustee who was compromised and the parent who took Miranda up on her offer, we'll track them down too." Lionel glanced over. "We may be down here for two or three days. Are you fine with that?"

SallyAnne prayed her voice didn't quiver when she replied, "It's part of the job, right? We're down here now, so let's make the most of it."

CHAPTER 5

All night long, Egan Gable had tossed and turned over the decision to take Lavinia up on her offer to come back to Ashbury Academy as its Upper Grades English instructor.

Even before the alarm went off, he was already awake. Egan felt like a convicted felon who had lost his last appeal and was now minutes from being strapped down for lethal injection.

Yes, I need the money, he'd reasoned. And yes, it'll only be temporary. Still, the world will see me as a loser to be back where I started before I was published.

Yeah, okay, so this is where I am in my life at this very second. I should make the best of it, right?

I mean, I'm a good teacher. The kids looked up to me. Heck, a few even idolized me. I made an impact on their lives.

Damn it, suck it up and just do it already!

He rose to shower, shave, and eat a cold bowl of cereal while gulping down his coffee. It was early, so congestion on the Golden Gate Bridge shouldn't be too bad. The city's traffic into the Haight was another beast altogether.

The sooner he left, the better.

When Egan got to the school, he was surprised by its many physical improvements. It was the same Victorian mansion, but it was no longer shabby. Fresh paint in a bright multi-hued pallet now accented the school's unique architectural details: turrets, gables, porch spindles, and fishtail shingles.

The decrepit storefronts and townhouses that had shared its block had been replaced by various structures that extended Ashbury Academy and complemented the architectural integrity of the original building. An ornate wrought iron fence connected the buildings, creating a private park between them. From the curb, one could see that the gravel paths intersecting the mossy lawn in the center of the campus were dotted with ornate benches.

These changes left Egan dismayed. He thought that, even some twenty-two years later, the school would have somehow stayed just like he remembered it. That, as in *Brigadoon*, the whole of it—building, students, and faculty—had gone into a deep sleep after he'd departed, only to be awakened again in his presence.

The school's future was very bright, whereas his star had fallen into a black hole.

Somehow, he had to climb out of it.

"Yoo-hoo! You're Egan, aren't you?"

Before he could answer, the woman reached out to shake Egan's hand.

He hesitated to take it, if only for a moment. When he did, she grasped it firmly and leaned forward. "I'm Miranda D'Arcy. Remember?" Her voice had a seductive tone to it.

He had to admit he liked it.

In fact, from what Egan saw, there was much about her he found pleasing. The blonde—slim, perhaps a decade his junior—was dressed in a suit that hugged every curve. The top two pearl buttons on her sheer blouse were open. A pearl pendant hung just above the V between her generous breasts.

Nice, he thought.

When he shifted his eyes to hers, she winked as if to say, *Gotcha.*

He didn't mind that at all. "Yes, of course I remember. We talked yesterday. So kind of you to be my welcoming committee." It was Egan's nature to hold any attractive woman's gaze and smile as if she'd already done something to please him. Experience taught him that, eventually, she'd want to.

And by Miranda's throaty chuckle, he knew she wouldn't want to disappoint.

This, above all, put to rest the niggling qualms he had about being back at Ashbury Academy.

Miranda placed her hand gently on his back as she guided him down the hall. "You'll have a full day, I'm afraid. Of your three courses, two you'll teach twice. You do have a period off, for lunch."

He nodded resignedly.

"Lavinia is already in the teacher's lounge," Miranda continued. "She is very excited to see you again! By the way, she took the liberty of reviewing and approving Mercy's syllabus, but she's open to any changes you may want to make. She trusts you implicitly."

Egan's grin wavered as he nodded mutely.

Even after all these years.

Even after what I did to Audrey.

But of course, Audrey would never have mentioned the incident to her mother.

Had she done so, he wouldn't be here now.

Miranda stopped in front of a door marked TEACHERS' LOUNGE. "I'll leave you in good hands."

Egan stared up at the sign and sighed. "I wonder if anyone I knew back then are still here?"

"Let's see: you were here for just one year, and it was over twenty years ago?" Miranda clucked her tongue. "I hear that there are still one or two of the original staff around."

"So, you're new here too?"

Miranda nodded. "I'm an alumna. But yes, I'm also new to the staff."

Noting his disappointment, she patted his arm. "Not to worry. I'm a friend, too, right?"

"I hope so," Egan murmured. He meant it. In a sea of doubt, she'd tossed him a lifeline. He wasn't about to let go anytime soon.

"Of course, we are!" Miranda chuckled. "We're old friends already, you and I."

She's quite a tease, he thought. Okay, two can play this game. "I feel that way too. Old souls, former lives."

Miranda winked playfully. "Yes, eons ago."

"I look forward to playing catch-up."

"No more than me," she assured him. "And we'll have plenty of opportunities to do so. As AA's in-house college admissions consultant, I seek out the teachers' opinions as to which seniors are excelling in their classes. In your case, perhaps their preferred college has a literary program that's a good match."

"I'm at your disposal," he promised.

"I'm sure you are," she purred. "And to return the favor, I'd like to make a suggestion. If the opportunity presents itself, volunteer to join the trustee board as the teacher representative."

Egan frowned. "That means staying later to attend the meetings."

"Just one night a month," Miranda reminded him. "It also means you'll be endearing yourself to the board members who are likely to underwrite your chair here at Ashbury Academy. Trust me. It will pay off handsomely." She winked seductively. "Not to worry. If you find yourself too tired to cross the bridge, I'm sure *someone* will be happy to let you sleep over."

She waved as she walked off, only to turn around after a few steps—

At which point, she caught him admiring the view.

Shaking her head at his audacity, she laughed all the way down the hall.

ALTHOUGH MIRANDA WASN'T A MEMBER OF THE TRUSTEE BOARD, JUST that morning she'd suggested to Lavinia that she attend its first meeting of the year. "As an administrative asset and sounding board, if you will," was how she had positioned it to the headmistress. "The school's crowning achievement is the number of students who have been accepted by their first-choice school. I've been hired to play an integral role in building on this success. Meeting with the board as soon as possible gives me an opportunity to answer their questions."

"I think it's a great idea," Lavinia agreed, albeit she then added firmly: "But remember, Miranda, the school's—and therefore the board's—first and foremost goal is to provide the students with the skills that allow them to make the best choices for their lives, now and into the future. If an academic path is what they decide, then yes, of course, you'll be a wonderful resource for them. But college isn't necessarily right for all students. We must respect their choices."

Miranda noted the gentle rebuttal with a meek nod.

In fact, she knew AA's bylaws by heart. It was the best way to protect herself should any of her illegal activities go awry. It had almost happened in her last position.

At least she had accomplished her immediate goal: an introduction to the trustees.

The endgame: a permanent seat on the board.

"You haven't changed a bit." Lavinia beckoned Egan closer for a hug. There was no standing at attention with her.

She felt frail in Egan's arms; noticeably smaller somehow.

Instinctively, he looked down at her head. Where gray strands could once be glimpsed in its formerly thick curly brown mane, now only a few dark threads stood out in the almost sheer drape of white hair pinned primly to the nape of her neck.

The naïvete of her statement pierced his heart. He sighed. "If that were true, it would be a travesty."

"Would it?" As if surprised that she may have offended him, she laid a hand on his arm. "When you were here, you thrived! Ashbury Academy was the start of so many great things for you!"

His laugh was fierce and joyless. "'Was' is the operative word there. Whatever greatness I had, Lavinia, I've since failed it."

"Your life isn't over, Egan. Granted, our circumstances are in constant flux. But our mistakes create detours on our journey, not dead ends."

"Apparently, my road has turned into a cul-de-sac." He looked around the teachers' lounge. Despite new furnishings and walls now painted crisp beige as opposed its former dingy taupe hue, it was the same room he remembered. "Lavinia, you know I adore you. And I meant no offense to Ashbury Academy because my time here was special in so many ways. I guess what I'm trying to say is that being back where I started... Well, I feel like Dante: stuck in some soul-sucking circle of Hell."

Lavinia chuckled. "I read your novel, Egan. It strikes me that your time at AA was more like *Vanity Fair*."

He laughed. "Did you hate *Extracurricular*?"

Did Audrey? Does she hate me as well?

Lavinia shook her head. "Each person's perception of the same incident is going to be unique." She raised a brow. "And it was fiction, after all."

He let that lie.

"Although, Egan, I must say: until I read your book, I hadn't known you'd placed Audrey on such a high pedestal."

"As you said: it's fiction." Egan shrugged. Before he'd lose his nerve, he asked, "How is she, anyway?"

"You can ask her yourself." Lavinia winked. "She's no stranger to AA. In fact, she'll be here tonight. She wouldn't miss it."

"Does she know I'm back?" His heart pounded heavily at that thought.

Lavinia laughed. "I'm sure she will, before tonight's open house…Oh, didn't Miranda tell you? It's at seven. We're all in for a long day! Speaking of which, before the other teachers start filtering in, we should go over the syllabus Mercy prepared for her—that is, *your* classes…"

CHAPTER 6

*B*y nine the next morning, Lionel and SallyAnne had entered the lobby of the Century City law firm that bore Robert Edelson's name along with those of three of his partners.

According to the receptionist, Edelson had been there since at least eight. And yet, he kept them waiting almost an hour.

Finally, an assistant arrived to show them to Edelson's office.

It was on a corner and almost the size of a ballroom. Like his home, it boasted floor-to-ceiling windows that afforded him a westerly view of Santa Monica and the ocean.

It's the office I would have chosen, given the opportunity, Lionel thought. The alternate corners—staked out by the other partners, he supposed—would have looked directly east onto the regularly traffic-congested Santa Monica Boulevard, or southeast toward amber-hazed downtown Los Angeles, or north toward the stark Hollywood Hills.

I wouldn't have lasted as long as that sun-baked potted plant in the corner, he realized. Corporate law offices like this one made him happy he'd chosen the FBI instead.

Rob stood as they entered and motioned to the chairs facing his massive desk as opposed to the more comfortable leather Corbusier couch and side chairs that made a conversation pit in the middle of the mammoth office.

We are the enemy, Lionel reasoned.

The goal now was to find out why.

"What can I do for you, Special Agents"—Rob nodded to Sally-Anne first—"Jagger? Great name! My favorite rock-and-roller." His eyes shifted to Lionel. "And, um, Polk, right?" He chuckled. "Not such a great president. No relation, I assume."

"Yes, as a matter of fact." Lionel admitted. "Great uncle, six times removed."

Rob seemed taken aback by that. "Well then...I guess we're all related to someone."

Lionel and SallyAnne let that sit. They knew Rob wasn't really trying to make small talk.

"Mr. Edelson, we're investigating a case of potential fraud," SallyAnne explained. "A woman by the name of Miranda D'Arcy is currently a person of interest. If you have any evidence that, in her capacity as a college admissions counselor, she established a network of university administrators who are willing to, for lack of a better word, 'facilitate' admissions of students for a fee, it would help us establish that she is, in fact, a prime suspect in our case."

The color drained from Rob's face. "I see."

"Additionally, Ms. D'Arcy's illegal activities may have included tampering with, or falsifying, standardized test scores," Lionel explained.

Rob nodded slowly. "How did you get my name?"

Lionel shrugged. "Our sources are confidential."

"I still don't understand why you're here talking to me."

Lionel and SallyAnne exchanged glances. Lionel knew they were thinking the same thing: *something is not right here.*

SallyAnne pulled out her cell phone, clicked on an audio recording app, and laid it on Rob's desk. After stating the date, the time, the agents present, and Rob's full name, she began: "Rob Edelson, you sat in a trustee meeting in which felonies were discussed. As an officer of the court, you had a fiduciary responsibility to bring these matters to the attention of the appropriate authorities. Not doing so makes you—not to mention the other trustees—suspects in a criminal conspiracy."

"Wait... *Wait just a minute!*" Rob stood up. "How do you know what was discussed in the meeting?"

"For the record, are you telling us that you do not know of anyone, including Ms. D'Arcy, who may have committed illegal acts such as fraud, or bribery, or cheating to facilitate student admissions to U.S.-based universities?" SallyAnne asked.

"I…I didn't say that!" Rob stammered.

"Then, exactly what are you saying?" Lionel countered.

Rob glared at him. "Level with me. It was that bitch who sent you here, wasn't it?"

Bitch?…

Is he referring to Helene? Did we give her away?

Lionel and SallyAnne's stares met. Apparently, she was confused too.

Rob's lip curled into a smirk. "Agents, I'm no fool. I know how this plays out. I become a felon! My law license gets suspended—or worse, I lose it for life! My wife divorces me, and my children are shunned. Robbie will hate me because I didn't believe he'd get into USC on his own. And all because that bitch flipped first—"

Oh, I get it now.

"Sir, please…*Calm down*," Lionel's voice was soft but firm. "We've yet to talk to Ms. D'Arcy."

As Lionel's words sunk in, Rob dropped back into his massive captain's chair.

He stared out the window: two minutes at the most, but it seemed like an eternity. Finally, he looked up at Lionel. "Well, then, I guess that works in my favor doesn't it, being the first up to bat?" His attempt at a smile was weak at best. "You'll note I'm a cooperating witness, correct?"

"Yes, absolutely." Lionel glanced at SallyAnne.

She nodded. "As an officer of the court, you're sworn to tell the truth. Not to mention, as a possible suspect yourself, any misstatement will be seen as obstruction of justice and dealt with accordingly."

Rob sighed. "Alright. Let's move forward then, shall we? So, what is it you want to know?"

Thank God for cooperating witnesses, Lionel thought.

SALLYANNE BEGAN: "MR. EDELSON, FOR THE RECORD, CAN YOU NAME the individual perpetrating the college admissions fraud?"

"Her name is Miranda D'Arcy. She was formerly the college

placement counselor at Bobbitt-Hennings Prep School here in Los Angeles."

"How were you made aware of these acts?"

"She approached me with an offer to attain acceptance to a top-tier university of my choosing for my son, Robbie. She named other parents who had had success with her, um, methods."

SallyAnne nodded. "Did she explain these methods to you?"

"Yes. And there are numerous opportunities for fraud. In many cases, the students' standardized tests are taken by, or substituted with others provided by a professional test taker. This is done by getting approval from the school to take the test off-campus, at a certified testing center. In this case, it was University Prep & Test." He shrugged. "Additionally, false narratives about a student's extracurricular activities are established to give the student a non-academic advantage over others."

"Was Ms. D'Arcy paid for these services?"

Rob scoffed. "Yes. Serious money."

"How much?" SallyAnne asked.

"The fees varied substantially, depending on what Mandy—that is, Miranda—thought she could get."

Mandy…? That sounds cozy, Lionel noted.

From the way SallyAnne's brow lifted, she also caught the nickname. "Can you give us a range?" she insisted.

"Yes. Fees ranged as small as ten thousand dollars. But those were rare. As Miranda put it, she'd cut some slack for the desperately poor."

"How generous of her," SallyAnne muttered.

Rob flinched at the jibe. "Yeah, well, that's Miranda for you. To answer your question, most parents paid in the mid- or high six-figures. A few paid over a million, if you can believe that."

Lionel's eyes opened wide.

SallyAnne paused, then asked: "Mr. Edelson, how much did *you* pay to have Robbie's SAT test falsified?"

"One hundred thousand." Just admitting this, Rob deflated like a hot-air balloon stabbed with a cold knife.

Lionel remembered Helene's pride in her children's accomplishments, both in and out of the classroom. "Why do it?" he wondered aloud. "Robbie's grades were better than good. And he had at least one solid extracurricular. He was a soccer champion."

Rob looked up sharply. "How do you know that?"

Damn it, I may have just outed Helene.

Lionel was relieved when Rob muttered, "Never mind. I know you guys don't bother asking a question unless you already have the answer." He looked down at SallyAnne's phone and shrugged at the recording. "Robbie... well, he's a lousy test taker. Just freezes. His real SAT score wouldn't have been enough to get him into my alma mater."

"But he would have gotten into other good schools," SallyAnne countered.

"Maybe," Rob conceded. "But it wasn't worth risking. Not for such a paltry fee." He grimaced when he saw SallyAnne's eyes narrow.

This case rubs her raw, Lionel realized.

So that Rob wouldn't just close up, Lionel knew it was time he jumped in: "How were the fees paid?"

"The testing center was paid directly, but I wouldn't be surprised if Miranda took a cut of what it got." Rob shrugged. "As for the counseling fees, they were paid to a non-profit corporation called the Best Foot Forward Club. That way, parents get to write it off as a tax-exempt donation. It's a win-win."

The IRS would surely be interested in this revelation, Lionel thought.

Annoyed, SallyAnne clenched her fists. When she finally released them, she asked, "How and when did the Bobbitt-Hennings trustee board discover her actions?"

"Mid-July. Someone made a formal complaint. I couldn't let the other members know I was one of her so-called 'concierge clients,' so I suggested that, as the school's legal representative on the trustee board, I negotiate a settlement with her."

SallyAnne shook her head in awe. "As opposed to telling the authorities about her illicit activities?"

Rob shrugged. "As far as the board was concerned, it was all hearsay. It wasn't the board's place to prove or disprove the allegations. In the meantime, to maintain its stellar reputation, it was best that the school quickly distance itself from her."

"You said that Miranda D'Arcy's average fee was the mid- six-figures," SallyAnne pointed out. "And yet she charged you only one hundred thousand. Why is that?"

Rob's face turned bright red.

Suddenly, Lionel knew what Rob was trying hard not to say, so he asked: "How long had you been having an affair with Ms. D'Arcy?"

Rob muttered, "It wasn't like that! We…we only did it once." He shrugged. "I told her we had to meet because the board was onto her. At her suggestion, we met at her place. She insisted she didn't want to make trouble for the school. She was upset and worried about the possible consequences of her actions." He shook his head. "One thing led to another… You know."

SallyAnne allowed a minute to pass before asking, "And, for that, she walked away with a severance five times her salary—and a reference?"

"No—not for '*that!*'" Rob retorted. "She knew her reputation was in tatters. If she tried to Me-Too me, it would be her word against mine." He frowned. "She needed insurance. She made a video of us —*together!*"

SallyAnne looked from him to Lionel and back. "A sex tape?"

Rob nodded. Then, remembering he was being recorded, he murmured, "Yes."

"You're saying she blackmailed you?" Lionel asked.

Rob's response was so soft that Lionel wondered if the recorder picked it up.

"Again, please, Mr. Edelson," he prompted him.

"Yes! She told me if I couldn't convince the board to pay up, not only would she take the school down with her, she'd send the video to Helene." Shamed by his confession, Rob closed his eyes. "As it turned out, Miranda didn't need the video anyway. The board gladly gave her what she wanted to put the incident to bed without a scandal."

Lionel waited until Rob opened his eyes again to ask, "Can you name any others who were also… you called it, 'concierge clients,' right?"

"Yes. Janna and Eric Calisher. They live in Beverly Hills. He's in financial management. The firm is Dewey-Calisher. Their kid, a boy, isn't the sharpest tool in the shed," Rob rolled his eyes. "The other client is Tanner Simpson."

SallyAnne perked up. "Tanner Simpson, the director?"

"Yeah. He doesn't let anyone forget it, either. If he could, he'd carry around his Oscar to remind the rest of us." Rob's scorn was evident in his tone as well as his words. "His daughter—Lacey, is her name—skirts by on his reputation."

"Are there any others?" Lionel asked.

"Probably, but I can't think of anyone else. My guess? It's just the tip of the iceberg for Miranda." Rob opened his hands wide. "Agents, I'm doing what I can to earn brownie points. Consider me part of the team."

"I'm glad you put it that way, Rob. And, as part of your agreement to cooperate fully, we'll need all correspondence between you and Ms. D'Arcy," SallyAnne explained. "By the way, within the next twenty-four hours, an FBI tech team will be at your office and home with subpoenas to go through all your computer and other electronic devices."

"Understood."

"In the future, we may also ask you to make a call to Ms. D'Arcy and ask her specific questions. The conversation will be recorded."

"No problem." Rob nodded. "Agents, I know I have no right to ask you this, but… if my wife finds out…" His voice trailed off.

Lionel nodded. "Like you, we're sworn to keep our findings confidential. Remember, we've only just begun the investigation. At this point, we can't say how long it will take to build the case and issue subpoenas for Ms. D'Arcy and her network of bribed administrators."

"A year, maybe?" The hope in Rob's voice made SallyAnne grimace.

"Even so, eventually the parents who participated in Miranda's scheme will be named in court documents and have trials of their own," SallyAnne replied. "How a judge may rule in your case… well, it's hard to predict. You know that better than most."

Rob sighed. "I just pray whomever is appointed is not someone I've already pissed off."

———

DIVISION DIRECTOR MELAMED AGREED WITH LIONEL AND SALLYANNE that they should spend the rest of the week in Los Angeles, perhaps even longer, checking out the leads that had come their way via Rob Edelson.

Melamed also approved the search and seizure of all of Edelson's devices, and the wiretaps on all of now prime suspect Miranda D'Arcy's communication devices. As soon as these could be analyzed and assessed, the deep dive into Miranda's background would begin.

"I'll send Riley Kemp down there to facilitate on tech," he promised.

In larger markets, the bureau had travel accounts with Marriott. Because it was spending taxpayer dollars, whenever possible agents were encouraged to take the less expensive brands within the chain. With this in mind, for this trip Lionel had chosen the Marriott Courtyard in Century City beside Beverly Hills, which was within ten miles of most of the Bobbitt-Hennings Prep School parents who were currently potential suspects.

After returning to their rooms, Lionel joined SallyAnne in hers. Their task: create a profile on Miranda from anything they could pull up on their suspect from public records and online sources, such as social media, news clippings, college transcripts, and her company's website.

SallyAnne watched as Lionel's eyes perused every photo they could find on Miranda D'Arcy, née Mandy Blackwell. They felt they'd struck gold when they located an online version of her high school yearbook.

As a teenager, Mandy had been pudgy and pimply, with a tightly coiled mass of bright red hair. But from what SallyAnne could see from the pictures of Miranda D'Arcy on her latest driver's license, passport, and company website, the once ugly duckling had grown into a slim, blond swan.

By seven, the agents were famished. Lionel suggested that they use their allotted per diem to eat at a casual Italian restaurant.

SallyAnne gave him an immediate thumbs-up. She loved spending time with him when they were officially off the clock. When fatigue and a glass of wine kicked in, she gleaned a few more touching tidbits of the man behind the badge.

That night, they spent the balance of the meal discussing the approach they'd take with the potential suspects: the movie director, Tanner Simpson, and Janna Calisher and her husband Eric, the financial manager.

"Perhaps tomorrow's first stop should be Simpson," SallyAnne suggested. "We could approach him when he's leaving his home for the movie set. That way, we won't have to be announced by studio security."

"Sound theory," Lionel murmured. "Later that morning we can then interview Eric Calisher at his office."

"He'll tell his wife immediately afterward," SallyAnne pointed out.

"Probably. But by getting Eric on record first, we can then explain to her what he could be facing so that she makes the best decision for herself and their children. They've got two others who are currently in middle school."

In other words, Janna may want to cut a deal to avoid or reduce her jail time.

SallyAnne held up her wine glass. "Here's to securing our first witness willing to turn on Ms. D'Arcy, and, hopefully, three more to come."

Lionel tapped his glass to hers. "I can't wait to meet her in person."

SallyAnne raised a brow. "Why is that?"

Lionel met her question with a shrug. "I'm always fascinated to see what it is about our suspects that beguiles their victims. Or, in this case, co-conspirators. She must be quite a smooth operator to have convinced these parents to secure her services regardless that they'd be skirting the law."

SallyAnne knew him well enough to realize he, too, felt Miranda should do jail time for creating this enormously profitable scheme.

Once again, she tipped her glass toward his. "I'll drink to that."

It made her proud to have him as her co-worker.

How she wished they were much more than that.

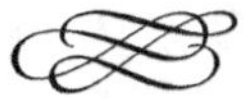

CHAPTER 7

I'm the man.

This declaration had been reverberating through Egan's mind all day.

At first, it was the mantra he needed that morning to propel himself out of the house and into his car—really, his father's ancient Camry—for the trek over the Golden Gate Bridge and through the city to Ashbury Academy.

But then Miranda D'Arcy's flirtatious greeting (make that her obvious come-on) bolstered the phrase into an honest-to-God possibility.

Any doubts still lingering faded in the very warm welcomes he received from the two former colleagues still on staff.

Odette Pettigrew's rib-bruising hug was accompanied with an alarming whisper: "When I read *Extracurricular,* I was touched to learn I was your muse! Perhaps we should explore that role in depth, on our off time?"

Egan covered his horror at that thought by chuckling benignly. Apparently, she hadn't recognized the character he'd based on her: Lilliane Canard, a frowzy, flirtatious tippler with a heart of gold.

Far be it from him to correct her.

Cornell Rothchild's response was even more surprising. Egan had fully expected the slight, effete chemistry teacher to chide him for leaving him out of *Extracurricular* altogether since any actions that could have been attributed to him went to an über-masculine hulk who went by the name of Oscar. Instead, Cornell nodded toward the exclusive blend of beans now steeping in his private portable French press.

"Stay away from that swill in the communal coffee urn," he warned Egan. "In fact, I've got enough of this for another cuppa or two, if you care to join me."

Egan winced at the thought of having to drink from one of Cornell's prissy little cups. He was relieved when the brew was presented in a mug engraved with Ashbury Academy's logo.

As Egan sipped the excellent coffee, Cornell pulled out a copy of the book and asked Egan to autograph it. With a broad wink, he added, "Please make it out to 'Oscar.'"

As Egan signed, it brought to mind the most famous stanza from Robert Burns' poem, "To a Louse, On Seeing One on a Lady's Bonnet at Church":

O would some Power the giftie gie us
To see ourselves as others see us!

Burns was spot on, Egan thought. Most people are blind to any truth about themselves.

Egan's version of their truth, anyway.

EGAN'S ANXIETY WAS FURTHER ASSUAGED BY LAVINIA'S HEARTFELT introduction of him to the rest of the teaching staff: "In the solitary year Egan's presence graced Ashbury Academy, he was an eager volunteer for school events, a true friend to his fellow teaching colleagues, and an inspiration to his students."

His twenty-eight new coworkers instinctively turned to peruse the recipient of Lavinia's praise. All were younger than him, some by two decades.

To cover his chagrin, he did the one thing that never failed him in anxious times: he grinned broadly, then sought out the prettiest woman in the room and winked at her.

As in every other incident, the chosen one blushed even as she returned his wink.

This was not lost on the others. Curiosity abounded. Nonchalant glances hardened into outright stares.

One of the male teachers in particular—tall but wiry, a twenty-something sporting hipster chin scruff—scowled outright. When he caught Egan's eye, he glared. Egan held his gaze until the man finally looked away.

Egan imagined what he must be thinking: *Has a new pecking order been established?*

Hell, yeah it has, Egan thought.

I'm the man. And don't you forget it.

"...And remember, staff: a catered dinner will be prepared for teachers who won't have time to go home prior to the parent open house, which begins at seven tonight." Lavinia's tone was gentle, but firm. "The parents will be following their student's class schedule, so there will be a total of seven meet-and-greets. Each will run only fifteen minutes. I'd suggest structuring your time so that you give a short introduction to your course—no longer than five minutes. Take their questions for the balance of the time. The parents have only five minutes to get to the next class. Any questions?"

Lavinia waited a moment. Hearing none, she added, "We have one last bit of business before we join the students in the auditorium. Berney Neufeld's retirement leaves the academic staff without representation on the trustee board. We'll need a replacement." Lavinia scanned the room. "The board meets once a month, in the evening: usually on a Wednesday. The position means presenting the collective faculty issues that merit the board's attention. As you can imagine, diplomacy is of the utmost importance, as is the ability to appreciate the opinions of the parents who sit on the board. They have a tendency to..." Lavinia hesitated as she struggled to find the right phrase.

"Be complete assholes?" Someone grumbled.

Egan noticed it was Hipster.

"Forget all that we do to keep their kids from turning out like them?" Another declared—this time, a female instructor. From her shorts and tee shirt, Egan deduced she was a PE teacher.

Lavinia's eyes shifted from Scuff to the woman and back again. "Ike, Candice, if that was your audition for the position, you missed the mark."

Nervous chuckles resonated through the room.

"What I'm trying to say is that these parents feel the school's wellbeing is important enough to take the time to meet and offer their unique skills on its behalf. They come from all walks of life. They help us with legal issues that may arise. They help us balance our books. They raise funds from outside sources for AA's scholarships and other important programs. And they donate. *Yes, we need them.* But have no doubts: it is a symbiotic relationship. They need us too. More to the point, their children need us to work together so that we have a school that makes each and every one of us proud." Lavinia's voice seemed to fade away.

She seems so tired, Egan thought.

Finally, Lavinia took a deep breath. "Any takers?"

No one raised a hand.

Egan kept still too.

Today's drive from his parents' house in Greenbrae had taken him an hour. The main vein of the county, Sir Francis Drake Boulevard, was always a traffic nightmare during rush-hour. When he'd finally reached US-101, there was still the issue of getting over the Golden Gate Bridge, not to mention the stop-and-go traffic through town as he drove toward the Haight.

Suddenly, he remembered Miranda's advice: that getting onto the board would be the best way to curry favor with those who could underwrite his position.

And besides, I'm sure Lavinia will appreciate having another board member advocating her vision of the school.

He raised his hand. "I'd be happy to sit on the board."

Lavinia beamed gratefully. "Thank you, Egan. You'll be a welcomed addition."

He waved away her appreciation. Suddenly, he felt guilty for being selfish at her expense.

"That guy Lavinia just introduced—our seventh-period teacher —he's the one who wrote that book!" Manya Patel nudged her pals,

Charly McKittridge, Sienna Belluci, and Zina Sisley-Calder, so that they'd quit gossiping and take notice.

The girls followed their friend's gaze at the man now making his way to the podium.

Charly was particularly interested in him. She was ecstatic when she learned that, like her friends, she'd been accepted into AA's advanced placement Shakespeare Comparative Lit class. It would look great on her college transcript. The scuttlebutt from AA alumni was that the course had prepared them well for similar classes on the university level, especially those who went on to post-graduate degrees in Literature, Fiction, or Creative Writing.

The new teacher, Egan Gable, looked to be about the same age as her parents: in his mid- to late-forties. He wore a navy blazer over a gray tee shirt tucked into his slim-cut jeans. Caught in the beams of natural light slanting through the auditorium's high windows, the silver strands entwined with his dark hair flickered like tinsel.

There was a confident air about him. His grin grew wider as his eyes scanned the crowd. When he took a deep breath, it was as if he were drinking in the energy bouncing around the room.

Quest Wishart-Jammerhead, who sat right behind the girls, stuck his head between Manya and Charly. "Yo, so, what book did he write?"

Manya sighed as she rolled her eyes. "Why do you care? You can barely read."

"Oh yeah? I've read…um…*Lord of the Rings*!" he retorted.

"Read it, or saw the movie?" Charly teased.

Quest's blush made his freckles pop even more. "I…read it. Really, I did."

"Okay, then what's the name of the elf?" she asked.

Quest thought for a moment. "Arwen."

"You're right—*in the movie*. In the book, it's Glorfindel." She wagged her finger at him.

"*Shhhh!*" Odette glared up into the bleachers to see who was talking. Satisfied with the pending silence, she turned back to Egan.

"Seriously, what's the name of his book?" Charly's lips barely moved as she asked the question.

"Don't tell me you haven't heard of it!" Zina put her hand over her mouth as if she were shocked. "It's called *Extracurricular*. It's a novel about a private prep school."

Sienna squinted. "I've heard of it too—through Mom. All I know is that it came out before I was born…so it's *ancient!*"

Quest shoved his head back between them. "He must have written other stuff since then."

"That would just mean more stuff you haven't read." Charly shoved him back into his row.

"The guy sounds like a one-hit wonder," Quest mumbled.

Charly glared at him. "So was J.D. Salinger."

Quest stared blankly at her.

She shook her head, amused. "*Catcher in the Rye?*"

He frowned cluelessly.

"Remember? We read it in the ninth grade," Charly insisted.

Quest winced. "That was, like, a lifetime ago."

Charly sighed.

"*Extracurricular* was considered racy back in the day." Zina raised a brow.

"Seriously, how much could doing the dirty have changed between then and now?" Charly asked.

Zina snickered, "If you were doing it, my sweet little virgin, you wouldn't have to ask."

Charly stared back at the podium. Zina and Manya had relationships with their boyfriends that began in their junior year. When the girls broke the news to her, it was quite matter-of-fact. They seemed relieved that their virginity was no longer an emotional burden.

Charly doubted their folks knew any of this. Manya's mother, Nira, was a single parent who was determined that her daughter follow in her footsteps and become a physician. Had she known that Manya was already playing doctor with Theo Dempsey—now a freshman at Stanford—she'd put her in a convent or something.

Zina's parents knew she and Sven Jorgensen were dating. They weren't pleased by it. "You're too young, and he's too white," Gemma had warned her daughter. "If Grandpa Sisley knew, he'd hit the roof!" Gemma's father was a renowned civil rights attorney who had made his name defending Black Panther activists.

"If we want an inclusive world, it has to start somewhere," Zina had argued.

"Honey, I don't see it starting with you," Darius responded.

He backed off, albeit warily, when he heard Sven in last year's county debate tournament defend the legitimacy of W.E.B. Du Bois' statement: "The price of culture is a lie."

Now, listening to Egan, Zina sat up straight. "Hey, did you hear that? This Egan guy just said that he taught here before."

"Does that mean the book is about AA?" Manya wondered out loud.

Sienna and Charly's eyes grew large at this possibility.

"If so, I'll bet my mom has a copy," Zina mused. "I'll ask her."

"Mine would too," Charly murmured. "I'll do the same."

"And the school would have it in the library, wouldn't it?" Sienna asked.

"If not, there's got to be a few copies floating around the public library system," Manya countered.

Quest whispered in Charly's ear: "You're seeing this dude in seventh period. Before you get all hot and bothered about the darn book, why not just ask him if it's about AA?"

He was right.

For once, she didn't swat him away.

WHEN INTRODUCING EGAN TO THE STUDENT BODY AT ITS MORNING assembly, Lavinia again spoke from her heart as she lavished praise on the latest addition to the teaching staff.

Although she mentioned his previous tenure at AA and his bearing as a "celebrated published novelist," Egan had no expectations that the students would find yet another middle-aged instructor the least bit intriguing. He was pleasantly surprised that her introduction garnered some impressed nods and curious murmurs.

As he took the podium, Egan realized that the last thing he wanted to do was disappoint his newfound audience. After thanking Lavinia for her kind introduction, he vowed to keep his classes interesting and entertaining. ("Not on a *Game of Thrones* level, but I'll do my best to come close...") He then sprinkled in a few humble brags. ("I haven't felt this appreciated since my editor called to tell me I'd made the *New York Times* Bestsellers list..." and "For those of you who grew up reading Harry Potter books, I can assure you, J.K. Rowling is every bit as whip-smart as Hermione Granger—even after a cocktail or two...")

Egan's words had the hoped-for effect: a few outright chuckles, murmurs of excitement, and finally enthusiastic applause.

Undoubtedly, for someone with Egan's pride, publishing offered a tantalizing prize: fame and fortune.

Having achieved this in his first book, he'd garnered his fair share of acolytes: mostly awed readers, although every now and then another author would grace him with a grudging compliment. And he could always count on his publicist to stroke his ego.

But as a novelist, Egan had felt he was constantly in competition. The expectation of success for his next book—from his publisher, his editor, his agent, his readers, and himself—was stratospheric and therefore unrealistic. Not only were its sales to be measured against those of *Extracurricular,* it would also be compared to the novels of every other best-selling author— debuting and established.

In his case, a second chance at the brass ring never happened. Egan's fear of failure had him second-guessing every plot point, every line of dialogue, and every turn of phrase in his second novel. His uncertainty proved to be his undoing. The manuscript missed its submission deadline by three years: just in time to catch a recession that wiped out many of the independent bookstores that had championed *Extracurricular.* Without the enthusiastic support of his publishing house, his second novel lost its way in a vast, endless universe of digital releases.

Egan was no longer the "shiny new thing." In time, as far as the publishing industry was concerned, he wasn't a "thing" at all.

How he longed to prove them wrong.

As a teacher, his role wasn't to compete, but to lead; to inspire.

If he stayed the year, he'd have time to regroup; to plot out his comeback novel. Ashbury Academy had inspired him once. Perhaps it would do so again.

Being here isn't so bad, he thought.

For the first time all day, Egan was okay with admitting this to himself.

By Egan's last class— his second course of *Advanced Placement*

Shakespeare Comparative Lit for seniors and juniors—he realized what he missed most about teaching: sharing what he knew with students who were eager to hear what he had to say.

As with the earlier Comp Lit class, Egan began by making a simple request: "Write down one line from William Shakespeare. It doesn't matter which play. You've got five minutes."

Before the gentle clack of keyboards went silent again, Egan got up and strolled down the center aisle. His game plan: choose a student at random.

He scanned their faces until one caught his attention. The girl was slim and by the height of her torso, he could tell she was also tall. Her hair, the color of young mahogany, was mussed and cut pixie short. This accentuated her wide green eyes in a perfectly heart-shaped face.

"What's your name?" he asked.

"Charly," she replied with a blush.

Perfect, he thought. It was the name he would have chosen, had he conceived her as a character in a novel.

He grinned down at her. "Hello, Charly. Would you be so kind as to read me your quote?"

She nodded, then cleared her throat: "'Everyone can master a grief but he that has it.' It's from *Much Ado about Nothing*."

"Correct. Now, tell me: what does it mean to you?" Egan leaned in as if hoping to divine some grand secret.

"Well..." Charly paused as she collected her thoughts. "We may tell someone we feel their pain, but the reality is that unless you've experienced a similar tragedy, you can't really understand another's grief."

Egan nodded, as if intrigued. "I take it you would agree with Shakespeare on this premise?"

Charly thought a moment. "Yes, certainly. It's why people at a funeral will say, 'Sorry for your loss.' Even someone who's never experienced the death of a loved one feels obliged to say it. But then, during the reception or wake, they converse and laugh without any thought as to how it may affect the grieving family."

"An excellent example. Have you read a book recently that epitomizes Shakespeare's contention?"

Charly thought for a moment. "One that comes to mind is Edith Wharton's *House of Mirth*."

"Why is that?"

"The main character, Lily Bart, is running out of money. Although her so-called friends pity her, they're willing to let her starve, to fall from grace, while they gossip about her."

"Great choice. Then your first assignment shouldn't be too challenging: turn your contention in an essay of, say, a thousand words." Egan scanned the room. "Tell me, Charly, would you say that anyone you know exemplifies Shakespeare's quote?"

Charly rolled her eyes. "Like, here at school?"

"That's a good place to start."

"Well, then yeah—probably everyone."

The other students laughed at that. Seeing that Egan was grinning too, Charly smiled shyly.

Suddenly, someone yelped: a girl, who then whined, "*Chuuuuck* —shhh! Cut it out!*"

It wasn't a desperate plea. More like a taunt; a dare.

If there was any doubt of this, the plea's theatrical delivery—the seductive tone in which the girl crooned the boy's name, allowing it to linger deep in her throat—robbed it of any sincerity.

Charly's smile faded. Instinctively, she turned toward the commotion.

So did Egan and the rest of the class.

Apparently the kid named Chuck—broad-shouldered, with light brown hair, his long legs stretched far in the aisle—had been flirting with the girl in front of him.

Granted, she was a stunner: fair-haired, big blue eyes, full pouting lips, generous breasts under a form-hugging tee shirt.

Both looked up when they heard the room grow silent again. When the girl's eyes met Egan's, she held his gaze as if pleased to have his undivided attention.

Chuck saw the look too. He didn't seem to like it.

Good, thought Egan.

Frankly, he was annoyed that the girl even assumed that, like the boy, he'd be enticed by her all too obvious simper. They were disrupting his class, undermining his authority.

This was his domain. Here, he was the master.

Time to prove it.

He nodded at Chuck. "I'm not interrupting anything, am I— *Chuck?*" Egan's deliberate emphasis of the boy's name hadn't had the same drawn-out cadence as the girl's. Still, it had the desired effect: the other students snickered.

Chuck grinned as he leaned back in his seat. "No, sir, not at all. We're enjoying the class immensely."

"Good to hear." *Smart-ass.* "Tell us—*Chuck*: which of Shakespeare's many passages will you be honoring us with today?"

Egan was prepared to be underwhelmed with one of the more common quotes; say, "Romeo, Romeo, wherefore art thou, Romeo..." or "To thine own self be true..." or "To be or not to be, that is the question..."

Had that been the case—and worse yet, had Chuck failed to identify the chosen phrase's origin—Egan was prepared to use the boy's ignorance as a warning to him and any other slackers: if they didn't take the class seriously, they'd receive a grade that would kill their GPAs.

And if that unnerved Chuck into requesting a transfer from the class, Egan would gladly accommodate him.

Instead, Egan was dismayed when Chuck responded, "'A fool thinks himself to be wise, but a wise man knows himself to be a fool.'" He then added, "It's from *As You Like It,* by the way."

Surprised, Egan nodded. "And your thoughts on its meaning?"

"If you have any real intelligence, you'd realize that you're never as smart as you'd like to think you are."

Egan's approval was grudging at best. "A decent analogy. Tell me, *Chuck,* do you agree with Shakespeare?"

Chuck squinted as if he were taking the answer seriously. "Not necessarily. But I know my mom does because she says it every time I sass her."

To Egan's dismay, the class broke out in a fit of giggles.

Great, I've got a class clown on my hands.

"Yes, well, I for one certainly feel *her* pain," Egan declared. "Tell me, *Chuck*: does any book come to mind that may exemplify your quote?"

Chuck grinned. "Does a comic book count?"

Laughter roiled through the room.

"I think you know the answer to that. Tell you what, since you're at a loss to come up with one, I'll assign it: *The Beautiful and the Damned.* There's a character in it who always thinks he knows it all. You'll identify with him, I'm sure."

Chuck's grin disappeared. "But…but…"

It was Egan's turn to smile. "Oh, and by the way, although Disney has yet to make an animated film of it, there are other cinematic versions. Should you be tempted to use one as a shortcut, I'd prefer you drop the class instead. It will save your poor mother another heartache when your report card comes out."

Egan's tone put everyone on alert: *Don't fuck with me.*

So that the others understood that he much preferred handing out carrots as opposed to sticks, he exclaimed, "Class, now that you have the gist of your first assignment, take another five to ten minutes to write down a novel with a plot you feel embodies the phrase you've just chosen. I'll call on a few of you, to see if you're on track. By the way, you'll have until Friday to turn in a paper. I'll expect footnoted excerpts that help you make your case."

The rest of class time went just as Egan had hoped: the students brought their A game.

He was glad about that. He'd be seeing Lavinia at the trustee board meeting and he wanted to be able to tell her that his day had been a love fest between him and his students.

Some smart ass wasn't going to ruin that for him.

***

Damn you, Chuck!

Her brother's wisecracks made Charly want to crawl under her seat.

All this, just to impress Fawn, she fumed.

Charly had felt she'd established a real connection with Egan. He seemed to appreciate her thoughtful choice and the insight she had into its relationship with Lily Bart's plight.

Why must Chuck always be the center of attention—and at my expense?

It was not lost on Charly that, amongst their three children, each of her parents had a personal favorite.

In both cases, it wasn't Charly.

She knew her parents loved her dearly. And that they appreciated the hard work and determination she put toward her studies. They were verbal in their admiration of her dutiful nature. They always took her at her word, no matter the issue. They showered her with gratitude, never once withholding their affection for her.

At the same time, their actions toward her brothers spoke volumes.

For her mother, Chuck was the clear choice. He never failed to make her laugh at his silliness. Whenever Chuck got in trouble, if he couldn't convince Mom that the crime was one of ignorance or impulse, eventually he'd sweet-talk his original sentence down to a misdemeanor. She'd never understood why her mother allowed Chuck such leeway.

Charly had always modeled her behavior on her grandmother and mother: work hard, do your best, be gracious, and think of others.

It would mortify Charly to disappoint Audrey. But should it ever happen, no doubt her mother's dismay would come with consequences.

For Dad, the favored child was Noah. This was to be expected, considering the twins shared a natural closeness and buoyant personalities: traits their mother felt best fell under her watchful eye. Add to this the fact that the younger boy's thoughtful deliberateness mirrored their father's, Noah was the natural choice.

It helped, too, that Noah was just as passionate as their father about cycling.

As soon as the McKittridge kids learned to maneuver a two-wheeler, they ecstatically joined their father in what became a weekend tradition: exploring the rugged trails and old fire roads that coiled around Marin County's Mount Tamalpais.

Before Noah was old enough to join them, the family would drive over the bridge and start their trek from the nearest town: Sausalito. At first, toddler Noah was their mother's excuse for passing on the excursions. But when even he was ready to join the others, she gave a somewhat weaker rationale: without them underfoot, she'd have time to prepare the picnic that would be waiting upon their return.

When the older children reached high school age, the four McKittridges cycled over the bridge. Afterward, they'd enjoy a meal in Mill Valley, one of the small towns nestled at the foot of the mountain.

Occasionally, their mother would drive in to join them. They'd ride back into town with her, the bikes tethered to the extended rack on the back of the family's SUV.

Eventually, Charly realized what their mother was really doing: gifting them precious time with their father during his much-deserved respite from a long week spent managing his law firm.

Charly now wondered if Chuck or Noah had also figured this out. Maybe Noah. He seemed to have been born wise. His actions bore this out.

Chuck was the opposite. The universe revolved around him and no one else.

His behavior in Comp Lit was proof of that.

Charly was still steaming over her brother's antics when AA's bell tower chimed the end of the school day. As her classmates rose to their feet, Egan's next words succeeded in breaking through her tortured thoughts:

"…and by the way, Debate Team tryouts are in three weeks. If you're interested, feel free to take the handout on the corner of my desk. In the year I was here, I was proud to coach AA's very first team to the state quarterfinals. I'd like to best that record with some of you."

Manya nudged her. "What do you think? Should we go for it?"

"I'm in!" Zina exclaimed. "I know it helped Sven get into Stanford."

"Me too," Sienna declared.

Charly shrugged. "Sure, sounds like fun."

Despite her nonchalance, she was determined to do one more thing that might set her apart from her brothers—especially Chuck.

Not that a jock like him would dream of trying out for Debate Team. And even if he did, after today's incident, there was no way he'd make the cut.

That was fine with her.

ell, well, who is this handsome devil?
More to the point, why is he here?

Miranda had caught sight of the tall, dark stranger just as he'd entered the parents' lounge, where Ashbury Academy's trustee board meeting would soon take place. She had long ago tuned out Egan's humble-bragging about his first day back at the school. He hadn't noticed because she'd been *oohing* and *ahhing* in all the right places even as she scoped out the rest of AA's board members.

In one corner of the room, that pompous fool—the investment fund manager, Seamus McCoppin—held court with his allies: Warner Crawford, Jess Smallwood, and Darius Calder. All were superb golfers and always part of Seamus' foursome at the gold-plated Olympic Club.

Miranda had spent the past evening memorizing their names and faces. She'd researched their work histories, wives, and university alma maters. She'd perused their presence on social media.

Like Seamus, Warner and Jess were financial titans who rode roughshod over other people's money: in Warner's case, union pensions. For Jess, it was limited partnerships created for angel investors interested in tech start-ups.

As for Darius, he was a lawyer. And although the firm he'd started with his wife—Miranda's old Debate Team nemesis, Gemma Sisley—was renowned for defending the civil rights of underdogs and death row inmates, its cash cow was another sort of clientele, handled solely by Darius: drug kingpins and other shady entrepreneurial clients looking for creative ways to shelter their undeclared earnings.

All of this intel was to give her some idea whether they'd be potential concierge clients.

If their newsworthy endeavors and social media accounts were to be believed, the answer was a resounding yes. Everything about the men and their wives oozed status and privilege.

Miranda had also looked up their children's names and GPAs. Sadly, for Warner, Jess, and Seamus, their children's grade point averages were lower than the acceptable standard for topflight universities, but would get them into a mediocre technical school or a junior college that fed into a state university.

The great news for Miranda: neither option would be acceptable to men with their inflated egos.

Warner's son, Buck, was a handsome devil. But be it sports or academics, he'd never applied himself at either, and it showed.

In the dictionary, the boy's picture could appear beside the word *sloth,* Miranda thought.

In her opinion, Jess' son, Hugo, was less of a loser but only by a thin margin. The best thing he had going for him was his entrepreneurial skill: he was the school's go-to drug dealer.

Only Darius and Gemma's daughter, Zina, could be a shoo-in. First off, she was an excellent student. Being a person of color would also work in her favor. Had she also participated in sports, she would have been a slam-dunk for an elite university. But, from looking at Zina's test scores, Miranda could tell that the girl's Achilles heel was math.

Maybe that's my way in with Darius, she thought.

One thing Miranda knew: after her shameful incidents during the Debate Team tournament, she certainly had to stay away from Gemma.

If Egan, Audrey, Tallulah, and Bliss don't remember me, maybe Gemma won't either, she reasoned.

Bottom line: she'd have to win the men's trust, which meant playing to their egos.

Miranda watched as the stranger made his way to Lavinia. At first, the headmistress didn't notice him because she was deep in discussion with the trustee who had been on the board since the school's inception: US Congressman Harris Blanchard. Despite a slight stoop inherent with surviving seven decades of life, the revered statesman towered over the headmistress.

When the stranger offered her his hand, she pulled him in for a quick hug instead.

Interesting.

Then again, Lavinia was touchy-feely with everyone. For all Miranda knew, the guy was her accountant.

Tallulah and Bliss stood on the other side of Lavinia. After shaking hands with Blanchard, the stranger offered pecks to the women.

A spark of jealousy charged through Miranda. It was disappointing how little either of them had aged. Instead, they'd become sleeker, posher versions of themselves.

They wear their success with such ease, she thought enviously.

When they'd arrived, the two women had nodded hello to Miranda. Other than that, they ignored her. It was high school all over again, what with the two of them murmuring animatedly between chuckles.

Like that idiot, Audrey, they haven't put two and two together as to who I am, Miranda realized. Otherwise, they'd probably spit on me.

All the more reason to keep them clueless as long as possible.

Periodically, Bliss and Tallulah's eyes scanned the room but didn't linger on anyone, not even the men. Not surprising. Considering their personal success and the size of their bank accounts, they certainly weren't in the market for breadwinner husbands.

And with how quickly my wealth has grown these past few years, neither am I.

Miranda smiled at that realization.

"What, did I say something funny?" Egan asked.

She stifled the urge to roll her eyes. *He's such an egomaniac!*

Instead, she batted her lids and simpered, "If I could, I'd follow you around all day. I wouldn't want to miss any of your scintillating *bon mots.*"

Gag me, please!

Egan puffed up at that. He must have taken this as her invitation to continue because his blathering began again.

She'd had enough. Miranda had just devised an excuse to sidle over to Seamus and his cronies when Lavinia proclaimed, "Now that we're all here, shall we get started?"

Miranda didn't need a second invitation. As if regretting the intrusion, she murmured, "Excuse me, Egan. Time to sing for my supper," then made her way to the circular conference table.

She waited until Seamus took his seat before choosing her own; to his right.

As it turned out, the handsome stranger chose the chair to her right.

Perfect.

Egan grimaced at this turn of events. So as not to look silly, he took the chair to the stranger's right.

This put him across from Tallulah and Bliss.

Tallulah eyed him curiously.

The guileless Bliss couldn't resist: "You look familiar."

"You do too." Egan's smile went full wattage. "But up until recently, I've lived in New York. Do you have occasion to go there?"

"Occasionally," she replied coolly.

He nodded. "I'm a member of the Metropolitan Club."

Bliss shook her head.

"Core Club?"

"Sorry, no."

"Let me guess. Soho House?"

"Nope. Wrong again," Bliss replied. "With all your friends back there, I suppose we should be honored to have you all to ourselves!"

Egan's face warmed with embarrassment.

Tallulah turned her head so that Egan wouldn't catch her smirk.

Oh my God, how emasculating for that horn dog, Miranda thought.

She pursed her lips to keep from laughing.

LAVINIA GOT RIGHT DOWN TO BUSINESS. "FIRST OF ALL, I'D LIKE TO introduce our newest members and a guest." She nodded at Daniel. "When Phillipa Garner resigned, AA's board lost its legal advisor.

As the managing partner of one of the city's largest international law firms, I'm grateful Daniel McKittridge accepted my invitation to take Phillipa's place. I'm sure you'll agree that he'll be an integral and appreciated addition to the board."

Though Miranda's hopes for the vacancy were dashed, she was more determined than ever to gain access.

No better place to start than Audrey Thorpe's husband.

"It's also with great pleasure that I introduce Bliss Thackeray Belluci and Tallulah Wishart as this year's PTA co-chairs." Lavinia nodded toward the women. "As you're already well aware, Ms. Thackeray Belluci is an iconic face around the world and a leader in the fashion industry. Ms. Wishart manages two of the most celebrated musical artists of our time. Thank you, ladies, for making the time for us too."

Daniel winked at his friends.

When Egan's jaw fell open in shock, Miranda had to stifle a snicker.

The board members nodded appraisingly. They were well aware of Bliss's fashion celebrity and Tallulah's standing in the music industry. That both were now on its trustee board gave Ashbury Academy additional bragging rights.

"It will be a pleasure to work with you, gentlemen. One suggestion: I won't believe all your bad press if you'll do me the same favor." Bliss' honeyed-tone request was met with chuckles and preening.

Tallulah added: "Because this is the school's twenty-fifth anniversary, the PTA is playing a critical role in fundraising for the scholarship program, which supports fifty percent of the student body, either partially or fully. This is also AA's edge over the city's other private schools." She looked each man in the eye. "As much as Bliss and I admire each of you for your many accomplishments, we're all sitting at this table because we understand one simple rule: money talks. We look forward to your support in this endeavor."

Seamus scowled at Tallulah's audacity.

The other men shifted uncomfortably in their seats.

"Thank you, ladies, for your candor." Lavinia then nodded toward Egan. "There are several new programs offered this year. Our more generous parents will be asked to underwrite them. In fact, the accomplishments of our new academic trustee"—she nodded toward Egan—"merit a special chaired position in his honor." Lavinia was practically beaming at him. "Once again, AA is lucky to have on staff the *New York Times* bestselling author, Egan Gable."

---

*J*ESUS*...B*LISS *AND* T*ALLULAH ARE...*
Women.

Egan forced himself to gaze at a spot on the wall beyond Warner's bald pate so that he wouldn't be tempted to stare at his former students. Instead, his mind created a double exposure: here they were in Technicolor, superimposed over his sepia memories of them.

Bliss had always been a stunner. Egan was impressed to see that two decades of maturity hadn't dimmed the innate charm of the leggy, wide-eyed wild child of his memories. Back then, her stream-of-consciousness exclamations had been like a handful of Skittles thrown up in the air, its sugar-coated innocence falling willy-nilly on confounded ears, albeit its sweet logic hard to swallow. This new Bliss voiced her opinion sparingly with a savory sultriness that left listeners longing for seconds.

As for Tallulah, the halo of bright red curls was now tamed into a blunt auburn bob. Chic designer skinny jeans and a sheer blouse worn under a fitted jacket had replaced her slip dresses and bulky denim vests. Louboutins now took the place of her standard-issue army boots.

Her tart bluntness is still intact, Egan thought wryly.

And now that he'd been singled out, he noticed that they too were surprised to see him.

Really? Do I look that different?

He knew the answer to that.

It was inevitable that muscle and flesh would soften and sag after twenty-two years of gravitational pull, abetted by too much fine dining, heavy drinking, and summer fun in the Hamptons. With each passing year, the tiny lines etched around his eyes, nose, and mouth had deepened with the seismic events that shook, rattled, and rolled through his life.

When he'd had the money, personal trainers and hairstylists helped greatly to stave off life's cruel vagaries. As his funds dwindled, Egan had convinced himself that jogging and push-ups would fight off the pounds just as quickly. But all it took was one clumsily administered at-home dye job to accept the silver creeping through his hair.

Glancing at Warner, he thought: At least I still *have* hair.

And now it was time for him to turn on the charm, to impress all these movers and shakers; these pillars of the Ashbury Academy community.

Including two of Audrey's dearest friends.

Had they read his book? And if so, had they been flattered or appalled at his depictions of them?

Hard to tell. Now that the shock of seeing Egan again had worn off, their benign smiles were back in place.

Time to find out. "It's a pleasure to be back at Ashbury Academy. It holds a special place in my life, having been the inspiration for my debut novel."

Whereas the men murmured their approval, Egan noticed Tallulah and Bliss exchange grimaces.

Ah, heck, he thought, they hate their characters.

He forced himself to keep his voice on an even keel: "Today was my first day back as an educator, and I'm already impressed with the skills and determination of my students."

"In fact, Seamus, your daughter, Fawn, is in Egan's seventh-period Shakespeare Comparative Literature class," Lavinia pointed out.

Seamus leaned over Miranda to scrutinize Egan.

Egan groaned inwardly.

The blond fembot is this guy's kid? Great. Just…great.

Egan hadn't had time to look over the class rosters let alone memorize his students' names. Hell, he'd barely had time to review the lesson plans.

Despite this, he forced himself to grin. "Ah, yes! She is quite the charmer, that one."

He panicked for a quick moment over the thought that Seamus might ask him to elaborate.

Lavinia saved him by adding, "And Daniel, Charly is also in that class—"

"Charly is your daughter?" Egan cut in excitedly. "She certainly knows her Shakespeare! She made quite an insightful comparison with one of my favorite Edith Wharton novels, *House of Mirth*. I was very impressed."

"Yes, Charly is a great kid. She never ceases to amaze me too." Daniel smiled appreciatively, adding, "I won't play favorites, but I feel blessed."

Perhaps blessed enough to donate generously for the Comp Lit chair?

I'll be seeing him in the last open house, Egan remembered. Before this meeting breaks up, I'll ask him if he has time to go out for a drink sometime soon and discuss it.

"WE ALSO HAVE A VERY SPECIAL GUEST WITH US TODAY," LAVINIA pointed out. "Miranda D'Arcy is Ashbury Academy's new college admissions consultant. Besides being one of the most sought-after professionals in her field, Miranda has been retained by our school to assess each student's admissions criteria and guide them to the university that's best suited to their unique talents and interests."

"Based on that criteria, my kid may end up in my basement for the rest of my life," Warner muttered.

Jess Smallwood shrugged in solidarity.

No argument there, Miranda thought.

Instead, she said, "Don't sell him short! I know I won't. I'm proud to say my track record for getting my clients' children in at least one of their top five schools rivals that of AA's." Miranda smiled winningly. "My goal here is to beat both records with this graduating class."

Warner nodded grudgingly. "I would imagine the easy cases take care of themselves. Does that give you more time to work on those who are harder to place?"

"Each student, no matter their GPA, receives equal attention. Obviously, the seniors are my initial priority. I'll be scheduling a session with each of them to discuss their admission goals, and to assess their grades, standardized test scores, and extracurriculars before they tackle the applications under my watchful eye." Miranda sighed. "We have over a hundred seniors, so I have my work cut out for me. I've already started scheduling meetings with the more—for lack of a better term, *ambitious* students and their parents—"

"I'll be blunt," Jess interjected. "Can you work a miracle for a lazy student?" From the anxious look on his face, she knew he was only half-joking.

"For those students who have been sitting on the fence for some reason or another—I call them late bloomers—I will be meeting with their parents first. For their children, I may suggest a more aggressive plan of attack."

Jess nodded vigorously.

"You called yourself a 'consultant,'" Seamus pointed out. "Does that mean you're not part of the administration?"

"Very perceptive of you, Mr. McCoppin," Miranda replied crisply. "I accepted the position as a consultancy because my practice includes private clients as well. Most of them have two, sometimes even more children. I've placed their eldest in their dream schools. They want assurance that I'll do the same for their siblings."

"In other words, you're filling in your schedule with our kids," Seamus argued.

"Hardly," she countered. "My retainer agreement with AA puts me here on campus every hour the school is in session, and it calls for me to be available by appointment after school hours as well. In other words, I'm at your beck and call." When she leaned forward, it had the desired effect: his eyes went to her cleavage.

He nodded grudgingly.

At least that shut him up, she thought.

"Any other questions?" Lavinia asked.

"Do you walk on water too?" Jess joked.

The others chuckled.

"Since we'll only have a half hour to enjoy our catered dinner before the parent-teacher open house, I'd like to call for adjournment."

"I second the motion," Darius declared.

The others quickly exclaimed, "Aye!"

As Miranda rose from her seat, Jess waved her down. "Do you have a minute to chat?"

Ca-CHING!

Egan turned to shake Daniel's hand. "It was a pleasure meeting you."

Daniel smiled. "Likewise."

"And I meant what I said about Charly. She's a gem."

"I appreciate your saying that."

"Daniel, listen, if you can take the time some night, perhaps we can meet for a drink soon. Lavinia views my return as a viable fundraising opportunity. I want to do everything I can to help her make that happen, and I'm sure you do too. Since you have a far better lay of the land, maybe you can suggest a couple of likely candidates."

"Sure, anything I can do to help." Daniel looked at his watch. "We get done tonight at, what, nine? Nine-fifteen?"

"Yeah, about that," Egan replied. "And since Charly's in my seventh-period class, you're in my last open house. We can walk over to Magnolia Brewing Company afterward, if you'd like."

"Works for me. My wife and I are in separate cars, so I won't be holding her up if she needs to get home to help our youngest with his homework."

Before Egan could say any more, Lavinia tapped him on the shoulder. She was holding a covered plate. "I didn't want to interrupt you, Egan dear, but you'll barely have time to make it to your classroom for your first open house." She handed him the plate. "Take this with you, so that you have a little sustenance between meet-and-greets."

Reluctantly, he got up. After nodding goodbye to them, he headed for the door.

Maybe it was for the best. Egan noticed that Tallulah and Bliss were heading his way. He wasn't ready to answer their questions about his fall from grace. Or about his book, for that matter.

The last thing he wanted was their pity.

He'd much prefer information on Audrey.

Not that he could ever ask for it.

CHAPTER 9

Cross-town traffic was so bad that Audrey made AA's first period parent-teacher meet-and-greet with only ten minutes to spare.

As promised, Daniel had waited for her at the classroom's door. His kiss was quick, but as always, passionate.

When he pulled away, Audrey sighed. His lips always had that effect on her.

She murmured, "So, how was the board meeting?"

She hoped she'd kept the anxiety out of her voice even as she wondered: *Did Lavinia seem ill?*

She was afraid that if it were apparent to Daniel, the others would have noticed too.

"It was interesting and uneventful," Daniel replied. "You'll be happy to hear that the Tallulah-and-Bliss tag team made quite an impression."

"Thank goodness!" Audrey pretended she meant that about her friends, but in truth, she was relieved that he hadn't started out by mentioning Lavinia. Had Daniel noted anything unusual about her, it would have been the first thing he'd have mentioned.

Daniel grimaced. "By that, I gather you expected a death match between Seamus and Tallulah."

Audrey sighed. "It may not have happened today, but I know them well enough to say it's inevitable."

"I wouldn't take that bet," Daniel conceded. "The one time Tallulah showed her claws, Seamus bristled like a porcupine."

"Well, you know what they say about pricks," she muttered.

Daniel laughed. "What a naughty remark, Ms. Thorpe! In most schools, it would merit a trip to the principal's office."

"Thankfully, corporal punishment has never been acceptable at AA." She wiggled her brows. "However, I'm sure all kinds of dirty deeds have played out in the many nooks and crannies of this old building."

"If you're offering a tour, I'll happily take you up on it—"

Daniel's quip was interrupted by the chime of the school's clock tower, announcing that the first open house would commence in five minutes.

"Ah well, I guess that little excursion will just have to wait." Audrey pretended to pout. "This year, Charly and Chuck only have two classes together. As in the past, we'll have to split up for the others." She handed Daniel a notecard. "Charly's classes are on this card. You were very kind to take on the board, so I figure you deserve to hear glowing reviews all night long as opposed to the winces and sighs that come with examples of Chuck as class clown."

"That's very generous of you." Daniel rolled his eyes. "Still, maybe it's best that I take Chuck's schedule. You know, in for a dime, in for a dollar. And besides, if anyone is going to scare the kid straight, I think it's going to be me. You've got too much of a soft spot for him."

"Now you're beginning to sound like Charly," Audrey huffed.

"Sorry, but it's true, whether you want to acknowledge it or not," Daniel countered. "Letting him slide isn't doing him any favors, Aud."

She plucked Charly's schedule out of his hand and replaced it with Chuck's. "Okay, then, by all means, run roughshod over him."

"Not to worry. I won't let you down."

"You never do." This time, Audrey initiated the kiss.

When they came up for air, she added, "The twins share this first class: Trigonometry. A guy named Ike Melton teaches it. He's been on the staff a couple of years, but our two scholars haven't had him before. I hear he's a real taskmaster and a hard grader." She frowned. "Chuck can do the assignments, but that doesn't mean he will. You'll have your work cut out for you."

Daniel shrugged. "Duly noted."

"We'll join up at the last class of the day, Comp Lit. Wait outside if you get there first. I'll do the same."

Daniel nodded. "Speaking of which, you'll be happy to hear I already received a compliment about one of our children. From the Comp Lit teacher."

"Really?" Hope rose in Audrey's heart. "About Chuck?"

"Guess again."

"Ah! So Charly's already made an impression on her new teacher! What did the woman say, exactly?"

Before Daniel could answer, the warning chime sounded. He nodded toward the class. Ike Melton was closing the door.

Instead of answering her, Daniel ushered Audrey inside.

She'd meet the twins' instructor soon enough, she reasoned. Even one accolade about her daughter would make up for all the winces that would greet her when she introduced herself as Chuck's mother.

If Cornell hadn't been scolding Audrey about Chuck, Audrey would have been on time to the twins' seventh-period class. "It doesn't take much to memorize the Periodic Table," he pointed out to her. "By Chemistry II, he should know it!"

"If he doesn't, why do you keep passing him?" Audrey asked, defensively.

"Trust me, if he weren't so charming, I wouldn't."

At least Cornell is honest, Audrey thought.

She ran up the stairs to Comp Lit. Reaching the door, she had a déjà vu moment. It awed her that, even with all of AA's renovation and additions, twenty years hence the course was still being taught in the same classroom.

As they'd agreed, Daniel had waited for Audrey outside the door. They had a second for a peck but then Daniel's phone rang.

He stared at the Caller ID. "It's our Kyoto office. I should take it. Go on in. Save me a seat."

Audrey nodded and hurried through the door.

THE TEACHER, A MAN, WAS WRITING SOMETHING ON THE WHITE BOARD. Embarrassed at her tardiness, Audrey scurried toward the only two adjacent empty seats: in the back of the row closest to the window.

At this point, the teacher made some joke about wishing Lavinia had let the teachers set up full bars in their classrooms. "It might help us be candid with each other—you'd be more forthcoming about what I've gotten myself into, and I'd be honest about what they've really been up to." He paused. "As if you'd really want to hear that, right?"

The parents laughed heartily.

He's got a nice voice…

Hmmm, sounds familiar…

Just as she'd reached the empty seat, she realized where she knew it:

Egan…

She whipped around:

Yes, there he was.

Audrey felt faint. As the blood rushed to her head, her pounding heart drowned out all sound. She forced herself to sit down very slowly.

Get ahold of yourself! Breathe!

BREATHE.

Even as her heartbeat steadied, emotions surged through her:

Excitement. Rage. Shame—

Sadness.

OPEN YOUR EYES.

She forced herself to look at Egan; to see that he was real.

Physically, age had blunted the sharpness of his features. The angle of his jaw was somehow softer. His shoulders were rounder. His once slim girth was now fuller, just as his hair was graying.

But his wit was still as crisp and dry as ever. His audience drank him in like an Oakville sauvignon blanc, savoring each tart aside, every nuanced rejoinder.

He lets them in on the joke, she thought. It's what makes him so desirable.

But not to me.

Not anymore.

Not after that afternoon.

As her heart stilled, Egan's voice seemed to grow louder: "…and the joy of having your children in my class—"

The children…

Our children.

Oh my God…Chuck and Charly…

It dawned on Audrey that Egan was now glancing around the room. She would have ducked, but he'd have seen her anyway. The seat in front of her was empty.

It was the one she was holding for Daniel.

Oh my God—Daniel!

At that moment, Egan's eyes met hers.

JESUS…

She's here.

Egan had been scanning the room, doing a headcount, trying to figure out if his chatter was getting enough laughs; hoping that it seemed meaningful to the parents, perhaps inspirational, maybe even life-changing for their children.

Otherwise, for what AA charged as its annual tuition, why not buy a Tesla instead?

Granted, it would be the cheapest one in the showroom—the mid- five-figures Model 3—but a Tesla nonetheless.

Then again, considering the average household income of the AA families paying full-freight, odds were that most of them already had a garage filled with Teslas—

And that's when his eyes lit upon Audrey.

The desire to linger on her face was a visceral one: it was pretty and therefore pleasing. But what caused him to want to scrutinize it further was that it seemed familiar as well.

When recognition finally snapped into place, his eyes widened and his voice faded away.

Audrey.

She's here.

She came.

For me.

Egan forced himself to say something, anything; to remember the patter he'd come up with; the jokes that seemed to be working.

He was just about to go back into his rift when, behind him, the door opened.

Annoyed, he turned to berate the intruder.

It was Daniel.

Having caught Egan's eye, he apologized with a contrite nod.

By rote, Egan waved him in and waited politely for him to take a seat.

Daniel strolled to the aisle where Audrey was seated. But before taking the seat in front of her, he bent down to kiss her.

In that quick, sweet second their lips met, Egan felt himself deflate as if she'd punctured something deep within him:

His purpose for being.

WRAP IT UP — NOW.

"Any questions, folks?"

A couple of hands went up.

Including Daniel's.

Fuck you. How dare you!

Egan pointed to a woman sitting front row center. She was too tanned, with skin that was tight and brittle like wrapping paper. He forced himself to tune her in: to hear her blather some nonsense about *Titus Andronicus*: "...perhaps encouraging the students to compare such a timeless play to some of the Serbian and Bosnian authors who have emerged after their civil unrest in the 1990s?"

Really, lady? THIS is what you want to ask?

Egan hated show-offs. Still, he forced himself to smile. "Interesting analogy...and quite sound! I'll take it under advisement, for sure. But if anyone whines, 'That was *soooo* last century,' I'm sending them your way." He shot her with his index finger as if to say, *Right back atcha!*

Everyone chuckled.

"Anyone else?"

A guy in the third row on the left, shouted out: "Do you grade on a curve?"

Another joker, like that Chuck kid.

Egan took a closer look to see if there was a resemblance. Nah. The dude looked like an overripe toad. Chuck's father was probably some high-testosterone braggart already on his third wife, who indulged his son because the kid was a chip off the old block.

He chuckled, as if in on Toad's joke. "Yeah…right. Quick answer: *NO.* This is an AP course. And before anyone asks, I don't grade in iambic pentameter either."

Again, a spate of laughter.

"Any other questions?" Egan gazed down at his watch in the hope that they'd all take the hint: *It's time to wrap things up.*

He waited a beat—just long enough to ignore any hands that may have been raised. Then, clapping, he exclaimed loudly, "Wow, folks, congratulations on making it through seven open houses— without a *single cocktail!*"

They fell for it. Applauding his cleverness, they rose en masse.

Acquaintances hugged farewell. Others made their way to the front to shake Egan's hand, hoping to make some impression, perhaps because they knew their children weren't going to leave much of one, or worse yet, the wrong one.

That is, everyone except Daniel and Audrey, their heads together deep in discussion.

About what? Me?

Is she telling him—

NOW?

At that moment, Daniel caught his eye and waved at him.

Then Egan remembered why: Oh, hell—I invited the asshole out for a drink!

Shit—is Audrey joining us?

He could see it now. Audrey would hate every minute of their little gathering. Every glance in his direction would sting like a pinprick. He'd be smarting from hurt and jealousy, whereas she'd be reliving the shame of trusting him to be her first lover.

If only she'd told me that was the case. Things might have been different…

I'd be him—Daniel.

If she came along, there would be deadly silences between small talk that hit every topic except the ones that mattered most:

How they felt about that fateful night.

How they feel about each other now.

Instead, they'd pretend that nothing happened.

But something did happen. It was the end of the beginning.

I wanted to spend the rest of my life with you.

Instead, you're spending your life with him.

It angered him that she never gave him the chance to tell his side of the story, let alone apologize for...

It.

Okay, yeah, I broke your cherry. But to be fair, you broke my heart...

So, can we call it even?

He guessed the answer to that was *NO*.

Oh, shit, Daniel's an attorney. Can he sue me for that?

...No. I'm being...ridiculous...

Right?

He suddenly realized they were making their way toward him. Trying not to panic, he swiveled to make eye contact with one of the few parents still lingering in the classroom—

Too late. Daniel tapped his shoulder. "Egan, sorry I interrupted that great song and dance." His apology came with a shake of his head.

"No problem. It was bound to happen. Seven times up to bat. Got to hit a foul every now and then." Egan shrugged. He forced himself to keep his eyes solely on Daniel. If he dared to glance at Audrey, he didn't know what he might do.

Kiss her?

Curse her out?

Slug Daniel?

Cry?

Maybe.

"Understandable response—especially on an empty stomach." Daniel nodded toward the dish Lavinia had made Egan. It was still covered and obviously untouched. "You've got to be starving by now. Listen, are you still up for that drink and maybe a burger? I don't think Audrey would mind. Would you, hon?" Daniel's hand went to the small of Audrey's back as if propelling her forward.

"Audrey..." Her name tumbled out of Egan's mouth as if finally freed from the prison of his shameful memory.

To his own ears, it sounded like a choking cat that had fallen down a well.

Instinctively, Audrey looked at him, her eyes opened wide in panic. What Egan saw in them made him sad:

Fear.

Pleading.

"Audrey…Thorpe?…as in my former student?" Egan smiled blandly. "What a pleasure to see you again."

"Thank you," she murmured. "It's good to see you too, Egan. Congratulations on all your success."

Our success.

I couldn't have done it without you. You know that.

You hate that.

You hate me.

He knew they expected a response. But none of what he was thinking was appropriate. Finally, he answered, "So, you're Charly's mother."

As if shocked, she bolted upright. Finally, warily, she replied simply, "Yes."

"And we're Chuck's parents, too," Daniel added with a grin. "But don't hold that against us."

"Chuck…is *your* son?" Egan's eyes roamed from Audrey to Daniel and then back to her.

She nodded defiantly. "They're twins. You didn't notice the resemblance?" Her tone was as cold as ice.

Egan laughed weakly. "Now that you mention it."

She mesmerized him with her stare. "Daniel just told me you've joined the trustee board as the new academic liaison." Audrey's voice took a softer tone. "I'm sure Lavinia appreciates your support."

"Thank you. I think so." Egan was relieved they'd shifted to a safer topic. "She's been a lifeline to me…now, and…then."

When we fell in love.

But now you love him.

He couldn't just stand there, staring at her like a love-starved puppy. He blurted out: "Will you be joining us?"

Audrey stiffened, then shook her head. "Our youngest, Noah, is waiting up for me. He likes it when I check his homework."

"How old is he?"

Audrey shifted her gaze to Daniel, but her attempt at a smile died before it reached the corners of her mouth. "Thirteen. He'll be here at AA next year."

"I look forward to teaching him someday." Egan was lying. He'd be long gone.

If he could, he'd resign now, this very second.

I can't keep letting you break my heart, Audrey Thorpe.

"Enjoy your chat, gentlemen." She held out her hand to Egan. "I'm sure I'll be seeing you around school."

He took her hand and pressed it firmly, taking in its warmth and softness a tick too long as if daring her to break away first.

Egan was disappointed when she lived up to his prediction and pulled away.

He felt bereft.

Angry.

Daniel nodded toward the door. "Let's go. I'm buying."

You're living the life I wanted. Hell yeah, you'll pay, you son of a bitch.

CHAPTER 10

*A*udrey staved off her panic attack until she got into her car. Once she was in the driver's seat, she allowed herself to gasp. But soon her gasps turned into sobs, which became wails, which morphed into screams accompanied by her fists pounding on the steering wheel.

It was inevitable that she'd accidentally hit the horn.

Those parents still in the parking lot jumped nervously, craning their heads to see if a car was barreling in their direction.

One woman was close enough to make out Audrey's face: Nira Patel, whose daughter, Manya, was one of Charley's closest friends. She had also been in Egan's last open house. She waved. Concern etched her brow.

Audrey waved back, and quickly started her car's engine. It was the best way to keep Nira at bay; to send the universally understood non-verbal message, *there's nothing to worry about. Everything is fine and dandy.*

Nothing could be further from the truth.

Slowly, she inched her way out of the lot and onto the street.

He will soon know, she told herself. My God, how could he not?

Even a mere hour a day, five days a week, would be enough time to recognize his scratchy chuckle in the twins' laughter. To catch himself in their profiles and notice the similarities to his own: their height; their wide-set eyes the shade of seafoam.

She'd rue the day he'd make a panicked call begging her to meet him so that she could look him in the eye and tell him to his face:

Yes, they are yours.

And, no, I'm not sorry.

Not for keeping them from you.

Not for marrying Daniel.

Not for the one time we spent in the frenzied rapture that created those two precious beings.

Then she remembered all the things Egan had gotten wrong about their relationship—heck, about himself!—and her fear subsided.

I guess that's one good thing about being a self-centered son of a bitch. You don't see beyond the nearest mirror.

<hr>

It was late enough that Daniel and Egan could grab one of the pub's tall-back booths.

Until and after the waiter took their orders for beers and burgers, they made small talk: the Giants' chance at another pennant, if the Warriors could bring home another NBA title, the cost of living in San Francisco—safe topics for two men who should be getting to know each other and were supposed to be allies for the same cause.

Egan ached with hate.

Eventually, he mentioned that he commuted from Marin County.

Daniel perked up at that. "We live on this side of the bridge, but I love Marin for the trails. The kids and I bike to Mount Tam on most weekends."

"Audrey doesn't go too?" Egan asked.

Daniel shook his head. "She's always been welcomed. And she's certainly fit enough. She won't say it, but I think she really wanted it to be 'our thing'—you know, just mine and the kids'."

"That sounds like Audrey," Egan muttered.

"Yeah, she's always thinking of others," Daniel acknowledged. "I'll bet she was like that even when she was the twins' age."

"She was…" *…perfect.* Egan gulped his beer. "How did you two meet?"

"At Berkeley. We met in the law library. She was working there in her junior year. I was already a lawyer, but I was looking for a particular case law book. She helped me find it." He paused as if transported back to there and then. "It was love at first sight." He munched a fry. "Before then I'd never believed such a thing was possible."

Egan shrugged. "I know what you mean."

"Hey, believe it or not, you and I almost met a few years back," Daniel exclaimed.

Warily, Egan looked up. "How?"

"You did a reading at Berkeley when your book came out, right?"

As Daniel motioned the bartender for their tab, Egan nodded cautiously.

"Audrey went to it. You signed a couple of books for her. Remember? I was supposed to be her date, but I got held up at work." Daniel drained the last sip from his glass.

"Yeah, I do remember that." *As if I'd ever forget that day.*

Egan gulped his Pilsner for the courage to ask, "Did you get a chance to read it?"

Daniel shook his head. "Sorry, no. But now that I know you, I'll make it a point to do so." He thought for a moment. "I'm sure we still have it...."

Egan frowned. "You don't sound too certain."

Daniel laughed. "Only because it could be anywhere. Our house is filled with books. Like Audrey, the kids are avid readers." He shrugged. "Well, two of them anyway. We're still working on Chuck." He smiled. "Speaking of scholastic miracles, consider your chair underwritten."

Egan choked on his beer. "I...I appreciate that. But ...shouldn't you talk it over with Audrey first?"

"Not necessary. If you've got Lavinia and Audrey's *Good House-keeping* seal of approval, you've got mine too." Daniel clinked his mug against Egan's. "The prodigal son is always welcomed home."

Egan sat there, stunned.

If only you knew.

By the time Audrey got to the house, the kids had completed

their homework assignments and were huddled together on the couch, watching *Stranger Things.*

The boys, caught up in the show's bump-in-the-night suspense, barely mumbled their hellos.

Charly waved at her mom, albeit distractedly. "So that Noah could watch with us, we triple-checked his homework. Not to worry. He aced it." Lovingly, she tousled her little brother's hair.

"Thank you," Audrey kissed her forehead and then did the same for each of her sons.

Chuck smiled, but teasingly brushed away the dampness with an "Ew, yuck!"

Anxiety had parched Audrey's lips. What he'd felt were her tears.

<hr>

Like the children, Audrey was already in bed when Daniel arrived home.

She pretended to be asleep, rolling over on her side, away from his part of the bed. Better that he not read the anxiety in her face.

If Audrey had asked, she knew he would have relayed his conversation with Egan. But asking would make her seem concerned, which was the last thing she'd want him to think about her.

Besides, if Egan were to say something stupid (in the back of her mind, she imagined him boasting, "I had her first, you know...") Daniel would flip on the light and awaken her so that they could discuss it.

Instead, she breathed a sigh of relief as he washed up and changed before coming to bed.

Audrey felt his body curl around hers. An arm folded snugly around her waist.

Feeling his warmth, she scooted back against him. This is what she lived for: those pitch dark hours when they held each other, seemingly far away from the rest of the world. She couldn't see him, but the touch of his skin never failed to make her tingle.

And it never failed to have an arousing effect on Daniel.

Behind her, Daniel's cock hardened. Instinctively, his hand

curled around her breast. His index finger barely touched her nipple, but it stiffened nonetheless.

Audrey turned her head, her lips hungry for his. He was just as voracious for her. While his kisses wandered down her neck and over her breasts, his thumb and finger strummed her: gently then deeply, stirring an insatiable desire to feel him inside of her.

She stroked his cock with her fingers before her hand tightened around it. When she released him, they were both ready.

He plunged so deeply within her that she gasped.

Ecstatic with desire, she tightened around him. His moans set the tone of their rhythm: steady and slow at first. But then an urgency took hold, elevating their mutual pleasure to a fevered pitch.

When he burst within her, she had to clench her lips to keep from screaming out.

No one can take this away from us.

AFTERWARD, HE STROKED HER CHEEK AS THEY LAY IN EACH OTHER'S arms.

"Hey, um, this isn't exactly pillow talk, but because I have to be at the office at five this morning for a confab with our European offices, I do have to mention something before we both drift off to sleep."

"I'm all ears," Audrey purred.

He chuckled appreciatively. "Oh no, you're much more than that. Having just taken a complete inventory, I can vouch for the fact that you have other body parts just as delectable."

"Thank you, kind sir. Now, what's so important that you've stopped mid-snuggle?"

Daniel rested his head on his elbow so that he could gaze into her face. "If you remember, right before my mother passed, she told me she wanted me to use a portion of her estate for our children's education. I know she felt guilty that I had to do all kinds of jobs while getting my undergrad. The partial scholarships helped, of course. Still, Mom was so concerned about my student debt that she did her best to talk me out of law school. She suggested that I teach instead." He winced. "She was so proud that I got a job offer from a prestigious law firm. But she knew that an associate's salary wasn't going to make much of a dent in my debt—not with the twins still in diapers and all."

"I wish she were here to see you—and them—today." Audrey wiped away a tear. She'd loved Ruth and appreciated all the traits Daniel shared with her: patience, kindness, and a wonderful sense of humor.

Soon, Lavinia will be gone too, Audrey realized.

How she longed to tell Daniel of Lavinia's plight.

"Since the kids' college fees are now funded, I've been trying to come up with the perfect use for Mom's legacy," Daniel continued. "Lavinia provided it at the trustee meeting. She's looking for bene-factors to underwrite specific academic chairs. The first one starts this year."

"Sound interesting What does it entail?"

"The sum goes toward covering the salary of the prestigious recipient—an instructor of some renown—who will serve as an inspirational role model. It also allows for a very generous stipend toward their living expenses."

"How generous?"

"A quarter of a million."

Audrey whistled. "Well, that should attract some great press, and yet one more reason for parents to fight for their children's acceptance to AA. Not to mention a few qualified applicants!"

"This year's chair is already filled."

Audrey stared blankly at Daniel. "Really? Who?"

"Egan, of course." Daniel chuckled as he kissed her nose.

Had he not then snuggled back around her, she would have leaped out of bed to—

To do what, pace the floor while she cursed Egan for coming back into her life?

Or, perhaps explain to Daniel that his mother's life savings shouldn't go to the man who was the twins' real father?

It would kill Daniel if he ever found out. But I have to say something—

"I can't wait to tell Lavinia tomorrow," he whispered.

A moment later, he was snoring softly.

I can't do this to him.

Or to Lavinia.

Everything would be perfect if it weren't for Egan.

CHAPTER 11

At five-thirty the next morning, SallyAnne and Lionel were parked across the street from Tanner Simpson's sprawling Spanish hacienda overlooking Benedict Canyon.

Within fifteen minutes, a black luxury sedan had pulled in front of the movie director's long, gated driveway. Five minutes later, the gates opened, and the director—dressed in his signature attire, a black tee shirt and jeans—stepped out of his house.

The driver got out of the car to open the back door. Lionel and SallyAnne also jumped out of their vehicle. By the time Tanner reached his driver, they too were standing beside the town car.

Tanner looked over at his driver. The man's crestfallen face reflected his shock.

Lionel and SallyAnne pulled out their badges. "Mr. Tanner, we're with the Federal Bureau of Investigation," Lionel announced. "We'd like a moment to discuss your knowledge of a possible act of fraud."

Tanner grimaced. "I'm on my way to my movie set at Paramount Studios."

"We can talk out here, or inside the house, if you prefer," Sally-Anne suggested.

Instinctively, Tanner looked up toward his home. "No! My daughter is there..."

"We can ride along with you," SallyAnne offered. "Fair warning

89

though: this regards a confidential matter." She'd already glanced into the town car and noted it had no privacy screen between the front and back seats.

"Or you can go along with us," Lionel suggested. "Your driver is welcome to follow behind."

"Yeah…okay." Tanner nodded to the driver.

SallyAnne let Tanner and Lionel walk ahead of her. Tanner's gait —slow and hesitant—was that of a guilty man. When he got to the agents' car, SallyAnne was surprised when he opened the back door for himself: another telltale sign of guilt.

She startled Tanner by sliding in beside him. It was the best way she'd be able to assess his answers while Lionel drove.

THEIR OPENING REMARKS WERE ALMOST IDENTICAL TO WHAT THEY'D said to Rob Edelson: that they were investigating Miranda D'Arcy for the fraud she'd committed in her capacity as a college admissions counselor.

Tanner leaned against the backseat's headrest. "What did she do?"

"So, you know her?" Lionel asked.

Tanner thought a long moment, then sighed. "I guess you already know I do, or you wouldn't be here."

"Then the question is, Mr. Simpson, exactly what services did she provide for you?" SallyAnne asked.

"Um… Well, she was my daughter's college admissions counselor."

"I'll be audio recording this conversation, Mr. Simpson." Sally-Anne pulled out her phone, clicked onto her audio app, and placed it between them.

Tanner inched away from it. "I have nothing to say except that I want to call my lawyers."

"Sure, feel free," Lionel replied casually.

Tanner treated that as a dare, jabbing his index finger on a saved number in his frequent contacts. "Artie… Yeah, sorry for the early hour. Listen, I'm sitting with a couple of FBI agents…. No, not for a picture, nothing like that. I'm—I'm being questioned about my, er, involvement with someone they're investigating… regarding

Lacey's college application...." Tanner glanced furtively at Sally-Anne. "Um.... yeaaahhhh." He frowned. "Yes."

There it is, SallyAnne thought. His admission of guilt.

The muttering on the other end of the line stopped. When it started again, Tanner's eyes got glassy. Turning to SallyAnne, he muttered, "He asked that I put the call on speaker."

She nodded.

Artie Abrams barked out an introduction. SallyAnne responded with her name, and Lionel did the same.

Then in the expected tone—that is to say, brusquely—Artie Abrams launched into the anticipated questions:

Was his client under investigation?

"Currently, he's a Person of Interest," Lionel answered.

Did they have any evidence against him?

"I'm sure a search warrant, which we'll have in hand within twenty-four hours, will bear more light," SallyAnne replied. "We'll also be searching the electronic devices belonging to Mr. Simpson's daughter, Lacey, as well as those of his ex-wife, Cassandra."

Tanner's eyes went wild. "My ex? Why her? She didn't know about Miranda's..." His mouth snapped shut.

"Miranda's illicit activities on Lacey's behalf, that were sanctioned by you?" SallyAnne prodded.

Artie barked, "Don't say another word, Tanner!"

All the color left Tanner's face.

"Listen, Tanner. It's gentlemanly of you to admit that your ex-wife knew nothing of your activities. I'm sure she'd greatly appreciate it if we got that on the record," Lionel suggested gently. "Lacey would too, for that matter. Having only one parent arrested for fraud is better than two."

"The DOJ will ask for leniency from the court for parents who have hired Miranda and are willing to cooperate quickly and fully," SallyAnne added. "It's already happening. No one wants to be out on that limb when Miranda is sawing it off."

"What do you mean by that?" Tanner stammered.

"Ask Mr. Abrams. He'll be the first to tell you that the moment we arrest Miranda, she'll be looking for ways to get the judge to reduce her sentence," Lionel replied. "She'll surely turn on those parents who haven't already decided to give evidence against her.

How ironic it would be for her to turn on you when you've been protecting her."

Tanner barked, "Artie, is that true?"

Artie's silence went on a beat too long. "It's certainly a consideration, yes. But if you were to plead 'not guilty,' a jury might be more receptive to your position than a judge."

Tanner's celebrated dimpled chin jutted out. "I'll take my chances that a jury will find me not guilty."

"Seriously? Do you want to take the chance you'll walk, just because you've got something the jurors don't—money and celebrity status?" Lionel asked. "Don't you think they'll resent that you did something they couldn't: buy your daughter's way into a great school by cheating and lying?"

"Worse yet, what if they hated your last movie?" SallyAnne muttered.

She knew she hit a nerve when Tanner winced. His last film was eviscerated by movie critics.

SallyAnne's jibe crumbled Tanner's stony gaze. Broken, he stared down at his hands. "If I go to jail, it'll ruin me! I'll never be able to work in the industry again!"

"We're truly sorry about that." Lionel's sincerity was real. "But Tanner, fraud is a serious crime. If you have any realistic hope of a lighter sentence, help us put Ms. D'Arcy behind bars."

"Okay—*Okay!*" Tanner croaked. "What do you want to know?"

SallyAnne's eyes caught Lionel's slim grin in the rearview mirror. Like her, he was ecstatic. They were now two for two.

"So, my daughter's math scores were sub-par," Tanner explained. "Miranda had a separate program for her private students. She called it 'concierge college admissions counseling.'"

"How much did you pay her, and how?" Lionel asked.

"Half a mil. I have the dough, so I thought, sure, why not?" Tanner shrugged. "Miranda asked that it be paid directly to her non-profit—the Best Foot Forward Club."

SallyAnne frowned. "So that you could take the fee as a tax deduction?"

Tanner hesitated, but finally, he nodded.

"What did she do for her fee?" SallyAnne asked.

"Well, the very first thing was to connect Lacey with a tutor. The guy also ran some sort of testing center."

"University Prep & Test," Lionel replied.

"Yeah, that's the one," Tanner acknowledged. "And, as Miranda promised, Lacey's SAT Math score was significantly higher than when she took the test at her school."

"By how much?" SallyAnne asked.

"Enough to earn a score of 1440 overall." Tanner shrugged. "Lacey isn't much of an athlete, so Miranda suggested she play a game or two of volleyball—you know, at the beach. Her mom took the Malibu house, so she could easily catch a game there. Miranda took a few photos, and it went in with the application." He rolled his eyes. "Miraculously, Lacey ended up on the team—for all of five minutes. She was sort of disappointed when the coach told her she wasn't up to the team's standards. But hey, it got her on campus..." His voice drifted off.

SallyAnne could guess what he was thinking: *until now.*

"I paid for the testing center separately."

Just like Rob Edelson, SallyAnne thought.

When they reached the studio, Tanner stuck his head out the window. Recognizing him, Paramount's security guard motioned them through the gate.

Tanner directed Lionel through the lot's maze of narrow streets to the studio's warehouse-sized stage where he was shooting his latest production, *Beyond Heavenly.*

As Tanner opened the car door, Lionel reminded him, "We'll have a search warrant by the end of the day."

"Yeah, whatever. I'll call the housekeeper and tell her to expect someone." Tanner shrugged. "Hey, listen, seriously: at this stage of the game, do Lacey and Cassandra need to know about this crap?"

"Sorry, but yes—if you want them cleared as suspects," Lionel replied.

"Of course I do! I just don't want them to...you know, hate me!"

Lionel grimaced. Sally realized he didn't want to lie.

Of course, they would. Tanner's ex-wife would hate him for smearing the family's reputation. His daughter would be hurt that he didn't trust her to make it into such a great school on her own.

For some reason, SallyAnne felt compelled to say, "Your daughter may be upset at first, but in time, she'll forgive you."

Tanner looked up at her. Hope filled his eyes. "You really think so?"

She nodded. "Yes, because she'll realize you acted out of love."

He nodded and then shuffled off.

When SallyAnne got into the front passenger seat, she noticed that Lionel was smiling at her.

She blushed. "What is it?"

"I ...I didn't know you had that in you."

SallyAnne cocked a brow. "Had what in me?"

"Such…kindness." He patted her hand.

His touch charged through her. She didn't pull away.

He didn't either. That is, not immediately.

By the time his hand went back to the wheel, she'd made up her mind. She didn't always have to be the hard-ass.

CHAPTER 12

"**Y**ou'll never guess who we saw last night!" Tallulah's voice boomed through Audrey's car's speaker.

Oh, no, Audrey thought.

There is no way I'll allow the kids to hear this conversation.

"Can't talk now, Tallulah! We're driving to school!" So that Tallulah would take the hint, Audrey tooted the car horn, causing an elderly man strolling in the crosswalk with his teacup poodle to bolt upright. He grabbed the dog, wrapping the pooch in his arms protectively.

As the tiny poodle yelped hysterically, the man raised his hand in a one-finger salute.

The kids burst out laughing.

"Oh, my God! Is everyone okay there?" Tallulah asked.

"Ma just scared the bejeezus out of some poor old guy, is all," Chuck proclaimed. He tapped his mother on the shoulder. "Want to pull over so I can drive?"

Charly scoffed, "Like heck! I'm the safest driver in the family—"

"No way!" Noah piped up. "It's Dad by a long shot!"

"Tallulah, I'll call you back." The only thing good about the conversation was that it gave Audrey an excuse to hurry off the phone.

"Don't bother, love! Just meet Bliss and me for lunch—Rose's Cafe, one-ish! We've got to tell you how—"

Immediately, Audrey tapped her phone off the speaker.

"Mom…*MOM!* You're passing the carpool line!" Through the rearview mirror, Audrey saw her youngest son smack his head with the palm of his hand. She skidded to a halt.

The car immediately behind her honked its horn. She sped up again and swerved to the curb, just beyond the drop-off point. The carpool monitor gave her a scowl.

Audrey's mea culpa was a wave.

She caught her youngest son's eye in the rearview mirror. "You've made your point, sir. Now, give me a kiss before your walk of shame."

Noah's smack on the cheek was too quick for her to corral him for a kiss of her own.

Never mind, she thought. I've embarrassed him enough.

Anxious to find out what the twins thought of their seventh-period teacher, Audrey wracked her brain for some way to raise the subject. She need not have worried. Five minutes into the fifteen-minute ride from Noah's school to theirs, Charly paused the twins' usual verbal jousting to declare, "Hey, guess what, Mom? I'm going to try out for Debate Team. Our seventh-period teacher is the coach."

Chuck scowled. "And that's why I'm not."

Audrey gripped the steering wheel so hard that her knuckles turned white.

"The teacher? Who is it again?" To her own ears, Audrey's voice sounded like a squeak.

"His name is Egan. And he thinks he's hot shit," Chuck muttered.

"He's not the only one. Everyone thinks he's hot—*especially Fawn*," Charly taunted. "In fact, she's trying out for Debate Team too."

Chuck's jaw fell open. When he caught his mother's eye in the mirror, he shut it and shrugged. "Then, maybe I will too," he declared.

"Ha!" Charly crowed. "After how you sassed Egan on his very first day, what do you think your chances are of making it?"

"You got into an altercation with your teacher—*on his very first day of school?*" Audrey exclaimed.

This time, Chuck avoided the mirror and looked out his window instead. "I was asking Fawn something—"

"She squealed while Egan was making his point," Charly corrected him.

Chuck retorted, "Well, I proved to Mr. Big Shot Gable that you weren't the only one in the class who could quote Shakespeare, Little Miss Show-Off." To prove his point, Chuck nudged his mother. "You see, Mom? All those times you quoted the Bard to put me in my place finally paid off!"

This time, Audrey turned red. "Wow, I'm so proud," she murmured sarcastically.

Chuck nodded vigorously. "Yeah, well you would have been if you'd seen his face." Chuck slapped the back of Charly's head. "Don't worry, you'll be the teacher's pet in no time, just like you are in all your classes."

The blush that crawled up Charly's neck was not lost on Audrey. She felt as if the pit of her gut was on fire.

That's why Charly wants to try out for Debate Team—to impress Egan. History is repeating itself.

I can't let that happen.

Audrey glanced at Charly. "Honey, do you even have time for Debate Team? You have so many other extracurriculars! And almost all your courses this year are APs. Isn't it more important to focus on your grades?" She took a deep breath, then added: "In fact, why don't you drop Comp Lit and do something fun like… I don't know, Glee maybe?"

Charly looked at her as if she'd lost her mind. "*Glee?* Are you kidding me?"

"She's got a point there, Ma," Chuck exclaimed. "Haven't you heard her sing?"

Charly turned to pound Chuck's arm. He inched away just in time to avoid it.

"I will not be dropping out of the AP class I've waited two years to take," Charly growled. "And as far as Debate Team goes, I'm not trying out just because it'll quote-unquote look great on my college apps. I'm doing it because it'll be fun. So, if you want me to have more fun this year, mission accomplished."

Audrey's heart dropped into the pit of her stomach. Still, she nodded silently.

Don't push it. Don't make her suspect anything.

"And besides," Charly continued, "don't you want me to follow in your footsteps and lead the debate team to victory?"

"I?...Oh...well..." Audrey stammered. "How did you know about that?"

Charly rolled her eyes. "I saw the trophy in AA's display case. There was an *LA Times* article attached. It said, quote, Audrey Thorpe argued succinctly yet poignantly, leading her team to its next win, end-quote." Charly grinned. "Mom, I get it: you've set the bar pretty high. But I'm going to do my best to beat your record."

"To be frank, it was a team effort," Audrey insisted. "And it was a lot of hard work, believe me." *Yes, it was exhilarating—but for all the wrong reasons.*

"Mom, since you already know the ropes, you can help me make the team too," Chuck declared.

Audrey panicked. "But...Why would you even go out for it? Between basketball and baseball, don't you have enough on your plate?"

Charly snorted. "Because of Fawn. He's afraid he'll lose her to Egan. At least, that's how Fawn's playing it."

"She isn't 'playing' anything," Chuck shot back. He caught Audrey's eye in the mirror. "I need an academic extracurricular. Something like that will look great on my college apps. Isn't that what you keep telling me? So, you'll help me—right?"

Chuck's gaze said it all: *You love me. Of course, you will.*

How could she say no?

As far as Audrey was concerned, they couldn't reach Ashbury Academy's student drop-off queue soon enough. While their car idled in line, Charly's peck on the cheek goodbye came with a question: "Since you were on Debate Team, you had Egan too, right?"

"'Had'... him?" Audrey stammered.

Shit... SHIT.

"For Comp Lit. Isn't that why you're such a Shakespeare nerd?"

"Oh! Yes, of course! I mean, that one year Egan was here, I was in his class."

"Then you must have been excited when his novel came out. It's called *Extracurricular*."

"Everyone was." Even to her own ears, Audrey sounded defensive. She turned her head to hide her frown.

"Do we have a copy in the house?"

"No…" Technically, she was right. Her copy was buried in the back of the closet of her old bedroom in Lavinia's house.

"Oh," Charly shrugged. "That's okay. Zina thinks her mom may have a copy because he taught her too. If not, I'm sure there's a copy in the school library."

"Why do you want it? So that you can impress Egan by giving it a glowing review in class?" Ignoring his sister's glare, Chuck grabbed his book bag. "Or do you just want to read the sex scenes?"

Charly's eyes went wide. Turning to her mother, she asked, "Are there sex scenes in *Extracurricular*?"

Audrey's answer was a flushed face.

Chuck hooted with laughter. "Wow, Mom! Really? His porn is that hot?"

"I wouldn't know," Audrey huffed. "Frankly, I never opened it."

I didn't have to. Egan read it to me—along with an auditorium filled with others just as moved by his erotic fantasy of…

Me.

"I'm sure they'll have a copy in the school library," Charly reasoned.

Oh my God—she's right!

Hearing the honks behind her, Audrey lurched the car forward before squealing to a halt in front of the school's entrance. "Out, kiddos. Make your mama proud today!"

The twins took the hint and scrambled out of the car.

After pulling away from the curb, Audrey took the first parking space she could find. She waited for AA's clock tower to chime the final bell announcing the start of the school day and then rushed through the campus to the library.

THE LIBRARY'S ORIGINAL BUILDING WAS STILL ITS ENTRANCE, BUT A NEW wing had expanded it considerably. There, the bookcases were tall enough that a rail holding a rolling ladder was needed to reach the highest shelves.

The students were in their first period classes, so the library was empty. Audrey waved at the librarian—Suri, a woman in her twenties, who was tattooed from her wrists all the way up to her shoulders. There were several earrings in the younger woman's nose and ears.

Suri smiled and waved back. "Great to see you, Audrey! Call me if you need anything." As the PTA chair, Audrey had helped raise tens of thousands of dollars for the books that now filled the newly renovated library.

Audrey nodded casually, then sat down in front of one of the online catalog monitors and put in the title she sought. Yes, a copy of *Extracurricular* was in the system, and it was currently on the shelf.

Audrey easily found it. She slipped it into her valise. But as she made her way toward the front door, she noticed the security arch.

I can't just walk out with this. And I certainly don't want to be seen checking it out!

I've got to hide it somewhere…

Casually, Audrey strolled back toward the library's non-fiction section, in the library's new wing. She glanced around. Suri's desk was too far away for the librarian to see her.

Audrey scanned the shelves, wondering what topic would interest the students the least. Architecture, perhaps? Maybe Mathematics or Science. For her, it would be Technology and Engineering, but that might not be the case for the AA students whose parents saw Silicon Valley as the right career path for them.

In any case, she started there, climbing the closest ladder as high as it would take her. She found a row of books on the topic of Fracture Mechanics and opened one.

Perfect, she thought, it's about concrete. Dull enough.

The books were tall, whereas Egan's novel was only nine inches in height, and relatively slim. If she pulled out four of them and put *Extracurricular* behind them and on its side, it would likely never be found.

In seconds, the deed was done.

She hurried down the ladder but slowed her pace by the time she reached Suri's desk. The librarian, engrossed in a book, looked up. "Did you find what you were looking for?"

Audrey shook her head. "It was already checked out, so I roamed around a bit to see if something else might strike my fancy. But I just realized I'm late for a coffee date and I've got to run. I'll be back later in the week."

H AD A UDREY WAITED EVEN A FEW HOURS TO HIDE THE BOOK, SHE'D have failed in her mission. As it turned out, Charly stopped by the library at lunchtime.

After perusing the online catalog and seeing that *Extracurricular* was indeed listed and on the shelf, she headed to the fiction section, where the books were shelved in alphabetical order by the authors' names. She found a gaping hole where the book should have been.

On the off chance that it had been misfiled, Charly eyed each shelf above and below, then through all the authors filed under G. Still not finding it, she went through the Fiction section shelf by shelf.

Finally, she stopped at Suri's desk. After greeting the librarian with a welcome-back hug, Charly explained, "I'm looking for Egan's novel, *Extracurricular*. The catalog says it's checked in, but I can't find it."

Suri's brow knotted with concern. She tapped a few keys on her computer screen and nodded. "You're right. It should be back there."

"Could it have been misfiled?"

"Maybe. The last time it was checked out was last February."

"Could it be in the return cart? Maybe someone could have walked it up here and then changed their mind?"

Suri shook her head. "Doubtful. But you're welcome to take a look."

It took no more than a few seconds to see that it wasn't there either. "Ah, well. I'll check the public library after school." Charly waved as she walked away.

"Oh, Charly, I forgot to mention to your mom that if she calls me with the name of the book she was looking for, I'll be sure to hold it for her."

Charly stopped and turned around. "My mom was here?"

Suri nodded. "Yes. She was in Non-Fiction looking for some sort of science book."

Charly shrugged. "Oh... Probably for her job. I'll be sure to tell her."

CHAPTER 13

SallyAnne and Lionel's next stop was the Wilshire Grand Center, where Eric Calisher's brokerage office was located.

The firm took up three floors of Los Angeles' tallest building. One of its three receptionists, all of whom were wearing wireless headsets, stood up from behind a desk that looked as if it were modeled after the flight deck of the latest *Star Trek* movie. She greeted them the moment they walked into the lobby.

In a town of gorgeous women, she—all three of them, really— ranked up there with some of the supermodels who graced the fashion magazines that stared out at SallyAnne during her late-night runs to the local Mollie Stone's Market.

Was the woman a failed actress or an aged-out model? Perhaps her role was that of a human work of art? In any event, her presence relayed the message to Calisher's clients that his firm provided them with the best of everything—even waiting room eye candy.

The receptionist stared when they declared they were with the FBI but didn't flinch when they presented their badges. Instead, she whispered so low that SallyAnne couldn't hear what she said to the person at the other end of the phone line: presumably Eric.

Finally, she turned to them and murmured, "Follow me, please."

Their path began through a pair of double doors paneled to fade into the wall. There were no handles. Instead, the doors slid open the moment the receptionist was within a few feet. SallyAnne deduced the woman emitted a security clearance signal.

The hall was long, and doors within it were recessed. They weren't taken to an office but to a conference room adjacent to where they'd entered.

There was a surveillance camera in the corner of the room. Sally-Anne wondered if the conversation would be audio-recorded as well. If so, by California law, this would have to be disclosed upfront. Not that it mattered. What the agents would say to Eric followed the letter of the law anyway.

Eric kept them waiting ten minutes. He was a tall man, impeccably dressed, with the lean muscular build of someone who worked out religiously. Although mid-fifties according to his birth record, he'd had enough nips and tucks to fool anyone into believing he was a decade younger.

They rose to shake hands and show their badges. The brief second their palms touched, SallyAnne noted that Eric's was dry.

"So, agents, what can I do for you?" No pleasantries. Just right to the point.

Lionel's introductory remarks were the same: their investigation was into Miranda's activities as a college admissions consultant, and that Eric, as a client, was a Person of Interest.

They expected him to interrupt them at that point to ask how they knew this, but he didn't take the bait: to either confirm or deny their allegation. Instead, with no emotion whatsoever, he replied, "If that's the case, I'll be contacting my attorney. Feel free to do the same. It's Phillip Isaacson, at Conley Bell & Brownwell. Good day, agents."

He stood up to leave.

"Mr. Calisher, we'll be back with a search warrant," SallyAnne said matter-of-factly.

He waved that tidbit away as he walked out the door.

Lionel glanced at SallyAnne. As she stood up, her eyes moved to the security camera.

He got the hint and silently followed her out the door.

SallyAnne waited until they were outside the building, then asked, "Next up, the wife, right?"

Lionel nodded. "Yeah. But like you said, he's probably calling her right now and telling her to lay low. In which case, if she's home, she won't answer when we ring the doorbell. We have to prepare for that."

"We may be in for a stakeout," she countered. "Still, eventually she'll have to leave to pick up the kids or return home with them. And she may not want to play this his way."

"We'll know when we get there," Lionel replied. "At least we know what she looks like, so we won't miss her."

As with Miranda, they'd pulled photos from online sources, mostly social media. In the case of the Calishers, the fact that they gave significant donations to a number of charities made them regulars in the society columns.

When they're indicted, I wonder how many of their friends will stand by them, SallyAnne wondered.

———

The Calisher home was a post-modern mansion on a corner lot in Beverly Hills. An ornate wrought iron fence ran the home's full perimeter.

A gate opened onto a circular driveway in front of a grand portico. There were no cars out front.

Lionel parked the car in front of the home. He and SallyAnne walked to the gate and rang the security buzzer.

No answer.

They rang a second time, leaning on it longer.

Still, no response.

"I guess we have a wait ahead of us," Lionel grumbled.

SallyAnne shrugged. "Late lunch, then. If we get hungry in the meantime, I took some apples, bananas, and a couple of granola bars from the hotel breakfast buffet."

Lionel chuckled. "You think of everything."

To get her mind off his compliment, she murmured, "There's got to be a garage. Perhaps in the back?"

Lionel drove the car around the corner. SallyAnne was right. An alley ran behind all the houses on the Calishers' block.

He pulled the car across the street from the alley and up a few feet. "This way, we can watch if anyone comes out of the front or the back of the house," Lionel explained.

While they waited, SallyAnne called in the search warrant requests for the Simpson and Calisher homes. She then asked to be transferred to Riley to learn if anything had been found on the Edelsons' computers.

"There was no correspondence between D'Arcy and the wife or the son," Riley confirmed. "And we've downloaded all correspondence between D'Arcy and Edelson, including the payment to the Best Foot Forward Club. We also found an electronic receipt to University Prep & Test."

"Thanks, Riley. Call with updates."

"Will do."

SallyAnne had just hung up when Lionel nudged her. A car was pulling into the alley. It stopped in front of the Calishers' garage and idled.

A man was driving. A woman sat beside him.

"Hey, the woman in that car is Janna!" Lionel tapped the photo sitting on the dashboard. It showed a stunning redhead—as beautiful as the receptionist, but about fifteen years older.

SallyAnne craned her neck. "But that's not Eric...is it?"

Lionel pulled out a pair of binoculars for a closer look. Suddenly, his mouth dropped open. "Nope," he murmured. "And they're kissing!"

"If she's been quote-unquote indisposed, maybe Eric hasn't reached her with the news that we might be on our way over." SallyAnne took out her cell phone and took a picture of the car's license plate. In answer to Lionel's quizzical stare, she declared, "Leverage. It may come in handy."

He laughed. "Janna is opening the car door," he noticed. "We'd better storm the castle now before she pulls up the drawbridge."

Spoken like a true knight in shining armor, SallyAnne thought.

THEY PASSED THE CAR AS IT PULLED OUT OF THE ALLEY. THE DRIVER didn't look twice. In fact, he made a point to turn his head: a clear indication that he didn't want to be noticed by a couple who might be Janna's neighbors.

By the time Janna tapped the garage's security code, they were at her side. "Ms. Calisher, FBI. May we have a moment?" Lionel asked.

Startled, she froze even as the garage door rose slowly in front of her.

"Who…me?" she stammered.

"Yes, thank you." Lionel smiled down at her. "You see, we're investigating a case involving an acquaintance of yours: Miranda D'Arcy."

"Miranda?" Janna frowned. A faint buzz emanated from her purse. Instinctively, she opened it to reach for her phone. Reading the caller ID, she said, "Oh! I…I have to take this! It's my husband. He's been trying to reach me all morning."

"You mean that wasn't him in the car?" SallyAnne asked. "The man you were kissing?"

Janna froze. She stared down at the phone's screen as if it were radioactive. Finally, the call rolled into voice mail.

No one moved.

At long last, Janna muttered, "What do you want?"

JANNA CALISHER TOOK THEM INTO AN EXPANSIVE, BEAUTIFULLY appointed living room. As was the usual procedure, SallyAnne made it a point to mention that the conversation would be recorded and then placed her phone in plain view.

Janna nodded silently, and listened as they explained the situation:

That they already knew about Miranda's crimes;

How they knew Miranda had worked with Janna and her husband for their son David's application to USC.

And why she needed to be truthful about her role and that of her husband.

"You still have two children at home, don't you?" SallyAnne nodded toward the large family portrait on the wall behind the sofa.

"Have you already talked to my husband?"

Lionel nodded. "He wasn't forthcoming."

Janna shrugged. "Then I suppose I shouldn't be either."

"It won't matter," SallyAnne warned her. "We'll have a search warrant by early evening. When we do, the texts, emails, and photos on your husband's cell phone—and yours—will tell us a good deal."

Janna blanched at that thought.

She's thinking of how Eric will react to the news of her lover, SallyAnne realized.

"Janna, was hiring Miranda your idea or Eric's?" Lionel prodded.

She grimaced. "It was Eric's. He'd heard from some of her other clients that she always delivered. He wanted a sure bet. Heaven knows our son, James, isn't exactly a shoo-in to the schools Eric would have liked to see him attend."

"Had you known about the tactics used to get your son into the university of his choice?" SallyAnne asked.

"I…I guess I suspected. It sounded too good to be true." Janna grimaced. "But Eric's response was, 'don't ask, don't tell.'"

"Janna, I must warn you: if you follow your husband's lead and hold out for a jury trial, like him you're chancing jail time. You'll also be doubling down on whatever verdict it delivers," Lionel explained. "And don't expect any leniency in your sentence. A judge won't appreciate that you attempted to skirt the law. Now, are you sure that's what you want?"

Janna dropped her head. "I…I don't know! I just know that it'll be worse if I cross him." She wiped away her tears.

"Janna, listen: you strike me as a woman who doesn't like to take chances," SallyAnne said. "If Eric wants to take the fall, so be it. But if you cooperate, you'll put this behind you more quickly and can get on with your life sooner than later."

Janna shrugged. "One way or another, this is over, isn't it? This life, I mean."

"Just the things that are wrong about it," Lionel murmured.

"If you say so." She stood up. "Yes, okay, I'll cooperate. In fact, if you'll wait here a moment, I think there's something that will help make the case even easier for you."

"Providing crucial evidence will go a long way with a judge," Lionel murmured.

Janna nodded sadly. Then she stood up and walked to the staircase that led to the home's second story.

"Did you see the relieved look on her face?" SallyAnne whispered. "Whatever she's got, it must be important."

The answer came with a single gunshot.

"Holy shit!" SallyAnne exclaimed.

She was on Lionel's heels as he ran up the stairs.

CHAPTER 14

There were three more copies of *Extracurricular* in different branches of the San Francisco Public Library. Audrey barely had the time to track them down and check them out before her luncheon with Bliss and Tallulah.

She was the last one to get there. Bliss and Tallulah had already snagged an outside table. They waved her over.

She'd barely had time to sit down and unfold her napkin before Bliss exclaimed, "Guess who's back in town?"

"Egan." Audrey replied bluntly.

"Darn it!" Tallulah exchanged disappointed pouts with Bliss. "Let me guess. Charly told you because she's in one of his classes."

Ha! If only she'd mentioned it before I walked into the seventh-period open house...

"Nope. Daniel mentioned that Egan was the board's teacher liaison," she reminded them.

Bliss slapped her forehead. "How could we have forgotten that!"

"I know someone who would have remembered," Tallulah winked playfully. "That college counselor —Miranda D'Arcy."

Audrey frowned. "Why is that?"

Bliss arched a brow. "Let's just say she perked up when Daniel entered the room. For a moment there, I thought she was going to throw Egan over for him."

Audrey felt her cheeks heat up. "What do you mean, 'throw Egan over'? Were they doing something other than talking?"

"Not during the meeting," Tallulah admitted. "But there was some heat between the two of them. I'd be willing to bet lunch that she didn't go home alone."

Bliss patted Audrey's hand. "By that, she means Egan, not Daniel."

At least that gave Audrey something to laugh about. "Good to know. But in either regard, lunch is on Tallulah. After the last open house, Egan went out with Daniel for a burger and a beer."

Tallulah shrugged. "I'm still banking on Egan and Miranda becoming an item."

In a way, I hope she's right, Audrey thought.

Should Egan be struck with a sudden crisis of conscience, a lady friend would give him added incentive to keep his mouth shut about their first and only outing.

As if devastating my marriage wouldn't be reason enough.

Audrey waited for their waiter to take their order before asking, "How did Egan react to seeing you?"

"He remembered us, but he didn't recognize us," Bliss replied.

Tallulah giggled. "Yeah, it was quite a thrill seeing his jaw drop on the table, especially after his attempted come-on—to Bliss, anyway."

Audrey ignored the remark. Still, it bothered her, although she knew it shouldn't. It had been eighteen years—plenty of time for Egan to ruin a lot of women's lives.

Bliss shrugged. "In his mind, Audrey was the intellectual, you were the renegade, and I was the airhead. I took great pleasure in letting him know how successful we'd become." She turned to Audrey. "And how did he react to you?"

"He was polite, nothing more. If Daniel hadn't introduced us, I don't think he would have recognized me." Audrey truly believed that.

"Poppycock! Just look at you. Lean, firm—and more muscular than when we were teens," Bliss argued. "It's all that cycling you do."

"I thought you never went out riding with Daniel and the kids," Tallulah interjected.

Before she could answer, Bliss replied, "She doesn't. Last week I just happened to be walking by one of those indoor cycling studios, and there she was"—she pointed a thumb at Audrey—"pedaling away furiously."

Audrey held up a finger to her lips. "It was supposed to be our little secret."

Tallulah shook her head, awed. "I don't get it. Your whole family spends almost every Saturday morning cycling over the bridge, up a mountain, and back, and you don't want to join them?"

"They see too much of me and too little of Daniel. I can spare them those precious few hours a week together," Audrey insisted.

Tallulah looked skyward. "This, from a woman who never keeps secrets from anyone, let alone her husband."

If only you knew, Audrey thought.

She spent the rest of the lunch listening to her friends chitchat about PTA business and their work.

Bliss was proud that Sienna had suggested the net proceeds from her favorite pocketbook in the Belluci fall collection be earmarked for Ashbury Academy's scholarship program.

The generous offer left Audrey speechless. When she found her voice again, she murmured, "What a great idea!"

"I thought so too. In fact, I suggested to Raffaele that since it was Sienna's idea, she would be the perfect person to walk it down the runway during Fashion Week. But he's adamant that she participate only on the business side of Belluci," Bliss explained. "Instead, I'll take it onto the runway. Still, Sienna insists on mentioning it on every vlog post she does between now and then. She's so close to many of the kids who get scholarships to AA." Bliss beamed proudly. "Hanging with them has been a reality check for her. I know that's true for many of AA's well-off students."

For Tallulah, the news was that Maggie was all in for headlining the twenty-fifth birthday gala for Ashbury Academy, and not just because it would raise money for her dearest friend's life achievement.

"She also wants to do new recordings of all the songs from the album that came out the year AA was established," Tallulah announced. "You remember: *Make Lust, not Love.* All proceeds will go to the school."

"Oh, my God!" Audrey exclaimed. "That would be incredible! Have you mentioned it to Lavinia?"

It was a perfect message to take her mother's mind off her illness.

Tallulah shook her head. "I suggested that Maggie break the news to her in person. Bliss did the same with Maude and Reggie. Her parents will be carrying the handbag in all their boutiques. They've arranged to take Lavinia to dinner tonight so that they can tell her together."

Audrey blinked away her tears. "Lavinia and I don't have dearer friends than you and your parents."

"Group hug!" Bliss exclaimed.

The three friends threw their arms around each other. Audrey sighed. "I wish Davis were here too!"

Tallulah's eyes sparkled. "Let's call him now! He'll flip out when I tell him about Egan."

She didn't wait for permission.

Davis picked up on the fifth ring. "Wow, I was just thinking about you guys!"

Tallulah guffawed. "Sure you were—in between taking meetings with studio suits, right?"

"In fact, I'm on my way to Netflix now, which means sitting in traffic for at least another half hour. So, what gives?"

"Bliss and I are sitting here with Audrey. I told her you may have something to tell her."

"I sure do! Hi, sweet cheeks!"

Despite the noise level in a busy restaurant during lunch, those at nearby tables glanced over at them.

Audrey blushed. "Hey, this is on speakerphone! I don't need the whole restaurant knowing about our love affair."

"Too bad. You have that effect on everyone, lassie. In fact, to stay always in your heart, my latest random act of kindness will be premiering my next indie film there in San Francisco to coincide with Ashbury Academy's gala fundraiser. All ticket proceeds will go to the scholarship program."

Audrey's eyes glistened with tears. "Oh my goodness, Davis! Lavinia will be so touched."

"I was just one more kid kicked to the gutter when she found me and invited me to our school. I owe her everything, Audrey. You know that." He sighed. "And by the way, I'll also have a private screening for AA students in the school auditorium. The stars and some of the tech crew will be with me to answer the kids' questions."

"They'll be over-the-top ecstatic!" Bliss declared.

"No more than me. I can't wait to give all of you—and Lavinia—a great big kiss."

Audrey turned her head to wipe away a tear. *The tribute may be coming just in time.*

"Speaking of big deals at the school, guess who's back at AA?" Tallulah teased Davis.

He chuckled. "Don't leave me in suspense."

"Egan Gable. He's teaching again."

The silence on Davis' end went on for so long that, finally, Audrey asked, "Are you still there?"

"Yes! Sorry. It blows me away to hear that," Davis admitted. "I have to tell you: my first reaction is 'my, how the mighty have fallen.' But, frankly, like us, the best thing that ever happened to him was because of Ashbury Academy, so maybe it's not such a wrong move on his part."

Audrey bit her tongue to keep from shouting, *It's awful!*

She finally managed to say, "So, you liked his book?"

"Yes, of course! Didn't you?"

"Frankly, I never got around to reading it," she murmured.

"It was a real tearjerker, as I recall," he replied. "I do remember he made me look swell, so I have no complaints. Ah, good times."

She waited for the other shoe to drop: for him to ask her what went on between Egan and her that had inspired such sensual prose—

But nothing.

So, Davis didn't recognize me in the book either, she realized.

If Egan had had the good sense never to return, she might have been disappointed about that.

"Yeah, well, you were one of the lucky ones," Tallulah pouted. "I came off looking like some kind of rebel without a cause, and he wrote up Bliss as some clueless love child."

What about me?

As if reading her mind, Bliss replied mournfully, "And poor Audrey..."

"What do you mean by that?" *SO THEY KNOW.*

"Well, it's just that..." Bliss winced. "I guess you didn't make much of an impression."

"Are you kidding me?" Audrey turned to Tallulah. "Is she kidding me?"

Tallulah raised her hands in surrender. "Hey, don't shoot the messengers! We just figured he didn't find you interesting enough. And since you never mentioned it, we certainly weren't going to bring it up."

Davis whistled. "Yeah, boy—but that thing he had for Mandy! Talk about love being blind!"

Audrey's relief was so intense that all she could do was laugh hysterically.

Bliss, shocked, murmured to Tallulah: "At least she's not crying."

CHAPTER 15

The gun Janna Calisher shot herself with was an S&W M&P Shield.

The Beverly Hills Police Department's CSI unit appeared just minutes before the FBI unit tasked with the search warrant showed up.

BHPD deduced what SallyAnne and Lionel already suspected: she'd been sitting at the foot of her bed when she pressed the gun firmly against her chest. In order to pull the trigger, her hand had to be at an awkward angle. Still, she succeeded in hitting her heart directly. The force propelled her backward onto the bed. The blood, thick and crimson, had washed over her torso before spilling onto the duvet.

Had SallyAnne not seen Janna prior, she would have never guessed that the dead woman's silk blouse was white.

She found it strange that Janna was smiling.

Having received Lionel's call, Eric came in just as the FBI's search and seizure was concluding. He was accompanied by another man.

The lawyer he mentioned, Isaacson, SallyAnne deduced.

Ashen and silent, Eric stood in the middle of his living room, his eyes darting at the activity around him: the swarm of federal agents going through all the electronic media devices they'd found; BHPD

CSI cordoning off the crime scene; its sister unit, Forensics, wheeling away the body.

The sight of the body bag containing his wife infuriated him.

He glared at Lionel. "What the hell did you say to Janna?"

"All we did was explain why we came here to meet her," Sally-Anne explained. "She agreed to let us record her."

"As his attorney, I want a copy of the recording." The man at Eric's side handed her his business card. As she suspected, he was Phillip Isaacson. She handed him her card as well. Lionel did the same.

"I'd been calling Janna since you left my office. Are you the reason she wouldn't pick up my calls?" Eric snarled.

"No," Lionel replied. "Janna ignored an incoming call in our presence, but it was a decision she made on her own."

SallyAnne was glad Lionel didn't feel the need to elaborate.

"By the way, Janna acknowledged your involvement with Miranda D'Arcy," Lionel added.

Eric opened his mouth. But before he could say anything, Phillip put his hand on his client's shoulder. "Just because she said it doesn't make it so. In fact, Eric claims no knowledge that Ms. D'Arcy's activities on his son's behalf were illegal."

"Eric's correspondence with Ms. D'Arcy may prove otherwise," SallyAnne countered. She nodded toward a man standing behind Eric: Riley was there now too.

"In fact, we've discovered several email addresses for Mr. Calisher," Riley piped up. "And one was used exclusively for correspondence between Ms. D'Arcy and him, including the one in which a fee was paid to a non-profit controlled by her."

"What is the email account name?" Isaacson asked.

"It's a Gmail account: the name Calisher followed by the numbers zero six zero six," Riley replied. "It's a desktop computer in the upstairs office, off the master bedroom."

"Even if there was correspondence between this account and Ms. D'Arcy's, it doesn't mean the correspondence was conducted by Mr. Calisher—especially if *Mrs.* Calisher also had access to the office, the computer, and that specific email account. And considering Mrs. Calisher's state-of-mind—especially as it concerned David's anxiety about the college admissions process, all of the dealings with Ms. D'Arcy may have been conducted by her instead." He turned to his client. "Isn't that true?"

SallyAnne frowned. *Damn him—he's leading his client.*

Eric got the message. He nodded vigorously, insisting, "I don't remember ever opening, let alone using, that email address. Did I meet Miranda D'Arcy? Sure, a couple of times at David's school. Did I know about her work on David's behalf? Yes—but I was only told what my wife must have wanted me to hear: that Miranda's process was legal and above board." He opened his hands wide. "To put it bluntly, my job was to bring home the bacon. The kids and their schooling were Janna's domain."

Noting SallyAnne's scowl, Isaacson added, "Look, agents, my client wants to cooperate fully. He'll tell you everything he knows about your suspect. But that doesn't make him complicit in his now-deceased wife's actions."

"That's very good of him," Lionel muttered. By his tone, Sally-Anne knew he wasn't buying their bullshit either.

Eric's smirk proved he couldn't have cared less. "My younger children will soon need to be picked up at their school. If you'll excuse me, agents, I've got to break the news to them and to David about their mother's death."

"We're sorry about your loss, Mr. Calisher," Lionel murmured. "Our IT forensics analysis should take a week or two. Afterward, I'm sure we'll be back in touch."

WHEN THEY GOT INTO THEIR CAR, LIONEL DIDN'T START THE ENGINE immediately. Instead, he stared down the street.

Three houses away, a gardener was using a leaf blower to clear away fresh grass cuttings. Another gardener was across the street, trimming a hedge. Workmen were coming out of a house farther down the street. The only pedestrian foot traffic was two au pairs wheeling baby carriages.

"Where are the people who live here?" he wondered out loud.

SallyAnne rolled her eyes. "Working, I guess. Or shopping. Or eating lunch out with the girls—or the boys."

"Exactly. This isn't a neighborhood where people talk across fences to each other while their kids play in their yards. Beverly

Hills is a collection of *Architectural Digest* showrooms! These homes are entertainment write-offs."

"So, what's your point?"

"Janna was lonely. It's why she was disconnected from her husband. It's probably why she was having an affair."

"I can't say I blame her. Talk about Mr. Freeze! I got frostbite just being in the same room with that cold fish!" SallyAnne shivered. "But if she was unhappy, why not just leave?"

Lionel shook his head. "Not everyone is strong like you."

SallyAnne laughed weakly. "I'll take that as a compliment."

"Good, because it is."

She shrugged so that he wouldn't know how touched she felt by it. "Speaking of Janna's lover, shouldn't we have a talk with him?"

"Agreed. I'll call in the car's license plate to get his name and address."

A few minutes later, they were on their way to Santa Monica to talk to someone named Van Pierce.

THE CAR, AN OLDER MODEL PRIUS, WAS PARKED IN THE DRIVEWAY OF A stucco duplex located just a few blocks from Santa Monica's beach.

SallyAnne and Lionel's knock was answered by a man in his mid-thirties: the one whose driver's license matched the name attached to the car registration. Van Pierce's hair was dark, thick, and on the longer side. The hair on his face was scruff more than beard or goatee. He was slim and almost as tall as Lionel.

Van wore sandals, cargo shorts, and a loose *Game of Thrones* tee shirt. On it, the words WINTER IS COMING was emblazoned in a circle.

He wasn't exactly who SallyAnne was expecting. Like Lionel, she held up her badge. "Are you Van Pierce?"

"Yeah." He nodded, surprised. "What can I do for you?" he had a soft Southern drawl, more Georgia than Texas.

"You have an acquaintance—Janna Calisher," SallyAnne stated.

Van's smile faded. "Yes. We're friends."

"May we come in, Mr. Pierce?" Lionel asked. "What we have to say is somewhat personal in nature."

Warily, Van stepped aside so that they could enter.

The place was a typical man cave: a leather couch, a matching leather easy chair, a big screen TV, and not much of anything else. It wasn't exactly tidy, but it wasn't a pigsty either.

To encourage Van to sit down in the chair, they took the couch.

"Coffee? Water?" Van asked.

"Thanks, no," Lionel replied. He said no more until Van finally plopped down in the easy chair.

"Mr. Pierce, what I have to say isn't easy. You see, earlier this afternoon, Mrs. Calisher took her own life."

Van leaned back in the chair. All color left his face. He moaned as if he'd been punched.

When he finally talked, it was to whisper one word: "Why?"

"We were hoping you could shed some light on that very matter," SallyAnne replied. "In our very brief conversation with her, we got the feeling she was an unhappy person."

"Yeah, well, that's an understatement! Frankly, I don't think she and I would have...I don't think we would have connected like we did if she were happy." Van shrugged. "I mean, I'm not exactly her type."

"What type do you think that is?" Lionel asked.

Van scowled. "The guy she married thinks he's Master of the Universe."

Lionel leaned in. "Was it a happy marriage?"

Van snorted angrily. "Are you kidding? She hated that asshole! He'd had affairs on her—sometimes with her friends! He didn't think twice of flaunting it in her face. Heck, Janna wanted out of it, badly! But she knew if she divorced him, she'd lose everything: his money, their house, her social standing...maybe even the kids. He's a winner-take-all asshole."

The perfect M.O. for Miranda D'Arcy, SallyAnne thought. "How did you meet Janna?"

"I was David's tutor. Since his freshman year and up until his senior year. Then Eric insisted David go to some bogus testing center instead: University Test & Prep." Van rolled his eyes. "David wasn't a great student. That drove Eric up the wall. The sad thing was we were finally making progress."

Lionel frowned. "The test center was *Eric's* idea?"

Van nodded. "I mean...that's what Janna told me. She was upset about it. More than me. She even insisted on taking me out to dinner to break the news." He attempted a smile. "It was the first time we really talked—not like client and vendor, but like two people. Afterward...we had our first kiss. She was a sweet person. Sad, but sweet." He shook his head, sadly. "I'm going to miss her."

"Van, you called the prep center 'bogus.' What did you mean by that?" SallyAnne asked.

"Frankly, that was Janna's word for it. She felt David wasn't improving at all. Just for the heck of it, I wanted to see if she was right, so I dropped in to see if they were hiring. The more successful places always are, especially in the more affluent areas. Lots of parents want their kids tutored, and there are only so many after-school hours for that to happen; less if the kids have lots of extracurriculars. But University Prep & Test is a one-man band, if even that. I went three times in the after-school hours. No one was there! Only once did someone open the door—some guy. He must have been expecting a client."

"What did the place look like?" SallyAnne asked.

Van grimaced. "He wouldn't let me get through the threshold. But I peeked over his shoulder. All I saw was a couch, a coffee table and a couple of desks." Van rolled his eyes. "When an operation is that small, usually the private tutoring takes place at the student's home. A private tutor certainly doesn't need the overhead of an office in a high-priced neighborhood."

"Thank you for your time, Van." Lionel stood up. SallyAnne rose too.

Van nodded. "I'm stunned—just blown away! I knew she was unhappy, but this...Poor David!"

SallyAnne paused. "One last question: what were David's extracurriculars?"

"Other than video games and TV?" Van forced a grin. "Nothing I can think of. He wasn't really into sports." He looked at his *GoT* shirt. "This was a gift from him. I watched enough of the show to pass as a gray worm."

"A what?" Lionel asked.

"It's a *GoT* fan who thinks Stannis is the true King of Westeros. It was how I connected with David."

From the car's speaker phone, Director Melamed declared, "A bird in the hand is worth two in the bush."

"With all due respect, sir: what the heck does that mean?" Sally-Anne asked.

"It means that we've got a cooperating witness willing to give evidence against our prime suspect. The fact that Eric Calisher's hands aren't dirty in this case doesn't matter."

"But it does—because *he's the perp!*" SallyAnne insisted. "He's the one who hired Miranda, not his dead wife!"

"From what Riley says, there isn't any evidence that Calisher ever talked to her directly, let alone met her. And the emails on the shared account aren't signed by either of the Calishers."

"But Van Pierce just told us that hiring Miranda was Eric's idea!"

"Unless Mr. Pierce has proof, what he told you was hearsay," Melamed interrupted. "And for that matter, a disgruntled, unfaithful wife who was depressed enough to kill herself isn't exactly a reliable resource, even alive and first-hand. Wrap it up down there, agents."

Melamed clicked off.

"I need a drink," SallyAnne muttered under her breath.

"Food first," Lionel countered. "Neither man nor woman can live on bananas and granola bars alone."

"Sure. Absolutely." Sh knew he was right. Besides, if she drank on an empty stomach, she might say the wrong thing.

She might even tell Lionel how she felt about him.

"Maybe we shouldn't be doing this," SallyAnne blurted out.

"What? We can't leave now!" Lionel looked down at his watch. "Our food will be out any minute. At least, that's what they keep telling us."

They'd ended up at the lounge at the Hotel Casa del Mar. From their oceanside table, high above the walkway that catered to the continuous flow of walkers and cyclists, they'd spent the past half hour staring out at the waves lapping at the beach.

"No! I didn't mean leave here. I meant, leave *this case*." Really, SallyAnne couldn't have left even if she wanted to. She'd barely touched her salad. To top it off, somewhere along the line she'd switched from wine to martinis.

Now she was feeling tipsy. And guilty. "If we hadn't approached Janna, she'd still be alive," SallyAnne stared down into her empty martini glass. "If I hadn't told Janna we'd be looking at her phone messages and texts, maybe she wouldn't have gone upstairs and… and…" She slumped down in her seat.

"Hey, listen: *Janna's death wasn't your fault.* She was a very sad person. Van told us that." Lionel laid his hand over SallyAnne's. "And besides, who kills themselves over a college admission crime?"

"That's my point!" SallyAnne straightened up. "Miranda preys on parents who are insecure enough to take her up on her offer. They have money, and they'll use it to do anything for their kids— even illegal stuff! Even stuff that no one in their right mind would do if they weren't egotistical, or paranoid for their kids—or depressed!" She waved her fork at Lionel to make her point. "People are out there murdering. They're selling and transporting drugs! They're robbing banks! They're committing acts of terror! And what are we doing?" She smacked the table with the fork. "We're arresting parents who have more money than brains! It isn't even a crime of passion! It's… It's a crime of *privilege!*"

Lionel grabbed SallyAnne's wrist with one hand. With the other, very gently he pried away the fork. "You're right—about one very important thing: *it's a crime.* Period. Bribery to create fraud is illegal. Paying by interstate commerce is illegal. And don't forget: universities receive taxpayer dollars for their programs. We, the taxpayers, are paying for the education of these fraudulently admitted students. And as for those who missed out on that university seat: what would you say to them? That what was stolen from them wasn't as important?"

SallyAnne meekly shook her head.

"Good, because the course of their lives was changed too. They missed out on jobs, and experiences—maybe even friendships that may have changed their lives."

SallyAnne nodded silently. "You're right. I'm sorry."

"So, you're not going to ask for a transfer to the Domestic Terrorist unit?"

The worried look on his face sobered her up quickly.

She shook her head. "No. You're not getting rid of me that easily, Mr. Polk. Partners forever."

"I'll drink to that," he murmured.

Thank goodness, when he raised his glass to his lips, he was grinning again.

Jesus, I almost blew it, SallyAnne thought.

For just a second, she thought she saw a haze of longing in his eyes.

Now I'm imagining stuff? Jesus, Mary, and Joseph—no more booze tonight!

CHAPTER 16

awn McCoppin stood in front of her closet's full-length mirror, scrutinizing every inch of herself.

Her make-up had been applied as meticulously as a supermodel's, and with the same effect: polished perfection that emphasized her large eyes, sharp cheekbones, and generous mouth.

As always, she'd placed a small beauty mark on the left side of her lips. Her hair was loose, its long locks gently teased into a messy mass.

She wore a cheerleader's uniform: not the one she used while leading shout-outs to Ashbury Academy's football and basketball teams, but one of several she'd had custom-made and wore exclusively when uploading new content to her premium-subscription erotic website, CheerFullyYours.Club.

The uniform she chose for today's video was a hot pink little number, except for the material inside the pleats of its tiny skirt, which was Easter Egg blue—the same hue as the letter "F" sewn below the cleavage created by the uniform's skintight, low-cut shell top.

Under the skirt, Fawn wore blue "spankies"—Spandex briefs, cut high on the thigh. To complete the outfit, she accessorized it with hot pink and pale blue pompoms.

This particular outfit had never been worn before, but Fawn already knew it would be a crowd-pleaser. A daily analysis of the viewing habits of the website's subscribers—primarily males between the ages of thirty-five and sixty-four, with household incomes of over two-hundred thousand dollars—hinted at this by what they'd enjoyed previously on the site.

It wasn't just the website's clicks and views that Fawn assessed. Besides knowing who watched which video and when, she also knew how many times the viewer had done so. Just as important, Fawn could see when a subscriber lingered on a certain portion of the video in order to enjoy a particular part of her sensual routine.

As always, Fawn dressed quickly and off-camera. But when she disrobed, it would be on-camera and at a snail's pace: a slow, languid striptease that intercut regimented gymnastic moves with the slower, sensual undulations of an experienced pole dancer. She scripted every camera angle, every action, every word, every inflection.

Cameras were hidden behind the mirrors placed throughout the room—not just the mirrored closet doors and the mirror over her makeup table, but the ones hanging behind and over her bed as well. This allowed her to watch her performance, assuring her that she was amping up the heat at the right time and in the right place.

The cameras were controlled by a miniature remote control secured in the palm of Fawn's hand. Her greatest skill was found in the tip of her index finger. With a single tap, she could manipulate a specific camera to turn on or off; to zoom in or out.

To follow her every move.

By trial and error, she'd learned that her audience—her "sugar daddies," as she called them—craved fantasy and sensuality; dirty talk and primal action. Her video vignettes were erotic, yes; but no more salacious than what you'd see while watching a well-choreographed burlesque show.

Certainly not porn.

Still, her cosplay came close enough to keep her almost half-million subscribers panting and heaving for their weekly dose of Fawn.

In her post editing sessions, the real thrills were added. A mere glance at bare skin—a peek-a-boo freeze shot of the top of her thigh below her skirt, a close-up of a fully covered breast, a slo-mo zoom-in on her cleavage, or something as simple as allowing the camera to linger on her pouting lips—was why her sugar daddies watched her videos over and over again.

Afterward, the spankies worn in the routine would be auctioned off to the highest bidder. Of all the ancillary items Fawn sold on her website—sex toys, blow-up dolls in her image, even cheerleading attire—the biggest money-makers were things that had actually touched her body.

Fawn had no doubt her clueless parents would blow their tops if they knew what went on under their very roof.

Well, too bad. CheerFully Yours was Fawn's way of breaking Seamus and Gretchen's chokehold on her life.

Heck, they didn't even know that she'd skipped every class today up to AA's lunch break. On Friday mornings, her mother met with her tennis foursome. Afterward, the ladies got massages and indulged in a long, liquid lunch. By the time her mother returned, Fawn would be back at school.

Skipping her morning classes was worth it. What CheerFully Yours had earned her to date wasn't just pin money. It was giving her the financial arsenal she'd need to combat Seamus' dictatorial edict:

That she waste the next four years of her life as a college student.

It wasn't because he thought she was smart. Far from it. Seamus made no bones of his contention that she was too flighty, too lazy, and too dumb to make anything better than just a passing grade in any of her classes.

Realizing he had no other expectations, Fawn lived down to them.

Seamus did have one mandate. She should do what other pretty girls had done before her: marry well.

When she was fourteen—already a willowy budding beauty catching the eye of every male who crossed her path, he explained it this way: "A beautiful girl is catnip to boys who know how to make money. They find the girls they want to marry in college. And not just any university, either, but the *créme de la créme* schools. That's why you've got to focus on what counts."

"My grades?" she asked.

He laughed heartily at that. "Yeah, well… Look, no one is telling you not to try your best. But let's face facts, Fawnie. Life deals each of us just an ace or two. Yours wasn't brains. It's *your looks*." He patted her on the head. "A man who has made his way in the world has earned the right to have a pretty wife by his side. I'll get you into the right college. Once you're there, set your cap on some MBA student at the top of his class and you're home free. If he has a trust fund, all the better."

She'd smiled blandly and nodded to indicate she understood: *Be that girl. Marry money.*

NOT.

No way was she going to end up like her mother, Gretchen: an arm charm to a vainglorious man.

Granted, Fawn owed her parents a lot. Her beauty, now in full bloom, had been Gretchen's genetic gift. Seamus' legacy was the Machiavellian cunning that drove every relationship she'd ever had.

And, like him, her God was the Almighty Dollar.

Someday, her parents would be proud that she showed such entrepreneurial ingenuity. In the meantime, her goal was to keep the clicks coming and the money flowing.

It's why each of CheeryFully Yours' posts was a work of cinematic art; not just its production values but the stories too. Each ten-minute video had a provocative beginning, a middle ramped up with a series of subsequent actions, and a very satisfying ending. If Fawn's only interest in school—literature—had taught her anything, it was that these criteria were the essence of every great story.

Fawn worked hard to build her persona; to create her *brand.*

But she knew she couldn't play the role of the provocative cheerleader forever. If her mother's numerous cosmetic surgeries had taught her one thing, it was that within a decade—maybe fifteen years, if she stayed out of the sun and cut all sugar from her diet—she'd have to segue to some other business.

A natural career choice was to produce pornographic films. Fawn had already learned a lot about erotic cinematography. By the time she was ready to pack her cheerleading outfits away once and for all, she would have earned enough to finance a porn studio.

But as quickly as that idea came to her, she dismissed it. By their nature, actors were temperamental creatures. She couldn't even imagine the amount of cajoling needed to get a few well-endowed porn actors to perform sex acts under the camera's glare with the same realism she put into her own mini-movies. Right now, Fawn was the producer, the director, and the star. Whatever she did next would have to further embellish her brand—not someone else's.

Before choosing her senior year school schedule, it had occurred to Fawn that a better use of her storytelling skills would be writing erotic books. She'd done a happy dance when learning she'd been accepted to Ashbury Academy's Advanced Placement Comparative Lit class. She looked forward to studying the works of master story-writers.

All the more reason to create a strong impression on Egan. As a bestselling author, he'd hacked the code to success in the publishing industry.

Fawn's mission was to compel him to share it with her. She wouldn't be too obvious about her quest to become teacher's pet. But to do so, she knew she had to dump Chuck McKittridge, and pronto.

A shame, too, because he was actually great in the sack.

And boy, did he appreciate her for all her talents.

In fact, every time the cameras rolled, Fawn's thoughts went to Chuck. She pretended it was him she undressed for; that it was Chuck who coveted every inch of her.

But it was obvious that Egan abhorred Chuck. And since Fawn had no intention of associating with anyone who rubbed the teacher the wrong way, she'd have to drop him—and fast.

She'd do it this afternoon, in fact.

Perhaps, in Egan's classroom. That way, Egan would realize how serious she was about Comp Lit.

Chuck's sister presented a different problem. Intuitively, Fawn could tell Egan was intrigued with Charly; that he'd been impressed with her knowledge and insights on the course's topics.

If Fawn weren't so jealous, she'd actually admire Charly for it.

She noticed that Charly's friends—Manya Patel, Zina Sisley-Calder, and Sienna Belluci—were cut from a similar cloth. They seemed as true-blue to her as she was to them.

Fawn had never had friends like that. Her entourage was made up of sycophantic wannabes who stroked her ego and played yes girls to her.

Needless to say, none of them knew of her side business. She planned on keeping it that way. She vowed she too would someday have friends she could count on; friends who were her equal. More than likely they'd be pop stars and supermodels; a few Famechangers, maybe—if they were at least in the Mega-Influencer category, like Sienna Belluci, whom she despised almost as much as Charly.

The second she turned eighteen, Fawn would thumb her nose at Seamus' grand plan for his little girl: to be his bartering chip in his corporate playground.

She chuckled softly when she thought of how many of his colleagues and clients were actually her subscribers.

Unfortunately, her eighteenth birthday was still a full year away. Until then, she'd have to play along. Sure, she'd do his bidding and enroll in some elite college. She was certain he'd be good to his word and make sure her entree was as easy as possible.

In the meantime, she'd build up her getaway stash.

With that in mind, she clicked on Camera One's button. Under its watchful eye, slowly and seductively, she picked up her pompoms. Then in a Kewpie Doll voice, she shouted out this cheer, choreographed to a bouncing bump-and-grind that, by the end of it, left her naked and panting:

You think you're bad? You think you're hot?
You think you'll score? Not till I show you what I've got!
Say, what? You want to come again?
Not so fast. Not 'til I say when.
You say you're uptown? Let me take you down...
Down!... Down!

"CONGRATULATIONS!" MIRANDA'S SLAP ON EGAN'S BACK WAS HARD enough to make him wince.

But what she said next, delivered with a gleeful giggle, had him cringing: "I just heard that Daniel McKittridge is sponsoring your chair! How fortunate is that?"

Egan felt his face warm up. "I don't know why you find that so amusing," he retorted. He glanced around the teachers' lounge to see who else might have heard her.

Turns out it was everyone.

By pretending to be seemingly engrossed in his class's Comp Lit textbook—ironically, one written by his former college mentor, Clive

Munt-Luckinbill—he'd hoped to spend his lunch hour working through the conundrum he'd now found himself in because of Daniel's generosity.

He could only imagine what Audrey thought when she'd heard the news: that somehow Egan had coerced Daniel into funding his honorary chair; that it was payback for the horrible way they'd split up;

That he had done so to make a mockery of her.

By taking his lunch in the teachers' lounge as opposed to hiding in his classroom, he'd hoped to catch Lavinia to suggest that Daniel's donation go to a different purpose and to promise that he'd work doubly hard to secure another gift in its place.

But Miranda's declaration proved it was much too late for that.

Where was Lavinia anyway?

Egan stood up. "If you'll excuse me, I have some tasks to do in class before the bell."

"Oh...I'm so sorry!" Her smirk puffed outward into a pout. "I would have thought you'd think it great news. It was one of your goals in taking the position, wasn't it? Making sure it paid to make it worth your while?"

Heads turned. Brows arched. The math teacher, Ike, rolled his eyes.

"With or without the sponsorship, I find it an honor to be here at AA," Egan huffed.

"I'm sure you do," Miranda murmured.

She didn't sound convinced.

The snickers of some of the other teachers echoed that sentiment.

Egan was too upset to sit there any longer. He headed out the door and up the staircase.

Egan was already at his classroom's threshold when he realized Miranda had followed him. With a sigh, he asked, "Is there something else you wish to say?"

She nodded contritely. "Only that I'm sorry. And, frankly, I'm confused as to how I upset you."

He shrugged. "Miranda, seriously...it's not you. It's just that... well, I don't feel comfortable taking Daniel's money."

"You mean, you don't want the chair?"

"Yes!...I mean, *no!*...I mean, yes, certainly, I *want* the chair."

I want the money. I need the money.

"And I feel honored to have been given the gift. But I just don't want *the McKittridges* to be my sponsors."

She frowned, perplexed. "Why not?"

"It's..." He was about to say, *it's personal*, but that would lead to even more questions—all of which had embarrassing answers. "It's just not right. Not with their children being in my class. Someone may assume they were buying my favors. You know, a better grade or something."

Miranda scoffed, "Doubtful! In the first place, Charly's grades are impeccable. Granted, Chuck's are a bit—well, shall we say less than stellar? But from what I hear, he talks his way out of all sorts of shenanigans." She winked. "He is quite the little charmer. Our female students certainly think so, anyway."

"Yeah, well, that's what I mean. I don't want it to seem...*odd*."

"A shame! Lavinia was ecstatic to hear that Daniel stepped up— and so enthusiastically too. You'll break her heart if you turn down the gift." Miranda poked him with her finger. "Look, Egan, in academics—especially in schools like this one—no one looks twice at donations, especially for such a great cause." She put her hand on his chest. "Do yourself a favor: *just take the money and run.*"

"I don't know..." Maybe she has a point, he thought. If it's chickenfeed to Daniel, who was Egan to assume anyone would take it the wrong way—even Audrey?

Miranda leaned in. "Are you at all concerned because of Audrey?"

Egan did a double-take at the thought she'd read his mind. Warily, he asked, "Why would you say that?"

"Oh...nothing." Miranda shrugged. "I guess I shouldn't be talking out of school. It's just that...Well, from what Lavinia mentioned you'd made quite an impression on her."

"What? You mean, last night at the open house?"

"No, silly! *Back in the day.* You know, when you first taught here." Miranda grinned slyly. "I guess she had a little crush on you." Suddenly her eyes widened. "I hope I didn't make you uncomfortable, pointing that out."

"No, not at all." Egan smiled uncertainly. If Lavinia knew about it and it hadn't bothered her, she would have never asked me back if she thought it would make Audrey uncomfortable, he reasoned.

Suddenly, he felt very silly about the whole thing.

And intrigued at the thought that Audrey still cared about him.

"Okay, since you put it that way, I'll graciously accept it. Why look a gift horse in the mouth, right?"

Miranda giggled. "I won't tell Daniel about your almost change of heart if you don't. I'd hate for him to get jealous."

Egan muttered, "There's nothing for him to be jealous about."

Miranda raised a brow. "Oh, I wouldn't say that, exactly. From the way Tallulah and Bliss reacted to you, I imagine there might still be embers in that old flame." She glanced down at the book in his hand. "I've taken up too much of your time. I'd better let you get back to work."

As she sauntered out, he wondered, *Could she be right?*

He smiled at that thought.

THAT NARCISSISTIC HORN DOG LAPPED IT UP!

The whole time Miranda was stroking his ego, she'd had a hard time keeping a straight face.

She'd seen how Tallulah and Bliss had reacted to him: first with disdain, and then with pity.

Good. To Miranda's way of thinking, Egan deserved both.

Her instinct had told her that even if Audrey had outgrown her crush, Egan's pride wouldn't let him believe it.

Especially if someone else confirmed it.

And since he trusted her, she was that perfect someone.

No woman in her right mind would see Egan for anything less than what he was: an egotistic asshole.

Certainly not one who had a man like Daniel wrapped around her finger.

So now, if Egan acted on his worst instincts—those instincts being to flirt with the prim and proper Mrs. McKittridge—he'd be sure to repulse her *and* lose her husband's donation in the process.

And Lavinia would have no other recourse than to ask him to resign.

The thought of engineering Egan's imminent downfall sent a thrill through Miranda.

Still, trifling with Egan was *petite amusement*. At happy hour today, real business was at hand. At the board meeting, she'd piqued Jess Smallwood's interest in her private consulting services.

They were to meet for a drink at six, at Palmer's on Fillmore. She'd already reserved a private banquette.

In the meantime, she had only a few hours to review the intel she'd pulled up on Jess' son, Hugo. What a piece of work! She found easily decoded messages on SnapChat and Instagram that bore out the rumor he was the school's busiest drug pusher. If she could sniff this out, so could a savvy university admissions officer.

If Jess's goal was to erase all traces of Hugo's illegal activities as well as pump up his SATs and extracurriculars, it would cost him a pretty penny.

CHAPTER 17

*C*huck had waited all day for seventh period for one reason: Fawn was avoiding him.

She hadn't shown up for Ike's trigonometry class. And when she came in during lunch period, she took great pains to avoid Chuck.

Nor had she responded to his texts, and she let his calls roll into voicemail.

By the seventh period, anxiety had set in. Fawn had played the tease all summer long. But then, right before school, when she knew her parents would be out for the whole day, she'd invited Chuck to the McCoppin's Presidio Heights home.

Located on a high hill adjacent to the historical national park that gave the neighborhood its name, the imposing Beaux-Arts mansion commanded an incomparable view of the Golden Gate Bridge.

Fawn's bedroom—cotton-candy pink, its round bed lined with plush stuffed animals—was nothing like his sister's small, prim attic garret room that overflowed with books, its walls papered with maps of the world.

But there was nothing juvenile about Fawn's approach to sex. He didn't need to cajole her into foreplay. And from how she responded to his touch, he had no doubt that she appreciated his handiwork.

In no time they moved beyond the usual slap and tickle to prodding and probing, and finally to the main event.

Other girls had told Chuck he was, like, hung. *Hugely*. It didn't faze him to hear that except for the fact that he felt it came with the expectation of a worthy performance.

Before Fawn, he'd had enough practice to pace himself. So, between her initial moans and her final gasp, he was sure he'd satisfied her.

Why else had she smiled and commanded, "Yummy! Again, my noble steed!"

By their third go-round, she was sated.

He was in love.

Chuck envisioned their senior year as an alliance. Every second together would be badassical.

Every moment apart would suck.

But now, in only the first week of school, something had changed. Why?

What the hell had happened?

The second he walked into his seventh period classroom, he saw who was to blame.

Egan.

The teacher was leaning against Chuck's desk. Fawn was chuckling at something he'd just said. She was in her seat—well, sort of. Really, she was sitting on her desktop. With her arms placed behind her, she was partially reclining. The top two buttons of her blouse were open, exposing her generous cleavage.

What …the hell?

So, that's how it is!

By now, other students were meandering into class—Charly, Manya, Sienna, and Zina included. Like some of the others, instinctively their eyes fell on their teacher. Curious, they tuned into the conversation.

Angrily, Chuck walked over. Egan, who was listening intently to Fawn's animated dissertation, hadn't realized someone was beside him until Chuck declared, *"Do you mind?"*

Though still intrigued by whatever tale Fawn was spinning, Egan nodded distractedly. As he moved from the desk, he patted Chuck's shoulder.

Chuck shrugged off his hand and then slammed his backpack on the desk.

Fawn frowned. "Gee, seems someone sure woke up on the wrong side of the bed!" She winked knowingly to Egan.

Egan shrugged.

Chuck was glad Egan didn't attempt some clever rejoinder. Otherwise, he might have socked him.

He was relieved when the final seventh-period warning bell chimed because Egan strolled to the front of the classroom—

Only to turn back to Chuck. "By the way, I never told you I was very impressed with how you were able to come up with the *As You Like It* quote so quickly."

Taken aback, Chuck muttered, "It was easy enough for me. As I told you, it's been thrown in my face enough times."

"I'm sure your mother says it only because she loves you, and she believes you can accomplish anything you set your mind to."

The audacity of this guy!

Incensed, Chuck grinned at Egan. "You taught my mother too, right?"

The question seemed friendly enough.

Egan nodded hesitantly. "Yes. Audrey was a conscientious student."

Chuck smirked, "That's nice of you to say, considering the stuff you put in your book about your students."

Egan frowned. "What do you mean by that?"

"Wasn't your novel based on Ashbury Academy?"

Egan's back stiffened. "It's a work of fiction."

"Fiction..." Chuck wiggled his brows. "Like, what...*porn*?"

"Critics consider it contemporary literature," Egan countered coolly. "But, yes, there is sex in the book, if that's what you're hinting at."

"Let me guess: between a teacher and his student?"

At that very second, every other conversation in the room ceased.

Everyone stared at Egan.

"I take it you haven't read it. Otherwise, you'd realize that's an asinine question." He smiled as if the joke were on Chuck.

"I haven't," Chuck admitted. "Still, I'll take that as a yes. Am I right?"

"Tell you what. If you take the time to actually read it, we'll have an honest discussion as to the plot, the characters, and my inspiration."

Fawn licked her lips, fascinated by Egan's rejoinder.

Chuck could have kicked himself. *Fuck! Fuck! Now she'll read it for sure. And she'll want to be his next inspiration.*

"Sure," Chuck muttered. "Looking forward to it."

When Chuck's gaze met Fawn's, she rolled her eyes. Then she grabbed her books and moved to an empty seat—beside Charly, of all places.

Charly's reaction cut the deepest: she closed her eyes tightly and shuddered as if watching a baby seal getting clubbed to death.

Fuck Chuck!

Egan fumed silently, even as he called on various students to read aloud their homework assignments;

Even as he pretended to listen, then gave bland atta-boys before calling on the next student.

Egan had wanted to give Chuck a clean slate. Really, he did. But if the kid was stupid enough to jibe him because he was jealous— and over a silly simp like *Fawn McCoppin, of all people!* —then so be it.

As soon as Egan's sixth-period class had cleared out, Fawn had made her entrance. She was juggling a stack of books that just so happened to slip from her hands as Egan noticed her—

Allowing her to bend over seductively to pick them up.

By then, Egan knew the game she was playing: Easy A.

To put an end to it, he walked over, knelt down, and picked up the books she'd missed.

That would have been the end of it, but she then mentioned that she felt confused by the debate pamphlet he'd left for those interested in the tryouts. She'd perched herself on top of her desk then leaned back seductively so that he'd be sure to notice that her breasts had somehow breached the top two buttons of her blouse. Then, in a kittenish purr, she asked to meet him after class so that he could explain the debate rules and definitions to her.

He'd said no—firmly—and recommended instead that she buddy up with another contender and become critique partners to sound out their arguments and rebuttals. "You know, like your boyfriend, Chuck," he pointed out.

Fawn giggled at that like it was the funniest thing she'd ever heard.

That's when Egan knew she'd already decided to dump Chuck.

She was still laughing when the poor kid walked into class.

Chuck, kiddo, you reap what you sow.

In Fawn's case, Egan could only imagine how many others had plowed that field before Chuck. Maybe he should warn Audrey to have the kid checked for STDs...

Oh, hell—*Audrey!*

Egan had almost freaked out when Chuck prodded him if *Extracurricular* was about a teacher-student tryst. He was glad he thought of asking Chuck outright if he'd read it.

He'd felt a wave of relief when Chuck said no.

No doubt, though, that the first thing Chuck would do when he got home was to ask Audrey if they had a copy of her former teacher's book, *Extracurricular.*

At first, she'd be taken aback. Then, cautiously, she'd ask. *Why do you want to know?*

Chuck would tell her that Egan had assigned him the book for a report.

Audrey would be horrified, Egan realized.

She'll trash it, or burn it—

If she hasn't done so already.

In any regard, Audrey would assume Egan had assigned Chuck the book to humiliate her.

She'll hate me all over again, Egan thought miserably.

Then he remembered what Miranda had said: "The way Tallulah and Bliss reacted to you, I imagine there might still be embers in that old flame."

If she's right...

Then what?

Then maybe I'll have a chance to show Audrey how much I love her.

And do what—break up her marriage? Wreck a seemingly happy home?

Egan glanced over at Chuck. He wasn't surprised to find the boy still scowling at him.

No. Never. It's not worth it.

But maybe...

We can be friends?

Reality charged through him like a blast of frigid air:
As if.

JUST AS THE SCHOOL CHIMES RANG OUT THE END OF CLASS, FAWN tapped Charly on the shoulder.

Charly turned around. As Fawn anticipated, she was surprised to see who'd summoned her. Because Fawn ignored those she considered a waste of her time, she was used to this reaction. For guys, it was a shock. For other girls, it was awe. Go figure.

She fully expected Charly to stutter something that indicated she was flustered and flattered by Fawn's attention. Instead, Charly, bemused, replied, "What do *you* want?"

For once, Fawn was taken aback. "Well…Okay, see, I was thinking…" *Damn Charly! Why was she always acting so superior to everyone else?* "I guess you're going out for Debate Team. Am I right?"

Charly nodded warily.

"Well…so am I. And…I wondered if you'd like to be, you know…critique partners?"

Charly glanced over to the classroom door, where Manya, Sienna, and Zina were waiting for her.

Fawn followed her gaze. Charly's friends, relaxed and confident, gossiped and chuckled together, totally oblivious of the exclusive offer she'd just made to their bestie.

They are all so damn smug. Well, wait until Charly dumps them —for me.

Charly would do it too, because it was an honor to be included in Fawn's inner circle. The girls already there—Kaylie, Sophie, and Mackenzie—met a certain standard. They were pretty enough, but not gorgeous like her. They were smart, but no geniuses and had none of her cunning.

And like Fawn, they were snobs.

Better yet, their greatest fear was being banished from her posse.

Just then, Chuck, still stunned at being humiliated so publicly, was shuffling out the door.

Charly nodded toward her brother. "Wouldn't you rather partner with Chuck?"

Fawn sniffed, "*Are you serious?* Do you actually think he's going to try out too?"

Charly shrugged. "He claims he is."

Fawn frowned. "Either way, the answer is no."

"Why not?"

Fawn studied a nail. "I'm sorry if this hurts you to hear it, Charly, but your brother is a loser. Plain and simple, he doesn't have your smarts."

Charly tilted her head as if she hadn't heard Fawn correctly. "Wait, let me get this straight. You enjoy fucking my brother, and you love that he's head over heels crazy in love with you. But because you're angling for a better grade and you think Egan will hold it against you that you're dating Chuck, you dumped him?"

Fawn stiffened. "It sounds cruel when you put it that way."

Charly snapped her fingers in Fawn's face. "Earth to Fawn: *that's because it is cruel.* You used Chuck, and now he's not important to you anymore. *So, you're ghosting him.*" Charly stood up. "You know, there should be a word for a female who acts like a player. Until someone comes up with it, I guess 'bitch' will have to do."

Charly left to join her friends.

At first, Fawn was too incensed to do anything but stare after her.

Why, that little nobody! How dare she talk to me that way!

In Fawn's world, only she had the right to turn down an offer of friendship. Just the thought of this slight made her furious.

She grabbed her books and headed for the door.

As she passed Egan's desk, she noticed he had his back to her. Still, she could tell he was chuckling about something. It mortified Fawn to think that he might have heard Charly put her in her place.

She quickly dismissed that thought. Egan was enthralled by her. Perhaps even smitten. It was why he'd found it necessary to put Chuck in his place.

Now more than ever she wanted to take something away from Charly: Egan's respect.

She knew how to do it too: she'd impress him at the debate tryouts.

CHAPTER 18

Miranda arrived at Palmer's fifteen minutes earlier than the designated time for her appointment with Jess Smallwood. She'd pulled up everything she could from AA's files on his son, Hugo.

No doubt about it, Hugo was a smart boy. When he was a freshman, his grades were exemplary. But sometime in the middle of his sophomore year, he dropped two grade-points on average for each subject.

This was bound to happen when his only purpose for going to school was to distribute drugs to his clients—that is, a few trusted AA students, Miranda reasoned.

Some teachers included a few insightful notes for other faculty and staff:

Hugo keeps a low profile.

(Teacher-speak that meant he didn't participate well in classroom discussions).

Hugo is constantly tethered to his phone.

But of course he was. It was how he procured orders. Miranda was willing to guess that the code for his various products—weed, coke, Ecstasy, whatever—was simple enough code to crack.

Miranda looked forward to hearing Jess' take on his kid. She wondered if he actually knew anything about his son's lucrative side business.

Her guess was no.

But if Jess were aware of it, she was willing to bet it simply didn't matter to him.

It was worth bringing up if only to gauge how much he was willing to pay to make his son squeaky clean.

She didn't have to wait long. Jess walked in promptly at six o'clock. As they waited for their cocktails—martinis for both—they made pleasantries: about her take on AA's students; and his upcoming trip to Bangkok.

Once the drinks arrived, Jess got right to the point: "You mentioned some sort of private concierge service. What does that mean, exactly?"

"A student's best attributes aren't always apparent via a university's standard admission criteria: you know, grades, extracurricular activities, awards and other achievements."

"In Hugo's case, his GPA stinks, he's not on any teams, and he's not exactly a do-gooder." Jess rolled his eyes. "So, how would you enhance his, for lack of a better phrase, 'best attributes?'" He took a swig of his martini.

"Do you mean the fact that he's a successful drug dealer?"

Jess spewed his drink. "Well, you certainly come right to the point."

"So, you do know about his extracurricular activity. Good! We won't have to beat about the bush." Miranda leaned in. "But in order to make him appealing to college admissions officers, I'll need complete honesty from you—and him."

"Sure, okay," Jess murmured cautiously.

Miranda smiled broadly. "Believe it or not, you've given me a lot to work with."

"Are you serious?" He motioned the waiter for a second round.

"Yes—depending on how we spin it, Hugo's triumph over substance abuse—and his desire to help others fight it too—could make for an inspirational essay."

"Stop it. You're giving me a woody," Jess murmured. "Oh...

Wait! I just went soft at the thought that Hugo is an awful writer. Not to mention he doesn't preach against drugs. He *sells* them." Jess gulped his drink.

The sexual innuendo annoyed Miranda. Still, she was willing to ignore it if he accepted the price tag for her services. "Not to worry. I'll get Hugo a private tutor who will help him write a gripping saga of his triumph over cocaine."

"Marijuana—but, yeah, from the way he's talking, he wants to take that on too, as a secondary product line," Jess replied. "He's like a capo—you know, got to keep the troops marching."

"He has a battalion of foot soldiers to do his bidding? What an industrious overachiever! How does he deliver his, er, product?"

"It's really quite creative! Only edibles—lollipops, in fact. Great high, but no smell. And he sells them in airtight sealed metal containers: like the kind used to sell mints, only larger."

"Genius! Unobtrusive and raid-proof!" As if awed by Hugo's ingenuity, Miranda applauded slowly. "Now, about your son's SATs: *abysmal*. He'll need a tutor."

"Yeah, no shit. Or more importantly, a miracle," Jess muttered.

"They do happen, you know." She grinned mischievously. "With the right tutor. Mine. How does a score of fourteen-fifty sound?"

"I think I just came! This is better than phone sex." He leaned in and put his hand on her thigh.

"Do tell," she muttered. Although if she were to be honest with herself, he was looking more desirable after a second martini. "Was Hugo ever a substance abuser?"

"He was, but he's clean now." Jess grimaced. "He's got an entrepreneurial bent. He saw a way to scratch an itch. Big deal. Besides, most kids his age are only recreational users, right?"

Until they're not, Miranda thought. "When Hugo got clean, did he do it in rehab?"

Jess nodded again. "Yes. Two months, the summer between his sophomore and junior years. One of those fancy airy-fairy dry-out spas."

"Has Hugo ever been arrested?"

"Not yet. But worrying about it keeps me up at night." Jess' face seemed to fold into itself like a fallen soufflé. "So how much do these so-called miracles cost?"

"One million dollars," she purred.

This time he choked on his olive. "You're kidding!" he gasped.

"I never joke about money," she huffed. "Put it in perspective, Jess. You've already paid much more than that for twelve years of private schooling. Am I right?"

Jess nodded grudgingly.

"All of it has been leading up to this: *admission into a top-drawer university*," Miranda added. "You don't want to fumble the ball on the five-yard line, do you?"

Jess thought for a moment. Finally, he muttered, "I'm a sucker for whores. But despite the *Pretty Woman* reference, usually when I dole out that kind of money, at the very least I get a blowjob."

"This isn't Bangkok, Mr. *Smallwood*. The fee is non-negotiable."

Miranda's emphasis of Jess' surname made him wince. He sat silently.

"Shall I continue?" she asked.

He nodded.

That's when she knew he was hooked.

"We'll make sure to tick all the boxes. That starts with getting him into the *right* university—that is to say, one in a state that has already passed laws that make it legal to sell marijuana."

"Like here in California," Jess pointed out.

"Bingo! Home of Berkeley, Stanford, UCLA, and USC. Do you think he'd be interested in any of those schools?" Miranda batted her eyes at the obvious.

"Jeez, I'm hard again," Jess declared.

"We'll narrow the choice further to universities with Business Administration programs underwritten by Big Pharma." Miranda tapped the table as she thought. "Which is all of the above—oh, except for Berkeley." A shame, she thought, considering that once upon a time mind-blowing recreational drugs were practically part of the curriculum.

Jess grimaced. "Does your million-dollar fee come with a guarantee?"

"First of all, it's a 'donation,' so you get an IRS write-off," she pointed out. "And an SAT score in the mid-fourteen-hundreds or higher means serious consideration by every university. Now, top that with the right extracurricular or two, and he's a shoo-in."

"He can't very well join Future Business Leaders of America," Jess scoffed.

"In fact, the specific purpose of the non-profit you'll be donating to—The Best Foot Forward Club—is to align graduating seniors with an inspirational mission. For Hugo, I would imagine a few photos of him and his distribution crew—those he's helped get on their feet financially by selling his colorful candy tins for a great cause—will do the trick."

"What's the 'great cause'?"

"Why, the Best Foot Forward Club, of course!" Miranda patted his wayward hand, but she didn't move it.

Instead, she used her other hand to motion the waiter for another round. She had one more pitch to make. Another drink might help him see the advantage of agreeing to it. "Now that we've gotten Hugo's conundrum out of the way, I'd like to talk a little board business."

Jess looked up, surprised. "You're on the board? But I thought you only sat in that one time, to introduce yourself and make a quick presentation."

"My point is that I *should* be on the board—for a couple of reasons. First of all, despite Lavinia's contention otherwise, the most important mission of our school is really how well our students get placed upon graduation. Shouldn't it be a board imperative to have my ongoing insights on this?"

"Yes, certainly!"

"Secondly, the way the board is set up now—with eight members, since there are now two PTA representatives—there can never be a voting majority. Should push come to shove on the issues important to your little clique—say, reducing that illogically enormous budget for scholarships, or some student perk that Lavinia may balk at—I imagine you boys would find a tied board to be a bit cumbersome."

"I see your point," he said gravely. "I'm sure Seamus will too."

"I thought you would." She tipped her glass to his. "Here's to Hugo's success."

As he tapped hers, he murmured, "And yours."

Miranda was sipping the last of her martini when she felt his fingers crawling higher between her legs.

Ah, the quid pro quo.

Miranda had already made up her mind that she was up for Jess' antics. She'd need a powerful ally on the board. Of all its members, he was the most desirable.

As she'd done with Rob Edelson, she'd be video-recording their trysts. She saw it as an insurance policy. Jess Smallwood's first marriage had already cost him dearly. He couldn't afford for his second to implode as well.

"Why don't we take this celebration back to my place?" Miranda murmured. To make her position clear, she cupped him firmly.

To her dismay, what she felt there came up short. Apparently poor Jess lived up to his name.

CHAPTER 19

*W*ithin minutes of learning that they were back from their weeklong Los Angeles fact-finding investigation, Director Melamed summoned SallyAnne and Lionel to his office. Then, for the next hour, he sat, stone-faced, throughout their briefing session.

Granted, he'd been ecstatic that they'd secured three cooperating witnesses against Miranda D'Arcy. But like them, he was disappointed when they acknowledged having hit a stone wall.

Or as he put it: "So, your LA-based cooperating witnesses had no leads on other possible parent suspects?"

"That doesn't mean more aren't out there," Lionel replied. "It's just that most of them knew better than to talk about it in public."

"University Prep & Test also came up empty," SallyAnne admitted. "Janna Calisher's boyfriend—the private tutor, Van Pierce—was right. It's a shell company. In the three days we staked it out, no one went in or out of the place."

"We left a detail on stakeout. Eventually, someone has to show up," Lionel added.

"The building's leasing agent must have a contact," Melamed countered.

"Yes, it's someone who calls himself 'John Smith,'" Lionel replied. "The agent took that at face value. I guess he felt it wasn't worth questioning, considering the guy paid a full year's rent in advance."

"When we called the facility's phone number, it prompted us toward three different departments: Consultation Requests, Test Appointments, Test Results." SallyAnne explained. "We called each one to see if someone would actually pick up. All of our calls rolled into a voice mailbox."

The agents never left a message. There was no need to alert Miranda and any employees of the FBI's interest in her activities.

"We also checked state business license records and the IRS as to whether University Prep & Test filed with either," Lionel added. "We came up blank. The company must be pocketing the fees from the parents, or funneling it through the Best Foot Forward Club, which isn't even registered with the California Secretary of State as a non-profit."

"No surprise there," Melamed muttered.

"Sir, we suspect it's nothing more than a virtual voicemail service. Still, we'd like to get a trace initiated on the calls coming in and out of it," SallyAnne suggested. "At the very least, they'll lead us to parents whose children are using UP&T. Some—maybe even *all* of them—will be tied to the prime suspect, Miranda D'Arcy."

"And when she calls into it, too, we've hooked our whale," Lionel added. "Metaphorically speaking, that is."

"You'll have it by Monday, along with one for Ms. D'Arcy's phone," Melamed promised.

Lionel smiled. When he noticed SallyAnne's congratulatory nod, he winked at her.

"Go home and enjoy your weekend." Melamed nodded toward the door.

As they walked out, he muttered, "Too bad the testing facility was a bust."

As far as the case was concerned, Melamed was right. Still, Lionel wouldn't have called it a total waste of time.

He'd gotten to learn a lot about SallyAnne.

University Prep & Test occupied one of three suites on the top floor of a low-rise office building in Beverly Hills with a private gated garage. The other two suites were empty. The agents spent three days camped in the hallway outside UP&T's door.

The whole time, not a single person crossed their path.

To bide their time, they talked through every angle of the case. Then they gossiped about their colleagues. When they ran out of small talk, SallyAnne had suggested a game called Never Have I Ever.

"Sounds...intriguing," Lionel admitted. "How did you hear about it?"

"It's one of those things people play at parties. You know, as part of a drinking game." She shrugged. "But you don't need to drink to play—like now, I mean."

Right then and there, Lionel learned something he never knew about SallyAnne: she actually made time to go to parties.

He wondered what it would be like to run into her at one.

He wanted to—so badly.

Noting his grimace, SallyAnne quickly added, "Look, we don't have to. I just said it to, you know, pass the time."

"No! ...I mean, yes, let's do it," Lionel insisted. "Okay, so, how does it work?"

"I ask you a question—a daring one." SallyAnne's face reddened. "And I'll preface it with the words, 'Never have I ever.' Now, the key is that you have to answer truthfully, 'Yes' or 'No.' If you elaborate, you get to ask the same of me. If you want to keep it to yourself, you have to come up with another question."

"Sure," he murmured.

Heck, what will I ask?

Is there anything I shouldn't ask?

My God, there's so much I want to know about her...

"Do you want to go first?" He wanted to see how far she'd take it.

"Okay..." SallyAnne thought a moment. "Never have I ever farted in the office?"

"Um...No. In fact, I have."

Lionel admitted it so sincerely that SallyAnne snickered, "I guess I've been lucky enough to be upwind!"

"Lucky you. I'm sure it's because I eat too much fiber...but hey, the stuff's good for you."

This time, she doubled over with laughter.

When she finally got ahold of herself, he asked, again in all sincerity, "Too much information?"

"I'll let you know if it ever comes to that," she replied solemnly. "Okay, your turn."

"Wow. Okay, let me think…"

There were so many questions he wanted to ask—

Play it safe. Don't scare her away with something too personal.

"Never have I ever, um…tattled on a sibling?" Did she have brothers or sisters? They'd never discussed stuff like this. She was so damned buttoned up and by the book.

It was another thing he loved about her. One of many.

She grinned. "My brothers are older than me. They were a couple of scamps, for sure. Teased me unmercifully! But I got back at them." Her eyes twinkled. "One had a girlfriend who lived just around the corner. They used to make out on her front porch. I took a picture of an intentional nip slip with his hand around it." She rolled her eyes. "Let's just say my mother was so appalled that he was grounded for a month. From then on, the girl was known around our house as 'the harpy.'"

Lionel laughed.

She joined in.

And on it went, just like that:

Questions about family, close friends, pets;

Favorites—colors, flowers, teachers, travels, books, sports, cars, so on and so forth;

Hopes were divulged, fears admitted, and secrets revealed via questions couched playfully, but nuanced with more than a mild curiosity.

On the first two days, a little after six, they reluctantly threw in the towel. His disappointment was more about leaving the game than missing out on anyone who could shed light on their suspect.

Lionel wondered if SallyAnne felt the same way.

On their last day in LA, Friday, the stakeout was cut short so that they could make it back to the San Francisco office in time to catch Melamed before his weekly jaunt north to his Russian River cabin.

On the flight home, Lionel wondered if their little cross-examination games meant as much to her as they did to him.

No. Ridiculous thought. Surely, she saw it as no more than a distraction from boredom.

As for him, her responses were like childhood treasures: each one tucked away in an old shoebox to be scrutinized periodically, cherished secretly, and always remembered in context with every blush, grin, and errant touch that accompanied it.

There would be other stakeouts. If SallyAnne again suggested playing Never Have I Ever, he'd be up for it.

CHAPTER 20

 shbury Academy's monthly Friday Fun Nights were something the entire school community looked forward to with anticipation.

From what Egan gathered from Odette, this AA tradition had started a couple of years after he'd resigned. "Initially, its activities were simple: a potluck and a sing-along or improv skits put on by anyone who wanted to get involved—students, staff, or parents."

"But in the past five years, everything about it went from the ordinary to the *extraordinary*!" Cornell added. "Granted, it's great to have a gourmet chef on campus. But that gives it the feel of a must-see, must-attend event."

Tonight's catered buffet featured organic roasted chickens and grilled wild salmon; a harvest bounty mélange made of vine-ripened tomatoes, fresh chickpeas, and fingerling potatoes; and for dessert, apple pie and homemade ice cream.

A student jazz trio would play during the buffet. Afterward, AA's full student orchestra would accompany a laser light show designed by the physics club.

Because the teachers had a few hours off before the event, Egan allowed Cornell and Odette to talk him into joining them for an off-campus happy hour.

Apparently, their favorite hangout was a place called Barvale, on trendy Divisadero Street in San Francisco's NoPa neighborhood.

They walked over after Egan signed the lease on a small one-bedroom apartment located just a few blocks from the school—something he could now afford, thanks to the additional stipend provided by Daniel's endowment.

Leaving his parents' old house would be a relief—not just because of the torturous drive into town but because it held too many memories of his failed dreams. Whereas his position at AA wasn't ideal, it was a step in the right direction—

One that had put him back in Audrey's world, if only as an uneasy acquaintance. As long as he was at the school, he'd have to live with that.

But just as they snagged a table and ordered a round of drinks, Egan realized his cellphone was buzzing.

It was his literary agent, Chastity Blunt. Since the bar was much too noisy, he excused himself and went outside.

In the grand old days, when *Extracurricular* had soared to the top of various bestseller lists, Chastity was sure to touch base daily: if not to read him sales numbers or drop the names of editors jumping over each other to work with him, then to prod him toward the completion of whatever current work-in-progress she hoped to sell on his behalf.

But when each subsequent sale brought in a smaller advance or failed to earn out the advance she'd wrangled from his current or even a new publisher, Chastity's calls slowed to a trickle.

He realized the worm had turned when he did all the dialing.

On the few occasions when Chastity deigned to take one of Egan's increasingly desperate calls, invariably a client whose sales were higher would ring up. At that point, Chastity would leap off the phone with less grace than a streetwalker turning her back on one john in order to wave down another whom she knew paid more.

In the past year, whenever Egan called Chastity, it was inevitable that her assistant would inform him that her boss was on another call and would have to get back to him.

Naturally, the callback never came.

Seeing her name now on Caller ID, Egan tamped down the desire to sneer out something he'd regret. Instead, with as much pleasantness as he could muster, he proclaimed, "Well, well, Ms. Blunt! To what do I owe this pleasure?"

"I wish it were something that would make us some money, Egan. Really, I do. Unfortunately, I've got bad and even worse news. Which do you want to hear first?"

Egan felt a cold chill run down his spine. "Start with just plain bad."

"In that case, you should know that your publisher, Signal Press, has been slapped with a defamation of character lawsuit for publishing *Extracurricular*. Some woman is claiming that one of your characters—the one called 'Fannie'—is based on her."

"Let me guess—her name is Mandy Blackwell."

"Oh… So, it's true?" Before he could answer, Chastity quickly added, "No, no, don't tell me! I'd rather not know in case I have to take the stand." She paused, and then added, "And by the way, you're named as a co-defendant. Since my agency represents you, the subpoena was served here. So you better lawyer up."

"I wrote the damn book twenty years ago! Isn't there some sort of statute of limitation?"

"Depending on the state, one year; maybe two. However, her attorneys are making the case that since the novel is still in print, each subsequent purchase, print or digital, makes the suit valid— that is, until it's out of print entirely."

"Why, that's absurd!" Egan exclaimed.

"I agree," Chastity replied mournfully. "Believe me, Egan, I do."

"You know what they say: no news is bad news, right?" Egan countered. "Why doesn't Signal Press use the publicity of the lawsuit to stoke sales?"

"Frankly…" Chastity paused. Egan guessed she was dragging on a cigarette. "That brings me to worse news. Just in case some judge agrees with Ms. Blackwell's contention, as a way to placate her Signal Press felt it smarter to halt publication immediately."

"Does that mean digital copies too?"

"Sadly, yes. In fact, Signal has already sent takedown orders to all the online bookstores—as well as the public libraries. To motivate the latter, those libraries that do so within twenty-four hours get a free replacement: anything else from Signal's extensive catalog." Chastity paused, then added: "Additionally, they extended an olive branch to the plaintiff."

"What does that mean, 'an olive branch'?" If the term were

literal, he'd offer to deliver it himself—and soundly lash his nemesis with it.

Chastity sighed. "A cash settlement."

"Signal Press isn't going to put up any sort of fight?" Egan couldn't believe his ears. "They're just going to let Mandy set some bogus precedent for future suits?"

"Apparently so. And the settlement is substantial—a quarter of a million."

"Oh, well—hell." He massaged the ache in his forehead. "Let me guess what's next: they want me to write another book for them, gratis, to pay for the loss."

"Um…No. In fact, there's even more bad news: because of how your contract is written, Signal Press is suing *you*."

"Wait, wait…"

This is all a bad dream!

"You've always made sure I was indemnified from any lawsuits deriving from my books!"

After a frosty silence, Chastity growled, "You forget, Egan. You were a very eager, very desperate debut novelist. You insisted that any clause that got in the way of the sale of *Extracurricular* be jettisoned—including your indemnification."

"It was your job to warn me against that!" Egan shouted. "Maybe I should countersue Mandy, Signal Press, and *YOU*!"

As soon as the diatribe left his mouth, he regretted it. Chastity was his lifeline to the only thing that still mattered to him: his writing career.

"Oops! Sorry, Egan! My phone system put you on mute because another call just came in. I'm sorry but I really have to take it. The author—a debut novelist—just hit the *USA Today* list and is simply *overjoyed*—"

Egan clicked off.

Then he threw the phone at the wall, breaking it.

Damn, he thought. I can't afford a new iPhone…

Dismayed, he threw up his hands and stormed back inside.

Then he proceeded to belt down a double Scotch.

"Whoa, cowboy!" Cornell warned. "Don't you want to wait for the tapas we just ordered? Lavinia won't like it if you set some parent's hair on fire with your breath."

Lavinia.

Shit.

Cornell was right. And not just because Egan couldn't afford to get fired, either.

To sober up, he gulped water, lots of it, with his tapas.

As the fog of Scotch dissipated from his brain, he thought about the few times in the past week that his path and Lavinia's had crossed. He'd noticed a difference in her. The headmistress' naturally rosy complexion had paled. The quickness of her response to questions was off, if only a beat. When around those she loved unfailingly—her students—there was still a buoyancy in her demeanor, but an unmistakable scrim of sadness had darkened her eyes.

Egan was worried about her.

He wondered if Audrey was too.

But he knew she'd be the last person he could approach with his concerns.

I'm sure I'm just imagining it anyway.

"Fawn!...*FAWNIE!* Where the hell are you? The damn driver is here!" Seamus' bellow came through the home intercom. It was as loud as a cargo ship's horn while sailing through the Golden Gate passage on a fog-shrouded night.

Fawn's response was a litany of curses—one she knew no one could hear from her wing of the three-story twenty-room mansion. It had nothing to do with her father's obnoxious summons and everything to do with Fawn's frustration at her inability to pull together some semblance of a debate argument.

It wasn't for lack of trying either.

For the past week, she'd gone back and forth on which two subjects she'd choose from a list of four that each contestant was to argue, both pro and con:

• *Is the current approach to illegal immigration too harsh or too lenient?*

• *Are there ramifications for teens in the "hook-up culture," and if so, are they emotionally or physically harmful?*

• *Does the death penalty constitute a cruel and unusual punishment?*

• *Should scientists be allowed to clone humans?*

She'd finally decided to tackle the cloning question (the research should be easy enough, she reasoned) and the one on teen hookups. (A subject that everyone would assume she was an expert in it anyway. For once they were right,)

Making arguments for cloning was harder than she'd anticipated. There were lots of ethical cases already prepared for the con part, but it seemed as if no one agreed with her that making carbon copies of those revered by others—celebrities, the wealthy, the powerful—might actually save humanity from itself.

"I don't really have time for this shit!" Fawn shouted. "I have a dynasty to run!"

She was right. Her website had shot into the stratosphere. And to keep it there, she had to feed the beast, as it were.

When her parents were home, they pretty much left Fawn to her own devices. Despite this, posting even one video a week was an arduous process for someone who was also a real cheerleader enrolled in a competitive prep school with several AP courses on her schedule.

It dismayed her to no end that her ploy to secure Egan's attention had backfired. She'd dropped Chuck to give their teacher the message that, like him, she saw Chuck as a loser. Instead, Egan ignored her ploys to get his attention. If anything, it seemed as if the animus Egan had previously felt for Chuck was now directed at her.

At the same time, Chuck was repositioning himself as a good student. By participating in class discussions, making decent grades on tests, and showing interest in trying out for Debate Team, he was earning Egan's grudging respect.

When did they kiss and make up? And why hadn't she been invited to do the same—figuratively if not literally?

But of course, she already knew the answer to that. She'd shamed Chuck in front of the whole class. Because of that, now he wouldn't even look in her direction.

To top it off, she'd then gotten her comeuppance at the hand of his caustic nerd of a sister—in front of Egan, no less.

Instead of being grateful for the invitation and falling into line, Charly had insulted her. First, she'd called Fawn out for dumping her twin. Then she'd called her a bitch.

Fawn couldn't have felt more humiliated.

It wasn't supposed to happen that way. A summons by Fawn for friendship was as rare as the Queen of England granting a Dame Grand Cross. Those who received it were honored to do so and showed their appreciation with total submission.

Knowing Charly, she's already gotten her debate arguments all worked out. And if not now, soon…

At that moment, it occurred to Fawn that if she could confirm it, she'd have the perfect way to get back at Charly.

Steal her arguments.

It would surely be easier than going through the time-suck of creating her own.

But to do it, she'd need Chuck.

He'd spent the past week stewing in the misery of being dumped, Fawn reasoned. By now, he'll be more than ready for a reconciliation.

And no better time than tonight—when everyone could see that their spat was over; that she'd finally forgiven him.

Yes, Chuck would be so grateful.

Even if it meant selling out his sister.

And the makeup sex would be awesome.

She smiled at the thought.

Fawn fairly flew down the floating staircase and out to the grand foyer to the limousine waiting in the McCoppins' circular driveway.

Her parents were already in the backseat. Seamus grumbled, "About damn time! If you'd taken any longer, we'd have missed the damn laser light show—which my firm has sponsored!"

Although a steady regimen of Botox made it impossible for Gretchen's anxiety to show in her face, Fawn heard it in her voice as she hissed, "Your father almost left without you!"

Fawn shrugged. She knew this would never have been the case. Without her, neither of her parents would have had any reason to go to Friday Fun Night.

She was their trophy child.

CHAPTER 21

"You know, it would have been okay for you to miss one Friday Fun Night." Audrey's admonishment to Lavinia was delivered with a hug.

Her mother didn't know it, but Audrey's hugs were how she gauged her mother's condition. Although Lavinia's flowing tops made it difficult to see the subtle changes happening to her body, by wrapping an arm around her mother's waist Audrey could tell that, in just a few weeks' time, Lavinia's body was in full retreat.

Since being sworn to secrecy, Audrey had made it a point to spend as much time with her mother as possible. Dropping the twins to and from school gave her a reason to stop by her mother's office with some make-believe excuse: tidbits about Lavinia's grandchildren, a reminder about some public discussion that might be of interest to her, a quick chat about current events, or, say, the latest news about what project she'd currently initiated for Congressman Blanchard.

If no other excuse presented itself, Audrey would drop off a bouquet of flowers.

On Saturdays, while the rest of the family biked over the Golden Gate Bridge and into Marin County, Audrey cycled over to her mother's house.

Whether it was to return a borrowed book or to drop off fresh fruit from the farmer's market, Lavinia always saw through her excuses. "You'll be here on Sunday, with the rest of the family, helping me in the garden," she reminded her daughter.

"That's different, and you know it. Sometimes I like it when it's just the two of us."

Their time together was more precious than ever before. They both knew that.

They'd sit on the back porch and talk. Lavinia would give updates on her prognosis. If there was none, they gossiped about school business.

Other times, they simply reminisced. It never seemed to surprise Audrey how the prism of time bent their perspectives in different directions. One subject neither had yet to bring up was Egan's departure after Audrey had graduated, nor his triumphant visit three years later.

Audrey wondered if Lavinia had suspected the attraction they'd shared.

Not that it mattered now.

Audrey warned Lavinia that Daniel was working late at the office but had promised to get to the school before the laser light show started. Although it was late September, the days were still warm until the sun set beyond San Francisco's seven hills and the evening's crisp chill set in.

The crowd milling around on AA's central campus green was thick and animated. Chuck was nowhere to be found, but Audrey spotted Charly sitting on a picnic table with Manya, Zina, and Sienna, laughing and talking.

Like moths drawn to a lamp on a dark night, a few boys hovered nearby. Audrey recognized Quest among them. His parents were on tour through the weekend. Just a month older than the twins, the three had grown up together like siblings, along with Sienna and Zina.

They'll always be there for each other, Audrey realized. Just like Bliss, Tallulah, and Davis are for me.

As it should be.

Sensing her daughter's pride, Lavinia murmured, "There is so much of you in sweet Charly. And her father too, of course."

At the thought of Egan, shame flamed in Audrey's cheeks.

Lavinia didn't see it because she leaned into her daughter. Her sigh indicated what Audrey already suspected: Lavinia's regimen of chemotherapy was sapping her vitality.

Not that she'd ever admit it.

Additional evidence of this: the note card in Lavinia's hand with prompts for the announcements she'd make before the light show. In the past, Lavinia had always been able to ad-lib in front of audiences.

Lavinia has to tell the school. They are her family. They are her community.

Now, having noted the concern in her daughter's eyes, Lavinia answered Audrey before the question was even out of her mouth:

"Yes, I'm tired. And yes, sometimes I tend to forget a thing or two. But no, my sweet Audrey. *Not yet.* I can still fight this."

Audrey nodded. It broke her heart that Lavinia had chosen to battle her cancer in silence. But she also knew that she had to honor her mother's wishes.

To the very end.

Lavinia scanned the crowd. "The McCoppins are finally here. Good! Now I can thank Seamus for underwriting this event. Excuse me, dear." She pecked Audrey on the cheek and then made her way to the stage to address the happy, unsuspecting crowd.

"She's quite a lady." At the sound of Egan's voice, Audrey's heart raced.

She didn't turn around. She hoped—she prayed—that if he didn't get a response, he'd just figure that she hadn't heard him. Then, instead of repeating it—instead of making a fool of himself, of them both—he'd slink off into the night, burying himself in the crowd.

It would be just like Egan to run away again, she reasoned. He always looked for the easy out.

But no, that wasn't fair: damning him whether he did or didn't finish what he'd started.

In this case, a mere attempt at a conversation.

It was a long time ago. Daniel is funding Egan's chair.

Egan is teaching the twins.

Our children.

For everyone's sake I need to be civil.

I need to keep my cool.

She turned to face him. "Thank you for that. It's been a mutual admiration society, hasn't it?"

"Us?" His question seemed hopeful.

"Yes, of course!" She hoped to put him at ease by nodding. "Lavinia has always had such a high opinion of you too. You proved her right."

"Good to know." Despite his words, he sounded disappointed. Immediately, he tried to hide it with a smile. "Audrey, I was overwhelmed by Daniel's generosity! Shocked, frankly."

Audrey's guffaw was involuntary. Embarrassed by it, she added, "To tell you the truth, I was too."

"I see." He looked away, dismayed.

Her reaction had been honest. But she could see how he could have interpreted it as also being cruel.

Audrey shook her head. "By that, I meant to say it was *unexpected.* But Daniel loves Lavinia and the school. The money was a legacy from his mother for the children's education. They both see it as a worthy cause."

Her words seemed to put him at ease. "Thank you for that. Speaking of Chuck and Charly—"

Does he suspect? Her heart pounded at the thought.

"I'm truly impressed with their diligence in my class. They're both excellent essay writers and they have no problem with grasping some of the Old English nuances."

Realizing her fears were for naught, relief flooded over her.

A wave of surprise hit her next. Incredulously, she asked, "Chuck too?"

Egan laughed. "To be honest, he had a rocky start. Some male posturing. You know, playing the cock of the walk—"

Gee, I wonder where he gets that from…

"But he's fallen into line. He split up with the girl he was trying to impress. That helped tremendously." Egan took a deep breath: "Listen, Audrey, there's something I need to ask you."

Oh no, she thought, here it comes! He's going to bring up that awful day…

Suddenly he stopped. Apparently, something had caught his eye.

Audrey followed his gaze.

He was staring at Chuck and Fawn.

Arm in arm, laughing, they were slipping away from the crowd, but then paused beside the largest tree on the green—an ancient live oak. They looked around. Then, assuming no one was watching, they kissed.

Deeply.

Too long.

Chuck's hand slipped under Fawn's top.

She stopped it from reaching her breast. Instead, she held onto it, pulling him with her toward one of the school's buildings: the old gym.

The blood drained from Audrey's face when she realized where they were headed, and why.

"At least, I thought he'd come to his senses." Egan scowled. "Don't worry. I'll take care of this before things get out of hand."

He took off after them.

THE ROOMS THAT ONCE HELD THE OLD GYM'S LOCKERS WERE NOW USED for storage: mostly desks and chairs that had yet to be given away or junked.

The first door, to the old boys' room, was locked. Fawn giggled when Chuck hooted upon discovering that the second door's latch was broken.

The only light in the room filtered in through its high windows. Long shadows danced about the clutter.

Fawn pushed Chuck through the door and then shoved him down onto an empty backless bench. In no time, she was straddling him.

Her mouth was voracious for his. Their kisses—endless and sweet—concluded with hungry groans: Chuck's.

"I can't hold back much longer," he warned her.

"You'll have to," she declared. "I'm in charge here. Now"—she cupped him so hard that he grunted—"and forever. Do you get that?"

"Yes m'am," he murmured.

"That's better."

Before Chuck could stop her, Fawn yanked his tee shirt over his head. Next she went for his belt buckle. After pulling the leather strap from his jeans, she grabbed his arms. Flinging them over his head, she used the belt to tether them to the bench.

She then yanked off one sneaker and then the other, throwing them over her shoulders.

Finally, she slowly unzipped his jeans and pulled them to his knees. Chuck moaned, "Fawn...*please*...I'm busting here—"

"I said, shut up!" To make her point, Fawn tweaked his nipple.

Chuck yelped.

They both screamed when the lights went on.

———

WHEN THEIR EYES ADJUSTED TO THE LIGHT, THEY SAW HIM:

Egan. He was standing at the doorway.

Fawn leaped up too quickly, toppling to the floor with a thud on her hands and knees. "Ouch! *Shit!*"

Egan ignored her. He was too fascinated with the belt knot she'd contrived. Clapping slowly, he murmured, "Wow! I don't think a horny psycho sailor could have done any better!"

"What the hell are you doing here?" Chuck muttered.

"Saving you both from a suspension—I hope." He picked up one of Chuck's shoes and tossed it at him.

Unfortunately, it landed on Chuck's erection.

The boy groaned. Reflexively, his legs curled up toward his waist.

Catching Fawn's eye, Egan nodded toward Chuck. "Untie the poor kid."

Fawn smirked, "Is that really what you want? I mean, you followed us, right? Admit it. Wouldn't you rather watch?"

"What, you think I'd get off on some sort of teen porn amateur hour? I'll pass." Egan shrugged. "How old are you anyway?"

"Seventeen," Fawn looked up from the task of undoing her handiwork in order to wink at him.

"How about you, Chuck?"

"The same," Chuck growled. "What does it matter to you?"

"I'm trying to assess who between the two of you would end up in prison, and what kind of sentence you'd get, is all."

Chuck's shackle was loose enough that he could wrench away from it and sit up. "What the hell are you talking about?"

"In this state, even consenting teens under the age of eighteen can be tried for statutory rape. It would probably be considered a misdemeanor, but it would still carry some penalties: up to a year in a juvenile detention facility. Oh, and up to a thousand-dollar fine. Depends on the judge."

Fawn took Chuck's hand in hers. Solemnly, she declared, "I would never say you raped me. Cross my heart."

"That's really touching, Fawn." Egan pretended to wipe away a tear. "But the real question is whether Chuck feels the need to press charges against *you*." He pointed to the belt in her hand. "You lured him into this prison and tied him up. Hey, if Chuck's mom hadn't seen you coerce him down here, who knows if I'd have stopped you in time?"

Chuck stared at Egan. "*Shit! Shit!* My *mom* knows I'm down here?"

"She suspects...something." Egan shrugged. "But, hey, no one wants to get you"—his eyes went from Chuck to Fawn—"or you kicked out of school. So here's the deal. This sort of extracurricular activity doesn't happen on campus anymore. Understand? From now on, if you treat AA with the respect it deserves—that is, hallowed ground, considering all the time, effort, and money your parents give it—I'll pretend I didn't find you together down here." He pointed toward the door. "Fawn, you take off first."

He didn't have to ask her twice.

"Put your pants on," Egan muttered to Chuck. "If your mom asks, I never found you."

Mollified, Chuck did as he was told. But as he zipped up, he stammered, "So...so you're not going to tell her you saw me like— you know, like this?"

"And embarrass her?" *Yet again? Hell no.* "I have too much respect for her," Egan muttered. "And I know you do too."

Chuck nodded. He glanced around for the other shoe.

Spotting it, Egan picked it up and tossed it to him.

This time, Chuck caught it with one hand. "Thanks." His tone was sincere. "Mom...she has a lot on her mind these days."

"Oh? How can you tell?"

Chuck snickered as he untied the second shoe. "I've known her all my life! I can tell when something is bothering her."

I wish I'd known her all your life too…

For a second, Egan wondered what it might have been like to have a child with Audrey.

Now, knowing Chuck, he shook his head at the thought of all the drama he'd avoided.

And all the love he'd missed.

"Turn off the light when you leave," Egan muttered gruffly as he walked out the door.

EGAN REACHED AUDREY JUST AS THE LASER LIGHT SHOW WAS beginning. As each beam flared and pulsed to the syncopated music, the cheers grew louder.

Audrey leaned in close to ask, "Did you find them?"

"Yes!" He had to shout for her to hear him. "They were headed over to the buffet table. But just in case the chef's special works as an aphrodisiac, I checked all the doors to the building. They were locked, so I don't think—"

"Wait! I don't know if I heard you!" she shouted.

He moved in so close that their eyes were only inches away.

Their lips too.

Egan fought the urge to kiss her. And yet, he wondered if Audrey would have been shocked or upset by it.

Or if her mouth would have accepted his eagerly, willingly.

If Chuck were right and she was anxious about something, a kiss would tell him what he'd suspected:

It's because of me.

Egan looked into her eyes, hoping to find his answer there. Instead he found relief.

She was smiling again.

This was verified when she shouted, "Did you say the *buffet table*? And that the building was all locked up? Thank goodness! That's all Lavinia needs—some reason for Seamus to pull his little princess from the school!" Audrey grimaced. "Not with…everything else Lavinia is going through." The moment the words were out of her mouth, she pursed her lips as if daring anything else to come out.

There were so many lasers beaming up in the sky that Egan could see the single tear that had fallen onto Audrey's cheek.

How he longed to touch it.

But…why is she crying?

He then remembered that just before they'd seen Chuck and Fawn sneak off, he was going to mention his concerns about her mother.

She's not worried about me. She's worried about Lavinia.

"Audrey, before I went after Chuck, I wanted to ask you something. Remember?"

Her smile faded as she nodded solemnly.

"It's about Lavinia. Is she…well?"

Egan had seen such deep sorrow in Audrey's eyes only once before: the afternoon they'd made love.

She hung her head so low that he had to bow his head to hear her say, "Lavinia…has cancer. But no one knows about it yet." Audrey turned slightly so that he could see her lips as if assuring that he couldn't mistake what she said next: "You're the only other person who knows. I can't even tell Daniel because he's on the board, and he'd have a fiduciary responsibility to inform the others. Some of them would want to force her out!" Suddenly, Audrey clasped her hand to her mouth. "Oh my God! I forgot—*you're also on the board!*" The tears were now falling furiously. "Egan, please…I'm begging you…"

So that she'd calm down, Egan held tight to both her hands. "Audrey, it's okay! I'll do anything you ask! You know that. I… I love her."

And I love you.

Audrey was so grateful that she kissed his cheek.

Egan looked skyward, feigning awe of the colorful beams flaring over their heads. In truth, he was memorizing the soft touch of her kiss.

ALL NIGHT LONG, MIRANDA HAD BEEN WATCHING EGAN FOR TELLTALE signs that word of the Mandy Blackwell lawsuit had finally gotten to him. Unfortunately, he never had time to break away from the throng of fawning parents surrounding him—Gretchen McCoppin included—so that she could sidle over and wean it out of him.

Finally, when Egan had broken clear of the parents, he'd walked over to Audrey.

Old emotions surged through her:

Hate. Spite. Retaliation.

She'd vowed to destroy them. To that end, tonight couldn't have been scripted any better.

At the same time, Seamus cornered Miranda to gripe about the dearth of Easy-A classes offered at the school.

Or, as he put it: "With all the AP-class overachievers out there, how else is a normal kid supposed to get into Yale these days?"

When Daniel strolled onto the campus green, Miranda realized he was the perfect foil for both conundrums.

Seamus was the type who resented knowing someone else was a bigger priority. To interrupt his bellyaching, she declared, "You'll have to excuse me. I promised to take Daniel McKittridge over to Egan the minute he came in. It was so smart of him to underwrite our celebrity teacher, what with the twins taking Egan's AP Comp Lit class and all. Don't you agree? Not that I'm inferring that it'll guarantee A's to either Chuck or Charly. Why neither of them is *half* as clever as your Fawn…"

Seamus' scowl was proof she'd hit her mark.

And how convenient for Egan to be wooing Audrey at the very second her husband spotted her!

"Oh, gosh—*is that Audrey and Egan?* Looks like they're having a ball, catching up on the good old days!" Just in case Daniel missed the view of his wife through the clearing in the crowd, Miranda thought it worth pointing them out—

Locking lips, no less!

At least, it looked as if that were happening.

Granted, it was nighttime, and the light show was creating all sorts of shadows. Still, their body language was unmistakable:

Concern. Trust. Intimacy.

My God—they still feel something for each other!

To be heard over the band, Miranda cooed in Daniel's ear, "That's so Egan! Ever the flirt! He's been at it all night long!"

"Really? With Audrey?" Daniel squinted for a better look.

"Well, I don't want to speak out of school, but of all the moms, he's certainly sweet on her in particular—"

"Look, Miranda, you don't have to be so concerned." He put his arm around her. Then, leaning in so that she could hear him above the crowd and music, he added, "I mean, look at all you've got going for yourself! Any man would be proud to have you at his side. You're the full package: sharp, beautiful, and confident—"

Miranda let that sink in. *He's so jealous that he's coming on to me? My God, breaking up Audrey's marriage will be easier than I thought!*

And so much fun!

"—which is why there's no need for you to feel the least bit insecure. I'm sure Egan realizes that too. If not, hey, I'll be glad to give him a subtle heads-up."

What the hell? He thinks I'm pining over Egan?

"Frankly, I think you'd make a cute couple. All he needs is a little nudge in your direction." Daniel nodded toward Egan. "Oh, hey, look! Audrey's spotted us." He waved at his wife. "We should walk over."

"Sadly, I'm still on duty," Miranda purred. "You go ahead."

She didn't know what made her angrier: that he assumed she thought so little of herself, or that he had an unshakable trust in his wife's fidelity.

On both counts, she was determined to prove him wrong.

---

*R*ELIEF.

That was what Audrey felt when Egan reassured her that Chuck and Fawn weren't up to anything that would embarrass Lavinia.

She felt it too when, to her shock, Egan's solemn query hadn't been about the secret she feared he'd one day guess—that the twins were his—but the secret that now haunted her every waking moment: Lavinia's illness.

I can trust Egan.

Audrey saw it in his eyes. He too loved Lavinia and would do anything to protect her.

Exuberance had driven Audrey's desire to kiss him: chastely, on the cheek. With the appreciation one friend felt for another.

She knew he'd understand; that he wouldn't mind her taking

such a liberty. Lavinia had brought them together. Now, Lavinia's secret was what bound them.

That, and the twins.

The thought that she'd never be able to share that with Egan—with anyone—had the weight of a boulder tossed into an ocean and always tumbling through the black water of her shame.

Would its fall ever hit rock bottom? Could it ever find its way back to the surface?

Shamefaced, she turned away from Egan.

Her eyes fell upon a familiar figure: Daniel.

He had his arm around a woman—

Miranda.

The way their faces were angled, she could tell they were talking earnestly.

Or maybe they're…

Kissing?

Misplaced guilt, Audrey warned herself.

Or was it?

Just then, Daniel looked up. Having noticed that she was staring at him, he gave her a wave.

Whatever he said next had Miranda smirking. Her eyes followed Daniel as he walked to his wife.

The look on Miranda's face sent a chill through Audrey.

What did Daniel say to her?

She was still shivering when Daniel reached her side. Putting his arm around her, he declared, "You two look as if you're enjoying the show."

Audrey forced herself to smile before turning to him. Taking his arm in hers, she declared, "Just a couple of old friends, playing catch up."

She couldn't believe how normal she sounded.

She'd become such a casual liar.

Secrets do that to a person, she reasoned.

For the first time since they'd married, Audrey wondered how many secrets Daniel had kept from her as well.

e're live!" Riley shouted to Lionel and SallyAnne.

Hearing that, his team leaders high-fived each other. They then picked up their earphones.

Their court order not only allowed them to monitor Miranda's incoming and outgoing calls, but it also gave them the right to track text and emails sent out of, and going into, all of her devices, and to review previous messages.

Upon discovering that Miranda used a virtual assistant app—and that she also recorded every conversation, either on the phone or live—her cell phone also gave them a way to use it as a real-time listening device.

"Gotta love Siri!" Riley crowed. "She and Alexa are law enforcement's BFFs!"

"Where's Miranda now?" Lionel asked.

"She's still at the school. She has to stay late for some sort of board meeting," Riley replied. "But, hey, great news! Lover Boy will be there too." He wiggled his brows.

"Ha!" SallyAnne snickered. "This is better than a soap opera."

"So, who wants to wager whether Smallwood will do what he promised and get her voted onto the trustee board?" Lionel asked.

"With all the blowjobs she's given him to—well, shall we say 'pump him up'—I'd say it's a done deal," Riley retorted.

Lionel grimaced. "Ladies present," he muttered.

SallyAnne felt her cheeks warm up. Had Lionel just laughed, she would have too. She'd worked in law enforcement far too long to be offended by a high-testosterone quip. Still, she appreciated Lionel's sensitivity on her behalf.

Riley rolled his eyes. "SallyAnne's no lady. She's one of us."

To change the topic, SallyAnne snapped, *"Shhh*—listen! She's meeting with someone *right now…"*

TODAY'S THE BIG DAY, MIRANDA THOUGHT.

After what she'd observed on Friday Family Fun Night, she knew how it would go down:

Those who would vote to add her to the board would be Jess and Seamus, along with Darius and Warner.

If Lavinia was against it, those assured to vote her way were Tallulah, Blanchard, Bliss, and Daniel.

Egan was the wild card.

Maybe Blanchard would pull a no-show. True, his name added gravitas to the school and to the board. But after perusing minutes from the past two years, odds were fifty-fifty that he'd be absent.

And if not, the vote could deadlock at four against four.

No matter what happened, the only chance she'd have to get on the board was to flip one of them.

Egan was the likeliest choice.

Damn it, Miranda thought. I wasted my time flirting with Daniel on Friday Family Fun Night! If only I'd walked over to Egan and Audrey with him. It would have been so easy to flirt with him instead of trying to turn Daniel's head.

One thing would have led to another. Maybe he'd have suggested they christen his new apartment.

A disgusting notion, but hey—she would have said yes.

Anything to lock up his vote.

There was still time to do it.

Egan would be in his classroom, killing time before the meeting.

She knew exactly what to say.

Miranda knocked on Egan's door and waited for him to call out, "Enter at your own risk."

She peeked in. "Hey, got a minute?"

"Sure. What's up?"

Melodramatically, she looked down the hall—first one way, then the other—before stepping over the threshold and closing the door behind her. "I need someone I can trust. You were the first person who came to mind"—she forced a blush—"well, except for my mother."

"I guess I should be flattered," Egan muttered.

"If you knew her, you would be," Miranda dabbed away an imaginary tear from the corner of her eye. "Listen, I overheard something I shouldn't—about school business— and it concerns me! But it's not something I feel comfortable bringing up with the Trustee board because"—Miranda sighed mightily—"some members of the board are involved."

That got Egan's attention. "What are they doing?"

"They want to usurp Lavinia's policies! Can you imagine? I mean, her philosophy is why this school was founded in the first place! It's also why the school has been so successful! But here's the problem: right now, the way the board is made up, Lavinia is at risk of losing the majority vote."

"From what I can tell, Lavinia is usually opposed by Seamus McCoppin, Darius Calder, Warner Crowley, and Jess Smallwood. That's four members," Egan pointed out. "On the other hand, those who vote with her are lock-solid: Congressman Blanchard, Tallulah, Bliss, and Daniel are on her side on every vote. And, of course, me too. So that makes six. She's got a clear majority."

"Thank goodness for your loyalty," Miranda murmured. He confirmed what she'd suspected: Seamus could never win—

Unless she were on the board too.

And she controlled Egan's vote.

"But you're wrong about one of her lock-solids." Miranda made her lip quiver, then added: "Daniel."

Egan's eyes opened wide. "But…he's her son-in-law!"

"He's also the senior partner of a firm that counts Seamus, Jess, and Warner among its clients."

"Jesus!" Egan frowned.

"Tell me about it! Even if Daniel votes with Seamus' block, board rules call for a *supermajority*. That means sixty percent or more," Miranda explained. "To get it, tonight Seamus is going to ask the board to eliminate one of the two PTA representatives on the board. His rationale is that the bylaws only allow for one representative from the PTA. If he succeeds, he'll wipe out Lavinia's majority."

"I'd never vote against Lavinia. Neither would Harris and whichever PTA representative was left on the board," Egan declared. "With Lavinia, that's four votes."

"Still, she needs another lock-solid ally. That's where I think you can help." Miranda perched herself on Egan's desk: better to lean in and make her point, not to mention position her breasts at eye-level. "To counteract Seamus' ploy, why don't you suggest adding another member from the staff? In fact, if you suggest me, they may actually go for it since I play such a valuable role in helping their children." She rolled her eyes. "It's embarrassing, the things they'll say or do to coerce me into giving their kids special attention!"

"Well, sure! Anything to keep the status quo."

Miranda reached over and put her hand over his. "I knew I could count on you!" Her fingers stroked the back of his hand. She leaned in, so close that their faces were only inches apart—

Until Egan eased back. "Listen, Miranda…I'm flattered. Really, I am! But…"

He's turning me down? How dare he!…

Because of her:

Audrey.

So, I'm right—he still lusting for her.

Bingo!

"Forgive me!" Miranda forced her lip to quiver. "It was wrong for me to—to assume you might feel anything…" She bowed her head, as if shamed. "Look, I get it. The last thing you need is…is *another* rejection."

Egan frowned. "What are you talking about?"

"You…and Audrey." She shrugged. "What the two of you shared. It was beautiful."

Egan's hand stiffened under her touch. "How…do you know about that?"

So Audrey and Egan did have an affair!

"I was in the women's restroom in the teachers' lounge—in one of the stalls. Audrey walked in. She thought it was empty so she called someone. From what I could tell, she was on with her shrink. She was upset about...*about running into you.*" Miranda paused dramatically. "She said...she said it broke her heart to see you again after...after what had happened between you."

Egan hung his head.

It's true, alright.

"At that point, I couldn't just come out of the stall, could I? I was stuck in there until she hung up and walked out!" Miranda forced a sob. "You won't tell anyone I overheard, will you?"

"Of course I won't say anything! I mean—I certainly don't want anyone to know—" Egan put his hands on her shoulders so that she had to look him in the eye—"and neither would Audrey. Please, Miranda. Do you understand what I'm saying?"

"Daniel doesn't know, does he?" She stared back at him.

Egan eyes darkened with his sadness. "No."

Even if Egan hadn't said it, she could read it in his eyes.

"And...I promised myself he'd never hear it from me." He dropped his hands to his side. "So...I'm begging you..."

"You don't have to do that, Egan. Your secret—yours and Audrey's—is safe with me." She winked. "We'll always have each other's backs. Deal?"

"Deal." He held out his hand.

As if sealing their promise, Miranda pulled him in close—

But this time, it was for a chaste kiss on the cheek instead.

She slid off the desk. She knew his eyes were on her as she smoothed her tight, short pencil skirt back into place.

And she was sure his eyes were following as she walked out the door.

***

By the time Egan made it to the meeting, most of the others were already there, including Miranda.

She was standing between Seamus and Jess, and probably playing the suck-up, he reasoned.

She returned his wave with a smile and a wink.

Certainly, having Miranda at the meetings would make the damn things more palatable, Egan thought.

He remembered how she'd stroked his fingers. Obviously, she was open to moving their relationship beyond mere co-workers.

Maybe we can go out for drinks afterward. And if one thing leads to another…

I can't keep pining after Audrey. I have to open my heart to other possibilities, other women.

Maybe Miranda's the one.

Daniel was there too, of course. He was in another corner of the room, talking to Tallulah, Bliss, and some guy he'd never met but somehow looked familiar…

I know him…the rocker, Jammerhead. He's Tallulah's husband!

Jammerhead was dressed in the standard uniform for aging rock stars: a black tee-shirt, slim-cut tight black jeans, and boots. His long, graying hair was pulled back into a ponytail.

Tallulah was scowling. She had her arms wrapped around her waist as if shielding herself from assault.

The way she was shaking, Egan realized he had it wrong. She was holding herself back from doing something she'd regret.

And from the way she was glaring at Seamus, Miranda, and Jess, Egan guessed one of them was the culprit of her distress.

For some odd reason, Cornell had also shown up at the trustee meeting. Egan waved at him and walked over. "What, are you a glutton for punishment?"

"Not this kind, that's for sure." Cornell frowned. "Believe me, I wish I were here to beg for a grant for AA's robotics team. As it turns out, I've got a serious issue to report." He leaned in and hissed, "Student related."

Cornell was interrupted when Seamus barked, "Where the hell is Lavinia? This meeting was supposed to start fifteen minutes ago!"

"I vote we begin without her," Jess declared.

"I second the motion," Warner Crowley harrumphed.

"All in favor?" Seamus thundered.

"Excuse me, but I'm Lavinia's proxy until she arrives," Daniel reminded him.

Seamus waved his hand through the air as if shooing a fly. "Well, then get on with it, McKittridge."

Ah, great. This is going to be a hell of a night, Egan thought.

AFTER DANIEL CALLED THE MEETING TO ORDER, HE DECLARED, "WE'VE got several items on the agenda that need our immediate attention. First off, Miranda has an update on the senior students' college admissions process." He cleared his throat, then added, "We also have a student disciplinary issue to discuss."

"I called in with an agenda item too," Seamus said. "Why isn't it being noted?"

Daniel glanced down at the page on the table in front of him. "I don't see it here, but we can add it at the end."

"No. After Ms. D'Arcy's report, perhaps," Seamus countered. "It's short and sweet, and I'm sure everyone will agree."

"I'm glad you feel so confident about it." Daniel's sarcasm earned him a frown from Seamus. He ignored it. Instead, he glanced over at Tallulah, who shrugged.

Daniel nodded. "Okay, no problem. Miranda, why don't you begin?"

Miranda smiled sweetly. "I'm happy to report that eighty-four percent of our seniors did as well, or better, on their most recent SATs than on prior attempts. As for those who did not score as hoped, I've already sent emails encouraging them to attend the practice drills being held twice a week up to the last SAT date before the college admissions deadline."

"Great idea," Darius declared. "Zina will be signed up for it, that's for sure. She freezes during that damn test."

"That is certainly something I may be able to help her with," Miranda murmured. "Feel free to see me after the meeting so that we can discuss it further."

Darius nodded.

"Anything else, Miranda?" Daniel asked.

"Yes." Miranda pursed her lips. "Frankly, like Darius just pointed out, there are many reasons for tepid SAT scores. It's one of the reasons I'd like prep sessions to be compulsory as opposed to optional."

"Just do it," Seamus huffed.

"That's just it…" Miranda grimaced. "It goes against school policy."

"Maybe it's time for a new policy," Jess replied.

"But Lavinia's philosophy is that students shouldn't be forced to do anything; that they should be allowed to come to their own decisions," Miranda explained. "That includes prepping for college—or not."

"Bullshit!" Seamus retorted. "If that were the case, they'd all be parked on our couches watching reality TV twenty-four-seven! Let's put it to a vote, right here and now! I move that SAT prep sessions be compulsory for seniors."

"I second that motion," Jess added.

Daniel frowned. Finally he declared, "Those in favor?"

Jess, Seamus, Darius, and Warner raised their hands.

"Opposed?"

Daniel, Tallulah, Bliss, and Harris raised their hands.

Daniel turned to Egan. "What about you?"

Egan shrugged. "Here's a hypothetical: A student comes up to you and says, 'I know English I is mandatory, but I don't feel I need it because I already speak English, so I'm not taking it.' AA wouldn't allow him to graduate until he did. Am I right?"

Everyone nodded.

"We make certain classes compulsory because, at this time in their young lives, our judgment may be better than their own. Agreed?"

Again, the others nodded.

"Then I have to say that Miranda has a good point. AA students excel because we give them every opportunity to succeed. To that end, we hired the best college admissions consultant we could find, and she's doing everything she can to prepare them for the next stage of their lives—including ongoing SAT Prep." He nodded in Miranda's direction. "No one is saying that every AA student has to go to college, or when. But even if they never go, having taken the SAT when they were at their best and brightest will be yet another accomplishment. And if within five years they've changed their minds and want to further their education, *the test score is still valid.* They'll have one fewer admissions hurdle to worry about." He let that sink in. "So, yes, I vote that SAT test prep should be mandatory for those who score below a certain threshold. It's just as important as English I, or Algebra I, or any compulsory History class. It is the best skill preparation for the next stage of their lives."

The table was silent.

Finally Daniel said, "Then the motion passes."

For the first time all night, Seamus broke out into a smug grin.

Across the table, Miranda caught Egan's eye and mouthed the words, *thank you.*

For the first time in a while, he felt he'd done something right, and for all the right reasons.

———

"THANK YOU, MIRANDA, FOR YOUR REPORT," DANIEL MURMURED. "Now, for our next new business item. Seamus, you're up."

Noting that Miranda was gathering her notes to leave, Seamus said, "Ms. D'Arcy, if you wouldn't mind staying."

Miranda froze, wide-eyed.

"I'm very impressed with the initiative Ms. D'Arcy has taken on AA's behalf. In fact, I'm so appreciative that I'd like to like to move we expand the trustee board to include Miranda D'Arcy as a permanent member instead of a periodic advisor."

"I second that motion," Jess declared.

Egan noticed Cornell and Jammerhead exchanging flabbergasted stares. Blanchard's face lost all its color.

Instinctively, Egan's eyes moved to Miranda. Her face reflected similar shock and awe.

Well, what do you know! She's impressed Seamus enough that he's deluded himself that she'll be another of his trustee board pawns.

And now I don't have to bring it up, thank goodness.

"Wait...*Expanding the board*...without Lavinia's input?" Tallulah exclaimed. "That's not just audacious, it's obnoxious!"

"I agree, Tallulah. In fact, I refuse to put that to a vote without Lavinia present," Daniel replied.

"There is nothing in the bylaws that says Lavinia has to be present for every vote," Jess pointed out.

Realizing he was right, Daniel frowned. He turned to Miranda. "If offered, would you take the position?"

She glanced around the table as if considering the suggestion for the first time. Finally, she murmured, "It would be an honor! Yes, of course, I will!"

"The motion has been made," Seamus insisted. "We must vote on it."

Reluctantly, Daniel nodded. "Those in favor?"

Not surprising, Jess, Darius, and Warner voted yes along with Seamus.

And, as expected, Tallulah, Bliss, and Harris voted no.

Egan was surprised that Daniel also voted no.

Miranda was wrong about him.

Daniel pointed to Egan. "It's a tie. Which way are you voting?"

Instinctively, Egan looked at Miranda. She was staring down at the papers in front of her.

He remembered her earlier words: *We'll always have each other's backs.*

She'd already vowed to cover his—regarding his tryst with Audrey. Even if mere friendship was as far as their relationship were to go, at least his yes vote now would prove he too was as worthy of her trust.

And it certainly wasn't the worst *quid pro quo.*

"I'll always welcome another AA administrator to the board, especially someone with insights to the momentous task of running a school and whose life is dedicated to the students' success," Egan murmured softly. "I vote yes."

For Lavinia.

"The motion passes." Daniel cleared his throat. "Miranda, welcome to the board."

DANIEL THEN MOTIONED TOWARD CORNELL AND JAMMERHEAD.

"Cornell is here because of a student disciplinary issue that happened in his classroom." He turned to Cornell. "Do you wish to explain?"

Cornell nodded. "I intercepted the sale of five grams of cocaine between"—he nodded toward Jammerhead—"Quest Wishart-Jammerhead and Hugo Smallwood. I caught them in the middle of the act. Unfortunately, I couldn't tell who was selling and who was buying. And neither student will admit to bringing it into our school."

As if watching a three-way tennis match, the others shifted their gazes from Tallulah's scowl to Jammerhead's stare and then to Jess' smirk.

Jess pointed a finger at Jammerhead. "How dare your kid try to get my kid hooked on snow!"

Jammerhead's back stiffened. "Are you crazy? Drugs are forbidden in our home!"

"Bullshit!" Jess replied. "You rock stars are all the same—sex, drugs, and groupies all over the place!"

"Are you kidding me?" Tallulah stood up, glowering. "Everyone at school knows your son is one of the biggest high school dealers in the city!"

She stared pointedly at Seamus, who was smirking.

Tallulah guffawed mirthlessly. "See what I mean? Gee, Jess, if you really didn't know about it, I guess Hugo doesn't trust you enough with his revenue to make you his investment advisor."

Jess snickered. "Since when does the queen of the groupies care that her kid snorts, anyway?"

Tallulah leaped up.

Daniel placed his hand over hers. "Tallulah, please."

Still glaring at Jess, slowly she sat down.

"Let's continue, folks. Now, as we all know, the school's policy on this issue is strict: no illegal drugs on campus. If caught, it means formal expulsion." Daniel let that sink in. "Considering the severity of the offense, the board is entrusted to note for the record its adherence to school policy. Tallulah and Jess already know they must recuse themselves from the board's decision."

"Wait," Jess interjected. "If you have to vote on it, does that mean the board can vote *against* it too? You know, make an exception?"

Daniel shook his head. "AA's handbook is very clear on the subject. The vote is merely a formality."

Miranda raised her hand. "May I make a suggestion?"

"Yes, sure," Daniel replied.

"Quest and Hugo are seniors. Expulsion will ruin their chances for college." She scanned the faces around the table. "Is that truly what we want to happen for them?"

The room was silent.

Of course not, Egan thought. It might just as well have been one of their kids.

Finally, Harris spoke: "If word gets out that the trustee board made an exception for two of its own children, we'll have to do so for the next student who breaks the rule; and the one after that. And parents will expect leniency on other infractions as well."

"He's right," Tallulah muttered.

Jammerhead nodded as if accepting his son's fate.

"I'm not suggesting that we *don't* punish the students," Miranda explained. "Perhaps a suspension—say, two weeks—and two months of community service."

"I second the motion!" Seamus barked.

"You're jumping the gun again, Seamus." Daniel sighed. Turning to Miranda, he asked, "Is that a motion?"

She nodded uncomfortably. "I move that we offer these students a two-week suspension, along with two months of community service. Everyone makes mistakes, right?"

"Yes. And sometimes the consequences have an irreversible ripple effect." Despite this admonishment, Daniel added, "Okay, then, all in favor?"

Seamus, Warner, and Darius raised their hands along with Miranda.

"Opposed?" Daniel added.

His hand went up, as did those of Harris and Bliss.

Egan didn't know how to vote. The right thing to do was expulsion. Still—

"Please forgive me for being so late. I had to take care of a ...an emergency." Lavinia stood at the door.

She looked around the room. Noting the number of guests, she smiled quizzically as she took her usual seat. "Now, tell me. What did I miss?"

***

To Daniel's credit, his narrative of the meeting was both concise and positive.

Lavinia blinked twice at the news that the board had voted to make the SATs mandatory and testing below AA's historic average the litmus for mandatory prep as well.

"Egan had an interesting point about it." Daniel nodded toward the man in question. "Testing and prep are wonderful services that the school provides. However, considering the school's mission, it should be as compulsory as, say, English or Math. It doesn't mean the student has to actually *apply* to any university upon graduation or afterward. But it does assure them an easier acceptance should they decide to do so, either immediately or within five years."

"I see," Lavinia murmured. When she shifted her gaze to Egan, he couldn't help it: suddenly, he felt like a sellout.

He felt even worse when, resignedly, she shrugged.

She turned back to Daniel. "Go on."

"Cornell is here to report a disciplinary problem. Two students engaged in a drug purchase during class. Cornell confiscated the item—cocaine."

Lavinia sighed. "The school handbook is clear. AA enforces a strict policy for such matters."

"Yes, well..." Daniel hesitated. "The majority felt that, since two seniors were involved, we should lessen the punishment to a two-week suspension and two months of community service. That way, the punishment would have no effect on their college applications."

"The point of punishment is to teach a lesson," Lavinia replied.

"Why such a harsh one—for just one stupid mistake?" Jess countered.

"Was the student's mistake in selling an illegal drug, or selling it and getting caught doing so?" Lavinia asked. "And had it been off campus—say, across the street in the park—and the sale had been to an undercover police officer, wouldn't the consequence be even worse?"

"Of course, it shouldn't have taken place at all, either off or on campus," Jammerhead insisted.

"Says the guy who writes songs about his highs," Jess retorted.

Jammerhead smacked the table with an open palm. "Like I said before, asshole—*I don't sell drugs, and neither does my kid!*"

Jess shrugged. "In either case, Ashbury Academy isn't the police. And if it were, a donation to the Police Benevolent Society or our illustrious mayor's re-election campaign would get the matter taken care of with a hell of a lot less fuss."

"I'm sorry you find me harder to bribe than our local law enforcement," Lavinia replied.

"Some of us cover the costs of those who might have ended up as juvenile delinquents if they weren't here!" Jess snarled. "With all due respect, Lavinia, it should count for something!"

Lavinia closed her eyes.

She looks so tired, Egan thought.

Knowing her plight, his heart went out to her.

When Lavinia's eyes opened again, she said, "Yes, thank you, Jess. Having our scholarships covered by the families of those students who don't receive them is very much appreciated. Now, about the situation at hand: I take it that this motion for a more lenient disciplinary action is to be the exception, *not* the rule?"

"Yes," Daniel glared at Seamus, as if to say, *don't push it further.*

Seamus nodded once.

"Good," Lavinia said. "Anything else I should know about?"

Daniel nodded. "Well… It was suggested that we add an additional board member—Miranda."

Lavinia looked over at her.

Miranda nodded and smiled.

"And why is that?" Lavinia asked.

"Isn't it obvious?" Jess replied. "The board is evenly divided in its philosophies on how to run the school, which increases odds for a stalemate," he smirked. "I for one hesitated to vote for yet another staff person who may use it to curry favor with you, Lavinia. But considering it's in the school's best interests, I did so."

"How magnanimous of you," Lavinia murmured dryly. She turned to Miranda. "It's a big commitment. Considering you have private clients as well, will you have time for the board too?"

Miranda nodded fervently. "As I said when Daniel asked the same question, I'd do anything for this school."

Lavinia smiled wanly. "I appreciate your dedication, Miranda." She glanced around the table. "I'd like to add my vote to the minutes. Please let it reflect that I too wish to expand the board and that I also vote to include Miranda D'Arcy in this new trustee position."

Egan leaned back in his chair.

Thank God, I did the right thing.

"Since there is nothing else on the agenda, the meeting is adjourned." Lavinia knocked the gavel softly.

Egan watched as Miranda stood up. Jess was also on his feet. In fact, he was standing so close to her that it looked as if they were joined at the hip.

Make that joined at the hand—Jess', anyway. It had found its way to the center of Miranda's back as if she were some sort of life-size ventriloquist's dummy.

No, actually, Jess's hand was positioned lower.

A lot lower.

That son of a bitch…

So, it was Jess who'd divulged Seamus' Machiavellian scheme to Miranda.

Well, thank goodness he blabbed it to someone who has Lavinia's back.

Egan had met Jess' ex-wife, Lizbeth during the second-period meet-and-greet at AA's open house. She was the petite brunette with skin like leather. Too many tennis foursomes, Egan figured.

During Egan's short conversation with her, Lizbeth's eyes had darted fervently about the room as she searched for the man who had dumped her.

Although Jess usually brought his current, much younger wife—their son Hugo's former *au pair*—to the school's social functions like the Friday Family Fun Night, he'd come solo on the night of the open house. When Lizbeth finally spotted him, her one attempt to beckon him over was met with outright hostility.

During Egan's open house patter, Jess had done little to hide his boredom, preferring to spend the time continually texting.

Egan wondered if the asshole texted during sex too.

For a brief moment, the thought crossed his mind that Miranda might know the answer to that.

Immediately, he dismissed it.

Miranda is in a hard position. She has to pretend to like all parents, even the obnoxious ones.

Even the ones who cup your ass.

We're very much alike, he reasoned. We're strong people. We'd never let others use us.

"Jeez, that teacher guy is a sap!" Riley exclaimed.

"She played right to his ego," Lionel added.

Riley snorted. "Yeah, just like she played to Smallwood's joystick!"

Lionel frowned. Again, he nodded toward Sally Anne.

She shrugged off his attempt at chivalry. "Riley has a point.

Miranda D'Arcy is devious, to say the least. Besides wrapping a few members of the board around her finger, she's now on it herself—thanks to that teacher."

"Did anyone catch his name?" Lionel asked.

Riley and SallyAnne shook their heads. But SallyAnne thought she'd heard his voice before—

But from where?

"Anyone want to take the bet that she'll be able to keep him in play without jumping in the sack with him?" Riley asked.

Neither answered.

"Nah, I didn't think so." Riley sighed. "If she keeps it up, she'll have to hire an air traffic controller to keep her lovers from colliding!" He put on his earphones and waved them away. "Okay, back to the porn portion of our drama."

SallyAnne was glad neither she nor Lionel were tasked with listening or transcribing Miranda's sexploits. She doubted whether Lionel was turned on by Miranda's boudoir shenanigans. She could tell, however, he was certainly intrigued by how Miranda operated.

He likes strong women, SallyAnne realized.

She felt she met that criterion. But she also knew of agents who'd had relationships with co-workers. It always ended badly.

Better to admire Lionel from afar, she reasoned.

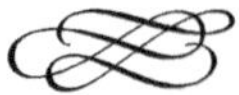

CHAPTER 23

"Can you believe that woman? The way she talked her way onto the board—with Egan's help, no less!" Tallulah's heels clicked fiercely on the floor as she paced in front of Audrey and Bliss.

Always a stickler for client confidentiality, the version of the meeting that Audrey heard from Daniel was less detailed and certainly much less emotional. Although, to Audrey's mind, the message was the same:

The fix was in to get Miranda D'Arcy on the board.

Now, the question was whether that was a good thing or a bad thing.

It hadn't helped that Lavinia had given her approval on the record.

"You know, if Lavinia had been there when Miranda's scam was going down, she wouldn't have bought into it," Bliss pointed out. "She'd have slapped it down *tout de suite.*"

Audrey didn't dare mention she'd been with her mother, at her doctor's appointment. Lavinia's chemotherapy was tiring her out. Still, she insisted on doing everything she could to stop the spread of her cancer.

And she insisted that Audrey say nothing to anyone. Not yet, anyway.

"If you could have voted on it, would you have voted to expel Quest?" Audrey asked.

"Hell, yeah!" Tallulah insisted. "I said as much too! Quest has seen how drugs can wreak havoc on a life! He was too young to remember how hard it was on our family before Jammerhead got clean, but, hey, he was old enough to see how it affected his own grandmother—Maggie!" She threw up her arms in dismay. "Thank goodness she's clean now too, but it took her half his life to get there! Why would he do something so stupid now?"

"Because he wants to fit in," Audrey explained. "You know, had he been at a public school, both boys would have been arrested."

"Maybe it would have been a wakeup call. Some of the AA kids are shielded from too much. And we, their parents, are enablers," Tallulah retorted. "I only wish Jammerhead felt the same way."

"He did look relieved when the board voted for leniency," Bliss admitted.

Tallulah frowned. "That's because my bullheaded husband thinks our son is ready for college. He's wrong. Quest is a musician. It's all he's ever wanted to be since he was old enough to strum a guitar. But no matter how many times I remind Jammerhead that *he* didn't need college to be a successful musician, he says we should view college as Quest's 'back-up plan.'"

"Jammerhead has a good point," Bliss countered. "Few musicians, with or without a college degree, attain his level of success. And with a kid like Quest, the right college could turn him onto a passion in a different field while giving him some additional skills that might be useful for a music industry career, if that's where his future lies."

"I'm not against Quest going to college. I just don't think *he* wants to go—at least, not right now," Tallulah explained. "Heck, if my son were more academically inclined, I'd be pushing him on his grades like every other mom. But he's a natural musician! He needs to follow his passion, hone his chops with a band, on the road in front of audiences. If not now, then when?" She threw up her hands in frustration. "But Jammerhead's big fear is that Quest will always be in his shadow and Maggie's. He insists if Quest goes to college, he'll be able to manage the business better."

"That's not such a bad idea," Bliss pointed out. "At least, that's the way Raffaele sees it for Sienna."

Tallulah raised a brow. "And we all know how Sienna feels about it. Frankly, she's right. She's already on her way to being a brand."

Bliss nodded resignedly.

"You can start college at any age. If the time comes when Quest feels he needs it, he can always enroll," Audrey pointed out.

"Exactly! Now, if Jammerhead would just let Quest do his thing —*play music*—the kid may prove him wrong," Tallulah muttered.

"Maybe that's what Jammerhead is afraid of," Audrey pointed out.

"I hope not." Tallulah blinked away her tears. "Jammerhead's father never told him he was proud of his success. It would be a shame if he did the same to Quest."

Audrey put her arms around her friend. "Stick to your guns on this one."

Tallulah nodded. "You better believe it." She leaned her head on Audrey's shoulder. "Speaking of the academically inclined, how are your two scholars?"

"Frantic!" Audrey sighed. "Sadly, between their studies and now Debate Team tryouts, I'm worried they've both taken on more than they can chew."

Bliss grimaced. "I hope Charly makes the team. Otherwise, she'll be heartbroken."

"Why do you say that?" Audrey asked.

Bliss laughed. "Because she idolizes you, silly! She won't be satisfied until she follows in your footsteps and becomes the team's captain."

Audrey shook her head. "I never had that title. It belonged to Mandy What's-Her-Name…Blackwell."

Tallulah snickered. "Bullshit! Don't try to rewrite history. You were why the team succeeded, and don't you forget it. In any case, that's how Gemma Sisley tells it—and she was there during that whole sordid weekend." She rolled her eyes at the thought. "By the way, I hear Chuck is also trying out for Debate Team."

Audrey nodded. "And, no surprise, he's approaching it as if he doesn't have a care in the world. I asked him if he was serious about making the team. I even offered to critique his arguments, but he insists he and his critique partner"—she made quote marks with her fingers—"have it down pat."

"Who is it?" Tallulah asked.

"Fawn McCoppin." Audrey stifled a shiver.

"Well, then, don't hold your breath for Chuck. That girl is nothing but trouble," Tallulah warned.

"Believe me, I already know it," Audrey retorted.

"He does seem to have a talent for charming his way out of things." Bliss chuckled. "Except with Charly. She's onto him. I pray for his sake that he never crosses her."

MIRANDA HAD BEEN EXPECTING DARIUS CALDER'S CALL.

She remembered how, at the trustee board meeting, he'd bemoaned his daughter Zina's, lousy test-taking.

And despite his acceptance into Seamus' boys' club, she could tell their relationship was one based merely on convenience (they were members of the same golf club) and strategy (Seamus needed his vote on Ashbury Academy's trustee board).

She also knew that, after almost twenty years of marriage, Darius and Gemma shared a "don't ask, don't tell" policy. Perhaps it had developed over the differences in their legal clientele, but Miranda guessed it covered many other issues as well.

So, when Darius suggested they meet for a drink to discuss Zina's college placement concierge program, Miranda knew the score.

She also knew his hot button: Zina was to follow in her grandfather and parents' footsteps in becoming a lawyer.

The girl had big shoes to fill.

And to do so, she'd first have to get into an elite college, and then follow up four years of exemplary grades in order to get accepted into a top-flight law school.

Miranda arrived precisely on time at their rendezvous locale: the tony Pied Piper Lounge at the Palace Hotel. Three men were sitting with Darius in the deepest corner of the lounge's wood-paneled anteroom.

One was a slim twenty-something man with the mien of a cherub: pouting lips, full cheeks, and ice blue-eyes. A highway of tattoos crawled up both arms bared by his sleeveless tee-shirt. This manboy's strawberry blond hair was shaved tight on the sides but spiked into a tall flattop.

Miranda recognized him immediately: a pop star who went by the single hyphenated name, Plug-Ugly. Despite his mobster swagger, he'd been raised in the heart of well-heeled and wealthy suburbia: Woodside, California. His latest song was blasting the airwaves—something touting big guns, big mansions, big-bootied women, and big bank accounts.

The two men on either side of him were scowling hulks twice his size. Plug-Ugly didn't look so happy either. Whatever Darius said had made the pop king somber and silent.

Seeing Miranda, Darius waved her over. Plug-Ugly and his security goons took this as their cue to vacate the booth, but it didn't stop them from staring and smirking at her as they walked away.

As she held out her hand to Darius, Miranda murmured, "So, *he's* one of your clients?"

Darius nodded. "You look surprised."

Miranda shrugged. "I guess…I guess I envisioned your clients as…"

"Let me guess—the stereotypical hip-hopper or gangster. Am I right?"

Miranda conceded with a nod.

Darius smirked, "Ms. D'Arcy, let me assure you, those who make their living on the outer banks of the law come in all shapes, sizes, *and colors*"—his eyes to roam over her—"and for that matter, genders."

"Good to know," she murmured coolly. "I now officially feel like a piece of meat."

Darius let loose with a deep-throated chuckle. "I'm sure you're used to it. You're a beautiful woman."

Miranda smiled. "Flattery will get you anything."

"Including admission to Yale?"

He goes straight to the point.

"That depends," she replied.

He listened intently as she made her pitch: how the best universities had an abundance of students to choose from, "…even those students from diverse populations."

Darius snickered at the term.

How some students were almost the full package but not

entirely. And acceptance was based solely on the subjective decisions made by the admissions staff's criteria for that year.

She admitted that the game was rigged for children of alumni. And opening one's wallet for, say, a building or curriculum program bearing your name was no longer the awesome sauce for consideration for a non-alum's child. "The worm has turned on that little game."

"Bullshit!" Darius scoffed. "There's always a way of gaming the system."

"You're right. And that's why you called me, correct?" She looked him in the eye. "Let me guess: Jess suggested you call me."

Darius nodded. "He mentioned you have a failsafe system."

Miranda stymied the urge to frown. The smaller the dick, the larger the piehole, she thought.

Word of mouth was a double-edged sword. Tell the wrong person, and the Feds would be swooping down on you. It was why Miranda liked to do her own recruiting.

As if reading her mind, Darius added, "I have a lot of clients whose business practices are creative, to say the least. Through the years, I've made sure to put systems in place to mitigate their worst instincts."

"I'll remember that in case I ever need an attorney with your skillset," she replied dryly.

"So, let's talk about your side door," Darius said. "Does it work with, say, Yale?"

"It's on the list," Miranda assured him. "Zina has great grades, so that's no problem. As for her SAT scores, I can arrange a prep session or two, followed by the test—which, this time, she'll take with a disability pass, so that she has all the time in the world with her proctor."

Darius grimaced. "For that, won't she need a doctor's note, or something?"

She waved away his concern. "The tutor will take care of that."

"If only all of life were that simple," he retorted. "So, be honest. What else does Zina need to be a slam-dunk?"

"Does she play a sport?"

He shook his head. "She'll hit a few tennis balls with her friends or play two-on-two basketball with her cousins. But, as she puts it, she doesn't want to be a stereotype."

"In this case, that's a shame," Miranda admitted. "Sports recruits are allowed to bypass the extremely competitive process set up for regular applicants. Instead, the university's student-athlete admissions committee would have reviewed their applications."

Miranda had some of the coaches in her back pocket. They added her client's children to their initial rosters and then cut those with what was officially called "limited ability" a few weeks later— just long enough for them to have formally settled into campus life.

"No need to worry." Miranda assured him. "Does she have any academic extracurricular activities, like, say, chess team or Spanish club?"

Darius paused in thought. "I know she's trying out for Debate Team."

"Perfect! If she makes it, that's a plus."

"Yeah, well, from what I hear, so is every junior and senior in the school. Even Smallwood's little delinquent is going for it!" Darius chuckled. "I guess he figures it's a way to expand his distribution channels into the other schools." He shrugged. "When the kid pulls that stuff on some university campus, he'll be stepping on some big toes."

Miranda couldn't care less. Jess had already paid in full, and she had a no-refund policy.

"I'll see what I can do to help Zina's cause," she promised.

Darius grinned. "I'm sure you will."

"What's that supposed to mean?" Miranda huffed.

"Hey, I'm not blind. Egan knows a pretty woman when he sees one." Darius arched a brow.

"You do know how to flatter a girl," Miranda simpered. She could tell Darius would be fun in the sack.

Until that situation presented itself—and she had no doubt it would—Darius did have a point: should Hugo and Zina make the team, it would certainly make them easier to place at their chosen universities.

The best way to influence Egan was to judge the tryouts with him. Piece of cake. She'd played him well thus far.

"Let's get down to brass tacks," Darius said. "How much are we talking here, to get Zina to Yale?"

"Half a million." She said it firmly and without blinking.

Darius laughed so hard you'd have thought she'd told him the best stand-up line in Vegas. "You're aiming too high. As you just said, Zina's almost the full package. Your job is to just tie a pretty little bow around her so that those admissions folk see it too."

Miranda frowned. "I can go as low as four hundred thousand."

"You'll go a quarter-million," Darius told her. He handed her his business card. "Half up front, half on delivery."

"Everyone pays my fee upfront," Miranda huffed.

Darius shrugged. "I'm not 'everyone.' I'm the furthest from 'everyone' you'll ever meet. And if you're willing to do business my way, I'll be the best friend you'll ever have."

"What's that supposed to mean?"

"I'm just saying if you scratch my back, I'll scratch yours—metaphorically speaking, of course." Darius winked knowingly.

Damn it! Is that loudmouth, Jess, telling everyone I'm an easy lay too?

Seeing the concern in her face, Darius burst out laughing. "Don't worry, Miranda. I take everything that blowhard Smallwood says with a grain of salt." He looked her up and down and smiled. "And even if it were true, I'd like to spare you any unnecessary grief that might befall either of us, should my darlin wife even suspect anything you did was untoward, be it business or pleasure."

"That's quite chivalrous of you," Miranda murmured. In a way, she wished it weren't the case.

"I'll have a hundred and a quarter, in small bills, delivered to your doorstep tomorrow."

"I'd prefer it through the Best Foot Forward Club. It's a non-profit that I support."

Darius snickered. "I'll bet you do."

Miranda slid a business card his way. "Here's its online address for donation information."

Darius reached into his pocket and pulled out a slim wallet from which he extracted a card. "And here's mine. Just in case your world ever comes tumbling down."

His words sent a chill through her.

She shrugged it off. "It won't. By the way, I'll call Zina in tomorrow and let her know I'm setting her up with an SAT tutor for a full assessment."

"Good. But mum's the word on any special treatment," he warned her. "Like I said, our arrangement is just between us."

"No problem there."

"By the way, I overheard Manya Patel's mother, Nira, talking to Gemma. Apparently, Manya also has test anxiety. Nira is a single mother—an MD. She insists that Manya follow in her footsteps. She feels it's the only way that Manya won't get burned in a relationship, like, apparently she did. Nira's ex gets half her earnings." He snorted. "Even divorce is an equal opportunity outcome."

"If you say so," Miranda muttered. Nothing new there. She had firsthand knowledge. "Well, thanks for the heads up on Nira."

"What are friends for, right?" Darius' eyes moved beyond her, to the front of the room. "Ah, my next appointment is early. I suggest you go so that you don't collide with Public Enemy Number 44. He's sure to have an undercover cop or two trailing him."

Miranda took the hint, nodded, and headed for the door.

The man walking in as she stepped out had countless gold chains around his neck, and a gold grill on his teeth to match.

The eye that wasn't covered by a patch followed her out the door.

"Oh, my God! We've got *Darius Calder*!" SallyAnne exclaimed.

Dumbfounded, Lionel nodded. "Hell yeah, we've got him! The lawyer for every drug-dealing badass in the Bay Area! Melamed will be over the moon about it!"

They slapped palms.

SallyAnne would have rather they had chest-bumped.

Better yet, if they'd held hands.

"So, when we arrest him, we'll suggest he sing about his clients to get some leniency with our charges," SallyAnne crowed.

"Boy, Miranda will be pissed when he throws her under the bus," Lionel predicted. "She's attracted to him."

SallyAnne frowned. "How could you tell?"

Lionel shrugged. "There's a different cadence to her pitch when she's truly interested in a guy, versus playing at it. It shows in how she nuances certain words."

"Does it?" SallyAnne sniffed. "I'm impressed. You've done quite a study of her voice."

"Thanks!" He sighed, "Yeah, makes me wish we had video too."

"I'll bet you do," SallyAnne muttered. She grabbed her purse. "Have a great night."

Lionel looked up, surprised. "Wait…what say we grab a bite to eat? Like me, I'll bet you have a few ideas on how we can use what we just heard—"

"Sorry, but I'm late for a date." She waved as she walked out the door.

In truth, she had no plans except go to a really nice hotel bar.

She needed a drink.

No—she needed *a man.* It had been a while since SallyAnne had had sex. If she picked up some guy and went back to his room with him, all the better.

For the past few years, most of her intimate liaisons had been one-night stands, usually initiated at some bar and with civilians who never knew what she really did for a living.

There was a reason she kept her job to herself: she'd learned early on that most civilian men were uneasy dating female agents. She could never understand why. Odds were that they weren't involved in illegal activities.

Even so, everyone has something to hide, right?

Mr. Lucky wouldn't know it, but they'd both be role-playing. While he assumed she was some out-of-town corporate lawyer who'd just finished a meeting with a locally-based client, and she'd close her eyes and pretend he was Lionel.

And unlike the real Lionel, he'd be one satisfied customer.

CHAPTER 24

"Mom! Dad! Read it and weep!" Charly ran into the dining room, her SAT score held high.

Her parents and brothers paused as she handed the official paper to her mother first.

Seeing it, Audrey's eyes opened wide:

Evidence-Based Reading and Writing: 782
Math: 719
TOTAL: 1501

She handed it to Daniel.

Reviewing it, his eyes grew wide. "Excellent!" Daniel gave his daughter a hug. He glanced over at Chuck. "Was yours in the mail too?"

Chuck frowned. "Yeah." He leaned forward to pull something out of his back pocket. He handed the paper to Audrey.

Her heart sank. Because I'm a soft touch, she realized.

Cautiously, she opened it:

Evidence-Based Reading and Writing: 486
Math: 713
TOTAL: 1199

Audrey winced. As she handed it to Daniel, she murmured, "Isn't this total less than your last try?"

Noah leaned toward his father for a glance. "Wow, you didn't even make it to twelve-hundred!"

Chuck's middle finger shot up in Noah's direction.

"Don't do that!" Audrey cautioned him.

"Your brother has a point," Daniel muttered. "What happened, Chuck?"

The boy shrugged. "Yeah, well, you know. With basketball season and all."

"Granted, your math score is decent. But how could you blow the reading and writing?" Audrey asked.

"I don't know! I mean, it wasn't like I did it on purpose."

"Apparently, it was," Daniel countered. "You're better than that. You got into AP Comp Lit, for Pete's sake!"

Charly snorted. "That's only because he kissed up to Mercy— you know, the instructor who would have been teaching it if she hadn't gone on maternity leave."

This time, Chuck tossed a middle finger salute in his sister's direction.

"Enough of that!" Audrey warned him.

"Look, Mom, Dad—maybe I'm just not college material. Or maybe I'm just not ready for it *now*—right out of high school. The Brits and the Aussies have the right idea: you know, take a year off—"

Charly interrupted: "It's called a 'gap year.'"

"Yeah, okay—*whatever!*" Chuck threw up his hands. "Like I was saying, if I took a year off to think about it, maybe I'd know better what's right for me."

Audrey shook her head adamantly. "Chuck, true: you can always go to college. But why drop out before you've even given it a try? Some people do, and…and they never go back. I did, granted— but almost two years later. With twins in tow. You see, real life gets in the way."

When Chuck and Charly exchanged startled glances, she wished she'd never said it like that.

"We all know you can do better," Daniel added. "Listen, guy: maybe you should resign from all sports to prove it."

"*Are you nuts?* I'm the basketball team's captain and starting forward! And I'm the starting pitcher on the baseball team!"

"Yes, you are—for teams that consistently place third or less in their division," Daniel argued. "That doesn't necessarily guarantee you a scholarship to any college." He leaned in. "Chuck, we're your parents. It's our job to make you buckle down. If you can give one hundred percent for your coaches, you can do it for us too."

All color went out of Chuck's face. "Dad, please! Don't make me quit!"

Audrey laid her arm on Daniel's wrist to caution him. "Your father is making the point that something's got to give. Something that gives you more time to study. So give us a solution, Chuck. What's it going to be?"

"I'll try harder on the next SAT session! I promise!"

Daniel rolled his eyes. "That's what you said before the last test."

"And there's only one SAT exam between now and when our college applications are due," Charly pointed out.

"Okay—*ALRIGHT!* Listen..." Chuck ran his fingers through his hair—something he did whenever he was at the end of his rope. "I'll raise my GPA!" His chin jutted forward. "I'll... I'll ace Comp Lit!"

"Egan did mention you were trying much harder in class," Audrey conceded.

Satisfied he'd made his point, Chuck nodded to his father. "See?"

Daniel shrugged. "That's a step in the right direction. But it won't help your SATs."

"I'll...I'll get a tutor."

"Okay, good." Daniel smiled. "We'll get a referral from Miranda."

At that suggestion, Audrey pursed her lips.

"I dunno. That lady scares me." Chuck rolled his eyes. "Hey! Maybe Egan won't mind helping me out."

Daniel frowned. "I would think he's got enough on his plate."

Chuck smirked. "He'd do it—if *Mom* asks him."

Audrey felt a blush creeping up her throat. "Why do you say that?"

Chuck shrugged. "He likes you. He sees you as some kind of...I dunno—*nun* or something."

Daniel choked into his water glass. When he recovered, he declared, "Well, then, by all means, ask him. It can't hurt."

"He'll say no," Charly declared coldly. "He's got Debate Team tryouts. And once the team starts up, he won't be able to make the time for you."

"Gee! Sounds like Teacher's Pet may be a bit jealous!" Chuck retorted.

"I have nothing to be jealous about," Charly replied smugly. "I have the highest GPA in the class—*because I care!* I work my ass off."

Chuck leaned out from his chair to examine his sister's backside. "Ha! Could have fooled me."

Charly tossed her bread roll at him.

Chuck caught it with one hand—quite a feat considering how hard he was laughing.

Incensed, Charly lifted her father's glass—

But Daniel grabbed her wrist before she could toss it on her brother. To his dismay, Daniel got back-splashed instead.

"Oh, shit! Sorry, Dad!" Charly yelped.

Audrey glared at Chuck. "You need to apologize to your sister!"

"Hey, I'm not the only one who thinks so. Fawn claims Charly's got some sort of daddy complex—"

Charly's jaw dropped open. "Why that—*bitch!*" Her eyes glazed up with tears.

"*Fawn?...*" Audrey frowned. "What does she know about... about something like that?"

"I would say it takes one to know one," Daniel muttered.

"Fawn knows *nothing* about Charly!" Audrey shot back.

Daniel raised his hands in mock surrender. "Calm down, folks! All I was saying is that everything Fawn does is to grab Seamus' attention."

This time it was Chuck who gagged on a gulp of water. When he recovered, he scoffed, "Ha! I wouldn't exactly put it that way."

Daniel raised a brow. "No, I guess *you* wouldn't." He shook his head. "Look, Chuck, I'm not telling you who to choose as your friends—"

"Good! Because as far as Fawn goes, I'm not dumping her." Chuck's voice shook. "We almost broke up once already."

"That's because *she* dumped *you*—and very publicly, too," Charly retorted. "What kind of girlfriend is that?"

"The kind who knows how to say she's sorry," Chuck declared.

"In fact, she wants to help me succeed. We study together. And she's my debate team critique partner."

Charly guffawed, "Wow! I can't wait to see how *that* plays out!"

"All those snide little remarks you make—just like that one—are the reason our parents think I'm stupid." With as much dignity as he could muster, Chuck rose from the table.

But before he could take off, Daniel reached over and grabbed his arm. "Let me make this clear: we've always judged you and your sister and your brother by your actions only. Only you can prove Charly wrong."

Chuck jerked his arm away and stormed out of the house.

Charly wiped her damp cheeks with the back of her hand. "What you said isn't really true, you know."

Daniel stared at her. "What do you mean by that?"

"You guys play favorites! We all know it too."

"That's not true!" Audrey protested.

"Sure it is," Charly insisted. She turned to Noah. "Kiddo, of the three of us, who would you say is Mom's favorite?'

Noah guffawed. "Duh! *Chuck*."

"How about Dad?"

Noah blushed. "I'd say…Me."

Charly's gaze went from her mother to her father. "I rest my case." She ran from the room.

They could hear her bedroom door slam.

Noah frowned. "I was going to tell her that she was the only one that both of you loved equally." The boy sighed. "May I be excused too?"

His parents nodded.

Audrey waited until Noah was out of earshot to whisper, "Doesn't Charly realize we love her?"

Daniel shrugged. "She knows it. But now we know she doesn't believe we love her *as much* as we do her brothers."

"We have three kids! There's no way we can—or should—have a favorite! We love them all equally!"

"Obviously, that's not how they view it. And if, like Charly, you believe you're the odd child out, it's got to hurt. Especially if the others see it too."

Audrey crossed her arms at her waist. "Exactly what do they think they see?"

"Well, in my case, since Noah was just an infant, he was my charge whenever you had to run shotgun over the twins. You know, when you ferried them to and from their big kid activities."

"I offered to swap duties," Audrey pointed out.

"I know," Daniel conceded. "But so many of their play dates were with Tallulah, Bliss, and Gemma's kids too. I didn't want you to miss out hanging with your best friends."

She nodded.

"As for you and Chuck…" Daniel sighed. "No matter what hot water he finds himself in, he can charm his way out of it"—he hesitated—"with you."

"Ha!" Audrey scoffed. "I take it you view yourself as the bad cop!"

"Wasn't that the pact we made at the parent open house? And even tonight, you didn't exactly back me up when I gave him the ultimatum about sports and the SAT."

Audrey had nothing to say because he was right.

Daniel stood up and walked over to her. Wrapping his arms around her, he murmured, "It's not as if we've taken a course in parenting. We both have made mistakes."

"I don't remember things being this complicated with Lavinia and me."

"She was one parent with one child. She adored you, and you felt the same about her. You never had to share your love with another sibling." Daniel chuckled. "I guess that means we'll have to scare up another parent somewhere."

Audrey couldn't laugh at that.

If only you knew, she thought.

"Slow…down!" Fawn's demand was adamant.

"I…I'm doing the best I can!" Chuck muttered.

But, sweet Jesus, it was hard!

So hard, what with the sight in front of him: Fawn's backside, rising and falling, again and again, on his cock.

Her reverse cowgirl was squeezing the Kickapoo joy juice out of him. She must have known that.

Not that she gave a hoot. He knew she was there for her own

satisfaction. The longer he could hold out, the longer he could hang onto her.

She's my little filly.

At least, that's what he told himself.

This was his mantra although she insisted on riding him as opposed to the other way around.

It was his mantra whenever he denied his parents' contention that she wasn't right for him.

It was his mantra whenever his sister arched a brow upon hearing Fawn's name.

And it was most definitely his mantra as he climbed over the high thick wall that separated the McCoppin estate from the Presidio—the best way to avoid the security camera aimed at their front gate, all the while fighting off his vertigo as he scurried up the lattice arbor next to her third-story bedroom suite.

When Chuck called Fawn, fuming over his fight with his family —about Charly's cruel taunts about his chances of making Debate Team—she cooed sympathy and promises to make him feel better.

She didn't have to ask twice to get him over there.

Even so, Chuck wouldn't have come over if Fawn's parents hadn't been out for the evening. After Egan's reality check about the legal consequences for underage sex, Fawn knew that Chuck was skittish about running into Seamus and Gretchen.

Ironically, Egan's warning had only whetted their appetites for each other. Suddenly, it wasn't just fun and illicit, but illegal too.

So yes, sex was on the agenda. But first things first: Fawn insisted that they look at the debate questions and decide together which ones to tackle.

"Which ones are Charly interested in?" She'd asked nonchalantly.

Chuck shrugged. "I forget."

"Well, Silly, it would help us develop our arguments if we could see how it was done," she pouted. "Where does Charly keep her classwork?"

"In our family iCloud account," Chuck admitted.

"Do you know her password?"

"Maybe. I mean, I can guess at it. But—"

"Listen, Chuck—tryouts are on Monday! *We've got less than three days to pull something together!* It'll take us a second to log in, copy her notes, and then log out again. But, hey, if you're too lazy, you can just leave because I'll have to pull an all-nighter." As if in anticipation of a long night, Fawn stretched toward the ceiling. (And, yes, he'd noticed that she wasn't wearing a bra.)

"Alright," he muttered.

Fawn handed him her iPad. "Use this to pull it up. We'll review it—*afterward.*"

Reluctantly, he went into the account. After a few tries, he rightly guessed his sister's password:

LisaSimpson6*

"Um… Sorry but that is too frickin' weird," Fawn muttered.

"Yeah well, it's the cultural icon she most identifies with, plus her favorite number. She once told me the star was her favorite keyboard character," Chuck admitted.

Remembering the same could be said of her own password—Kardashian5\$— Fawn realized she should change it immediately.

Just like that, she had both Chuck's and Charly's passwords. Quickly, she downloaded Charly's DEBATE NOTES file.

Chuck couldn't see it, but while he was admiring Fawn's undulating ass, she'd grabbed the iPad again and had logged back into the McKittridges' iCloud account.

With a click, she deleted all the documents within Charly's DEBATE NOTES file.

Best. Multitasking. Ever.

CHAPTER 25

It was the best of days.

It was the worst of days.

Over the next twelve hours, the day's ecstasies and agonies rose and fell like a seesaw commandeered by two very rambunctious preschoolers.

Miranda's first disappointment was Egan's response to the suggestion that she help him judge Debate Team tryouts.

"To celebrate our coup against Seamus' evil empire," as she put it, Miranda had come bearing gifts: a thermos of Blue Fog coffee and a canister of peanut brittle, which she claimed was her grandmother's recipe.

(In fact, she'd bought it off a clearance shelf at the local Safeway. It was right at its expiration date, but that didn't matter, since she wasn't going to touch it.)

Egan nodded, pleased. "Very kind of you—both the brittle *and* the brew." He opened the thermos and poured a generous portion of its contents into his mug. "But I've had the judges lined up for weeks. Thanks anyway."

"Even so, it would mean so much to me," Miranda purred. "You scratched my back—for Lavinia, I mean. I want to return the favor."

"It's a chore. Trust me. Besides, Cornell and Odette know the ropes already."

"I love learning new tricks, believe me," Her voice was husky with nuance.

By the way his eyes dropped to her breasts, she knew he'd picked up on it. "Look, Miranda…I don't want to step on any toes."

She frowned. "What are you saying?"

"I mean…you and Jess."

Jesus! First Darius, and now Egan?

Who else thinks that slime-bucket and I are an item?

If Lavinia hears rumors…

Miranda shook her head, angrily. "*Jess Smallwood?* Trust me, there's no 'there' there!"

"He seems to think there is," Egan pointed out.

"Well, he's wrong," Miranda insisted.

"Even so, I just don't think we're—"

The buzzing from Miranda's phone cut him short.

Miranda looked at the screen. Clare had texted her:

Jammerhead is here to see you.

Well, whattaya know! Tallulah's husband…

"Must run! Duty calls." She didn't wait for Egan's reply. She'd just have to pray that, by some miracle, at least a few of her new AA clients made the team.

JAMMERHEAD WASN'T WAITING OUTSIDE HER DOOR.

In fact, her door was wide open.

It steamed her to see that he'd made himself comfortable on her office couch.

Not that she could bitch about it to anyone. All of AA's staff was at every parent's beck and call, so why bother?

And besides, here at AA, Jammerhead was royalty.

She knew that because of his touring schedule, he rarely attended school functions. When he did, it was a big deal to the other parents. San Francisco wasn't as star-struck as many other places around the country. At the same time, it wasn't as blasé about its local celebrities as Los Angeles. Having seen the other parents gawking while in his presence, it was apparent to Miranda that old idols die hard. And despite Quest's lackadaisical study habits, she knew some of the parents with sons in the kid's class pushed them to hang out with him.

Miranda's eyes swept over Jammerhead. His black tee shirt hugged him like a second skin. Despite being on the far side of forty, he wore his hair down to his shoulders, as he did, what, twenty years earlier. And those skinny leather pants: had he used a crowbar to get into them?

Admittedly, as a teen, his *Bad Boy* album poster had hung over her bed, stirring up all sorts of fantasies.

And yet, life had not necessarily been kind to him. His face was pocked. He had bags under his eyes. Silver had threaded its way through his frosted locks. The Lycra in his shirt allowed it to cling to his biceps, but it also outlined the hardened pouch that had once been taut abs.

He looks as if he's going to a retro costume party as an aging rock star, she thought.

Playing at it was an apt analogy. Miranda had read somewhere that his last album had barely squeaked into the Top 100. His audiences were aging out. These days when he toured, fans sat in their seats during his new songs. The lighters only came out for the golden oldies, his classic hits.

Soon he'll be like all the other rock burnouts, she thought, *resting on his laurels and nudging his stockbroker for better market calls.*

"What can I do for you, Mr... I'm sorry, is Jammerhead your first name or last?"

"It's my only name. And you can drop the mister."

"I get it. Like Madonna." Miranda grinned slyly. "What can I do for you?"

"Pull another miracle for Quest. Get him into college."

BOOM! Just like that...

Jammerhead leaned in. "I have to be honest. I'm pissed—*outright pissed!*—at the accusation by those trustee board jackasses that it was my kid who was selling coke!"

"Is it perception, or reality?" Miranda challenged.

"What the hell are you trying to say, lady?"

Miranda had every intention of speaking her mind.

The world considers Jammerhead a legend. The city touts him as an honored son. And in the AA universe, he's married to an alumna. But despite his wife's do-gooder intentions for their son, this jerk is just like Seamus and his smug buddies. He thinks he deserves special treatment.

I'll give him the treatment, alright.

Miranda smiled encouragingly. "I'm asking you to look inward and ask yourself: 'Has my public persona given my son the wrong message of what he should be doing with his life?'"

Jammerhead frowned. "We are different people at home. Not freaks. Just everyday folk."

"In other words, you help Quest with his homework. You discuss colleges with him. You push him to raise his GPA, which now stands at..." She turned to her computer and tapped a few keys. Then, grimacing, she murmured, "Yikes!"

"So, um, no to all of the above," he conceded. "Okay, I get it. I'm shit as a parent! But now I want to make good on all that—*for Quest's sake.*" Jammerhead leaped up, pacing the room like a caged animal. "Look, don't get me wrong. Quest is one hell of a good guitarist—amazing, in fact! And he's got a great ear for lyrics too. But the industry is changing. Just to tread water you've got to spend more—and you still make less. Songs are pennies per download. Touring costs are through the roof! If Quest wants to survive, he'll need the business smarts to do it. Granted, it takes the fun out of it. But, shit—that's today's reality in the music business."

So, that's why he's worried, Miranda reasoned. To keep up the appearance of success, people like JammerJerk here run through their money at a quick clip. In case his next album sinks and his life-style burn rate leaves his son with nothing, he wants to make sure the kid can stand on his own two feet.

As if. Quest is clueless.

Miranda nodded sympathetically. "I feel your pain. But if we're going to pull this off, it'll call for some drastic measures. A full-court press!"

She got up, walked around to the front of the desk, and perched on it, crossing her legs demurely. "Recently, I initiated a special counseling program for those who are, um... stressed for help on admissions testing." Noting his interest, she thought it best to lean into the phrase. Quickly, she pulled together its acronym: "Or, as I call it, SHAT."

He guffawed. "'Shat'? What...*themselves?* Over getting into college?"

Miranda frowned at the irony of it. She shrugged. "Sure. I mean, a rose by any other name."

"Would smell *much, much* sweeter!" Jammerhead chortled.

"Yes, well, everything about the program is still in Beta," she huffed. "Rest assured, there is nothing like it anywhere."

"In what way? I mean, you all do the same things: practice tests, academic coaching, blah, blah, blah—"

"That is not *our* approach. I mean, yes, of course, we will offer those methodologies too—well, except for the 'blah blah—'" raising her frosty lips a few millimeters let him know it was a joke—"but we will...how shall I put this? Let me be blunt: we will be *reinventing* the student. *Including his SAT answers.*"

Jammerhead stared blankly at her. "What does that mean exactly?"

"We assess his SAT scores with a tutor—one I've already vetted —who will focus our efforts on correcting Quest's specific test errors. Down to each test answer. Do you understand what I'm saying?"

Just then, a ringtone on Jammerhead's cell phone howled through the room.

Miranda yelped, "What the hell is that?"

Jammerhead tapped a button to stop it. "Sorry! It's a riff from a song I'm working on." He stared down at the screen and grimaced. "Tallulah is texting me."

"Shall we include her in this conversation?"

"Hell, no! She'd hit the roof if she knew!"

"And that doesn't make you opposed to my unorthodox methodology?" Miranda's brow arched.

Jammerhead grimaced. "You're saying some shill will be taking the test for him, right?"

"To be clear, the tutor at my disposal is a very competent and well-proven test taker."

Jammerhead nodded. "Yeah, sure. Whatever it takes."

In your face, Tallulah!

Once again, the ring tone shrieked through the room.

Jammerhead sighed as he tapped it off. "Can you guarantee you can get a student into one of his top five schools?"

"Yes...and one in particular, for sure." She winked slyly. "It just so happens to have a great music program with a dual academic track: Composition and Music Business. And it's in Los Angeles, in fact, so he'll be right in the heart of his chosen industry."

"And which university are we speaking about?"

She reached for a pad and a pen. With a quick almost indecipherable scrawl, she wrote it down and handed it to him. She knew Jammerhead would leap at the opportunity to get his deadbeat spawn into it at any cost.

He peered at the note. His eyes grew large. Grudgingly, he gave a curt nod.

Time to go in for the kill.

Miranda steeled herself by placing both hands flat on her desk as she leaned forward. "Be duly warned, Mr...I mean, just Jammerhead"—the silliness of such a name was cringe-worthy. She shrugged it off with a sigh—"SHAT is exclusively for my concierge clients." She pursed her lips as if warning him not to get his hopes up. "And because it's still in the Beta phase, only a small number of students will be accepted."

"So, what will it take to move my kid to the front of the line?"

Miranda chuckled. "You're a funny one—as is every other parent who is begging for a slot in...*SHAT*."

Note to self: change that damn acronym, SHAT, to something more appealing!

Jammerhead shrugged. "The way these parents jockey over every little thing for their kids? I can only imagine."

"Frankly, I'm at the point where I'll need to hold a lottery to fill the slots equitably."

"How many slots are there?"

"Just, er...six."

"What do you say about making seven your lucky number?" He didn't even wait for her to answer. Instead, he pulled a checkbook from his jacket, scribbled away, then ripped out the check for her to see. "Will this cover it?"

Miranda stared down at it. *Seven hundred thousand dollars? Well, hell yeah!*

She was roused from her stupor by Jammerhead's impatient sigh. "Not enough, eh? Jeez, you people! Okay then, I'll round it up to a mil."

NO SHIT! A million dollars—for his kid's acceptance to some made-up malarkey program...

"Well, …okay." For once, Miranda's deadpan tone was from shock as opposed to disdain.

Not that Jammerhead could tell the difference. "When does he start?"

"During Quest's free period. Have him see me then."

"He'll be there. Or else the Tesla I just ordered for his graduation present is canceled."

Well, that should light a fire under the boy's ass, she thought.

Jammerhead whistled as he went out the door.

A million forking dollars…and from Tallulah's husband no less!

Payback was sweeter than she'd ever imagined.

Shit, she thought. Quest's math grade and his SATs *SUCK!*

I'll be earning every penny of it.

Dammit, maybe I should have asked for more…

The thought peeved her to the point of missing the soft purring of her phone: not her regular cell phone but the one she used to access remote messages for University Prep & Test.

Apparently, it had been buzzing off the hook with calls from desperate Los Angeles-based concierge parents. To a one, their messages said the same thing:

Why has Winslow rescheduled my kid's SAT test?
If we wait any longer, we'll miss the deadline!

What the hell was happening? Where the hell was Winslow?

Miranda was frantic. For the next two hours, she'd had her office door shut so that AA staff and students couldn't hear her assuaging her concierge clients over their distress that their children would miss the testing deadline in between frantic calls to Winslow's private number.

But he wasn't picking up.

Apparently, Winslow had gone AWOL.

Her lie was simple: Winslow had a family emergency. If they insisted that she elaborate, she gave some cock-and-bull story about his father getting run over. "Winslow is devastated," she'd say, faking a sob. "Not to worry, though! We'll call later with an update and a date to reschedule."

Her next course of action was to call every casino between LA and Reno to find him. Winslow always registered under an assumed name: usually the Henry James character named Caspar Goodwood from *Portrait of a Lady.* She knew this because he'd once asked her to cover his marker with a casino by wiring it under that name. "They'll jail me if I don't pay it," he'd pleaded.

At the time, Miranda had no recourse but to follow through.

She was sure he'd have the same excuse this time. She was fed up with it. She'd have to replace him. The sooner the better. Otherwise, the lawsuits would start flying.

If he wasn't already dead in a ditch, she might put him there herself—after the SATs, of course.

Miranda was about to call her eighth casino when she realized Winslow was finally calling back. Immediately, she answered. "Where the hell are you?"

"Macau." The phone connection was awful. He sounded as if he were underwater. "Listen, Miranda, I'm in a jam! I owe these thieves twenty-thou! Do you think you could—"

"Are you crazy? Twenty thousand dollars?"

"Euros, really."

"Jesus, Winslow! …How much is that in dollars?"

"I don't know! And seeing that I've got two goons ready to break my thumbs, I'm currently not at liberty to pull up a currency exchange app! I was about to board an EVA flight back to LAX when they caught me at the airport. I can still make the flight if you send the dough. I've just texted you the bank account number—"

Just then someone rapped on Miranda's door. She stifled the urge to shout, "Get lost!" Instead, she settled for "Enter!" in a tone that gave fair warning of her mood.

Egan stuck his head in the door. "Okay, yeah, I accept your offer," he declared.

Distracted, Miranda frowned. *"What?"*

"What the hell do you mean, 'what'?" Winslow's primal howl roared through her Air Pods. "I told you 'what'! Listen, Miranda— *OW! That hurt, dude!… Seriously, Miranda, I don't have a lot of leeway here! It's dismemberment…or…or worse! Please! Send the money! PLEASE!"*

Egan also assumed she was speaking to him. "Just what you said —you know, about scratching my back? That you want to reciprocate? Metaphorically speaking only, of course." He grinned as if tantalized, if regretful. "Cornell bit into your peanut brittle and broke a tooth. He's already on his way to the dentist. Needless to say, he's ditched on judging Debate Team tryouts this afternoon, so you're up to bat—"

With Winslow blathering in one ear and Egan yammering in the other, the only thing Miranda could think to do was to nod vigorously and exclaim, "Sure! No problem!"

"Thanks! See you after school then. In the auditorium." Egan gave her a thumbs-up, shutting the door behind him.

"*Oh, thank God!*" Winslow was blubbering so hard that Miranda could barely make out what he was saying.

"Don't miss that EVA flight," she hissed. "Or I'll kill you myself!"

The line went dead.

She sighed, checked her text messages, and followed the instructions Winslow had sent.

"Now he's my bitch," she muttered.

Exhausted, she laid her head down on her desk.

Until she heard her phone buzz again.

It was Clare, with another text:

Can you make time for Nira Patel? In lobby now.

Hell yeah, I can. Miranda thought.

Darius was already working his magic.

"So now, what you're saying is if I sign Manya up for your client concierge program, she will be assured entry into one of her dream colleges?"

From the look on Nira Patel's face, Miranda could tell that Manya's mother still couldn't believe her.

She's not leaving this office until she does, Miranda vowed silently.

"Face it, Nira. Getting into a topflight med school is *much* more competitive than when you got into Stanford."

Nira frowned. "I had the second-highest GPA in my high school class. Stanford was lucky to have me."

"You were a product of a *public* school. Had you been at a private prep with much higher standards—say, Ashbury Academy —that may not have been the case. Isn't that why you have Manya here at AA as opposed leaving her in public school—so as not to take any chances in today's competitive environment?"

That same thought must have crossed Nira's mind because she nodded slightly. "But, it's not just the student's grades they take into consideration, is it? Manya has been working as a hospital volunteer since she was fourteen. She has an excellent bedside manner. Her biology grades are exemplary—"

Miranda interjected, "And yet, she has never scored above 1240 on her previous SAT exams. At the same time, if her aim is Yale, Stanford, Georgetown, UCLA, or USC's pre-med programs, she'll be competing with every other applicant of diverse origins. And you know this better than anyone—especially when you toss in the international student applicants."

"Her ethnicity wouldn't—*and shouldn't*—be the only reason for them to consider her," Nira insisted.

"You're right. But, fortunately, putting that card in the deck is what broke the chokehold of all white and all male applicants. And now, by a mere eyelash, women physicians are the majority! That's because of women like you, Nira!"

Nira preened proudly at Miranda's display of sister solidarity.

"All the more reason to make this happen for Manya." Miranda placed both hands on the desk in front of her. "Let me be blunt. College admissions are a cutthroat process. We—Manya, you, and I —can't afford to be timid. When the opportunity presents itself, we should be gaming the system *just like countless others.*"

Reluctantly, Nira nodded. "What do you mean by 'gaming the system?'"

"Like you, I believe Manya is *almost* the complete package: bright, personable, and caring—all of which works in her favor. However, there are some criteria in Manya's application that need to be massaged to make her an even more obvious pick." She walked around to the front of the desk, taking the seat beside Nira. "Our best bet for Manya is raising her SAT score. I can make it happen—and I do, for my concierge clients. Its results are proven.

It guarantees that Manya will attain an SAT score of 1440 or higher."

Nira's eyes brightened at the thought. "How does your concierge program work?"

"As Manya's college admissions counselor, I can position the result of her low SAT score as a learning disability caused by emotional anxiety. It is an accepted prognosis that will enable Manya to take the test away from the school and untimed, with the help of a certified proctor who can explain the questions in a way that lessens her anxiety." Miranda paused to take a deep breath. "However, the program is a bit unorthodox.

"In what way?"

"The proctor will actually be taking the test for her."

Nira said nothing.

Jesus, did I blow this?

Finally Nira whispered, "I understand."

Miranda hid her relief with a stiff nod. "Good! I'll call Manya in for a one-on-one appointment with me so that I can start her assessment immediately. And of course, we'll look at other ways to enhance her application." Miranda gave Nira a reassuring smile. "I've noticed that Manya doesn't partake in sports, music, or drama."

"I've kept her focused strictly on math and science," Nina declared.

"It would help if she broadened her profile in other ways—"

Nira interjected, "She's trying out for Debate Team."

"That's a plus," Miranda assured her. Silently, she cursed Egan for once again stymying her success.

"And…the cost of your program?" Nira pursed her lips.

Miranda hesitated. She remembered what Darius had said to her: that Nira's ex-husband had secured half her earnings as alimony, and that she was still paying off her med school loans.

Even if Manya was on partial scholarship at AA, whatever was left in Nira's paycheck couldn't be much.

Finally, Miranda replied: "Fifty thousand."

Nira dropped her head in defeat. "That's…a little rich for my blood." She stood up to leave.

"Are you on scholarship here?" Miranda asked.

Nira nodded almost shamefully. "I know what you're thinking:

'She can't afford to pay for her daughter's tuition on a doctor's salary?' Sadly, that's my reality." Her head shook with anger. "I've made some mistakes in my life. Despite the lazy oaf I married, Manya wasn't one of them. She was the best thing that ever happened to me." Nira stared defiantly at Miranda. "I've raised her alone. She's seen me work hard. And when she's a doctor, she won't need to rely on…*on anyone.*"

Miranda shrugged. "Look…why don't we say…ten thousand?"

Nira clasped her hands to her cheeks as if she'd won the lottery.

Miranda reached over the top of her desk and plucked a business card from an open box. "Your payment will be made to this non-profit."

"Ah! So it's tax-deductible too!" Nira reached over and hugged her.

Miranda never felt so good.

And so bad.

And so angry with herself for being so foolishly generous.

Miranda closed the door gently behind Nira.

———

It suddenly dawned on her that somewhere between Jammerhead and Winslow and Nira, Egan had popped in to ask her something—

No, to demand something of her—

AS IF!–

And she had stupidly agreed to do so if only to get him out of her hair.

What was it again?…something about…

DEBATE TRYOUTS.

He wants me to help judge them after all!

Two new clients, University Prep & Test crisis averted, and a way to get three of my clients into a great academic extracurricular? It was the BEST of days!

———

Riley tossed his headset onto the desk. "My idol has clay feet," he groaned.

"What do you mean by that?" Lionel asked.

"I grew up listening to Jammerhead," Riley declared. "He was *THE MAN*. Now he's just some anxious *helicopter dad!* How pathetic is that?"

"Snowplow," SallyAnne corrected him. "Helicopter parents hover and nudge their kids. Snowplows actually do the work so that the kids never get a chance to learn from their mistakes."

"Gotcha." Riley saluted her. "Whoever thought that one of the most rebellious teen rockers of our generation would turn out to be such a pussy of a parent—sorry, SallyAnne."

"You're turning into Lionel," she muttered.

Lionel frowned. "Is that a bad thing?"

SallyAnne shrugged. "I...meant it as a compliment."

"Oh, no! The parents are fighting!" Riley put his hands over his ears. "On that note, I'm outta here. When I get home, I'm burning all my old Jammerhead LPs."

"That should cause quite a stink," SallyAnne warned him.

"No more than the bad publicity when Jammerhead makes his perp walk." He waved as he went out the door.

Lionel turned to SallyAnne. "We've confirmed that Winslow made it onto the plane flying out of Macau. The EVA flight makes a stop in Taipei before heading to LAX. It'll be in by five o'clock tomorrow afternoon. We should meet it."

SallyAnne nodded. "Agreed. With all the gambling bridges he's burned, he'll flip like a pancake. We'll get the names of all of Maleficent's clients."

Lionel frowned. "*Who?*"

"That's my new nickname for Miranda. Because she's so evil." SallyAnne shivered. "Just like the evil queen in *Sleeping Beauty.*"

"Oh, I don't know." Lionel shrugged. "She just cut Nira a break on her fee. That wasn't so evil."

SallyAnne snickered. "Yeah, right, keep telling yourself that! Have you forgotten that she's just convinced a single mom who worked her way through medical school to commit fraud?" She stalked the room. "You know, Lionel, if I didn't know better, I'd say you have a blind spot for our suspect!"

"Not everything is black and white," he argued. "And not everyone is all good or all bad."

"You are." SallyAnne could have kicked herself for letting that comment slip out.

"I'm...*what?*"

"You're...all good. Always by the book, I mean." SallyAnne stared down at her feet. "You'd never do anything wrong."

"In other words, I'm predictable," he muttered.

"Yes. But in a *good* way." She picked up her valise. "Unless you let it cloud your judgment."

Like now, she thought.

She could tell he'd read her mind.

Good. Fair warning.

Lionel let her walk out by herself.

CHAPTER 26

"Are you sure the file is gone?" Manya asked Charly.

"Yes, of course, I'm sure!" Charly's heart was palpitating.

"When was the last time you looked at it?" Zina asked.

"I don't know…about three weeks ago?"

Sienna slapped her forehead. "Damn, girl! That was practically when Egan handed out the debate topics!"

"What can I say?" Charly wailed. "I did my arguments really quickly. I wanted to get them out of the way of homework!"

"It's 'out of the way,' alright!" Zina declared. "It is *so* far out of the way that now you can't find the file."

It was lunchtime. The girls were in one of the group study rooms located on the top rotunda of Ashbury Academy's library.

"With Debate Team tryouts today, when and where you going to go over your arguments?" Manya asked.

"Now—and here." Charly shrugged. "I wanted it to be fresh."

"If you can't remember any of your research, it'll be more like improv," Zina muttered.

Charly winced at her friend's chiding.

In truth, she'd been fretting about it all weekend. But between juggling her school reading assignments with the family's Saturday bike excursion and their traditional Sunday gardening and dinner with Lavinia, she hadn't had time to look at it.

These days, Lavinia was uncharacteristically tired. The chuckles brought on by her grandchildren's joshing came a beat later than usual. And while Lavinia had come up with a few quips of her own, her tone was more wistful than lively.

Audrey's tender silence around Lavinia proved she was also concerned.

Last night, the family stayed until almost ten o'clock. When they realized Lavinia's eyes were closing, Charly had an overwhelming desire to linger. "Why don't I stay here tonight?" she pleaded to her grandmother. "Tomorrow morning, we'll walk to school together."

Lavinia shook her head. "The minute you leave, I'm going straight to bed." She tweaked Charly's nose. "You'd be bored watching me sleep."

Charly had reasoned she'd have plenty of time during lunch break to study the arguments she'd prepared. Now, to find the digital folder empty, she felt like crying.

I'm so stupid! I should have opened it long before now!

Where could those darned files have gone?

Sienna plopped down in front of Charly's laptop. "Maybe it's still retrievable. Let me take a look."

Charly buried her head in her hands. "Be my guest."

Sienna clicked some buttons. A moment later, she asked, "Hey, um…have you accessed the file from anywhere other than your home or the school's IP addresses?"

"What the hell is an IP address?" Zina asked.

"Every computer has one," Sienna explained. "It identifies the computer, its location and the service provider that it uses for its web access."

"Do you think I was hacked?" Charly asked.

"From what I can tell, yes." Sienna frowned. "I've got an Instagram fan who's a white hat hacker. I'll ask her to look at your browsing history to see if my guess is right."

"In the meantime, we should get cracking on recovering as much of your research as possible so that you can rebuild your arguments," Manya said. "What topics did you choose?"

"Human cloning and illegal immigration," Charly replied. "How about you?"

"I chose hook-ups and the death penalty," Zina said.

"I've got the death penalty and human cloning," Sienna added.

"For me, it's illegal immigration and hook-ups," Manya replied. "My mom almost had a cow when Miranda told her I'd chosen the last one."

The other girls snickered.

"Miranda is critiquing your debate?" Charly asked.

Manya nodded.

"Mine too," Zina added.

"That's nice of her," Charly murmured.

"Okay, so Charly, since I chose human cloning too, why don't you and I do the research on that?" Sienna suggested. "And since Manya has already researched immigration, she and Zina can research that topic. We'll have to leave after the lunch break, though. Charly, what do you have after lunch?"

"Odette, for French IV," Charly replied.

"Skip her class. I'll tell her your PMSing," Manya promised. "She'll understand."

"Hey, the research will go a lot faster if you check your browsing history from three weeks ago," Zina suggested. "Split up the links between us and we can pull them up and make PDFs for you."

"Brilliant!" Charly exclaimed.

The girls high-fived.

By the end of the lunch hour, they'd cobbled enough research on Charly's topics for her to make her arguments again.

"You're the best friends in the world," Charly declared.

"Don't get all sappy on us," Sienna warned her. "You can't afford to short out your computer with tears. Now, write your arguments and make us proud!"

She still got a peck on the cheek from Charly.

So did the other girls.

"So, TELL ME HOW THIS WORKS EXACTLY," MIRANDA COOED TO EGAN.

She flirting with me again, he realized. I wish…Nah. I can't.

He knew he was a fool to still be hung up on Audrey.

Miranda's come-on was appreciated nonetheless.

Because of the number of contestants, Egan had to change his grading system somewhat to choose the top eight who would make up the team.

"It's simple," Egan replied to Odette and Miranda. "We have about eighty or so contestants out there. You're to grade them on a scale of one to ten, on three criteria. Category One is organization and clarity. Category Two is argument support. And Category Three is cross-examination and rebuttal. This allows for a high score of thirty. That would make ninety a perfect score from all three judges."

"Easy-peasy," Miranda purred.

"I hope so," Egan admitted. He handed both women the pamphlet listing the four questions:

- *Is the current approach to illegal immigration too harsh or too lenient?*
- *Are there ramifications for teens in the "hook-up culture," and if so, are they emotionally or physically harmful?*
- *Does the death penalty constitute a cruel and unusual punishment?*
- *Should scientists be allowed to clone humans?*

"Each student was asked to choose two of these questions for debate," he continued. "The students are waiting for us now, in the main auditorium. They've divided themselves into four groups: one for each question they wish to debate first. They'll be called into this room randomly, two by two, prepared to present both sides of the argument, which will be determined by the flip of a coin."

"Got it," Odette said.

"Don't score brutally, but do score fairly," Egan insisted. "And *please! No playing favorites.*"

Odette rolled her eyes.

Miranda chuckled. "I'm too new here to have any favorites. I guess you could say that too, Egan."

Except, perhaps Audrey's kids…

She'd be watching to see how high he scored Chuck and Charly.

It's so obvious that he's still got a thing for that nitwit, Miranda fumed silently.

The way he had pointedly teased her about Jess, she wondered if he'd be wondering the same about her regarding Hugo.

Over the past couple of weeks, she'd already had two "tutoring" sessions with Hugo. From his broad wink, she'd quickly and angrily deduced that his loudmouth father had let him in on her scheme. "Anything to get me on a fat-cat campus," Hugo crowed. "Somewhere I can *really* clean up."

Miranda had made Hugo write a few test essays. She then placed all the writing samples in the University Test & Prep iCloud account. There, Winslow could access them. He'd copy the handwriting samples for the tests that would eventually be sent to the SAT's grading division.

She'd done the same with Manya, Quest, and Zina, all of whom were clueless as to how far Miranda's handholding would go on their behalf.

And all the more reason that, no matter how badly they choked on their debate arguments, they'd receive the highest grades possible from her.

CHARLY'S HEART LEAPED IN HER THROAT WHEN SHE SAW HOW MANY others had shown up for Debate Team tryouts.

There must be seventy, maybe eighty, other students milling around, she realized. It's practically half of the senior class and at least a quarter of the junior class.

As Charly signed in, a student volunteer asked her to write her name on two cardboard disks and place them in the bowls designated by the name of the argument topics she'd chosen.

She winced when she saw Quest sitting with Sienna, who, like Charly, had chosen "Immigration Arguments" as her first debate question. The competition was going to be stiff. She loved him as a brother. She didn't want to see his heart broken by a low score.

Zina and Manya waved at her from across the auditorium. They were sitting in the "Death Penalty Arguments" section.

Charly was dismayed to see that Chuck and Fawn were also sitting in the Immigration Arguments section. Fawn was practically sitting in his lap. Charly waved at her brother, but he barely nodded back. Since the argument at dinner two weeks ago, they'd scarcely said two words to each other.

If I make the team and he doesn't, he may not speak to me all year.

The thought saddened her.

Egan came out to say a few words. After thanking everyone for being there, he added, "As you read in the pamphlet, each round should take five minutes. If you win your first round, you move onto the second. If you don't, you've been eliminated."

The contestants grimaced.

"The top eight scorers make up the team. If there are ties for eighth place, the lowest-scoring contestants will be asked to face off with their second argument. Got that?"

This time, the contestants nodded.

"We'll start with the topic of immigration. To compete, two names in that bowl will be chosen randomly. We'll keep drawing until there aren't any more competitors. At that point, we'll move onto a different topic, then another, and finally the last one," Egan explained. "When you hear your name called, walk to the front table again. There, you'll pick from the bowl holding a pro and con disk." He clapped his hands. "Okay, the first category is 'Immigration." He reached down into the bowl and called the first two names.

SIENNA WAS CALLED BEFORE CHARLY, IN THE THIRD IMMIGRATION argument team. She drew the pro argument.

When she came out, she was smiling and gave Charly a thumbs up. She had her arm around her opponent, a senior girl, who was in tears.

Fawn was also called before Charly. She showed her triumph with a happy dance that caused her opponent to storm out of the auditorium.

Charly's name was the first one called for the eleventh pairing. When she stood up, Sienna whispered, "Break a leg!"

Quest was too nervous to say anything. When Charly patted his shoulder, he said, "I'm just glad I didn't have to debate you!"

Me too, Charly thought, as she headed down the bleachers to the front table.

Hearing the next name—"Chuck McKittridge"—stopped her in her tracks.

Chuck froze too.

Instinctively, the twins' eyes went to each other.

Their stares reflected their sadness at this anomaly.

Chuck pulled the pro disk, leaving Charly with the con argument.

Following the lead of the other contestants, they shook hands before entering the judges' room.

CHUCK IS MAKING MY PRO ARGUMENT.

The thought that her own brother stole her debate files felt like a punch to Charly's gut.

She forced herself to stay calm as he spoke her previously planned lines verbatim. He'd always been great at rote memorization.

He'd make a great actor, she thought, or a thief. He's well on his way to being either or both.

When it was her turn, she kept one thought in front of her:

I won't let Chuck rob me of my place on the team.

It drove her to make eye contact while making her opening remarks.

It gave clarity to the critical points in her argument.

She closed with an eloquence she never knew she had.

From the look on Egan's face, she could tell she'd wowed him.

From Odette's smile, she could see her French teacher was proud of her.

Miranda was smiling, too—also a good sign.

Chuck wasn't. He looked worried.

Good, thought Charly. That will teach you never to screw me over again.

WHEN CHUCK AND CHARLY WALKED INTO THE ROOM, MIRANDA HAD almost crowed at the situation before her:

The chance to make Audrey's life miserable, even in this small way.

With that in mind, Chuck got tens in all three categories.

On the other hand, she graded Charly with a six, a five, and a four.

Seeing her score sheet, Egan did a double-take. He whispered, "Wow! Don't you feel you graded Charly pretty harshly?"

Miranda shrugged. "She seemed too...I don't know, practiced, or something."

By Egan's frown, she knew he wasn't buying her answer.

Miranda was chagrined when Charly's overall score came in at seventy-five. That meant Egan and Odette had given her tens across the board.

She was dismayed when Chuck's score came in precisely the same.

"What do we do when there's a tie?" Odette asked.

"Both contestants are allowed to go through," Miranda muttered. She remembered this from past experience.

Egan looked sharply at her. "Yes! How did you know that?"

"Lucky guess," she replied.

⁂

CHUCK AND CHARLY WERE RELIEVED TO KNOW THEY'D AT LEAST MADE it into consideration. But both were thinking the same thing:

Is my score high enough to make the team?

The rest of the afternoon was just as dramatic.

The good news was that Manya and Zina also won their debates.

Even better, albeit surprising, was that Quest had as well.

But the best news of all was that Sienna, Manya, Zina, and even Quest had all made the team.

Surprisingly, so had Hugo Smallwood and Fawn.

When the eight top scores were called, Charly and Chuck were on the team—if barely.

"Gee," Quest exclaimed to Charly. "How did I score better than you?"

It was a great question.

Chuck walked over to his sister. Fawn was wrapped around him.

He looks as if he's being squeezed by a boa constrictor, Charly thought.

"Hey, looks like we're going to be teammates," Chuck declared.

"You sound as if you're proud of that," Charly retorted.

Chuck frowned. "Why shouldn't I be?"

"*Really?* You're proud of stealing my research and my arguments?" Charly poked his chest with her finger.

"I...we ...didn't steal anything!" The color went out of Chuck's face. "Did we?"

"*We?*" Charly looked from Chuck to Fawn and back again. "Why are you asking her?"

The smirk on Fawn's face told Charly all she needed to know.

Fawn clicked her tongue. "I heard in French class that you were feeling a little under the weather. Instead of taking it out on your brother, take a Midol or something."

To keep his sister from clawing out his girlfriend's eyes, Chuck leaped between them. As he hustled Fawn out of the auditorium, he looked back at Charly.

He's a clueless idiot.

Charly waited until everyone left the auditorium before going back into the judge's room. The score sheets were still on the table.

Miranda's scores were what had brought her down.

Ironically, Egan and Odette's scores for Chuck had pulled him even with her.

Fawn had only scored a point higher than the twins, as had Hugo. Again, Miranda had championed them with the highest scores possible.

Charly stuck the sheets into her backpack.

Then she changed her iCloud password.

CHAPTER 27

"What do you mean, Winslow Jennings wasn't on the flight?" Melamed was practically bellowing into Sally-Anne's phone.

She moved the phone away from her ear. Lionel winced when he heard their boss too.

They'd delivered the news while standing in an alcove off of LAX's international concourse.

Finally, when they could tell he'd quit talking, she replied, "He was booked through to Los Angeles, but he must have gotten off in Shanghai."

Lionel indicated for SallyAnne to put the phone on speaker. When Melamed's cursing subsided over this new bit of information, Lionel suggested, "We can put a tracer on his passport."

"He could be anywhere in the world," Melamed grumbled. "So, yeah, do that. It's not like we have a choice. When it comes to Miranda D'Arcy, he knows where all the bodies are buried."

"Don't we have enough to take her down now?" SallyAnne asked. "She's lining up new clients every day!"

"This is much bigger than just her college admissions fraud. She's a guppy, and there are bigger fish to fry," Melamed countered.

"You mean Darius Calder," Lionel deduced.

"You betcha. We have to keep her in play at least until she's delivered for him, not to mention the others," Melamed explained.

"Once we have him dead to rights, he'll flip on a few of his clients to lessen his own sentence." He rang off.

SallyAnne turned to Lionel. "In other words, we can't make any arrests until after her clients get their acceptance letters?"

He nodded. "Frankly, it may make sense. Once they accept the offers, it goes from being conspiracy-to-commit to a lock-solid fraud case. To pull off a scam like this, Miranda must have a number of co-conspirators on the college campuses. We'll need the extra time to round them up." Lionel looked at his watch. "If we hit the United terminal now, we can stand by for the SFO flight. It leaves in about an hour—if air traffic delays don't stretch it even longer."

SallyAnne nodded. "Sure, let's do it."

The memory of their last LA trip was still fresh in her mind. She wondered how he'd feel about a game of Never Have I Ever as they waited to board their flight.

She never imagined he was thinking the same thing.

What the hell is all that banging?

Miranda woke with a start.

Glancing at her clock, she saw it was only three o'clock in the morning. She was sorely tempted to ignore the pounding, but her gut told her she shouldn't.

Slowly, she got out of bed. Wrapping her bathrobe around her, she walked to her front door and looked out the peephole.

Winslow was standing in the hallway.

Before the racket woke her neighbors too, Miranda threw open the door.

"Why aren't you answering your phone?" he hissed.

"Because I turn it off at night!" Miranda sputtered. "What the hell are you doing here?"

"I came to warn you!" he hissed. "Something is fishy at the UP&T office. I've got a couple of hidden cameras in there and around the place—"

"You do?" Miranda was livid. "And you never told me?"

"It's insurance, trust me," he declared.

"Insurance against what?" Miranda asked. "Have you been recording me and our conversations?"

"No!... Okay, *yes*—but that goes with the territory." Winslow shrugged.

"What, you don't trust me?"

He snickered. "Tell the truth. Do you trust *me*?"

"You have a point there," she muttered. Suddenly, she was angry she hadn't thought of surveillance herself. "So what did you see that has you so concerned?"

"I had a stopover in Shanghai, so I thought I'd kill time by scanning the surveillance footage. It's a good thing I did, too. Someone was staking out the joint."

From his cell phone, he showed her some of the footage: a man and a woman, in suits, knocking on University Prep & Test's office door. After doing so several times and getting no answer, they hung out in the hall—for a long, long, time.

Three days, in fact.

"Wow! Talk about a couple of desperate parents," Miranda murmured.

"I thought so too—at first. But then I realized they could be a couple of goons from... I don't know, one of the casinos."

"Jesus! Did you get caught again, counting cards?"

"It's an occupational hazard—like broken legs." Winslow shrugged. "Listen, Miranda, what I'm trying to say is that, for whatever reason, UP&T is too hot right now for either of us to go back there."

Miranda took a closer look. "They don't look like mobsters."

"Don't be an idiot. These days, most of the casinos hire ex-cops. Not only do they know how to play rough, many of them still use their law enforcement connections to track down the bad bets." Winslow frowned. "In case they were tracking my passport, I ditched it in the Shanghai airport men's room."

"How did you get back into the states?"

He rolled his eyes. "What...you think I travel with only one?"

She jabbed him in the chest with a finger. "I've got *you* to thank for this! What the hell am I going to do with all the parents who've already paid me to get their kids into the college of their choice?" She paced the floor. "You'll have to set up shop somewhere else. Maybe Brentwood—"

"Are you kidding me?" Winslow snorted with laughter. "If they've already paid up, what do *you* care? Do you think they're going to run to the cops and say, 'Woe is me, I gave a crook a ton of money because she promised to illegally get my kid into some college, and now she's disappeared off the face of the earth'?"

"You're right!" Her eyes glistened at the thought of her great fortune. Her clients had already paid upfront. They couldn't implicate her without taking themselves down too.

"You should set up here instead," Miranda insisted. "I've already secured several new clients—"

He frowned. "To hell with that! You're on your own, lady. I'm plowing new pastures."

"But—you can't leave me, just like that…without notice!"

Winslow stared at her as if she'd lost her mind. He laughed all the way down the hall.

CHAPTER 28

"I'm sorry…what was that again?" Lavinia looked at Daniel, and then at Seamus.

The November board meeting was not going well. From what Egan could tell, Lavinia's mind was elsewhere.

If Harris hadn't been stuck in DC, she might have seemed more like her usual self, he reasoned. Seamus seemed to try harder to be an obnoxious prick when the congressman wasn't there to protect her.

Thank goodness for Daniel and me, Egan thought.

He was surprised, though, that Daniel hadn't noticed this too. Some of the other teachers were picking up on it. Egan could tell by the way they exchanged concerned glances when her thoughts drifted off mid-sentence.

And yet, no one said anything.

Were they afraid of seeming disloyal? Or, like him, did they prefer to be in denial of what was happening to the school's beloved headmistress?

Egan was tempted to divulge Audrey's promise to Lavinia and Daniel, but then he thought better of it. Audrey's trust in him was one of the few reasons for what little pride he had these days.

"We were arguing over Tallulah's budget for the damn anniversary gala," Seamus grumbled. "I told her that if she wanted to cut corners, instead of doing away with the ice sculptures, we should hire some of the scholarship kids as waiters. That way, the rest of us can see them earning their keep."

Lavinia blanched at the thought. Turning to Daniel, she murmured, "And you agreed to that?"

"No! Of course not!" Perplexed that she'd even think such a thing, he shook his head. "Since this has devolved into a discussion over ice sculptures and yet one more way in which we can shame our scholarship students, I'd like to call for an adjournment."

"I second that motion," Tallulah declared. "But first let me add that we've already promised *every* student a free ticket to the gala anyway—even our scholarship students. So, if any parents wish to volunteer as cater-waiters to defray costs, I'm sure everyone would appreciate it."

She stood up and stomped off.

Bliss was right on her heels.

"Well, that went well," Jess murmured. He looked around the table, but his gaze froze on Miranda. "Anyone up for a drink?"

Egan grimaced. But, yes, he was curious if Miranda would take Jess up on his offer.

He was surprised when she feigned a yawn. "Not for me, thank you. It's been a long day and an even longer night." Miranda stood up but was taking her time gathering her things.

Chagrinned, Jess walked out with Seamus, Warner, and Darius.

"I, um, should go too. It's been a very long day." Lavinia murmured. As she lumbered to her feet, Daniel reached over to steady her.

"Would you like a lift home?" he asked her gently.

Lavinia managed a chuckle. "Of course not, dear. I'm practically around the corner. But thank you for the offer." She pecked him on the cheek and waved to the others as she walked off.

Egan was going to ask Daniel if he'd like to stop off for a beer when he realized Miranda was whispering something in Daniel's ear. He pretended not to notice when Daniel nodded to whatever she was saying, or that they walked out together.

By the time Egan made it outside, Daniel was already driving off.

Miranda was in the car with him.

"I appreciate you giving me a lift." Miranda shifted so that she was angled closer to Daniel. "I'd forgotten how long these meetings can run! Otherwise, I would have never left my car with the mechanic today. He closes at six on the button."

The truth was she had Ubered to work and could have Ubered back home too. She knew Daniel was too polite to turn down her request for a lift.

To accomplish her next goal, she needed Daniel on her side.

"No problem," he assured her. "You're close enough to us—the Summit, right? On Russian Hill?"

She nodded. "Hey, I want to thank you again for your diplomacy with Lavinia about my addition to the board. I'd hoped she would approve."

Daniel grimaced. "She proved it with her own vote, wouldn't you say?"

"I'll always appreciate her vote of confidence." Miranda faked the emotional quiver in her voice. "Which is why I'm finding it very hard to bring this up."

Daniel glanced over at her. "Is something wrong?"

"Frankly, I was hoping you'd tell me." She sighed. "I've noticed some odd behavior from Lavinia."

"Like what?" Daniel's question was stilted.

"I can't put my finger on it, exactly. She seems tired. And then there's the weight loss—not that it should be an issue! Heaven knows we could all afford to lose a few pounds." She paused: "I guess it's the forgetfulness that is the most concerning. I'm just wondering…is there something I should know?"

Daniel shook his head. "I'm sure it's just the stress over AA's twenty-fifth anniversary events."

Miranda laid her hand on Daniel's shoulder. "I'm here for her. I hope you know that, Daniel. That being said, if there is any way you feel I can help—you know, to make things easier for her…or for the good of the school…" She let her fingers linger.

Until Daniel veered the car to the curb, at which point both hands went to the dashboard to brace herself. "We're here. Let me get the door for you."

Before she knew what was happening, he was out of his side of the car and beside hers. He opened the passenger door.

"You're such a gentleman," she muttered.

"Yes, I am," he said crisply. "Look, Miranda, if your questions are at Seamus' bidding, please make it clear to him that Lavinia is fine. She'd probably seem less haggard if, like most heads of school, she had a trustee board that did their best to support her as opposed to tear down what she has spent a lifetime building."

So that she took his hint the conversation was over, he drove off without saying goodnight.

———

Daniel waited until he and Audrey were in bed to say, "Lavinia was odd tonight."

Usually, Audrey's concern would cause her to flip on the light. Instead, she murmured, "In what way?"

"She was listless. Tired. Forgetful. Surely you've noticed her weight loss!"

"Yes, I asked her about it," Audrey's tone was casual enough. "Lavinia told me she's on a new diet. Apparently, it's working."

"Too well! Maybe she's not getting—oh, I don't know—enough nutrients or something!" Because Audrey hadn't flipped on her light, he turned on the one on his bedside table. "Honey, I'll be honest—*I'm worried about her.*"

Audrey didn't turn around. Instead, she said, "People change as they get older. I'm sure she's fine!"

Look me in the face and tell me that, he thought.

Instead, he turned off his light.

A few minutes later, Audrey turned over so that she could spoon him, wrapping her arms around his chest.

When he pulled her in even closer, he felt the dampness of her cheeks on his back.

If anything were wrong with Lavinia, she'd tell me, he reasoned.

As Daniel drifted off to sleep, he chided himself for making her worry; for causing her to cry.

That Miranda is such a bitch.

CHAPTER 29

*A*udrey hadn't realized how hard it would be to juggle three bags of groceries on her bicycle, even while going the short distance of the few blocks between the Haight Fillmore Whole Foods and Lavinia's cottage.

It was a week's worth of food for her mother. Audrey had also purchased the ingredients needed to prepare the meal Lavinia usually made every Sunday: pasta, an artisan bread, and peppermint ice cream, along with a salad from her garden bounty.

The family wouldn't know that it was Audrey's handiwork.

Before her illness, Lavinia had always made her own pasta and bread. But the effects of her chemotherapy put an end to that.

It was a bright, cool Saturday morning in mid-October. As always, Daniel and the children had biked over the Golden Gate Bridge, where they'd spend the day trekking over Mount Tam's many dusty trails.

Since learning of her mother's illness, Audrey's Saturdays were now spent with Lavinia. She wondered how many more they'd share.

Audrey carried the heavy bags onto the porch. The front door was locked, so she rang the doorbell, then waited nearly a minute before ringing it again.

Silence.

By balancing the grocery bags between the door and her hip, Audrey used her key to unlock the door and then slowly opened it.

She called out to her mother.

Again, no answer.

Not surprising. Lately, her mother's energy had been so low that Lavinia had taken to sleeping on the back sunporch or lounging in the backyard.

Instead, Audrey found her mother comatose on the kitchen floor.

She dropped the groceries. She didn't care that the eggs cracked and a jar of olive oil broke. All that mattered was that Lavinia still had a pulse despite not responding to Audrey's attempt to revive her.

When Audrey's hysteria finally subsided, the 911 operator was able to get her to verify Lavinia's address and answer a few questions about her mother's condition,

While they waited for the ambulance, Audrey patted her mother's face and arms. She ran to her mother's bedroom for a pillow and blanket with the thought of putting the former under her head for comfort and the latter to put over her body for warmth, but then she worried that perhaps it would have the opposite effect. Would the pillow angle her head in such a way that it would block her windpipe? Would the blanket make Lavinia so hot as to set off cardiac arrest?

Finally, Audrey heard the ambulance's wail. She ran to the door, flung it open, and waved the med techs into the house.

Lavinia moaned as they strapped her onto the gurney.

Audrey insisted on riding with her mother. She didn't want to navigate the city's busy streets and hills on her bike, and she didn't want to spend precious time looking for Lavinia's car keys.

It may have seemed as if it took the ambulance an hour to get there, but when it reached the hospital, Audrey realized it wasn't even lunchtime yet.

DOCTOR VIOLET JIMENEZ'S RESPONSE TO WHY HER MOTHER HAD reacted so violently to her chemotherapy left Audrey reeling: "I'd warned her that no two patients respond exactly in the same way to their specific cocktail."

"So you stopped her chemo?"

"No," Doctor Jimenez explained. "But we have had to change her regimen and attempt more aggressive treatment. As you can see by today's development, Lavinia's response to this change in protocol has not been good."

"My mother never told me any of this!" Audrey exclaimed.

The knot in her throat made it impossible for Audrey to continue asking questions. She knew from the beginning that Lavinia might not make it through her illness, but for the first time she felt the cold reality of living the rest of her life without her mother's love to buoy her.

Sensing her dismay, Dr. Jimenez took Audrey's hand. "Your mother has a lot of fight in her. We're going to do all we can to help her get through this. We'll keep her here overnight, for observation. Leave your number with the nurse, and you'll be called with a time to pick her up tomorrow."

"Thank you, doctor," Audrey whispered.

Audrey stared down at Lavinia. Despite the tubes tethered to her at one end and the monitors at the other, she looked peaceful.

Audrey closed her eyes for a bit. When she opened them again, she found her mother gazing at her.

Lavinia's lips were parched, and her eyes were damp. "So…you know?"

Audrey nodded. "I wish you'd told me your treatment wasn't going as well as you had hoped."

"Several times this past week, I was on the verge of telling you. But I couldn't bear the thought of causing you more worry."

Audrey wanted to cry, but she couldn't.

Not in front of Lavinia.

She saw her mother as never before: vulnerable.

Lavinia closed her eyes again.

For the next two hours, Audrey listened:

As the monitors chirped softly like crickets.

To her mother's gentle breathing.

To her own pounding heart.

Every half hour, a nurse would stop by the room to get a monitor reading or to write something on the chart at the foot of Lavinia's bed. Audrey finally dared to ask, "What is in the drip?"

"A little something to help with her pain, but mostly it's fluid to keep her hydrated," the nurse answered.

After the woman left, Audrey heard Lavinia say something, but it didn't make sense.

Audrey wondered if what was pouring into her mother's arm might act like a truth serum. If so, maybe now she'd get the answer to the one question she hadn't asked her mother since she was old enough to understand that it was something Lavinia felt, for whatever reason, should die with her.

But no, Lavinia. I need to know. And I want to hear it from you.

She took a deep breath. Then, softly she asked: "Lavinia, who is my father?"

Lavinia answered her with a gentle snore.

Audrey kissed her mother's cool forehead and left the room.

SHE TOOK A CAB BACK TO LAVINIA'S HOUSE SO THAT SHE COULD CLEAN up the mess in the kitchen.

The melted ice cream, the carton of broken eggs, the olive oil, and the now soggy loaf of artisan rye created a surreal, colorful tableau: pink, brown, and yellow goo on a black and white checkerboard floor.

It took half a roll of paper towels to sop it all up. Then Audrey mopped the floor. When she finished, there were no remnants of the sticky, smelly concoction. But Audrey wouldn't need to smell it to remember this day.

The sight of Lavinia, lying on the floor so helplessly, would stay with her forever.

WHEN AUDREY GOT HOME, DANIEL WAS ALREADY THERE. NOTICING how she looked around, he read her mind. "The kids walked down to Fillmore Street for sushi and ice cream. They were famished. Did you have a good day?"

How could she answer? Was this the time for yet another lie?

Or, should she tell the truth—and in doing so, break her promise to Lavinia?

Audrey said nothing.

Instead, she grabbed Daniel's arm and led him, running, upstairs to their bedroom, shutting the door behind them.

Slowly, she undressed him and watched his face intently as he did the same to her.

They made love silently. She let her mouth and her fingers and her sighs tell him all he needed to know:

She never wanted to lose him.

She *could not* lose him too.

CHAPTER 30

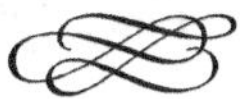

*A*shbury Academy's second debate, against University High School, was to take place on Wednesday.

And after handily defeating Marin Academy, the team was pumped for another win.

Well, most of the team, anyway.

To Chuck's eye, Manya, Zina, Charly, and Sienna worked together like a well-oiled machine. Even Quest—who would do anything Charly asked of him—proved to be a whiz at finding the necessary research on the four topics to be debated:

Should jobs be subcontracted into developing countries?
Do celebrities get away with more crimes than non-celebrities?
Is it appropriate for adolescents to be sentenced to life without
  parole?
Should more people choose adoption as opposed to having biological
  children?

Quest's research was then passed forward to Charly and her pals. Their tasks were to extract the relevant information that would best help the team form their own pro and con arguments, along with the necessary rebuttals.

Like Chuck, Fawn was watching the process from the sidelines.

"Call me when you have my argument written," she chided callously.

"You're supposed to write your own arguments," Charly argued.

Fawn snickered. "Why should I do that when you'll do it so much better?"

"It's why you supposedly made the team," Charly retorted. "Oh, wait…you're right! The only reason you're here is that *you and my brother stole my arguments!*" She glared at the two culprits.

Chuck felt his face heat up.

He was determined to succeed and prove Daniel wrong: that he could in fact manage basketball and Debate Team with equal skill.

But Fawn had put him in an awkward position. He'd only hacked Charly's debate argument folder at her insistence.

Okay, granted, it was much easier to memorize her argument than to build one from scratch. And he genuinely thought no one would find out.

Except Charly did. Up against Chuck, his sister had heard her hard work repeated verbatim.

This one act of thievery had severed their relationship. Charly no longer adored him.

In fact, she now ignored him entirely.

Oddly, Charly hadn't yet told their parents. Was it because she thought they wouldn't believe her? Chuck couldn't imagine it was because she was protecting him.

Because Charly had stated her accusation against Fawn loudly enough, Egan stopped mid-conversation with Manya to ask, "Charly—what did you say?"

Charly shrugged. "I think Fawn can explain it better." She nudged Fawn with her elbow—*hard.* "Go ahead."

"I was just saying that I thought it would be better for the team if those who were more adept at writing arguments could do it for those who weren't," Fawn huffed.

"And I told her that wasn't fair," Charly countered. "I mean, supposedly, that's why we're all here in the first place. We beat out others who actually took the time to create their own arguments."

"I've seen it work both ways," Egan admitted.

"See? Egan says it's best for the team!" This time Fawn nudged Charly—hard enough that Charly stumbled.

"That's not what I said at all," Egan countered. "In fact, Debate

Team is supposed to help you look at both sides of a situation. If all you're doing is memorizing someone else's argument, it defeats the purpose."

"Is that so?" Charly pushed Fawn so hard that she stumbled forward.

Fawn shoved back.

Charly slapped her.

Everyone gasped.

Except for Hugo, who crowed, "Catfight! *Meow!*"

Enraged, Fawn's fist went for Charly's nose.

Chuck stopped it by grabbing it with his hand. When it slammed into his open palm, he yelped from the pain.

"You three!" Egan growled. "In the hall with me—*Now!*"

"OKAY, WHO WANTS TO START?" EGAN WAS DOING HIS BEST TO STAY calm. The last thing he needed was for Lavinia to find out that her grandchildren were at each other's throats, thanks to Seamus's evil spawn.

The teens eyed each other warily.

Charly shrugged. "The team should vote as to whether it's necessary to carry those members who won't do their own research, let alone write their own arguments."

Fawn scowled at her.

When she balled her fists, Chuck moved between them again. "Charly is right. We're not all pulling our weight equally."

Fawn glowered at his betrayal.

"But we're all proud to be on the team, so those of us who are holding the others back will just need to try harder," Chuck continued. "That won't necessarily make us a winning team, but it will teach us some important lessons about ourselves—and each other, if we're willing to share what we've learned." He looked from one of the girls to the other. "I'm willing to work harder. And if others need my help, I'm there for them too."

Jesus, Egan thought. This kid sounds as if he's running for class president or something!

Egan nodded. "Okay, sure, with one caveat. Those who do research for others get help on their arguments. And for that matter, the whole team critiques all arguments. That way, building the strongest argument will be a team effort."

Charly, Chuck, and Fawn shrugged in agreement.

"Chuck, why don't you explain it to the others?" Egan suggested.

Chuck nodded enthusiastically—but then replied, "I'd rather Charly tell them. She's sort of the team leader anyway."

Charly's eyes grew large.

"Sure, works for me," Egan said. "But just a heads up. I'll be choosing the team's captain—and it will be someone who demonstrates leadership and fairness. If you want to be in the running—and I'd imagine you all do, considering how it would look on your college applications—start acting the part. *Capisce?*"

To make his point, he looked each of them in the eye.

As Egan watched them trek back inside, he wondered what had precipitated Chuck's peace offering to his sister.

For a brief moment, he felt such tremendous pride in both of them.

I guess this is what it's like to be a parent.

In good times, anyway.

No one expected the debate between Ashbury Academy and University High to be such a nail biter.

Certainly not Miranda.

AA was the home team. The audience reflected this: not just in the number of students and teachers present, but parents too.

Including Jess. As always, he'd somehow seen Miranda before she had a chance to see him first and hide.

"Hey, my kid did okay, right?" he exclaimed.

"A chip off the old block," Miranda cooed.

Far be it from her to point out that Hugo's score was the lowest on AA's team. But now that she'd burned her bridges in the Southland, it was essential to keep every San Francisco-based parent in play.

After this year, I can retire, she reasoned. No more lazy kids to coddle. No more sucking up to their snotty over-privileged parents.

After Winslow's visit, Miranda had checked out countries that didn't have an extradition treaty with the US. None of them were appealing. Ruling out war zones like Afghanistan or Third World countries like the Congo, she was left with a few European dictatorships or some Middle Eastern monarchies in which the *couture du jour* began and ended with whatever color burka was in season.

Thank you, but no thank you.

Until then, she'd continue to build her war chest.

With that in mind, she scanned the seats for her next victim.

Seamus was there with Gretchen. *They have me to thank for Fawn's inclusion on the team,* Miranda thought. *I'll be sure to let him know that.*

Gemma and Darius were also there, as were Bliss and Raffaele; and Tallulah and Jammerhead. To the crowd's delight, even the infamous Maggie Wishart had made an appearance.

Quest's family is just thrilled to see him on any stage, even if it's to stutter through a debate, Miranda reasoned.

Daniel was there too, with their youngest—the boy, Noah. They sat on either side of Lavinia. Blissfully, she held both their hands in her lap.

So, where was Audrey?

Miranda didn't have to look far. As she suspected, Audrey was standing next to Egan. Although they were looking at the stage, their heads were tilted toward each other as they exchanged comments.

He's still in love with her, Miranda realized.

The thought enraged her.

I have to kill his obsession with Audrey.

To do that, I'll have to make him fall in love with me.

Once, a long time ago, the idea of inciting Egan's lust had held some appeal, if only as a means to an end.

But now it merely seemed vile. Miranda's hatred for Egan went back to the day she'd learned how he'd successfully sabotaged her admission to Berkeley by writing a letter of recommendation that was anything but that.

And yet, were he to fall for her, Miranda would then have the votes she needed for her endgame: control of the trustee board, which was necessary if, sometime in the future, she needed to make a clean getaway, just as she had in Los Angeles.

The decimation of Audrey's mother's school—with Egan's unwitting help, no less—would be the ultimate triumph.

Out of the corner of her eye, Miranda noticed someone was waving at her: Seamus. He nodded for her to follow him out of the building.

What the hell does he want? Miranda wondered.

MIRANDA WAS PREPARED TO MAKE SMALL TALK—ABOUT THE DEBATE match, the board, whatever—but Seamus shut her down bluntly: "What the hell is wrong with you?"

"*What?* I don't know what you mean—"

"Cut the bullshit! Listen, missy, the only reason I supported you for the board was because—"

"Seamus, please—*calm down!*" Miranda huffed. "I have no idea what you're talking about!"

He leaned in so that they were nose to nose. "Your exclusive college admissions concierge program! Why didn't you tell me that I could *buy* my daughter's way into any school I wanted?"

Miranda slapped her hand over his mouth. "It's exclusive for a reason, as you just now so boisterously pointed out. *And I'd like to keep it that way.*"

Seamus's eyes darted up and down the street. Noticing something, he nodded slowly.

She saw them too: a couple of men, idling across the street, watching her and Seamus.

Shady characters, indeed. But it was the Haight, so shady was to be expected.

"Tell you what," Miranda whispered, "I'll call you, and we'll talk. *Privately.* Okay?"

"Yeah, okay. Just…make it happen! My Fawnie deserves it!"

"No problem, I'm on your side," she assured him. "How do you think she got on Debate Team anyway?"

His eyes widened at her revelation. "Thanks, then," he muttered.

"You're welcome. Fair warning, though: besides my fee, you'll need to do something for me, too."

"Name it," he muttered.

"Call an emergency board meeting for Friday. Ask for Lavinia's resignation."

He frowned. "We won't have the votes! Remember, Darius' wife is best friends with Audrey Thorpe."

"Sure, we will. Lavinia is going senile. I'm not the only person to notice it. Heck, Seamus, you saw it yourself in the last board meeting!"

He frowned. "She did seem distracted."

"Now is the time to push it through. And while you're at it, you can recommend me as her replacement—temporarily. Until a nationwide search proves I'm the best candidate anyway." Miranda grinned. "So, which university do you want?"

"The best, of course!"

"But of course." Miranda chuckled. "Perhaps your alma mater? What is it again? …Yale, right?"

"Why, er… yes." His winced as if dubious of such a pipe dream: Fawn at Yale.

"I may be able to arrange that," she assured him. "But first things first." She leaned in so that he'd have to look her in the eye. "Lavinia is out. Understood?"

"Okay, sure. You're on." Delighted, he chuckled as he strolled off.

After a minute, Miranda followed Seamus back inside.

Through the reflection of the auditorium's windows, she noticed that the men at the end of the street had never moved.

ASHBURY ACADEMY WON BY A MERE TWO POINTS.

The team, ecstatic, went into a group hug, pulling Egan in with them. "I'm proud of all of you," he declared, shaking hands all around. When he got to Charly, he winked his approval too.

But it was Chuck to whom he said, "Thanks for keeping everyone focused this week on the prize."

Chuck beamed at the praise.

He deserves it, Charly realized.

She reached over and squeezed her brother's hand.

Seeing her mother's happy face, Charly shouted: "Mom, tomorrow and Friday are teacher workdays, so we're off from school! Can I invite the girls back to our place for a sleepover cele-bration?"

Quest looked hopeful. "Boys too?"

Charly rolled her eyes. "You know better than that. No boys allowed!"

Chuck added, "Fawn too—right Charly?"

Charly pursed her lips. Finally, she shrugged. "Sure...if she wants."

If she wants.

Fawn could hear the disdain in Charly's voice.

Up until that moment, she'd been so proud of herself. She'd killed her argument!

And just seeing the look in her father's eyes made it all worth-while. For once, he saw her for who she really was: not only pretty, but brilliant as well.

Perhaps college was a viable option after all. And not just college, but anything she chose to achieve beyond it. Brains and looks made a heady combination, so why not?

She had to admit, having others critique her honestly had made her argument only that much stronger. In fact, it was Charly who'd come up with Fawn's killer closing line.

At the time, Fawn felt Charly might actually have wanted to be a real friend, not just someone who had to be nice to Fawn for the team's sake.

But now the look on Charly's face stopped this fantasy in its tracks. Apparently even giving a great argument wasn't enough to gain acceptance into Charly's little clique of nerdy girls.

It occurred to Fawn that there would always be nerdy girls—certainly in college—who would think they were superior to her. And, like her father, they would always judge her on her looks, not her smarts.

I'd better learn now how to deal with them; to hurt them before they hurt me.

Fawn knew just how to do that.

She'd seen how Charly sought out Egan's attention; how sullen

Charly had been when Egan accepted Chuck's resolution to their spat.

She's got a crush on Egan, Fawn realized.

Right then, she knew what she'd do—and tonight, too.

She leaned into Chuck and purred, "Honey, tonight let's make it just you and me, okay?"

That certainly put a smile on his face.

"I've got to go home with my parents, but why don't you pay me a visit...say, midnight?" she suggested.

Chuck's answer was a kiss. As he pulled away, he whispered, "You were awesome."

She shrugged off her guilt as she left the auditorium.

But instead of following her parents to their waiting car, she ran upstairs to Egan's classroom.

Egan's computer was on his desk.

She took a guess at his password. It was easy enough to hit it on the first time.

Extracurricular#1

Men are so predictable, she thought.

Through the school's open browser, she could access his private Gmail account, and wrote down its mailbox name.

She was out of the classroom in no time.

When Fawn got home, she went up to her room, locked the door, and opened her computer to set up two new Gmail accounts:

Egan.Gable
Charly.McK

The message Fawn sent from the first account went to Charly's real email account, and would undoubtedly pique her enemy's interest:

Dear Charly,
I know it seems strange to you that I'd reach out in this way, but I
can tell you've got something very important on your mind.
Your feelings are important to me. I hope you feel the same about
mine.

I guess Shakespeare said it best:
"Love looks not with the eyes, but with the mind."

If you're free, why don't you stop by my classroom at the end of the
teacher workday tomorrow. Say, four o'clock? It would mean
more to me than you'll ever know.

With tremendous respect, always,
—Egan

Of course Charly would show up. She salivated every time Egan threw a compliment her way.

Since Fawn controlled the password to Egan's fake account, she'd check it later to see if Charly had responded.

From the Charly.McK email account, Fawn wrote to Egan's genuine private email account:

Hi, Egan,
Look, I know it seems strange to you that I'd reach out to you in
this way, but there's something that's very important on my
mind. You seem to care deeply on so many levels that I feel I can
talk to you about it without feeling awkward.

I guess Shakespeare said it best:

"Love looks not with the eyes, but with the mind."

If you're free, would you mind if I stopped by your classroom after
the teacher workday tomorrow? Say, four o'clock? It would
mean more to me than you'll ever know.

With tremendous respect, always,
—Charly

Fawn imagined Charly would show up and make a fool of herself. Then, having done so, she'd be so embarrassed she'd drop out of Debate Team.

As it should be.

The others would wonder why. But Charly would be too ashamed to explain.

Fawn would never tell Chuck. If he ever found out what she'd done to Charly, he'd hate her for it.

She didn't know when Chuck's feelings started meaning something to her, but admittedly, they did now.

CHAPTER 31

*L*ionel was always the first one into the office, which was why he was at his desk when the call came in that Darius Calder's Mercedes-AMG S65 had been shot to smithereens while crossing the Bay Bridge last night.

Immediately, Lionel put in a call to SallyAnne. The news broke through her sleepy "Hello" and was followed with the anticipated alacrity by "Holy shite! It must have happened after the debate match! So, his wife and daughter—"

"As it turns out they weren't with him. The girl went to a sleep-over, and the wife went out to dinner with old friends. Darius was on his way back from a business meeting. The musician, Plug-Ugly, is under suspicion for Darius' murder. By the way, SFPD is keeping the murder out of the press until they've notified the deceased's next of kin."

"We need to tell the boss!"

"Agreed. I'm making that call next," Lionel promised.

"I'm on my way in," SallyAnne exclaimed.

"Two suspects dead—first Janna Calisher, and now Darius Calder!" Director Melamed fumed. "Not to mention that Winslow Jennings has disappeared off the face of the earth!"

"Maleficent is like a black widow," SallyAnne replied. "What piss-poor timing for us!"

"You can say that again," Melamed said. "And timing is every-thing. Since we can't afford to lose any more suspects, I say go ahead and arrest Miranda D'Arcy."

"Aren't we jumping the gun?" SallyAnne asked. "I mean, none of D'Arcy's promises with the AA parents come to fruition until this spring. If we arrest her now, even if D'Arcy were to get a guilty verdict, it would be for 'conspiracy to commit fraud,' which comes with a much lighter sentence than if the fraud were perpetrated."

"She may walk, anyway. She's very convincing with parents. A jury may believe her too," Lionel pointed out.

SallyAnne scoffed. "Are you suggesting we drop the case?"

"Not at all," Lionel replied. "But without a full list of the Los Angeles-based clients whose kids she got into some university by fraudulent means, the case is pretty thin. And the fact that Winslow has yet to return to the UP&T office suggests he might suspect it's under surveillance. Or else he flew the coop for reasons unknown to us. So I doubt we'll be getting the list from him."

"He's right," Melamed muttered. "We've got more cooperating witnesses who've flipped on Miranda than we've got parents who we can convict alongside her!"

"But what about the parents she's cultivating now?" SallyAnne asked.

"There are, what, only four of them here in San Francisco?" Melamed frowned.

"A fifth one came online last night—Seamus McCoppin," Sally-Anne reminded him.

"I heard the recording," Melamed replied. "Miranda didn't exactly pitch him, nor has she closed the deal. And no money has changed hands—*yet*."

"Another thing that may hurt our case is that one of those parents—Jammerhead—is a rock star with a huge following, and beloved because of his numerous charitable causes," Lionel pointed out. "If a jury lets him walk, it could soften the cases against other parent suspects, not to mention Miranda."

"If that's the case, one would think that the single mom, Nira, who paid only ten thousand dollars, could garner jury sympathy too," SallyAnne added. This particular exchange had saddened her.

"So, we're caught between a rock and a hard place," Melamed retorted. "If Winslow warned D'Arcy that University Prep & Test was under surveillance, she may also fly the coop. However, if we arrest her now, we can still make the case—especially if she's willing to turn on her LA-based clients we haven't already flipped."

"And if we let it play out through this school year's college acceptance period, we can convict her San Francisco clients of fraud too, as opposed to merely 'conspiracy to commit,'" SallyAnne added.

Melamed nodded. "Okay. You've got your marching orders."

Thanks to Miranda's online calendar, Lionel and SallyAnne were already in the lobby of Epic Steak Restaurant when Miranda walked in for her lunch with one of her university co-conspirators.

"What does this guy do again?" Lionel asked.

"Phil Brantley calls himself a 'Medieval games coach.' He's at USC." SallyAnne rolled her eyes. "Maleficent agreed to take the meeting because he claims he's got something golden to pass forward."

Lionel grimaced.

SallyAnne wondered if it was the nickname that made him wince, or that someone was willing to make Miranda's job that much easier.

She guessed the former.

When Miranda walked in, the agents purposely turned their backs on her. They waited until the hostess seated her before asking to be seated as well. They requested a table close enough to Miranda's that their listening devices could pick up every word.

Miranda and Brantley made small talk until their lunch courses were set in front of them. Brantley's pitch was simple: A week from Friday he'd have the answer key to the SAT test questions. "It's being sent to me by a contact in Beijing."

Ironically, Miranda's response was what SallyAnne would have asked: "The Chinese have hacked SAT headquarters?"

Phil chuckled. "Who knows? Maybe. But in this case, it's last year's international version of the test. It will be the version taken in the US this year."

"How much do you want for it?" Miranda asked.

"A million."

Miranda guffawed. "In your dreams." She glared through him. "One hundred thousand. Take it or leave it."

He choked as if his steak were stuck in his throat. Eventually, he shrugged. "One-fifty, and I won't go a penny lower. And I want it in small bills. Delivered to my hotel room by seven tonight. I'm catching the late flight back to LA."

"Done. I'll send it to you in a doggy bag." She picked up one of the bags left on the table for less ravenous patrons.

Miranda got up. She didn't bother to shake his hand. For that matter, she didn't bother to say goodbye. But she did toss down cash for the meal.

SallyAnne and Lionel followed her out the door.

—

"OH, MISS... MISS!" THE MAN WHO TAPPED MIRANDA ON THE shoulder had a pleasant enough voice: gentle, but persistent.

When she turned around, she found herself looking into a broad chest clad in bespoke Brooks Brothers.

The face above it was appealing: blued-eyed and square-jawed. His fair hair was cropped shorter than she liked, but she could work around it.

"May I help you?" she purred.

"You're Miranda D'Arcy, am I right?"

She hadn't noticed the woman standing off to the handsome stranger's side: short and slim, her dark, curly hair cropped short.

Miranda's simper faded. "Yes. And you are?"

They flipped open slim wallets holding small shields that clearly read:

Federal Bureau of Investigation

The rest of the odious woman's statements echoed in Miranda's ears but barely connected with her brain.

She deduced that she was being arrested.

The charge was fraud in relation to her college admissions counseling practice.

She could call an attorney, or the court would appoint one—

Darius.

"I want to call my attorney now!" she growled. She pulled out her phone and punched in his name—

Only to hear that his voice mailbox was full.

"Excuse me," the bitch beside her asked. "Were you trying Darius Calder just now?"

How did she know that?

Miranda was too surprised to stop herself from nodding.

"I'm sorry to be the one to tell you, but Mr. Calder was murdered late last night."

Darius... Dead?

Fuck...

The bitch—what did she call herself? Oh yeah: *Special Agent SallyAnne Jagger*—added: "Is there another person you'd like to call?"

Miranda scoffed. "Which son-of-a-bitch lawyer will make your lives the most miserable?"

The agents exchanged pitying glances.

"Wouldn't you prefer to be a cooperating witness?" Handsome suggested. "It would make everything much easier."

Easier? Nothing in life was easy.

Still, it would be great to know all the angles. Why not hear their pitch?

"Okay, let's talk," Miranda declared.

DESPITE HAVING THE DEMEANOR OF A MILQUETOAST ACCOUNTANT, Miranda's new lawyer, Gerald Breslin, was touted as the best balls-to-the-wall criminal defense attorney in the state, second only to the dearly departed Darius.

As if trying to prove this were the case, he held her hand as they listened to Lionel, SallyAnne, and Vera Gott—the U.S. attorney for the Northern District of California, who'd be heading up the prosecution.

"Right now, we've gotten testimony from three of your Los Angeles-based clients," Lionel explained.

Vera added, "Considering the number of multiple criminal fraud counts—including bribery, blackmail, as well as mail, wire, phone fraud, and IRS fraud—you could be looking at over fifty years in prison, and a fine of two million dollars."

Miranda almost chuckled at the fine.

However, the prison term was no laughing matter.

"And if Ms. D'Arcy is a cooperating witness?" Breslin asked.

Lionel shifted his gaze to Miranda. "How many families are involved?"

"Close to sixty," she admitted.

Breslin grimaced.

"Should you agree to be a cooperating witness—that is, name your co-conspirators at the various colleges, as well as give us a full list of your clients who have already paid you to commit fraud on their behalf—we will certainly take that into account when recommending sentencing," Vera promised.

"What would Ms. D'Arcy's role as a cooperating witness entail?"

"Besides a full list of her clients, she should indicate which of those had successful placements in a university, and which are to be accepted this spring." SallyAnne replied.

Miranda shrugged. "Sure, I'll provide it."

"If your contact with them happened before our surveillance subpoenas went into effect, you'll need to contact them again," Lionel added. "You'll explain that you want to curtail any flags that may pop up from the IRS on their quote-unquote donations to the Best Foot Forward Club. For our recordings, you'll get them to admit that their donation was really a payment for the placement of their child in the specific schools they requested, and to reiterate the amount paid."

"Got it," Miranda muttered.

"We know you're already getting word-of-mouth referrals on your special concierge college counseling here in San Francisco," SallyAnne explained. "We will have surveillance on you at all times. Should anyone approach you about your fraudulent services, we'll expect you to let the conversation take its course."

Miranda's lips rose into a smirk. "Are we talking entrapment?"

"Only if you actively solicit a potential client is it entrapment," Lionel explained. "Otherwise, if they approach you and agree to your stated terms, they formally become suspects."

"Potato, po-*tah*-to. I call them 'marks.'" Miranda leaned back and smiled as if enjoying their conversation. "By the way, a business like mine has expenses. For example, I've just agreed to pay a contact for a copy of this year's SAT test."

SallyAnne nodded. "You mean the one hundred and fifty thousand dollars you agreed to pay Phil Brantley before seven o'clock tonight?"

Miranda frowned. "My, my! Little pitchers have big ears!"

SallyAnne glared back at her.

"Posing as a courier, one of our agents will drop off the money to Mr. Brantley," SallyAnne replied. "He'll then be arrested. For a lighter sentence, no doubt he'll offer up your name. Another reason it's good that you've decided to play ball."

"I'm also expected to wine and dine my clients," Miranda added. "And considering their wealth, we're not talking the sort of tab you'd get at a taco joint. Who will be picking up my expenses?"

SallyAnne rolled her eyes.

"The FBI has an expense budget," Lionel explained. "If you can keep it in line, we won't charge it against your reparations."

Miranda snickered as if he'd made a joke. "In fact, I'm to set up a meeting with a parent who approached me just last night—"

"Yes, we know. Seamus McCoppin," SallyAnne interjected. "Since he's approached you, take the meeting."

"Gladly," Miranda murmured. "I'll set it up for this evening."

But the card she'd leave with him with instructions for his donation would go to an account the Feds weren't aware of. Nor would any other fees going forward.

And she'd make sure that Seamus kept spreading the word.

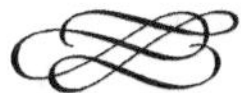

CHAPTER 32

When Charly got Egan's email, she was both surprised and pleased.

The way it was worded, she knew whatever he had to tell her was important. She could also tell that it wasn't something he felt like sharing with any of the others on Debate Team.

Did his cryptic message have anything to do with the fact that Debate Team hadn't chosen its captain?

Frankly, Charly would be thrilled if Egan chose her.

But after the argument she'd had with Fawn, Charly realized she might have blown her chances.

Maybe that was the news Egan wanted to deliver privately; that she'd somehow disqualified herself by her silly, petty actions, and that he was dismayed she'd done so.

Charly groaned. She'd just remembered that Egan had been standing next to her mother when Chuck had asked if Fawn could hang with the other girls at the house. Surely Egan had noticed that Charly's tepid response had made it clear the other girl wasn't welcome.

Fawn had certainly gotten the message. Charly could see it in the girl's glassy-eyed glare.

Had Egan noticed it too?

Charly was willing to admit to him—and to Fawn too—that

she'd made a mistake. She would explain that she'd already tried to make it up to Fawn by helping her with her arguments.

She'd make it clear that she would do anything he could suggest to make it happen.

EGAN HADN'T NOTICED THE EMAIL FROM CHARLY UNTIL HE WAS BACK at the school for Thursday's Teacher Work Day.

The gracious but strident way in which it was worded reminded him of Audrey at Charly's age.

He wondered what she wanted to discuss…

Egan chuckled at the thought of what he would have done had he ever received a similar missive from her mother those many years ago. Most likely, he'd have assumed it was her way of reaching out to express her feelings for him.

Would he have finally given in to his own longings for her?

With what he knew now, he realized the answer was yes.

Well, too late.

Whereas Audrey's feelings for him had once glowed hotly with desire, he'd missed the opportunity to prove himself worthy of her love.

Now he was willing to settle for the friendship she offered—one based on mutual trust and the memory of what they'd once shared.

Charly was so much like her mother. He looked forward to some one-on-one time with her; to hear what she had to say.

CHARLY'S KNOCK CAME RIGHT ON TIME.

Egan put down the paper he'd been grading and waved her in. "Having a good day?"

"Better than yours, I guess—since you had to work today, and tomorrow too." Charly walked in slowly as if deciding where to sit.

To make the decision easier for her, Egan moved out from behind his desk and leaned against it. He pointed to one of the front desks, indicating that she should feel free to do the same.

"Frankly, without you students here to harass me, I'm actually getting a lot of work done," he admitted. "Lavinia was only in for the first hour—" Egan stopped because he remembered Audrey's words of caution:

No one knows about Lavinia's illness yet…

"—which means when the cat's away, the mice will play," he concluded. "Some of the teachers left early, or are taking tomorrow off."

"So you hung around *just for me?*" Charly blushed at that thought.

So that she wouldn't feel so guilty, he replied playfully, "You're worth it."

Her smile is Audrey's.

Realizing this, he felt his face grow flush.

Charly saw it too. Embarrassed, she stammered, "Listen, Egan… I know I haven't been…well, I haven't been completely upfront with…with you…about…about how I feel about…"

As Charly formed her thoughts, she twisted her fingers.

It was a familiar gesture. Egan tried to remember when he'd seen Audrey do the same.

He chuckled to himself. *She's her mother's daughter, that's for sure: heartfelt, self-assured, passionate…*

Wait…

Is Charly trying to tell me that she…?

Oh…

Shit.

No.

Just…no.

SHE'S COMING ON TO ME!

If he was right—if Charly was professing some sort of *crush*—he knew he'd have to head it off at the pass.

He stood up. Nervously, he paced the floor. "Look, Charly…I…I know what you're trying to say…because…Well, let's just say, I've felt that way too."

"You have?" Charly looked relieved.

"Yes…I mean, *no!*" He wondered if he were making any sense. "What I'm trying to say is that I've done things I've regretted. Who hasn't, right? But whatever feelings you feel right now, at this specific moment…well, regret shouldn't be one of them."

"Wow! Hearing you say that…I feel so much better!" She almost seemed relieved. "Because…well, I was just hoping…that you'd—"

He moved away, shaking his head. "Charly—*I can't.*"

"But you just said..." Charly frowned. "So now you *don't* feel I'm—"

"Of course, I feel you're..." He held his hands in front of him as if that would stop the hurt she'd feel when he let her down. "Listen, I think we should just...*drop it.*"

Charly's face crumpled with defeat. So that he couldn't see her cry, she bowed her head.

Oh hell—I broke her heart.

Just like I did to Audrey.

He went over to her. Before he knew it, she leaned in.

Gingerly, he put his arms around her as she wept.

"I'm sorry," Charly sobbed. "I guess...I guess I didn't think it would affect me this way! But...*I just want it so badly!*"

Holy shit!

It took Charly awhile to collect herself. The moment she reached for a tissue from the box on his desk, Egan inched away.

Wiping her face, Charly sniffled, "You must think I'm an idiot because I care so much about it. Silly, isn't it?"

"No, it's not silly at all. It's life." Egan sighed. "And, frankly, I'm somewhat flattered."

"So then...you don't want me to quit Debate Team?" Charly asked meekly.

"Of course not! Charly, you're the team's heart and soul!"

She was so relieved to hear him say this that she did the unthinkable: impulsively, she hugged him again.

Stunned, he didn't dare put his arms around her.

When Charly pulled away, she was smiling sadly. But when she reached the door, she stopped and turned around. "Are you sure you won't reconsider?" she asked shyly.

He forced a chuckle and waved her out.

Shit.

SHIT!

This can't happen again.

I've got to tell Audrey.

CHARLY FELT TERRIBLE AND WONDERFUL, ALL AT THE SAME TIME.

She'd found it harder than she'd thought to speak her mind to Egan about her screw-up with Fawn. Then she'd fumbled her opening statement so awfully. She never even got out her pitch about why she should still be in consideration for Debate Team captain!

To her own ears, she'd sounded like a blithering idiot.

When Egan interrupted her and tried to put her at ease with his sweet "everyone makes mistakes" speech, she thought he intuitively understood that she was apologizing for her silly behavior. But when he adamantly told her he could never consider her for the position—that they should drop the topic immediately—she was heartbroken.

I can't believe I cried over it.

Egan was sweet to hold her until she'd quit blubbering. And it was kind of him to admit how touched he was by the depth of her feelings.

And when he declared she was the heart and soul of the team, she knew there was still hope that he might choose her for the team's captain, even if he'd refused to admit it at that moment.

That's okay. Charly was bound and determined to prove she was the best person for the job.

* * *

Audrey was still at her cubicle inside Harris Blanchard's campaign offices hashing out the topics for his next town hall meeting when her cell phone rang from a number she didn't recognize—one with a 212 area code.

Knowing Harris was in New York City for the day, she picked it up.

"We need to talk." Egan's voice sounded ominous.

"What...Why?" Cold dread surged through Audrey. "Is it...Lavinia?"

"No! It's about *Charly.*"

Audrey felt relieved and concerned all at once. "What about her?"

"I don't think we should talk about it over the phone. Can you meet me...maybe for a drink, or something to eat?"

He knows.

"Okay, sure, if you can give me an hour," she murmured. "Where?"

"I don't know… Osteria, on Sacramento at Presidio."

"I'll be there in an hour."

EGAN WAS ALREADY AT THE RESTAURANT WHEN AUDREY ARRIVED. HE'D secured a small banquette in an alcove against the back wall.

Thank goodness, it was nowhere near a window, she thought. She'd never seen him so upset.

Egan stood when he saw her. He didn't sit back down until she slid in beside him. When he beckoned, a waiter came over with two glasses of wine, and Audrey indulged Egan by taking a sip.

He did the same.

The waiter left them with menus.

Audrey said nothing until she couldn't stand the suspense any longer. Then she whispered, "Egan…please tell me what happened."

"Charly… Well, to be honest, I think she has a crush on me."

"*What?*" Audrey's shriek turned a few heads. She ducked. Finally, she hissed, "What…what did you do to her?"

Before he could answer, she realized her phone was buzzing. Audrey looked down at the caller ID: *Charly.*

Does she know I'm here—with Egan?

I'm being silly, she reasoned. Still, Audrey fumbled to turn off her phone altogether.

"What do you mean, 'what did *I* do to *her*?'" Egan huffed. "*I did nothing!*" Indignantly, he added: "How could you say such a thing?"

"Oh, bullshit, Egan! *You* know how you are!"

Frowning, Egan sat up straight. "What exactly is that supposed to mean?"

"Charming. Flirtatious. You live for our attention! Women eat it up!" The words flowed out of her as if a dam had broken in her heart. "Hell, I ate it up…once, a long time ago."

Egan bowed his head. "I never came onto her, Audrey, if that's what you're implying!"

"That may be the case," she conceded, "but girls that age can misinterpret the slightest action or phrase. And Charly is …she's vulnerable. Unlike some girls her age, she's still—she's still ...*innocent.*"

Audrey's thoughts went to the dinner she'd had with Gemma, Tallulah, and Bliss after the debate match last night. While talking about their children, Gemma had divulged that Zina had confessed to having sex with her boyfriend, Sven. "If Darius finds out, he'll hit the roof!" Gemma opined.

Noticing Audrey's sudden grimace, Gemma then patted her friend's hand. "Hey, you've got nothing to worry about with Charly. Zina let it slip that she's still a virgin—for now, anyway." She'd then chuckled. "But that Chuck and Fawn...*Oh, my God!* Did you know that Fawn is into making sex videos?"

First there's Lavinia's health, and then there's Chuck's infatuation with Fawn, Audrey thought. And now I have to worry about Charly too—

Because Egan is egotistical enough to play into it.

Her worst fears were reaffirmed when he retorted: "Quit trying to make me out to be the bad guy, Audrey. If you're so in tune with your seventeen-year-old self, you should respect Charly's feelings. I know I do. I proved it by—"

"By what? What did you do?" Audrey's eyes opened wide. "Egan...*what did you say?*"

"Gee, now, what would be the one thing I could say to break a teenage girl's heart?" He glared back. "What do you *think* I said?"

So, he told her...about us.

"You *fool!*" She was too ashamed to look him in the eye. Instead, Audrey stared down at the glossy white plate on the table in front of her. "Egan...the twins... *You're their father.*"

THEY'RE MINE.

Chuck and Charly—

How could he not have seen it?

The cadence of Chuck's laugh.

The way Charly tented her fingers when she was thinking her way through an argument.

They had his height, his crooked grin.

His ease with others.

Yes, they were his children.

Had they felt it too?

Maybe that's why Charly was so desperate to see me.

And I pushed her away.

What a stupid fool I am.

He leaned across the table. "Audrey…do they know?"

"No! Of course not!" Audrey looked shocked at the notion.

"Well…we *have* to tell them!"

Adamantly, Audrey shook her head. "No! No, we cannot!"

Egan couldn't believe his ears. "But they need to know! *They'll want to know!*"

"You're wrong!" Audrey hissed. "They already have a father, remember? Daniel! Quit being so—*so selfish!*"

"Me—*selfish?*" How audacious of Audrey to even think such a thing, let alone say it! "And you weren't selfish to keep it from me all these years—the news that I have a daughter and a son—*who have grown up without me?*"

"You didn't love me!" Audrey retorted. "What would ever make me think that you could love them?"

"I loved you with all my heart!" The same heart now beating so fiercely in his ears.

"You certainly had a stupid way of showing it—screwing anything that moved in the three years since I'd last seen you. It's been two decades, Egan! No—*longer!* Did you once call me? Did you once reach out to me?"

"Why would I? To have you shout out to the world how much you hated me?" He laid his hand on top of hers as if his grasp might make her realize she couldn't run away from him yet again.

"I had every right to hate you," Audrey spat out. "I wasn't important enough for you to stick around." She jerked her hand away. "Forget whatever fantasy you have about Chuck and Charly. They are Daniel's reality. *He* is their father."

"So he knows too?"

"No! Of course not!" She shuddered at the thought. "Daniel was so excited when I told him I was pregnant that I couldn't find the nerve to break his heart about…what I'd done *with you.*" Her words, strangled by her emotions, came out in a whisper. "Daniel believes the twins are his flesh and blood. He lives for them! And I've encouraged that," Audrey admitted bitterly. "It's why I don't partake in the family bike ride on Saturdays. After keeping such a big secret from him, I never felt worthy of taking away this precious time he spends with them!" Audrey used her napkin to dab away the tears clouding her eyes. "Why do you think I kept the name Thorpe? *Because I never felt I deserved his name.*" She raised her head defiantly. "But Charly and Chuck do, even if I don't."

Seeing her like that—so sad, so broken—and yet, so determined…

Egan tilted her head up so that she had to look him in the eye. "Audrey—*okay!* If that's what you want, I won't say anything to…to anyone. For now, anyway." He sighed. "But it's only right that they know, eventually."

"I know. When the time is right." Elated, grateful, Audrey kissed his cheek.

But she missed because Egan had been so startled that he'd lowered his face.

Their lips met instead.

Just an instant.

Just enough for him to savor their warmth.

Ah, Audrey! If only…

He felt her pull away. When he opened his eyes, the sadness in her gaze cut deep into his soul.

Shaking, Audrey stumbled to her feet. "Don't ever do that to me again." Grabbing her purse, she whispered more to herself than to him: "How can two supposedly bright people be so stupid about love?"

YOU MUST REMEMBER THIS…

Only now, it's from Egan's point of view…

CHAPTER 33

Egan hadn't realized how awestruck Audrey's confession had left him until he found himself wandering Sacramento Street in a stupor.

The double scotch he'd downed after her revelation might also have had something to do with the daze, he now reasoned.

At some point, Egan paused in front of one of the shops: a children's store called Dottie Doolittle. Its large window showcased a dainty pink Victorian dollhouse. It had been placed in the center of a moving train set amid a diorama of a town, a thicket of woods, and an antique railroad station.

I'll bet Audrey once bought the twins' toys here, Egan thought.

Had Audrey just let him explain away that awful day in Berkeley, he would have been around to help her pick them out.

He blinked away his tears.

How stupid of me to have kissed her just now!

The last thing Egan wanted was for Audrey to despise him. Now that she did, he wondered if he'd ever win back her friendship, let alone her trust.

I have to keep my vow to her, he realized. I can never tell our children who I am.

My children.

A montage of the moments he'd shared with them raced through his mind:

When his eyes first alighted on Charly, and how he thought she looked familiar;

Chuck's cocky attitude, especially when Egan had embarrassed him in front of Fawn;

How finding Chuck in the basement of the school's old gym had brought out some instinctual urge to protect the boy from himself;

The pride he felt at the twins' desire to please him, both in class and on Debate Team;

And when push came to shove, the allegiance they shared.

They are both so much like me, he realized.

I'd do anything for them.

Except that, right now, he wasn't in a position to do anything at all for them. Hell, he could barely keep his own head above the financial whirlpool swirling around him.

Throughout Egan's life, there had been many one-night stands. Every now and then, he'd enjoyed a particularly memorable lay. But he'd never had a long-term relationship.

Instead, he'd held onto a dream, a fantasy.

Audrey.

For far too long.

During that time, Audrey had created a life with a different man: Daniel.

And together they'd created a loving family.

They should have been my family, he realized.

The twins lived in Daniel's home. And Daniel's salary as a corporate attorney allowed them to live privileged lives.

What could he offer them instead?

Not much, he conceded miserably. Just debt—my parents' and mine.

And now, with those damn lawsuits he'd have to fight off—

That alone would eat up Daniel's gracious donation.

Daniel!

It had humiliated Egan when Audrey's husband had taken it upon himself to underwrite Egan's academic chair.

I wonder how Daniel would feel to know the truth about his children?

No—my children.

But he can never know because I promised Audrey.

She'd made a promise to Egan as well: That when the time was right, the twins would know the truth.

And when that time came, he'd be ready. He'd have written them into his will. He'd have a legacy to leave them—

I have to write again.

And it's got to be a bestseller.

It was the only way Egan knew to make money.

The toot of the toy train broke through the thick fog of his resolve. Realizing its engine had jumped off its track, instinctively Egan reached forward to nudge it back on—

Only to slam his fist into the shop's plate-glass window.

Fortunately, it didn't break.

Startled, the shop clerk looked up and frowned.

Egan waved in apology.

She shook her head as if to say, *loser.*

Of course, she was right.

His publisher hated him. His agent had kicked him to the curb. And no other pub house would touch him.

I need to eat something before I start blubbering like a baby.

I need another drink.

A block away was a restaurant called Spruce. He'd heard of it from Cornell. "Its duck sumo ditalini is *to die for,*" he'd rhapsodized. "And they've got a drink called the 'Sneaky Pete'—just absolutely yummy!"

I hope the joint lives up to its hype, Egan reasoned.

THE HOSTESS RAISED A BROW AS HE SLURRED OUT HIS REQUEST OF A table for one. "You'll be served more quickly at the bar," she suggested.

"Sold!" he exclaimed. He shooed away her offer to show him the way, declaring, "I can spot a bar a mile away."

"I believe it," she muttered under her breath.

He was in luck. Although the bar was filled, there was still one stool left.

Even luckier, it was next to a pretty woman: a petite, sloe-eyed brunette. Because she was perched facing away from the bartender, Egan got a good look at her slim, shapely legs.

Pretty, he thought. Like a sprite–a pixie.

Was she saving the stool for someone?

He tapped her on the shoulder to ask.

When she didn't turn, he realized it was because something happening in the closest banquette had caught her attention. Gently, he patted her again.

She swiveled around and tilted her head to one side, allowing her gaze to sweep over him.

If we don't know each other now, something tells me she wouldn't mind making my acquaintance.

He pointed to the empty stool. Grinning, he asked, "Is this seat taken?"

Pixie's eyes grew larger. "No, not at all—*Mr. Gable!*"

She said it loud enough that the man on the other side of her— tall and broad-shouldered, a blond Teutonic god clad in Brooks Brothers —turned and scowled at Egan. Like Pixie, he was also angled for a clear view of the banquette.

So this is Pixie's date? She can do much better.

Ignoring the man's glare, Egan dropped onto the seat anyway. Then, leaning in toward Pixie, he asked, "Do we know each other?"

She reeled back a bit.

Oh, hell! Maybe she's an Ashbury Academy parent. If so, and I'm flirting with her in front of her husband —

But then Pixie gushed, "I read your book, *Extracurricular.* In fact,"—she paused—"it's my favorite."

"Thank you for that." Egan chuckled, relieved. "In fact, THANK GOD for that! I thought you were another infernal AA parent!" He scanned her appreciatively. "But of course, you're much too young to have children of your own."

Pixie blushed at the compliment.

Not the Teutonic twit, though. He was still frowning.

"Um...AA?" Pixie stammered. "You... you mean Alcoholics Anonymous?"

"In this case, no," Egan guffawed. "Albeit, many of AA's—that is, Ashbury Academy's teaching staff are chip-carrying members—"

Unable to stop himself, he let out a burp.

Waving away her concerned stare, Egan added, "Not me, mind you." He nodded toward the bartender. "Speaking of which, may I buy you another"—he looked down, to see what she was drinking —"wine? Or, perhaps something a bit more adventurous? I can vouch for the fact that the barkeep makes a mean Sneaky Pete: whiskey, coffee liqueur, and just a splash of milk—"

Just then, Teutonic Twit leaned over and growled, "Sir, do you mind? The lady is on a date!"

Pixie did a double-take. Then she blushed.

Jesus, he's got nerve! The whole time they've been seated here, he's been staring over there, at the blond bitch in the banquette.

And now, he dares to stare me down?…

Oh…

Nope. He's staring at Pixie.

'Bout damn time he took notice of her!

Incensed for her, Egan declared, "Well, you've got an odd way of showing it, sir! Not only are you ignoring this, this"—

Egan burped again—even louder this time—

"—this *beautiful* young woman, the whole time I've been chatting her up you've been staring *over there*"—he pointed to the banquette—"at that over-inflated Barbie doll!"

He threw his arm open toward the object of Teutonic Twerp's fascination—

What the Hell…

That's Miranda.

With Seamus and Gretchen McCoppin!

Suddenly it all made sense:

Miranda's snide, backhanded remarks about Ashbury Academy's gentle, beloved headmistress.

The way Miranda put up with Jess's public manhandling.

Why she wangled a ride with Daniel after the last board meeting.

And why she finagled her way onto the board to be its deciding vote.

With my help, no less.

Stupid, stupid, me.

The realization that he might be having a hand in his mentor's downfall—*the grandmother of his children*— quickly sobered him up.

Does Miranda know about Lavinia's illness? If so, she may be positioning herself as the next Head of School…

Egan's eyes narrowed at the thought.

He realized his fan and her boyfriend were staring at him. To cover up his shame, he declared, "Well, well! It seems I know Barbie —and for that matter, her plasticine friends too—Ken and Midge."

Egan knew he hardly looked his best. The least he could do was straighten his tie, maybe tuck in his shirt again. "If you kind gentlefolk will excuse me, I think I'll mosey on over and pay my respects."

He walked off—not as steadily as he'd hoped, but that didn't matter.

For Lavinia's sake, he had to find out what Miranda was up to.

EGAN REACHED THE TABLE JUST IN TIME TO HEAR MIRANDA SAY, "Mum's the word..."

Interesting, Egan thought.

But what he exclaimed out loud was: "Well, I'll be damned! Small world, isn't it?"

The McCoppins met his unexpected salutation with shock and awe.

Jesus, they look as if they're seeing a ghost, Egan thought.

Miranda glowered.

Yep, apparently, I've interrupted a really important hootenanny.

Miranda tempered her frown into a simper, declaring, "Ah, well, look who's here too—AA's illustrious literature professor, Egan Gable!"

When Gretchen realized who he was, she actually gave him the once-over and a wink.

Jesus, now I know where Fawn gets it!

Just the thought that the mother of his son's girlfriend had just come onto him made Egan shudder.

"By the way, Mr. Gable is my top candidate for SAT proctor. I know how much Fawn dotes on him," Miranda cooed coyly.

Huh?... What the hell was she talking about?

"Oh? Well, ...that's great, I guess." Gretchen deflated a bit.

Egan was surprised that Miranda seemed to enjoy Gretchen's dismay.

Seamus nudged Gretchen. "We'd better take off." As Gretchen scooted out of the booth, Seamus muttered, "See you at the next board meeting" to Egan and Miranda.

As Egan slid into the banquette, Miranda declared, "Fancy seeing you here." She nodded toward the bar. "Slumming?"

For some odd reason, Pixie and the Twit were still staring at them.

Egan winked at Pixie. "What, with that pretty little damsel at the bar? Are you jealous?" He whistled low. "Surprise, surprise! Not that I blame you. She struck me as smart and beautiful—*and kind.*"

"She is also a…" Miranda stopped herself. "Jesus! Never mind! Enough of this bullshit—and enough of your little head games, Egan Gable!" Incensed, she added, "Oh, and as far as I'm concerned, our little deal is off!"

The deal…

Miranda was going to renege on her vow never to tell anyone about his affair with Audrey.

Egan's blood ran cold.

She could easily hitch another ride with Daniel. If she says something to him about Audrey and me out of spite—

"No… *NO!* You can't renege on what you promised!"

"Says who?" Miranda retorted.

"But-but…" Frantically, Egan grabbed her arm. "Please… *don't!*"

Miranda leaned back in the booth and smiled. "Well… Since you're begging. Perhaps we can work something out."

Egan sighed. "I told you twice already. I'm just not that into you—"

"Don't be a fool!" she sputtered. "I don't mean sex, you imbecile! I'm giving you back what you so desperately want."

She paused—not just because she hoped it would make the offer sound more enticing to Egan but because she needed her FBI tormenters to believe what she'd declared was true: "If you'll agree to be the proctor for Ashbury Academy's SAT test."

Egan frowned, perplexed. "Are you joking?"

"Not at all," Miranda insisted. "But you must do everything the job entails—*to the letter.*"

Egan shrugged. "How hard can it be?"

"Just the usual," she replied. "Of course, the most challenging task concerns the seven special needs students. Their math portions must be substituted. Will you have a problem with that?"

"Why should I? As you say, they're special needs, and all that implies."

Egan's response could not have been more ideal. Whereas he presumed a different test, the Feds would interpret it as she meant it to be: exchanged for a version already filled out with the correct answers.

"I thought not," she purred. "There's something I hadn't mentioned before. It is a necessary evil. It involves the essay portion." She sighed. "You're also to provide substitute essays for those students."

Egan frowned. "How is that even possible?"

"It probably means pulling an all-nighter, but, unfortunately, it goes with the job."

"Wait… I'll be staying up all night *with the kids*?"

Miranda's chuckle was devoid of any charm. "Don't play stupid, Egan. It doesn't suit you."

She counted silently to five as the reality of what she meant sunk in.

With each passing second, a different emotion shifted Egan's usual placidity. Incomprehension morphed into realization, which gave way to shock, then concern, and finally anger.

He growled, "You've got to be kidding me!"

"Suddenly, you have a conscience?" Miranda clucked her tongue. "I assure you, the pay will make it worth your while."

Egan's wary silence didn't concern her. She knew he was hard up for cash. In fact, the longer he stewed over his dilemma, the better.

Finally, he asked, "Oh yeah? How much?'

"Fifteen thousand," she replied.

Egan snorted. "Knowing you, you're pocketing at least a hundred thou."

"You arrogant bastard!…" Miranda paused. Then: "Alright then! Thirty-five thousand. Take it or leave it!"

Asshole.

Still, he had her over a barrel.

She took comfort in the thought, however, that if she were going down, Egan would too.

———

So that's her game—parents are paying her to cheat on their children's SAT tests!

It sickened Egan to think he'd allowed her to drag him into her scheme.

I'll do it because I have to.

For Chuck and Charly.

He shoved Seamus's plate out of his way but thought nothing of downing the last of the blowhard's wine. "So, how does this little scheme of yours work?"

"A week from Friday, I'm to get the SAT answer key for both math and reading, as well as the essay questions. That night, I'll drop them by your place along with the names of the students involved. After they take their tests, you're to substitute the math and reading portions with ones that you've already filled in correctly—especially the math portion, although, so that the tests look valid, you're to miss one or two answers in the reading questions. And Egan, just make sure they are different mistakes on each student's test, okay?"

Egan frowned. "Yeah, yeah, okay, whatever. And what about the essays?"

"The way the SAT board scores the test's sections, a well-written essay is merely icing on the cake," Miranda explained. "I know you well enough to appreciate your bullshitting skills. I'm sure elevating the students into the literary stratosphere should be child's play for you. And since you already teach these students, matching the essay topics to their voices shouldn't be that difficult for you."

Egan sighed. "If you say so." He was too weary to argue with her. Bone tired. Suddenly, he felt twenty years older. "One caveat, babe: I'll want my money a week before the test, or it's no go."

Miranda chuckled. "That's the easy part. In fact, tonight. Say, nine? I'll even give you the cash with a receipt for—let's call it 'services rendered.'"

He let that sink in.

Suddenly, he remembered something she'd said that had confused him. What was it again? Oh yes:

I'm giving you back what you so desperately want.

What did she mean? His writing career?

Audrey?

Right now, he was too tipsy to decipher her scheme. All he could do was shrug. "Sure, why not?"

Yes, he'd make love to Miranda. Keep your friends close, and your enemies closer, right?

But he'd pretend it was Audrey.

And tonight of all nights, he needed to be with someone, if not her.

Afterward, Egan swore, he'd figure out an even better way to screw Miranda D'Arcy.

The last thing he'd let her do was to take him down with her.

CHAPTER 34

*A*udrey drove home, lost in a tumult of emotions over finally having revealed to Egan the terrible secret that bound them forever.

Daniel should have been there already. Strangely, though, his car wasn't in the driveway. At that point she remembered she'd turned off her cell phone.

She flipped it on again before going into the house. Seeing that, in a mere hour, she'd received eleven messages, she stopped dead in the driveway and scrolled through Caller ID:

Charly - Gemma - Charly - Bliss - Charly - Tallulah - Davis - Daniel - Chuck - Charly - Daniel -

What the heck was going on?

It was Audrey's natural instinct to play the voicemails in order. However, she flinched at the thought of listening to Charly's pained dissertation as to why she felt it necessary to drop Egan's class and Debate Team.

Not that she would blame her daughter in the least, having gone through precisely the same heartache with Egan.

The egotistical jerk!

That he tried to kiss her proved yet again how insensitive he was to others' emotions.

Audrey was sure that her girlfriends' calls were to follow up on the innocuous gossip that had them laughing into the early morning hours, so not something that merited an immediate callback. Seeing Davis' name intrigued her, but his good news took a back seat to the drama happening in her own life right now.

She imagined Chuck's call was one long groan about how hungry he was and chiding her for the fact that there was nothing to eat in the house. If she had the time, she would have responded by texting him a map outlining the mere ten blocks from their home to Trader Joe's.

She knew she had to take Daniel's call.

She doubted Charly would have divulged to Daniel her talk of shame with Egan. Still, Audrey braced herself as she scrolled to Daniel's cell number.

Just hearing his voice would remind her that there was some normalcy to life.

Afterward, she'd have the nerve to deal with Charly's frantic calls.

"AUDREY—FINALLY!" JUST THOSE TWO WORDS RELAYED A DEPTH OF fear and sadness she'd never heard before in Daniel's voice.

"I—was at a meeting!" she stammered "I'm sorry... Why? What happened?"

"It's Charly—"

Oh no...Oh, my God...

She must have told him about Egan.

"She was in the Haight when she got a call from Zina...about Darius."

"Darius?" Audrey was confused. "What about him?"

"You haven't heard yet? He was murdered!"

"Oh, my God! I've got to call Gemma!" Guilt at not taking her friend's call surged through her. And of course, that was why Bliss and Tallulah had tried to reach her as well.

"Audrey, that's not all." She could hear Daniel breathing heavily. "Charly didn't know if Lavinia had heard the news, so she went over to her grandmother's house and...and..." Daniel paused. "She was passed out. Thank goodness Charly was there! Otherwise..." His words stuck in his throat. "She called an ambulance. We're at UCSF now—"

"I'll be right there!... But where do I go? Oncology?"

"What?...*No!* She had a heart attack! We're in the ICU." Urgently, he pleaded, "Audrey, hurry! Lavinia is fading."

I love you so much.

You can't leave me. Please don't leave me.

I need you.

Audrey longed to say this to Lavinia, but she couldn't. Not in front of her children, who were already shell-shocked with grief.

Charly, always the stoic one, had done the best in holding back her tears, but she held her hands cupped at her chest as if that might stop her heart from hurting so badly.

Chuck sobbed openly. Whereas he used the back of his hand to wipe away the tears rolling down his cheeks, he'd placed one hand over Lavinia's as if willing his life force into her.

Noah's tears flowed freely down his face, but his fist, held to his mouth, stifled his sobs. He leaned into Daniel, whose eyes were hazed with tears. Seeing Audrey, Daniel nodded, as if beckoning her to Lavinia's side.

Chuck stood up so that his mother could take his seat. Audrey hugged him dearly before inching the chair as close as she could to her mother's bed.

"I'm here, Lavinia," she whispered.

Her mother gave a slight nod. She gulped hard. Then, through parched lips, she whispered, "Love you...always."

"I'll always love you too." Audrey's words came out between sobs.

"Daniel..."

"He's here. The kids too."

"Yes. They'll...all be fine." Lavinia's voice faded away. Her attempt to open her eyes succeeded, if barely.

Audrey held her breath until Lavinia added. "You too." She released a sigh. "The school...my life's work..."

"It's your legacy. I'll make sure it will always stay that way! I swear!"

A smile rose on Lavinia's lips. "Family first. Always."

"Yes, of course. But—"

"Closer..." Lavinia's hands grasped her gently as if willing Audrey into silence.

As Audrey leaned in, Lavinia's eyes fluttered and then shut.

Her last words whispered to her daughter were: "Tell Daniel... about Egan."

*L*avinia's death catalyzes a power play for control of Ashbury Academy's trustee board. Daniel's covert actions, however, have Audrey questioning his vow to protect Lavinia's legacy at the school.

The arrests resulting in the FBI's investigation into Miranda's college admissions fraud bring tragedy to some of the families involved, and unexpected opportunities to others.

Can Ashbury Academy survive this scandal?

An even bigger question:

Will Audrey's marriage—and her family—fall apart after her long-held secret is finally revealed?

OTHER BOOKS BY JOSIE BROWN

The Totlandia Series (8 Books)

Books 1 - 4 (The Onesies: Fall, Winter, Spring, Summer)

Books 5 - 8 (The Twosies: Fall, Winter, Spring, Summer)

The Housewife Assassin Series

The Housewife Assassin's Handbook (Book 1)

The Housewife Assassin's Guide to Gracious Killing (Book 2)

The Housewife Assassin's Killer Christmas Tips (Book 3)

The Housewife Assassin's Relationship Survival Guide (Book 4)

The Housewife Assassin's Vacation to Die For (Book 5)

The Housewife Assassin's Recipes for Disaster (Book 6)

The Housewife Assassin's Hollywood Scream Play (Book 7)

The Housewife Assassin's Killer App (Book 8)

The Housewife Assassin's Hostage Hosting Tips (Book 9)

The Housewife Assassin's Garden of Deadly Delights (Book 10)

The Housewife Assassin's Tips for Weddings, Weapons, and Warfare (Book 11)

The Housewife Assassin's Husband Hunting Hints (Book 12)

The Housewife Assassin's Ghost Protocol (Book 13)

The Housewife Assassin's Terrorist TV Guide (Book 14)

The Housewife Assassin's Deadly Dossier (Book 15: The Series Prequel)

The Housewife Assassin's Greatest Hits (Book 16)

The Housewife Assassin's Fourth Estate Sale (Book 17)

The Housewife Assassin's Horrorscope (Book 18)

More Josie Brown Novels

Secret Lives of Husbands and Wives

The Baby Planner

The Candidate

Hollywood Hunk (True Hollywood Lies series)

HOW TO REACH JOSIE

To write Josie, go to:
mailfromjosie@gmail.com

To find out more about Josie, or to get on her eLetter list for book
launch announcements, go to her website:
www.JosieBrown.com

You can also find her at:

www.AuthorProvocateur.com

twitter.com/JosieBrownCA

facebook.com/josiebrownauthor

pinterest.com/josiebrownca

instagram.com/josiebrownnovels